Kathleen Rowntree grew
and was educated at Cleethorpes Girls' Grammar School
and Hull University, where she studied music. For the
last fifteen years she has lived on the Oxfordshire/North-
amptonshire borders. Her husband is a professor at the
Open University and they have two sons, Mark and Leo.
She gave up teaching in order to write full time. *Brief
Shining* is her second novel.

BRIEF SHINING

Kathleen Rowntree

CORGI BOOKS

BRIEF SHINING
A CORGI BOOK 0 552 13557 7

Originally published in Great Britain by
Victor Gollancz Ltd

PRINTING HISTORY
Gollancz edition published 1989
Corgi edition published 1990

This book is set in 10/12 Sabon
by Falcon Typographic Art Ltd

Corgi Books are published by Transworld Publishers
Ltd., 61-63 Uxbridge Road, Ealing, London W5 5SA, in
Australia by Transworld Publishers (Australia) Pty. Ltd.,
15-23 Helles Avenue, Moorebank, NSW 2170, and in
New Zealand by Transworld Publishers (N.Z.) Ltd., Cnr.
Moselle and Waipareira Avenues, Henderson, Auckland.

Reproduced, printed and bound in Great Britain by
BPCC Hazell Books
Aylesbury, Bucks, England
Member of BPCC Ltd

To Derek

BRIEF SHINING

Part One

THE DREAM

1

There was a time, before it all went wrong, when nothing could mar the glory of Willow Dasset. And although that time had gone, she could still recall how all pain, all obstacle – the discomfort of the journey, the whispered spite behind half-closed doors, the arbitrary rules, the rows – would melt into insignificance in the radiance of possession. Only to be there – where days sprang into life with the clatter of cattle in the yard, and closed with the pungency of pineapple weed fermenting in dew . . .

Yes, she could recall it in dispassionate detail: travelling down from their drab, Northern home in a car thick with pent-up feeling and the smell of dirty leather; her father at the wheel cursing the idiocies of other road-users, and liable at any moment to be propelled into a torrent of temper by an ill-considered remark from her mother who understood nothing of The Rules Of The Road; and her sister, squirming miserably at her side, about to turn the car into a tinful of wrath with a request that they stop . . .

'Stop?' Henry Robinson could scarcely believe it. Here they were on the great Fosse Way, stuck behind one filthy lorry after another, within minutes of the only straight stretch of road for miles . . . (Beside him, his wife's head quivered, but for the moment she maintained her lips in a tight, thin line.) 'Can't you wait?' he demanded of the wretch in the back.

11

An incoherent whine.

Meg Robinson's irritation burst forth. 'For heaven's sake stop and get it over with,' she advised.

That did it – as Sally, the elder of the two Robinson girls, had known it would. 'Get it over with? Don't you *understand*, woman – if we stop now we'll catch up with this lot again just in time for all those bends around Newark. Look!' he invited urgently. 'The road's clear. I could go now.'

'Go, then; go,' said his wife, feeling that a pool in the back might be a small price to pay – but too late.

'Damnation!' Henry cried, as a red Jaguar arrived from nowhere, passed the Robinsons with a toot of the horn and proceeded to occupy the empty road on the right of the lorry. For a few seconds Henry's rage was torn between the claims of drivers presuming a divine right to overtake and passengers prompting accidents with their contradictory advice.

Meg beat him to it. 'There's a gateway coming up. Slow down.'

'Where?'

'Slow *down*.'

'How'm I supposed to see . . . ?'

'Here it is. Now!'

Henry swung off the road and pulled up. He kept the engine running. 'I wish you'd understand that you're supposed to give adequate warning; I hardly had time to indicate . . . '

But his wife, after grappling with the handle of her door, had flung herself from the car and was now extracting her younger daughter from the back. 'Get on with it,' she admonished.

Alone on the back seat, Sally ventured a look in the rear driving mirror. Her father's fair, boyish face was

12

flushed, and his deep-set blue eyes gazed resentfully at the passing traffic.

'There!' said Meg, shoving Anne into the back. She got into the front seat and slammed the car door. 'Two minutes flat.'

In silence, Henry pushed the gear stick into first and waited for a chance to get back on to the road.

Sally looked briefly at her mother's untidy head. 'Two minutes flat' she had said, defending the stop by citing its brevity. Was she oblivious of the remark's significance – that it had undermined her husband's forthcoming, blow by blow account of their journey to a dinner table audience blank-eyed with boredom? 'Of course, we were obliged to stop for ten minutes or so, thanks to m'lady here; otherwise I reckon we'd have beaten our best time yet – that Easter run – do you remember?' Now, his wife having set a precise time limit, the stop was doomed to exist only as a remembered irritant, and had no future as a saving grace.

Henry was cheering up. For the time being all travel northwards appeared suspended, and he was able to swing out at will, overtaking half a dozen sluggish motor cars and, at last, the entire line of exhaust-belching lorries. One by one they disappeared from view. Henry's spirits soared. He became acutely conscious of his eyes' fine judgement, his hands' skilled control. He could even sense the admiration of his passengers . . . 'Oh, it's the open road for me!' he sang boisterously, wagging his head to exhibit his sudden good humour.

Wife and daughters continued to devote their unswerving attention to the passing countryside.

Henry was an abstemious man, despising tobacco, wary of alcohol. Driving was Henry's stimulant. When things were going nicely on the road he experienced a rare exhilaration, and requests for stops, sudden instructions to admire a feature of the landscape, pleas that he slow down, were cruel intrusions. At the wheel of his car Henry was a prince, and his testament was The Rule of the Road. Other drivers, as he liked to point out, constantly flouted The Rule, but Henry prided himself on applying it to the very letter. And The Rule was not without consequences for the passengers: it was a crime, for example, to impede the driver's rear view. Henry's cry of 'Someone's jogged the driving mirror' was guaranteed to sink hearts and set denials and accusations flying.

It was a satisfaction to Henry that his wife could not drive. One terrible summer she had set out to acquire the necessary skill; but, as Henry had foreseen, Meg proved blind to other road-users. (Her inability to recognize people in the street was a frequent source of offence in the town.) Now, he took a sly look at her and grinned – she was frowning short-sightedly at the view ahead through recently prescribed spectacles; yes, blind as a bat, poor girl.

To excel over his wife in this one particular was a relief, for, generally speaking, Meg was the more successful. He was a mere clerk to the court, whereas she was the head-mistress of the largest elementary school in the town. She served on this committee and advised that; was delegated to diocesan boards and county conferences; was asked to address meetings, to give talks, to open bazaars. She was a personage. Her views on civic matters were occasionally sought by the *Evening Mail*, and more than once her photograph had graced its pages. As a consequence she was recognized as she pedalled around town on her sit-up-and-beg bicycle, and when she and Henry called at The Tudor Café for a pot of tea and a toasted tea cake, the waitress would hurry to show Mrs Robinson to a table, and those already seated would call a greeting or whisper her name to companions as she passed.

In his humbler capacity, Henry had the consolation of knowing that he was appreciated. He was a stickler for standards, a keen observer of protocol, the smartest opener of doors ever to earn the gratitude of the great and good. Of course, there were one or two who failed to recognize Henry's worth – William Gawbutt, JP, came instantly to mind – but Henry felt he could safely disregard the idiosyncrasy of friend Gawbutt, whose flaunting of a lowly origin was a constant irritant undermining a comfortable theory of Henry's that were it not for his own lowly origin – which Henry had the good taste to disguise with careful speech and polished manners – he would have occupied the dais rather than the well of the court. And occupied it with style, for Henry had a flair for ceremonial.

A roundabout appeared ahead. He slowed and insinuated the car cleanly through a curvaceous manoeuvre, but as the road became straight and he pressed the accelerator, the response was disappointing. A Ford van pulled clear. Henry frowned. Evidently the engine required tuning; furthermore, he was not altogether happy about the gears. He glanced at his wife. 'You will have a word with the old man?'

'Yes, yes,' she replied impatiently.

'I mean, straight away wouldn't do any harm. Be nice to know where we stand. I could drive into Stratford later on in the week and get them to look at the gear box.'

In the back of the car, Sally listened and understood. She was a knowing child, given to hanging about in corners with a dreamy, abstracted expression while her ears and eyes missed nothing. 'A word with the old man' meant that her mother would closet herself in the dining-room

15

with Grandad while her father paced nervously in the bedroom. Her mother, looking pink, would eventually emerge and go upstairs, hand – without comment – a banknote to her husband and put the remainder of the money in her handbag. (The Robinsons were always short of money. If one was determined to maintain standards – and one was – motoring was an expensive business. Also, Henry insisted that his daughters be educated privately with the offspring of the great and good rather than the local riff-raff at a council school. Meg had demurred, but had not been prepared to spend time arguing about it.)

Sally craned her neck to peer between her parents' heads. They were getting near; soon they would turn off the main road and head for Whitton. Yes, there was the signpost. The car slowed and turned right. It went, as she had so often rehearsed it, down the lane, over the humpback bridge and through the village; then left at the fork and on to Dasset Saint Mary's. 'Dasset Saint Mary's' she breathed, marvelling; feeling the strangeness of things long imagined becoming reality. And in a moment . . . yes, *there*, on the village green, an oak so ancient that its hollowed trunk was girded with iron and its branches trailed over the ground. She put a hand to her throat. Sometimes, at home, as she lay in bed listening to the early morning wail of ocean-going trawlers and the sharp hoot of factory sirens, she felt empty, hollow as the oak; and the miles separating her from the place of her dreams made Willow Dasset as inaccessible as if roots held her to the ground. But now, miraculously, she was speeding past her imagined incarnation, leaving it behind. In a moment she would be there.

'Can I open the gate, can I?'

Sally did not deign to reply. Her sister had no sense of wonder.

Anne took the silence for assent. When the car stopped she almost fell from it in her eagerness. 'Me . . . I can . . . I'll do . . .'

The car moved on, paused to collect Anne, then continued: past the tied cottage and down to the pond where the willows streamed; up again, round to face the farmyard, then came to a halt by the side of a wall sheltering the yard of the house.

Two small girls burst from the car. Their pigtails flying, red-faced with the ambition to be first, they dodge an ankle-nipping terrier and pound over cobblestones to the steps. They scramble up, circumventing the joy of a tethered collie, and career across the yard to reach their prize. It is a dead heat. No matter – his chest is wide enough for two.

He is crouched, his arms are ready. They are seized, pulled close, squirming and squealing like puppies. Noses bury into his cheeks, and they savour the looseness of elderly skin, the bristle of afternoon whiskers, the lovely, laundered smell of him, and the faint, far off magic of an evening cigar. Grandad Ludbury is the most delicious person in the world.

'What have we here? Couple of rascals, I'll be bound. No – bless my soul if it ain't two nice little girls. But what's this, and this? Pigtails you say? Never! *Puppydogs'* tails. And I reckon they need docking!'

'Hello, Daddy,' said Meg.

They were set down at once – but gently. They ran into the house.

''Lo Megs. How y' doin'?' It was said carelessly, but there was a catch in George Ludbury's voice.

'Fine, Daddy. How about you?'

'All the better for seein' you, m'dear, all the better for seein' you.'

17

She allowed him to hug her, and when his grasp relaxed she kissed his cheek.

'Where's Bunny?' she enquired, walking quickly into the house to avoid hearing the faintly sneering tone that would coat his voice when he greeted her husband.

The children had discovered Aunt Bunny in the dining-room. She was kissing them carefully when Meg walked in.

''Lo Bun.'

'Meg.'

They looked at one another, then briefly embraced.

'Isn't this *nice*?' Bunny asked the children, and they agreed wholeheartedly that it was.

'Can I go out on the farm?' Anne asked urgently.

'Dinner first! Aren't you hungry? I don't suppose you stopped.'

'Well,' Meg said to her sister, looking stern. 'How is she?'

'Fine,' Bunny replied firmly. 'I dare say she'll come down later. She usually does in the afternoon.'

Meg gave a snort.

'Look . . .' But Bunny recollected the children. She took Meg's arm to lead her to one side, and was reassured to see Anne, the restless one, rush from the room and Sally, the dreamy one, become lost in a world of her own by the window. 'Please don't cause trouble. It's up to her, surely. She knows what suits her. You've only just arrived – we won't talk about it today.'

Sally stared thoughtfully into the garden. No, they wouldn't talk about it today. Today was the first day of the visit, and first days were always made artificial by the effort to shun controversy. Tomorrow they would start to get down to it – in huddles over the scullery sink, with lowered voices in the pantry, raised voices in the

18

dairy, and earnest debate on the back stairs – Mother and Aunt Bunny, Mother and Uncle Jim, Uncle Harry, dropping in after business in Warwick or Stratford to make it a foursome, probably siding with Mother – the two married ones who lived in the outside world, against the two unmarried ones, Aunt Bunny and Uncle Jim, who had stayed close to home – talking about her, talking about Grandma Ludbury.

As to why her grandmother provoked such endless discussion, Sally was unclear. Grandma Ludbury appeared as inoffensive as it was possible to be. In fact, she hardly seemed to be there at all – not as people are there – only there in the sense that the staddle stone is there by the path, or the quince by the garden wall.

'Hallo, Mama. May we come in?' Meg and her daughters hovered in the doorway.

Rebecca Ludbury was sitting in a basket chair drawn close to the window. An open book lay on her knee, but Sally had gained the impression as the door opened that her grandmother had been looking out at the garden. Grandma Ludbury, when not in her garden, seemed always to cling to it, sitting either here at the bedroom window or downstairs in her sewing chair which was placed permanently by the window in the sitting-room. Even when found in her bed – and morning visitors invariably found her there – her eyes would stray to the trees at the garden's end.

'So you're not down yet,' Meg commented, stating the obvious.

'Presently,' Rebecca murmured.

'That'll be nice. You can show me round the garden,' Meg said encouragingly, going to kiss her. She stood back

19

and nudged her daughters, who approached and stood on either side of the basket chair.

'Sally.' Rebecca's smile invited her senior grandchild to place lips against the fragile hollow beneath her prominent cheekbone. 'And Anne.'

But Anne was nervous. She saw that grace and delicacy were required and knew she lacked them. In her anxious haste, her lips made a rude smacking noise. She stepped back hurriedly, abashed.

Sally remained close to the side of the chair, replying automatically to a polite question concerning her schooling, her mind pondering the strangeness of heavy-lidded, dark-fringed green eyes gazing into her own with distinct amusement. Grandma Ludbury's pure white hair framed her face softly and disappeared behind her neck where it coiled loosely, but obediently, into a bun. In her afternoon dress of mauve silk she looked, Sally thought, as frighteningly ravishing as the figurine on the sitting-room mantelpiece that must never, never be touched.

The disturbing eyes turned. 'And what about little Anne?'

'I want to go out on the farm.'

'Of course you do. Off you go.'

Anne looked, for confirmation, to her mother.

'Change into your old things first. You can go, too, Sally.'

Sally went reluctantly, going slightly out of her way in order to finger a brass bedknob as she passed. It still wobbled. Good. Nothing at Willow Dasset should ever change.

2

Morning crept through the curtain chink. Waking slowly, Sally saw that her sister was already pulling on clothes and muttering encouragement to herself, impatient to be up in the fields collecting the cows with John, and anxious, too, to have John all to herself. When her feet clattered down the uncarpeted back stairs, Sally considered whether to follow her example. But, no — on this first morning of the holiday she would lie abed and relish the sounds of Willow Dasset coming to life. She closed her eyes and pictured herself in her wide, bumpy bed; in the room that was half bedroom, half corridor; in the long house full of light and air, its grey stone walls and blue slate roof spattered with lichen, its porches swathed in jasmine and clematis, its ancient window-glass wavy as water.

Outside a cow lowed, then faint bangings and clankings began. Soon, the most resonant sound was John's milking song: 'I'll *take* you home *again*, Kathleen . . .' In the kitchen, George Ludbury took a watch from his waistcoat pocket and consulted the German regulator on the wall. 'John's making good time this morning,' he remarked to the tabby cat looking in balefully from the window-sill. He raised the lid of a large silver teapot and stirred. Then he attended similarly to a small green china pot. All was ready. Carefully, he took up the tray and set off through the hall towards the front stairs.

The front stairs bore carpet, but they squeaked obligingly. Sally took note of his ascent and wondered whether

21

he would bring her some tea. First he would go to Grandma Ludbury and pour her special tea from the china pot. Then he would tap on the door to her parents' room, place the tray on the oak chest beneath the landing window and pour two cups from the silver pot. Her father would receive these at the bedroom door with a suitable morning greeting. Next Aunt Bunny would be served, and then . . . Yes, he was coming. Grandad Ludbury stepped into the room.

'Good gracious me! Still in bed? And I thought all the landgirls had gone out long ago. It's lucky I've brought an extra cup.'

When he had gone, a door on the landing opened. Sally put cup and saucer on the bedside table, shot beneath the bedclothes, and waited, peeping deceitfully over the sheet through half-closed eyes. A chamber pot appeared, followed promptly by its bearer, Aunt Bunny, grimly hairnetted, impregnably dressing-gowned, on her way through her nieces' bedroom to the bathroom. On her return journey, Aunt Bunny noticed Sally in the bed. '*What* a lazy bones. I thought you'd be busy milking.'

Her father would be next. Sally could picture him listening at his bedroom door for sounds of saucepan and plate banging – signals that Aunt Bunny had arrived in the kitchen and that Henry might proceed with safety to the bathroom, free from the danger of accosting a maiden lady with her chamber pot.

'Not up?' observed Henry Robinson. And on his way back: 'You'd better go to the bathroom now, before your mother.'

Sally ignored him. It was wonderful how Willow Dasset neutralized her parents.

*

'That's it, then, I'm done,' said George, giving his empty plate a shove.

This presumed reference to his consumption of frizzled eggs and salt fat bacon surprised his breakfast companions.

'More, Daddy?' asked Bunny.

He ignored her. 'Three score years and ten,' he announced portentously, and then turned pained eyes towards his son-in-law. 'And that's all we're owed, according to the Good Book – ain't that so, Henry?'

The authority on the Scriptures could not get his mouth around a suitable reply.

Henry's embarrassment seemed to restore George to good humour. He grinned, rolled up his napkin and slid it into a silver ring. 'Well, I must be off to Stratford to see the lawyer-chappie. Got to make a will.' But on his way to the door between kitchen and hall he shook his head and became gloomy again. 'Me allotted span – to think I've come to the end of it!'

There was silence when the door had closed.

Bunny was the first to speak. 'His seventieth birthday. Oh Meg, do you think we should have made something of it?'

'Of course not. We never bother about birthdays – except for the children, of course. Just imagine how he'd feel if we made a fuss about this one.'

Sally and Anne, who were puzzled, began to ask tedious questions.

'Did I hear a tractor start up?' Henry asked craftily.

'Arthur!' cried the girls, jumping up from the bench. 'Can we go now?'

They found Arthur in the tractor shed beside a throbbing Fordson Major, wiping his hands on an oily rag. He was gorgeous – his dark brown eyes shone in his

23

ruddy face, he smelt of tractor, and he spoke in the slow singsong of Warwickshire. On his head was a well-greased cap tilted up perkily at the front. Once, in the High Street of the local market town they had caught sight of Arthur bare-headed. Sally had banished the sighting from her mind. Without his cap, Arthur had not been Arthur. But here he was in his glory; as always, pleased to see them – unlike Benjamin the surly shepherd, and John the cowman who tolerated them but was not encouraging. Arthur allowed them to sit on the wide mudguards of his tractor for hours, ploughing, collecting muck from the farmyard or hay from the rickyard. During haymaking or harvest he allowed Sally to drive the old yellow tractor from stook to stook so that he could join the other men pitchforking sheaves into the cart. Anne was jealous of this privilege, and the arrival of a small grey Ferguson for John's use had a great deal to do with her cultivation of the cowman. Today it was the Fordson Major gearing up for duty – a giant not to be trifled with – even Arthur had been stern about this. They climbed aboard and perched on the mudguards, gripping its rim with their fingers and stuffing toes into crannies to maintain their balance.

'The Guv'nor's garn arff, then,' observed Arthur.

'Yes. To Stratford.'

'And it's nart market day.'

'No. He's gone to see about his allotted span.'

'Ah,' said Arthur, mystified.

But George had not gone immediately to Stratford. From Dasset Saint Mary's he drove three miles to Horley-in-the-Hedges where Jim, his elder son, farmed. He found Jim inspecting his wheat. 'Not ready. Not by a long chalk,' called George from the gate. He put his elbows on the gate-top.

Jim looked up, fumbled in his pocket for a tobacco

pouch, and ambled towards his father. He leant his back against the gate and filled his pipe.

'Another two weeks,' George insisted.

Jim felt for his lighter, then applied it to the bowl of the pipe.

'Two weeks at least. If the weather holds.'

Sucking noises. Puffs of fragrant smoke.

'I'm on my way to see Macheson.'

'Uhuh.'

''Bout me will.'

Jim withdrew the pipe from his mouth and examined it. In his pocket he found a spent matchstick and with this he poked the pipe's contents.

'M' time's up – three score years and ten.' He darted a look at his son, but there was no response. 'So me and your mother have been thinking things over – about the future – how time's getting on, I mean, look at this land.' (He waved a disparaging arm.) 'You'll never make anything of it. Terrible heavy stuff. How many ploughs have you broke since you came here? Give it up, boy, and come back to Willow Dasset. That's what your mother asked me to say. She'll never get any stronger, and she'd like to see things settled. We both would. We want to see the place carry on. You could start to take up the reins.'

Jim smiled to himself and took plenty of time to relight his pipe. So his mother had asked his father to say that, had she? A likely tale! Jim and his mother understood one another very well. The last thing she would do was interfere in his life. And she knew as well as he did what the old man was like.

'It wouldn't work,' Jim said, eventually.

'What d'ye mean?'

'Me taking up the reins. You'd never stand for it.

You'd always know better than me – you couldn't help yourself.'

George stared thoughtfully at the unripe wheat for a moment or two. 'You'll stay here, then?'

'Ay.'

'Ah well, so it'll be up to the four of you – when the time comes. At least I shan't be here to see what you all get up to.'

'That's true.'

George shot him a bleak look, but Jim's attention was still on the corn. 'Better not keep the lawyer-fellow waitin', I suppose – be sure to charge extra if I do.'

'I'll be over to see them all tonight.'

I dare say you will, me lad, George thought grimly as he took himself off. And I dare say you'll stoke up with a darn good supper.

That afternoon, George and Meg walked quickly across the house-yard, along the cobbled path by stables and barn, and through an open gateway at the edge of the farmyard. Sally, rushing from Dutch barn to house, almost collided with them, but they pressed on, as if unaware of the ten-year-old scrambling out of their path. The rutted track rose steeply and their steps slowed. George paused to lean on his stick.

'You say you called on Jim first,' Meg prompted, watching him closely.

George jabbed a warning with the end of his stick. They were still in sight of the back of the house. 'We'll walk on a bit, first.' And when the track veered to the right and sank between banks of hedgerow, he began to speak.

Sally, arriving in the house and running up the back stairs to the bathroom, was accosted by her father.

'Seen your mother? Or your grandfather?'

'Both. Just now. Going up the field.'

This was disconcerting news. Henry considered his daughter for some moments, while his hand turned over coins in the depths of his trouser pockets.

'Can I go now?'

'Oh . . . Mmm.' He turned into the room where his daughters slept.

Half an hour ago, he reflected, checking his wristwatch for accuracy – correction: twenty-seven and a half minutes ago – his wife had closeted herself with her father for the promised word. The business usually took a quarter of an hour, after which she came straight upstairs to report. He glanced around the room for inspiration. None came, so he went out on to the landing and then to the room he shared with Meg. On the edge of the big feather bed he sat down and waited impatiently for his wife's return.

'Can't understand the fellow,' George said, as he and Meg propped themselves against a gate and stared over it into a field. 'Seems he's got no feeling at all for Willow Dasset. Determined to stay on there, trying to make a livin'.'

'You can't expect Jim to feel anything. He was a grown man when you came here. This is just the place where he worked.'

'For twenty years.'

'For you. He even calls you the Guv'nor.'

George looked at her with narrowed eyes, as if he'd be damned if the fellow thought of calling him anything else. 'I told him – you can start to take up the reins, I said.'

'He'd have a hard job with you breathing down his neck. He's his own boss now, and I don't suppose he wants to come back here and argue the toss with you. Don't blame him.'

There was silence for a while.

'So – it'll be left to the four of you. Thing is, Meg, strikes me, now's the time you could do with a bit of help. It'd spare us both this rigmarole every time you come to stay . . .'

'Not every time, Daddy . . .'

'You don't like it. You do it for Henry. Bet it sticks in yer throat having to ask yer old Dad for money after all these years. You were always an independent madam.'

Meg, who had gone rather pink, caught his eye. They grinned.

'Expensive tastes, your husband's. Likes a nice motor, don't he?'

'We're busy people, Daddy. We've got to get about.'

'I dare say. But Henry Robinson, Esquire, likes to get around in style. Talkin' about a Rover at dinner time.'

'Oh, that's all it is – talk. Henry's always on about the latest car. Drives me mad.'

'Should think it does, old girl. Well, how'd it be if we put a nice little sum somewhere to tide you over these reg'lar difficulties – somewhere safe where Henry can't help himself. Be a bit infuriatin' if he turned up here in a brand new motor and I knew it was me who'd had the privilege of buying it for him, if you take my meaning.'

Meg hesitated. It would be pleasant to be free of these begging sessions with her father – and it was very decent of him to see how awful it was for her. But Henry had strong views about marriage, and particularly that there should be no secrets between husband and wife. 'Are you sure it could be done without Henry finding out?'

'If we put our heads together.'

'You are *good*, Daddy. Does Mama know about the will, by the way?' She had not entirely banished marital frankness from her mind.

28

'Oh, no. Couldn't worry your Mama. Wouldn't do at all.'

'It might encourage her to take an interest in things.'

George sucked in his breath. 'Ooo no. No, no, no. Mustn't be worried about anything. All the doctors have been clear about that; so was your Aunt Pip when she nursed her, and so was that terrible nurse-woman we had to put up with the last time she had a turn. I don't usually pay much heed to doctors – you know that – but I reckon they've been right about your Mama. How long has she been an invalid now?'

'Her first heart attack was in 1923. I'd just started teaching.'

'Well, well . . . twenty-three years. Just goes to show. As long as she stays nice and quiet she could last for years . . .' He smiled at the thought. Nice and quiet – that was Becky – quiet and gentle and calm; a superior specimen of womankind. He sighed, thinking of his good luck. Becky graced his house – yes, graced was the word for it. He pictured her coming softly into the dining-room with a bowl of sweet peas for the table, or kneeling in the garden to weed the border, charming as the flowers she tended; and at the close of day, propped on her mound of white pillows in their high feather bed, smiling her lazy smile, touching his hand with her own before closing her eyes to sleep . . . Ah, Becky. They had no need of words . . .

Meg broke into his complacency. 'I don't know, Daddy. She shuts herself away most of the time. What sort of life is that?'

'Her sort,' George answered promptly. 'And it suits her.' But they had got away from the subject of his financial arrangements. 'Come on. Come and take a look at m' new hunter. He's over in Bailey's Field.'

'He? You promised to stick to the mare after that last tumble.'

'He's a steady enough fellow, but there's a bit more go in him than Sherry.'

'Oh, Daddy!'

They moved off towards the great field – named after some long-forgotten soul – at the end of the track.

'Now, I'll tell you what I had in mind . . .'

Sally had been in a hurry to return to the Dutch barn where she and Anne had constructed a series of jumps – a stairway of bales affording ever more daring leaps into a mound of soft hay below. But she had lingered, and it was fatal to linger at Willow Dasset where immediate surroundings were so ensnaring. She had become transfixed on an upstairs window-seat, back pressed to one wall, toes to the other, hugging her knees. The house had drawn her in. She watched the yard, and the willow-draped pond, and the rough-turfed fields rising beyond. She watched the terrier jog purposely towards a cat hunched in the sun. He tried to mount her, but she spat and cuffed him, then jumped out of reach on to the wall. He pulled a paw over his boxed ear. (Serves you right, Tinker, she almost called, but was reluctant to dispel her indolence.) She watched these things, but all the time was intensely aware of the house and its faint hum lapping her.

She was roused by the insubstantial click of the half-glazed garden door. At the head of the landing a carved oak chest beneath the window made an excellent platform from which to view the garden. She climbed on to it and looked through the wavy glass of the window-pane. Grandma Ludbury was walking slowly along the path, shiny in her mauve dress, precise in her button-strapped shoes. She paused to stoop over the border, took secateurs from the trug on her arm, and snipped. She went on, then, at the point where the path turned a corner, disappeared behind a large rosemary bush. Would she reappear? It seemed she would not. Perhaps, as had happened yesterday, she would surprise them with her presence at the tea table. They would run in to tea to find her already seated there; and she would smile but not speak; take a half slice of bread and butter, cut it, move it occasionally around her plate; but not eat. And then, others having eaten heartily and discoursed vigorously, she would sigh, roll up her napkin, murmur something no-one could catch, and quietly leave the room.

Somewhere there was a robust disturbance. Sally abandoned the garden and climbed down from the chest. Evidently, milking had begun. She would go and disappoint her sister.

3

'Is it dinner time?' Sally asked, surprised, as the Fordson Major turned towards the gate.

'No. 'Tis Friday,' Arthur yelled joyfully, pulling on the accelerator to make the girls squeal.

'Go on, go sideways down the bank, Arthur,' screamed Anne.

And Arthur obliged, so that Anne soared high above them and Sally swooped near to the ground. Anne whooped and begged for more. Sally was silent, intent upon the mechanics of the performance.

Arthur, as he pulled and swung, saw her eyes upon his hands. 'Want to try it?' he called, flashing his teeth in a wide grin.

'Oh . . . yes!'

He slowed the machine, then swung a leg over the seat and indicated that she could sit there. She scrambled between his arms and grasped the wheel, his hands over hers. After a while he motioned her to pull on the accelerator. The tractor surged forward and they bounced along the track, the hedgerow rushing close to their faces, their breath snatched by the stinging wind. At the steep incline down to the tractor shed, Arthur stepped on the brake pedal. 'Now, push it right in,' he said in her ear, and placed her hand on the accelerator. 'Put your foot on here and kick arff the hook.' She replaced his foot with her own. 'Let it up slowly.' Under severe restraint, the roaring machine was brought into its stall.

Arthur cut off the engine. In the vast, still silence, Sally discovered that her legs were trembling.

'I'm arff to help John. Us has't be presentable of a Friday.'

Anne ran after him, beseeching that she, too, might have a turn on the Fordson Major.

'Nart till you'm big as your sister.'

Their voices and footsteps died. Sally was alone in the silence. Hot fumes still rose from the tractor's nose; the Fordson Major still glowed from exertion under her hands. She closed her eyes and relived every moment of her conquest. Arthur had contrived it for her. Gratitude and love overwhelmed her – she must *do* something – she would . . . she would write him a poem.

From the dressing table drawer in her bedroom she grabbed notebook and pencil. She had begun to arrange herself for composition on the window-seat when sounds of bathing disturbed her – soon the bather would emerge from the bathroom and pass through this room to the landing. Another place must be found. Downstairs, Aunt Bunny was savaging the sitting-room carpet with a Hoover. But the dining-room was deserted: here she chose a dim corner and sank to the floor, propping her back against the side of a walnut sideboard.

By the time George Ludbury entered the room, words were hitting the page with pleasing briskness. Sally was scarcely aware of her grandfather sighing at his bureau desk, occasionally groaning at the unpleasant nature of his toil. Absorbed, she wrote on.

There was a tap at the door.

'Come in.'

It was then that Sally looked up, startled into awareness by the novelty of his curt tone. She put her head around the corner of the sideboard to view the door. Benjamin came in, followed by John and then Arthur. They shuffled in line towards the bureau, each with a folded cap in hand, each hanging his head.

George did not look up. 'Reckon that's it,' he said at last. ''Ere y'are, then.' His voice was sneering, almost resentful.

Benjamin stepped forward and took the proffered notes and coins.

'Hatherton,' barked George.

Benjamin handed the money to Arthur, who jerked his head forward like a chicken and said: 'Thank 'ee, Sir.'

'Boyles.'

Benjamin took the second pile of money and gave it to John, who also ducked his head and mumbled his thanks.

'And you, Gurney.'

'Thank 'ee, Sir,' cried Benjamin, bowing respectfully over his own handful. Then he turned to his companions and indicated the door with cross impatience as though they had dallied there too long.

The door closed. Sally could hardly breathe. Her presence there was undoubtedly illegal – Aunt Bunny had once called her urgently from the dining-room one Friday morning when her grandfather had discovered her there, she now recalled. No wonder. It had been an inexplicably shameful scene. The men – John of the exuberant singing voice, Benjamin of the forbidding dignity, and wonderful matchless Arthur – had shuffled in and out of the room like half-men. As for Grandad . . . She could not take it in, this glimpse of a grandfather she did not know. He must not discover her.

George closed the lid of the bureau, rose and stuck out his elbows to expand his constricted chest. Ah – that was better. Desk work done with, thank the Lord

– George Ludbury wasn't cut out for it. He sauntered from the room.

With relief, Sally scrambled to her feet. She placed her notebook on the table and considered her next move.

'Hello, there. Given up farmin' for today?' George enquired, returning with the *Daily Telegraph*.

'Yes. I came in to write a poem,' she explained hurriedly.

'Well I never! Just like your great-grandmama! Famous for po'try writin', was your great-grandmama. Look.' He took a photograph from the mantelshelf and set it down by her notebook. 'Here she is. A wonderful lady. You couldn't do better than take after her, young Sal.' Well pleased with his granddaughter's confidence, he helped himself to a stiff drink from the sideboard – he deserved one, he reckoned, of a Friday. On his way to his armchair by the hearth, he gave her shoulder an affectionate squeeze.

Sally looked at the scowling woman in the silver frame and was not impressed. But at least Grandad seemed himself again. She turned to look at him, and he winked roguishly over his glass.

'I love you, Grandad,' she told him.

With matching seriousness he replied: 'And I love you too, my little dear.'

'You see what it *is*,' Meg said in urgent undertone to her sister, who was rubbing knives in a heap of Vim. 'A phobia.'

'How's that?'

'A phobia. An unreasonable dread.'

'But what *of*,' Bunny hissed, exasperated.

Meg hesitated. 'Of us, I suppose. At least,' she continued, gaining confidence, 'being with us in normal,

35

everyday circumstances. Can't *eat* with us, can she? Hardly a morsel at tea yesterday. Can't come downstairs and *be* with us – goes straight out into the garden, or sneaks into the sitting-room and hides behind her sewing. It's unhealthy. Not normal.'

Bunny's hands fell still. Her eyes rose to the window over the long, shallow, china sink and were captured by the defunct water pump in the yard. She was torn between the delicious importance Meg's theory put upon what seemed, on the face of it, to be an unremarkable state of affairs, and the danger of going down a path possibly riddled with pitfalls for the unsophisticated. Playing for time, she turned on the tap and held the scoured knives under running water.

'The trouble is, these irrational states of mind take people over. She may get to the point where she refuses to leave her room.'

'But Meg, she's an invalid. Doctor Parry says she ought to stay in her room when she feels like it.'

'Look: she's not such an invalid that she can't do two hours' weeding on the trot. I timed her yesterday . . .'

'I do quite a bit of the weeding – under her direction, of course.'

'Yes, well, you've fallen in with her. You're so close to things that you can't see clearly. You're at her beck and call – and Daddy's beck and call. You don't have time to think.'

This portrait of herself as martyr was rather attractive. Perhaps, after all, she would go along with Meg a little. 'Oh,' she breathed, 'you don't think Mama's . . . deranged?'

Trust Bunny to go overboard. 'Not *deranged*, exactly. There are degrees of instability. Mama's behaviour is irrational, and that sort of thing needs a firm

36

hand. What I'm saying is, we ought to tackle her with it.'

Danger. 'We must ask the boys first.'

'The boys! What do they know? I've studied psychology. I've taken exams in it. I've been to seminars, read articles . . .'

Without warning the scullery door opened. Sally stood on the threshold, observing how they fell silent then hurled themselves at sink and table as though nothing concerned them so much as well-scoured kitchen knives and brightly polished silver cutlery. Her father's frequent indictments against the whispering and plotting that went on over the Willow Dasset scullery sink were demonstrably justified – why else did they appear so guilty?

'What do you want?' snapped Meg.

'John wants to know about the milk. One can or two?'

'Oh . . . Two,' Bunny cried wildly.

'Well, go on then,' urged Meg as her daughter remained in the doorway.

Sally dealt them a severe look, then closed the door on their obnoxiousness.

4

It was Sunday. Meg was helping Bunny to change their mother's bed-linen before going to church with Henry and their daughters. 'Won't you come with us, Bun?' she asked for the second time that morning.

'Pull it *taut*,' instructed Bunny, preferring to concentrate on the job in hand.

'Well, I think it's a shame. This is what comes of tying yourself down – can't even go to church when you want to.'

'Don't be silly. Jim'll take me whenever I want to go.'

'Then why don't you take the opportunity to come with us?'

'I couldn't.'

'Why? Mama's all right. There's nothing the matter with her – nothing urgently the matter . . .'

'Nothing to do with Mama.' She pointed impatiently: 'The pillow cases are on the chair.'

'We could get the dinner started before we go.'

Bunny set about the pillows; but Meg, her stern watchfulness implied, intended to be answered. All right, thought Bunny, turning red, she'd jolly well come out with it: 'I won't go to church with Henry.'

'Won't go with Henry?'

'He shows *orff*.'

Meg sat down on the bed.

'Get up! Mama'll be back in a minute.'

'Look here, Bunny. What do you mean?'

38

'He shows *orff* – bobbing up and down, crossing himself, singing twice as loud as the choir, shouting in the responses . . . It's frightful – everyone stares. Don't ever ask me to go with him again.'

Well! This description of her husband's rigorous churchmanship was beyond belief. Furthermore, it was downright offensive.

The sisters completed their task in huffy silence.

'I'd better make sure the girls are ready,' Meg said coldly.

She found them in their bedroom, swinging their legs gloomily on either side of the bed; Sunday smart in clean white socks, newly polished shoes, pale print frocks with neat white collars, well-brushed blazers, and ribbons instead of elastic bands sealing the ends of their plaits – scarlet for fair-haired Anne, royal blue for dark-haired Sally.

'What are you doing here? Grandma will be out of her bath any minute.'

'Daddy said: Sit here and don't move.'

'Then go and don't move in the dining-room.'

They wandered downstairs and arranged themselves obediently on dining-room chairs.

George, waking from a doze over the *Farmers' Weekly*, was entranced. 'My – what a picture! Two nice little girls with ribbons in their hair. Goin' to church?'

They nodded glumly.

'Well, now,' – he straightened a leg and reached into a pocket. 'Say a prayer for your wicked ol' Grandad and put that on the plate for me.' He got up and gave each girl a shilling. 'Go every Sunday, do yer?'

'Yes, Grandad.'

'That's good girls.'

'Not just once – at least twice.'

'Yes, 'cos we go to Sunday School in the afternoon.'

'Sometimes we have to go in the evening as well – that's three times. *And* in the week if it's a special day.'

They stared up at him with big, mournful eyes.

Poor little blighters! George had always held strong views about church-going. These days he felt absolved from it on account of his advanced years and invalid wife, because church-going should be a family affair, an occasion to look smart like these little girls here, to parade solid citizenship and respect for a decent English way of life. But moderation was the essence of the thing. Once people took to hanging on to the vicar's skirt, to creeping off at all hours to kneel in a dingy church, or – worst of all – to churchifying everyday life, things had got dangerously out of hand. There was a time and place for everything. Too much church led to unhealthy goings on – foreign Romanish practices, or rantin' like those nasty Methodists. Oh, dearie me; what a thing to inflict on the children! He shook his head and reached again into his pocket. "Ere y'are,' he said, trying to make it up to them with two half-crowns placed on the table top. 'Next time you go to Stratford buy something nice.'

'Oh, thank you, Grandad.' Sally stood on tiptoe to kiss him.

'Yes, thank you, Grandad.' Anne enthusiastically clambered along his stooping body to kiss his other cheek.

'Nice little girls,' he said tenderly, and patted their shiny heads.

Upstairs in her room, Meg snatched a hat from the wardrobe drawer and marched on the dressing table. She sat on the stool and glared into the looking glass, seeing not herself but her sister beating pillows into shape. The trouble with Bunny was that she led a sheltered life; she had no idea as to what constituted proper and decent behaviour. As with church, so with everything else beyond the confines of Willow Dasset: she was an appalling companion to go out with – sniffy in restaurants, offhand in shops, an uneasy, disapproving visitor in other people's homes . . . Damn! A hank of hair had eluded a hairpin. Pin in mouth, Meg wound the hair around a finger. This time it was caught, she confirmed, holding a hand mirror to the back of her head. To forestall further mutiny she picked up the hat and rammed it over her hair, and for extra security inserted a stout hatpin.

Meg did not linger: lacking the sort of vanity that requires constant reassurance, she took for granted that she cut a pleasing figure. Tall and slender, youthful for her forty odd years, she had a certain beauty. In her college days she had been considered dashing – romantic even; and she had deduced from the adoration she inspired that all attempts at improvement were superfluous. Besides, she had no time for frippery. New frocks and coats to replace those that had finally given up the ghost were bought on the run after school. Her response to the question: And what had modom in mind? was invariably a vague Oh – something in green. Green, it had been agreed by an admiring throng on the day of her triumph as May Queen at Saint Ursula's College, was her colour. It was the only information she had absorbed pertaining to the enhancement of her appearance, and she had trotted it out ever since to ward off further time-wasting considerations. When she looked smart, it was by accident. Sadly, there had been no happy accident this present Sunday morning. She was wearing a green cotton frock with regrettable pink spots (Well, I suppose it's *primarily* green, she had said to the shop assistant, dragging it over her head to see if it would fit), a jacket of green tweed with blue and orange flecks, and her winter

41

brown felt hat. (In the rush to be ready for the journey to Willow Dasset, she had been unable to lay hands on her summer straw.)

Now then. Prayer book. Collection money. Gloves. Oh – and better grab a clean hanky. Good egg! – for once she was on time.

Henry had been warming up the car for the past ten minutes. 'Come on, come on,' he urged, as she ran down the steps.

'Bags of time,' she said, pushing her daughters into the back. 'Your watch is always fast.'

Henry's spirits were high. Meg's word with the old man – despite the unscheduled excursion – had proved as fruitful as ever. And Henry was looking forward to a trip to the garage. 'How about Stratford tomorrow? If we get the car to the garage by nine, we could be queuing for theatre tickets by half-past.'

'There's no matinée on a Monday. Anyway, it depends which day we go to see the aunts. I'll give them a ring tonight.'

At once the day darkened. The obligatory visit to The Grange, the home of Meg's three spinster aunts and bachelor uncle, was the item of their Willow Dasset holidays most feared by Henry. Whenever it loomed he steadied his nerve with a silent rehearsal of the holiday's utility – that the four of them ate heartily for two weeks or more, that they returned with a food-stuffed car boot, and perhaps shoes for the girls or a frock or two; not to mention attention to the car's requirements.

And there was an exchange of looks in the back of the car. There was a certain *frisson* about a visit to The Grange. Anne frankly dreaded it. Privately, Sally likened it to a jump from the highest bale in the Dutch barn – terrifying, but rather a thrill.

'Here we are,' said Henry, rallying at the sight of the church.

'And in loads of time. They're still ringing a full peal,' said Meg, vindicated.

Meg, with Bunny's words still fresh in her mind, was acutely conscious of Henry beside her in the pew. Usually, Henry was not beside her. Attending their home parish church of Saint Luke's, Henry would be in the sanctuary or the chancel, for Henry was the sacristan upon whose solid frame, rousing voice and eye for detail frail Father Timms depended. Saint Luke's was a parish renowned for High Churchmanship; and if the Robinsons, crossing themselves and genuflecting, now drew disapproving eyes from a Broad Church congregation, well, Meg was sorry, but it was something on which she was not prepared to compromise. In this matter she was stoutly at one with her husband. (Here, noting that the girls had only half-heartedly inclined their heads for the doxology, she gave them a nudge and a fierce glare. Miserably, they bobbed their heads to a more acceptable level.)

It was at Saint Luke's that Henry had met Meg – or, to be exact, that Meg had spotted Henry and resolved to appropriate him. (Meg was a determined woman.) Newly arrived in the town to take up her appointment as deputy head of Corporation Street Elementary School, she had cycled from church to church wondering where she would take her custom; for, as an old girl of Saint Ursula's College, Chelsea, she had a tradition to maintain. The moment she stepped into the scented gloom of Saint Luke's, she knew that her quest was over. There, just inside the door was the holy water, across the chancel steps the rood screen, and glinting reassuringly in the sanctuary the red glow betokening the presence of the reserve sacrament.

The following Sunday had been a festival. 'Hymn for the Introit' a voice had announced from the vestry door, a voice of such militant faith that Meg was awed, and when the organ sounded and the owner of that voice stepped forth, clasping a golden cross, fixing eyes on its topmost tip, singing like a passionate evangelist, Meg decided then and there that she would have him. Henry would be her indulgence, her reward for years of dedication to single-minded hard work, and compensation for earlier disappointments (a Viennese doctor with an unfortunate disposition to find her amusing, and a vicar who had assumed that she would abandon her career to become his unpaid curate). It did not cross her mind that Henry might have other plans for the disposal of his person. Fortunately, he was dazzled by this strong-minded, clever, intense-looking woman who saw such exciting promise in him, and impressed by her striking looks – her close-set green eyes, her frizzy auburn hair unsuccessfully caught up in a bun at the nape of her neck, her long, lissom figure (she was a little taller than he), and her air of unquestioning self-confidence. Furthermore, following the death of his doting widowed mother, there was a gap in his life that a wife might conveniently fill.

It had pleased Meg to discover that Henry lacked an education, for it seemed a romantic thing to liberate him from the bonds of ignorance. Henry's evenings became crammed with the perusal of text books. But Henry proved a poor scholar: the spirit was willing – he talked endlessly about the great things he would attain – but was never quite available when required. There was always an obstacle to his study – the fatigue of the day, the coldness of the room, the little tasks begging his attention; and finally, of course, in 1939, the war. He was exempted from armed service by the requirements of Law and

Order – only Henry, it was found, had a sufficiently comprehensive grasp of the town's legal affairs. (There was another reason: the fanatical set of his brilliant blue eyes was discovered to be the result of a cast, but this he kept strictly to himself, and soon eliminated it from his memory.) His evenings – and nights – were claimed by the ARP. Henry's stock rose, however, without recourse to further learning. The pressure on the courts was such that by 1945 he had a sizeable contingent of under-clerks to command. Lack of learning forever barred his way to a legal career – becoming clerk to the justices, for instance – but greater industry on the part of the criminal classes procured for him increasing status as an administrative official. For her part, Meg had understood the matter long ago: the securing of Henry's rightful position in life could be talked about, dreamed about, grumbled about; but would never, ever be acted upon.

Meg was not given to brooding. If an irremovable obstacle arose in her path she took note, shrugged, and made the best of it. Undoubtedly, marriage brought her a faint sense of disappointment, but it was by no means financial or social disappointment, for in these areas she had never relied upon anyone other than herself. It was loss of a *dream* of Henry that occasionally triggered a small ache – the knowledge that her husband's shining exterior hid an inertia of mind and a pettiness of spirit. 'Never mind,' she would mutter, discovering herself with these unfruitful thoughts, 'we've just got to get on with it.' She took the briefest possible breaks from her work to produce two daughters in swift succession. The shortage of qualified teachers ensured that her babies were welcome to lie in their prams in a school secretary's office or play on a rug in a staffroom minded by a couple of big girls or a school caretaker. By the end of the war she had achieved her ambition – the headship of a large school. At last, she was in a position to make mandatory the teaching methods recommended by Saint Ursula's. Educationalists came to admire, students queued to learn: she became, as she had always known she would, a success.

(Henry liked to claim a part of this success for himself. 'I have always encouraged my wife,' he confided at tea parties – and sometimes, when stung by perceived slight: 'I have always allowed my wife to work.' Overhearing him, Meg would merely mutter 'Silly man!' under her breath; it was nothing to get worked up about. Life was such that for as long as she could remember she had eased her feelings with Silly man! – the phrase had been a favourite comment of her grandmother and her Aunt Charlotte, resourceful ladies both, who had made an early impression upon her.)

Meg's mild disappointment was never present in church. Sometimes, during a particularly moving service, she could almost feel that her initial conception of Henry had been the correct one. Now, as they joined in the singing of the final hymn, Henry's voice rose to the rafters making even the effort of the choir seem lack-lustre and puny. Her heart applauded him. In the practice of his religion, her husband was as robust and meticulous as ever, and this aspect of Henry, no-one (least of all that silly Bunny) should be allowed to despise.

Jim always ate his Sunday dinner at Willow Dasset. He was a very satisfactory uncle, full of party turns and significant winks. Large and lumbering, one of his tricks was to jiggle the great mahogany table with his knees while stolidly eating. Sally, astounded by his audacity, would dart looks at her grandfather who steadfastly ignored the table's instability, and to her aunt who put on an

'Isn't uncle naughty?' face. 'Which hand?' he liked to demand of his nieces. And which ever one they chose he opened the other to reveal a coin. Uncle Jim had a hearty appetite, putting away mounds of bread with his meat and vegetables and always having seconds of pudding. After dinner he liked forty winks. 'Hush, Uncle Jim's having a nap in the boxroom,' Aunt Bunny would warn if they ran noisily down the back stairs; and sometimes: 'Good gracious me! Four o'clock and Uncle's still asleep. Run upstairs and pull his nose.' For some years Sally had been unsure whether to take this instruction seriously. Then, one holiday, noting the girlish fun suggested by Aunt Bunny's expression, she decided to try it, and thus became witness to an alarming transformation – easy-going, trick-loving, sleepy Uncle Jim into wide awake, very cross, possibly vengeful Uncle Jim. 'She told me to do it – Aunt Bunny did,' Sally had yelled before fleeing. Her aunt still persisted in the instruction whenever Uncle Jim overran his Sunday snooze; but now Sally received it in silence, marvelling at the chasm of misunderstanding it revealed.

Sunday afternoons were trying times at Willow Dasset. Apart from milking – unless the harvest was underway – there were no farming activities to divert children at a loose end. And Sunday frocks must reappear, unblemished, at the tea table. Whether it was permissible to change clothing for the afternoon had never been established: thinking it over, Sally decided that farming clothes on a Sunday might be provocative, suggestive of a blasphemous degree of activity. So it was in her Sunday best that she slid cautiously through the open kitchen door and scurried across the farmyard.

In the dim tractor shed she took in gulps of air deliciously perfumed by cow manure and tractor oil. (They had been muck-carting yesterday.) She climbed on to the Fordson Major and tried to make the seat bounce, but it was not as well-worn and springy as the seat on the old yellow tractor. Not that this was a shortcoming – no, no – the Fordson Major was her favourite, now. Her hands fondled the monster's steering wheel. Her eyes fell on the key, unexpectedly in the ignition. It was a provoking sight. She became still. Long minutes went by during which her mouth grew dry and her hands so sweaty that she was obliged to wipe them on the pale skirt of her Sunday frock.

George, emerging from the kitchen, was surprised to hear a tractor start up. He pulled watch from waistcoat pocket and discovered, as he had thought, that it was much too early for John. Moreover, he was sure it was not the Ferguson; his hearing was not all it should be these days, but he could swear it was that big blighter. He stooped to let the sheepdog off her chain and whistled for the terrier. Master and dogs set off.

After dinner, hearing his father-in-law declare an intention to inspect the wheat, Henry had thought it safe to settle in the dining-room armchair with a Boots library book. He always thought carefully before settling anywhere at Willow Dasset. The sitting-room, for instance, was an unreliable haven in the afternoon; Meg's disconcerting mother was sometimes discovered there, sitting with her sewing by the window; and however gallant the 'Pardon me' from the doorway, the 'Might one intrude?' or the 'Mustn't disturb the good work', the blessed woman said not a word, just lolled her head against the chairback, grinning at a private joke. Most embarrassing. But the worst danger by far arose during harvest. Then nowhere was safe. Nor was any able-bodied man, come to that.

Harry dropping in after a hard day's work, Jim's airman friend calling at Willow Dasset during his leave, business acquaintances of the old man; whoever the visitor the outcome was the same: jackets discarded, shirt sleeves rolled, and best foot forward for the harvest field. In his eager-to-please, brand-new-son-in-law days, Henry had done it all – fed wire into the snatchy baler, spread the load on top of a swaying cart, tied sacks, heaved bales, built stooks; but his enthusiasm had waned in the flying dust and deafening racket. These days at harvest time he was careful to demonstrate other obligations – a promise to drive the women to the shops, or the need to investigate under the car bonnet. If all else failed, it was prudent to seek out a secluded spot and to remain there with a book between mealtimes.

Jim, of course, had helped the women clear the table. It constantly amazed Henry to see these big Ludbury men showing keen with a tea cloth. Jim and Harry both seemed to gravitate naturally towards the scullery at the end of a meal, and on one memorable occasion, returning in the early afternoon from a rain-ruined expedition, the Robinsons had discovered George Ludbury drying away as Bunny washed. Henry had more care for his dignity. 'I don't mind you working,' he liked to inform the primary wage earner in the Robinson household whenever she complained about the chores, 'but I draw the line at skiv-vying. If you can't manage, get a woman.' It sometimes happened that visitors of some eminence in the town were expected when the Robinson home had turned grey with dust, and then Henry was obliged to set to with a vacuum cleaner – but always with a sense of grievance. As for the Ludbury obsession with the scullery, Henry made much of their offensive huddles over the sink: it was not pleasant to be made to feel he had stumbled upon, and interrupted, a conspiracy; and he trusted it would be understood if he declined to venture there again. Let Jim get on with it, he smirked, turning the page of his book.

Ambling between dining-room, pantry and scullery with dirty china and left-over food, Jim became aware of a certain tension between his scurrying sisters. Meg's expression indicated a determination to have it out and Bunny's a determination to avoid confrontation. When the table was cleared, Meg cried: 'Now look here, Bunny,' gave him a push and slammed the scullery door. Dismissed, he wandered into the hall and retrieved a brown paper parcel from the depths of a cluttered coat-stand. He returned to the kitchen and went to the back stairs which he ascended with as much resonance as possible. Anyone interested in his movements would conclude that he had repaired to the boxroom. In fact, Jim did not spend his entire Sunday afternoons asleep. He spent a part of them – the part when he was sure of each resident's whereabouts – in the master bedroom at the head of the landing.

'You've come nice and soon,' his mother observed as he entered. She was sitting in her basket chair by the window.

'Yes. Meg and Bunny are having an argy-bargy.' He leaned down to kiss her cheek and drop the parcel into her lap.

Calmly, she untied string and unwrapped paper. 'You got it! Thank you, darling. Have you read it?'

'No – brought it straight to you.'

'Well, you shall have it soon. You can take the Graham Greene, by the way. I finished it last night. And there's another one I'd like – I made a note of it on my pad – it was reviewed in the *Telegraph*.'

Jim crossed the room and went to the table drawer at the far side of the bed. From this he took a notebook, tore off a piece of paper and put it in his pocket. Then, in the cupboard beneath the drawer, he found *The Power And The Glory* and stuffed that, too, into his jacket pocket.

'While you're there, dear, look out a nice cover.'

Jim rummaged. 'This do?'

'Admirably.'

He brought her the book sleeve and soon *Goodbye to Berlin* was encased in a jacket announcing *A Posy of Garden Verse*.

'Now – sit down and tell me what you've been doing.'

Jim sat on the side of the bed nearest to her – his father's side. 'Went to the pictures Thursday night,' he told her. '*The Fleet's In*. William Holden, Dorothy Lamour. You'd have enjoyed it.'

'I haven't been for such a long time. When harvest is over and you've more time, you must drop round one afternoon to take me for a drive – when there's something nice on at The Regal.'

They smiled at one another, then lapsed for some minutes into comfortable silence.

'Going into the garden this afternoon?' Jim enquired eventually.

'Oh, yes. And I've something to show you. I've been clearing that difficult patch on the bank. I think hypericum would do there rather well. Can you get me half a dozen plants? That reminds me – bring me the box, and let's see what we've got.'

'There's still a fair bit left.'

'Fetch it, dear; it's nice to have plenty in hand.'

Jim collected a box from a dressing table drawer and put it into her hands.

Rebecca opened it and began to sort through her jewellery. 'Why on earth did I ever wear that?' she marvelled, holding up a length of jet. 'Miserable stuff. Now this might do,' – it was a gold and tortoiseshell brooch – 'yes, it might do very well. See what you can get for it.'

'All right.' He dropped it into his pocket. 'Better go and snore a bit now. But I'll be out in the garden directly.'

'Good. And Jim,' – she caught his hand – 'thank you for my book.'

Smiling, he took himself off.

The Fordson Major returned, rather abruptly, to its stall. As the engine died, blood roared through her ears, rushing to fill the sudden space of silence. Her teeth began to judder.

Had she been discovered? How near to tea time was it? (An age of time seemed to have elapsed. But no – that was the clang of a milk pail – John had arrived and Anne was undoubtedly at her post in the milking parlour.) She must hurry, she must escape before she was caught with a warm engine. Rising, she found that her feet had become giant feet – weighty, slow; too large to find an unencumbered foothold.

'I should stay put, if I were you, till you've stopped shaking,' George advised from the shadows.

Her heart turned over.

He came forward. The dogs matched his progress, the collie obediently low-bellied and watchful, the terrier squirming with thwarted exuberance. From her high perch she took in every detail.

He propped himself on his stick. 'You led me quite a dance, young lady.'

He had seen; he had followed her.

'Never seen anything like it in me life: little girl roarin' and bouncin' round Bailey's Field, pigtails flying, cheeks like a couple of boiled beetroots.'

She hung her head.

'You're a rare'un, Sal,' he said softly. 'Picked it up from watching Arthur, I suppose?'

She nodded.

'And you had to find out what you could do.'

She could not deny it. Tears of guilt welled ominously.

'Just like me when I was your age. Had to have a go.' He shook his head, recalling: 'The things I got up to 'ud made your blood run cold. Made off with me father's hunter – until I found it had made off with me; tossed me over a hedge, if I remember rightly. And once I climbed on to a railway line and got on a wagon while it was waiting at the signal. That made off with me as well: I had to jump clear while it was goin' in case I ended up in Birmingham . . .'

He was boasting! Astounded, she raised her head.

'But if we didn't try, we'd never learn, would we, Sal? I'll never forget the sight of you on that darn great machine. You know, you've got 'em all fooled with yer dreamy ways. You're a thorough goin' tomboy.'

What delicious flattery! Her sister was the official tomboy. Sally was stuck with less appealing labels – dreamer, book-worm, slow-coach. 'I love the Fordson, Grandad,' she confided, tenderly stroking the steering wheel. 'It's my favourite thing.'

'Well, well,' he marvelled, supposing that her unaccountable passion for the tractor resembled his own for a powerful horse. 'But you showed it who's boss. That's the main thing.'

He was pleased with her!

'You found the key'd been left in it, I suppose?'

She nodded, quite wild with happiness.

'Off you go now, then.'

Her feet took her to the ground with neat dexterity. Oh – but she ought to confess. 'Grandad . . . I bashed against the gatepost coming out of Bailey's Field. It's gone a bit wonky, I think.'

He considered this. 'Don't know what Arthur's goin' to say when I tell him he's got to start Monday mornin' straightenin' gateposts. I don't know at all.'

'Arthur won't mind,' she assured him, confidently.

'That's all right then. We'll say no more about it. But you'd better go in and scrub yer face – got oil on it.'

And on her dress, she noted with dismay. She had better shut herself in the bathroom. 'Are you coming, Grandad?'

'Directly. You run along, m'dear.'

When she had gone, he removed the key from the Fordson Major and put it in his pocket.

At tea Sally was self-conscious. A feeling of anti-climax had descended on her, she was inexplicably anxious, felt clumsy and fearful of suspicious eyes. But cautious scrutiny of her tea table companions confirmed that no-one other than Grandad Ludbury was taking the slightest notice of her. Grandad caught her look and winked. She stared at him solemnly, awed by his uniqueness; for her wickedness was thoroughly displeasing to those who regularly held dominion over her. Unaccountably, he seemed delighted by it.

Anne came to the end of a tortuous tale about a cow's tantrums during milking. Bunny, who had enjoyed it, wiped her eyes; and the ensuing silence allowed Henry the chance to deliver his thoughts on What To Do About The Miners. This closely argued thesis – which took in the solution of the cowardice difficulty on the Front Line and was inspired by an equally robust sense of purpose – had been rapturously received by Chief Inspector Weir and Mrs Massingbird-Formby during an idle moment at the town hall. Henry anticipated a similar reception from old man Ludbury. He was approaching the crux of his argument when his audience was suddenly distracted.

Rebecca got to her feet, smiled vaguely at a dish of hard scones, and wandered from the room.

'She doesn't like it if we get *excited*,' Bunny hissed reprovingly to Henry.

Well! Meg threw down her napkin. Were they to abandon all interest in the nation's affairs for fear of disturbing Mama's sensibilities? Was the world to stop because Mama chose to remain in ignorance of it? As for Bunny, Meg began to suspect that she had it in for Henry.

Sally and Anne exchanged glances. If Grandma had gone . . . 'Please may we get down?' asked Sally.

'Yes, I suppose so. All right with you?' Meg asked her sister, deferring belatedly to the presider over the teapot.

Sally rose.

'*What* have you got on your frock?' shrieked Meg.

Sally sank.

'What is it? Come here.'

Warily, Sally went to stand at her mother's side.

'A great black smudge. And you've tried to get it out – it's damp – you've been rubbing it. You *wicked* girl. Your best frock ruined!'

'Call that her best frock?' scoffed George. 'Look at her – she's busting out of it. Have to get her a bigger one. Grandad'll see you have a nice new frock for next Sunday, Sal.'

'That's very kind of Grandad. Say thank you,' Henry put in swiftly.

'Thank you, Grandad,' Sally whispered, too overcome to raise her head.

'There's the coupons – you can't just go out and get what you feel like, you know,' Meg reminded her father.

'I dare say we'll rustle some up. We usually do.'

Bunny leaned conspiratorially towards Anne (her goddaughter, a nicer, more straightforward child than that sneaky Sally). 'I'm going to do the hens. Like to come?'

'Rather!'

'We'll clear and wash up,' Meg told her brother.

'Just clear,' Bunny snapped. 'We'll wash up together when I get back.'

Meg, correctly surmising that Bunny wished to prevent a tête-à-tête between her brother and sister, rose to clear the table.

'We'd better do as we're told,' warned Jim when Meg began to fill a bowl in the scullery sink.

'All right.' She flung the dishcloth on to a stone slab. 'Let's go to the boxroom, then.'

Jim followed her slowly, pausing half-way up the stairs to light his pipe.

Meg went on ahead and opened the boxroom door. *The Power and the Glory* was lying open and face down on the bed. 'This looks interesting,' she said, surprised and encouraged by the title's religious tone.

He came in, closed the door and took the book from her. 'What's on your mind?' he asked, going to sit on the window-seat.

Meg sat on the bed. 'I'm worried about Bunny.'

'Uhuh.'

'She's worse than ever. Some of the things she comes out with are quite . . . eccentric.'

The pipe – never reliable – required a prolonged overhaul.

'You are taking this in? Something'll have to be done. It can't be healthy for a woman of her age to be cooped up here, miles from any form of mental stimulation, with a couple of elderly folk. She doesn't see anyone besides the family. She's out of touch. If you could have heard what she said about Henry . . .'

'Go on.'

'Not worth repeating. It was so wide of the mark it was pathetic – but indicative of her state of mind. What are we going to *do*?' She waited while her brother put a match to his pipe.

Plop, plop, Jim's lips smacked, and small round clouds drifted towards the bed.

'Well?' Meg asked, waving her hand to disperse the smoke.

'I'm not sure you're right.'

'What do you *mean*?' As head of Corporation Street Elementary School it was her business to be right.

'I reckon Bunny's got just what she wants.'

Why did the man require constant prompting?

'The Guv'nor,' Jim explained. 'She's got him all to herself, more or less. She runs the place just as he likes it. She's always wanted to please him – it's what makes her happy. And now I'm out of the way she's got him to herself. No-one to interfere.'

And that was another thing. 'Well, there jolly well ought to be. Mama is mistress of this house. If she took a proper interest, Bunny wouldn't have it all her own way.'

Now she had lost him. He stared blankly. 'You know, I reckon they all rub along pretty well . . .'

But Meg was not attending, she was too taken with this additional consequence of her mother's wilful decline –

57

the licence it conferred on Bunny, who, frankly, had never been up to wielding an unsupervised hand. 'I blame Mama,' she declared. 'This all stems from Mama shutting herself off from the world.'

He turned his head to look out of the window, but he carried her image in his mind and spread it over the rough tufty paddock to consider more thoroughly. It was the same old Meg; the same forthright manner, the same busy mouth and clear, certain eyes. No chance there of a pause for reflection; no hope of a saving smudge of doubt. It was a waste of breath talking to her; she would never understand ideas that were not her own. 'Funny the way you see it,' he observed ruminantly, more to himself than to Meg.

'See what?'

'Mama – shutting herself off from the world.' He began to smile, and irritation began to prickle Meg's flesh. When Jim smiled like that he was about to philosophize – a thing that always got Meg's goat. 'I suppose it all depends' – he paused to puff sagely once or twice – 'on what you mean by *the world.*'

She wasn't having this. The world was the world and that was the end of the matter. 'Come on. Better not let her find us having a confab.'

But the pipe was going splendidly now. 'I'll follow you directly.' He leaned back comfortably against the side of the window-seat. His eyes slid over the paddock while his mind pursued with contentment his pleasing train of thought.

The barn was a cathedral in the evening gloom; lofty, shadowy, stuffed with silence. The heady incense of grain knew nothing of the sharp sadness wafted by a censer; it breathed a balm of well-being. Reverently, she returned

58

to the yawning space left by the pinned-back doors, and squatted on the ledge across the bottom of the doorway to contemplate the farmyard. The weed-tufts between the cobbles were a special delight: tight yellow heads swathed in feathery green, long knobby pokers on leathery stalks jutting from tough, flat-leaved rosettes. As she walked, feeling the smooth, hard stones arch into her feet, she smelled the small plants' earthy pungency. The tractor shed was passed without a glance. She continued along the steep, rutted track of hard red mud and entered the paddock where long grasses slapped damply against her bare legs, and gnats rose from a patch of dead-nettles. She took careful note – the house, the barns, the trees – making a loving inventory.

(Bunny was passing the window on the back stairs. Whatever is the girl up to? she wondered, seeing Sally mooning about in the dusk – an unpleasantly furtive child, who ought, like her sister, to be getting ready for bed.)

There was a narrow path through the trees which led to a clearing where laundry could be hung to dry unseen by those who found the sight offensive. From there the trees were replaced by shrubbery, until, suddenly, the vista opened – a bank of lawn, a flower border, a gravel path to the house door, a rose trellis and a wide expanse of lawn and flower-beds falling to the tall, dark trees at the garden's end. She stood for some time on the well-mown bank watching a late bee in the fuchsia. Faint voices murmured in the house. Yellow gaslight glowed unsteadily at the dining-room window. And in the window directly above the dining-room a still white light shone against the wavy glass – Grandma Ludbury stood there, gazing over her beloved garden. Without a sound, Sally ran down the grassy bank to the door. Her prowl had assuaged her craving for possession. It was time for bed.

5

The Grange was a handsome house, a Georgian arrangement of orange-red brick, with pillared portico and regularly spaced tall windows. To the front of the house was a lawn and a monkey-puzzle tree, to the side nearest the road a screen of trees and shrubs, to the far side the farm buildings, and to the rear a kitchen garden and an orchard.

The Robinsons' car emerged from the shrubbery-bordered drive and drew up on the gravel forecourt. At once the aunts appeared, and Henry, who had been full of foreboding during the journey, was suddenly able to pinpoint the precise nature of his anxiety. 'For Pete's sake keep the batty one away from me,' he said in urgent undertone, as Aunt Pip tottered down the steps brandishing her walking stick. But Meg's mind was already on the task ahead, which was to accomplish this once-a-year visit with minimum distress.

The girls got out and braced themselves as each great-aunt fought to handle all, and carry off at least one, of their four visitors. The din was shocking; and the arm-tugging and pigtail-pulling alarming. Sally and Anne, it was established, had grown taller than any great-nieces had the right to grow; and their pigtails were longer, and their mother skinnier, and their father plumper than their great-aunts' wildest imaginings. They were to come in at once.

'With *me*, dear. Come with me.'

'Out of the way, you silly Louisa. You're holding us up.'

'And poor Charlotte's as deaf as a post. We have to *shout* . . .'

'Pip's going to fall over her stick. Be *firm* with her, someone . . .'

At last they were seated on the dusty sofas and chairs in the enormous drawing-room. The proceedings opened, as always, with a litany of names led by Charlotte, the senior sister. 'And how,' she enquired gravely of Meg, 'do you find your mother?' (Poor, *dear* Rebecca. Such a darling. And so brave; an invalid all these years.) 'And your father?' (Isn't George wonderful? Wonderful? Still farming, still riding to hounds.) 'Bunny?' (Bunny does her best. Yes, Bunny has always done her best.) 'And dear, kind Jim?' (He comes over so often to see us. Oh, he does. He gives poor Edward advice about the farm, and takes Charlotte to see her ear man . . . DOESN'T HE CHARLOTTE? HE TAKES YOU TO SEE YOUR EAR MAN . . . There is no need to shout, Louisa . . .)

'And he takes me to stay with Rebecca at Willow Dasset,' Pip said in her high, penetrating voice. 'Isn't that kind? And kind of Rebecca, too; because, of course, she sends him to fetch me. I love it more than anything in the world – going to stay with Rebecca at Willow Dasset. We talk and talk. And we laugh – oh, how we laugh . . .' Her words, charged with genuine emotion, diverted them from their ritual and provoked a thoughtful silence.

Charlotte heard them with the ferocious concentration of the partially deaf; and then her mind could not be done with them for they described the cruel truth. Pip, a constant menace to the good name of Ludbury (saving, of course, her brief glory in winning the Royal Red Cross Medal during the Great War) was a frequent visitor to

George's home, while she, Charlotte, who had loved and served him with passionate loyalty was unwelcome, tolerated occasionally from a sense of duty, and latterly not invited there at all. Charlotte thought about this every day of her life. Some days she decided that Rebecca had cultivated Pip with the sole purpose of emphasizing Charlotte's exclusion. On other days the fault was Pip's for having taken advantage of Rebecca's poor health to insinuate herself. Exploring this terrain was such a habit to Charlotte that Pip's words had sent her scurrying over the ground in search of new clues, new signposts, or new traps set by the wicked pair bent on keeping brother and sister apart. For George and Charlotte – let it never be forgotten – had once been all in all to one another. 'All in all,' she muttered, looking fiercely at the present company as if daring a contradiction.

But no-one took in Charlotte's sudden murmurings.

Louisa was recalling their girlhood days when she, alone of the Ludbury sisters, had been Rebecca's friend. In her whole life Louisa had made but two friendships, and both had wilted for want of a little courage. But then, she excused herself, Mama and Charlotte had always been so against friendships outside the family. Mama and Charlotte . . . She clasped her arms to control a sudden shiver.

Meg pushed her heels against the floor and tapped her toes irritably. Her mother's encouragement of mad, bad Aunt Pip had always angered her. And now the wretched woman was boasting of their intimacy, in full knowledge, no doubt, of Rebecca's reluctance to exchange more than a few pleasantries with members of her immediate family.

'Of course,' Pip added as an afterthought, 'Jim and Rebecca are very close. She trusts him. She sends a message to me whenever he calls . . .'

This further mention of Jim reminded Charlotte of her duty. It was time to invoke the name of Robinson. 'And how is Henry? He looks exceedingly well.'

'He looks wonderful,' Pip cried, gazing hungrily at the only man in the room, who was sitting – she had made sure of it – by her side.

'Very well, thank you,' Henry said in a clipped voice, edging nearer to the sofa's armrest.

'And Meg? Dear Meg. Busy as ever, no doubt?'

'She's always a busy bee,' Louisa confirmed.

'Too busy?' Pip enquired, digging Henry in the ribs.

'And the girls?'

'The dear girls.'

'Is Sally going to play for us?'

Indeed she was; she had been well schooled. She marched swiftly to the piano, sat on the stool and raised the lid. An experimental arpeggio revealed serious deterioration in the piano's condition – it had been bad enough last time . . . She grimaced at her mother, declining responsibility for what they were about to hear (or not to hear, for several notes were sticking); and Meg nodded her understanding of the situation. Sally played a jaunty jig by Bach.

The aunts detected no impediment.

'Wonderful!'

'How like dear Mama!'

'As a matter of fact she writes poetry like Grandmama, too,' Meg pointed out.

'Oh! Do you hear, Charlotte? SALLY WRITES POETRY LIKE MAMA.'

Charlotte craned forward, eager to miss not a word.

'I'll say my latest one,' Sally said, and took a deep breath. '"Arthur, the tractor king".'

'How's that? What did the girl say?'

'IT'S ABOUT KING ARTHUR.'

'No,' hissed Meg. 'Say "The First Snowdrop".'

'Not that silly thing . . .'

'Do as your mother says,' Henry ordered without moving his lips.

'"The First Snowdrop",' Sally announced.

'Oh!' said the aunts, falling back, disappointed, in their chairs.

'And what can little Anne do?' Charlotte wondered when applause for Sally had died.

Little Anne could do many things, but was unable to accomplish any of them within the confines of a ladylike drawing-room.

'"Thank you, gentle cow",' suggested Meg.

With flaming cheeks, Anne rose. She put her head on one side. 'Thank you, gentle cow . . .' she hazarded, hoping for a prompt.

Meg looked questioningly at Sally, who shrugged. 'And to think we pay to have the stuff dinned into them!' Meg told her husband witheringly.

'You said it nicely the other day,' Henry encouraged.

'I've forgot it.'

'Oh, well,' Meg shrugged. 'Anne's a bit of a tom-boy,' she explained loudly to her senior aunt – so could not, she implied, be expected to remember her lines.

Louisa rose. 'I'd better make sure dinner's coming along. I expect Henry's hungry. And then,' she whispered to the tomboy, 'we can go and see the hens.' Thankfully, Anne went off with Great-Aunt Louisa.

'We'll go to my room,' Charlotte told Meg. 'I've something to show you.'

This sounded promising, Sally thought, and decided to accompany them.

Henry found his voice, 'Er, my dear . . .' he called politely.

But treacherously, without a care for her husband's plight, Meg left the room.

Henry hesitated, searching for the right phrase. Stretch a leg, Look under the bonnet, See how the corn's coming on, were all rejected. She'd grab his arm and go with him. The lavatory was the obvious solution, but on a previous visit she had lain in wait for him outside the door, had nearly given him a heart attack with her 'Boo!', the silly old bat. If that Sally had not gone off with her mother . . . He had it! He'd call Sally back, impress upon her with a strict look and a firm hand that she was to stay and entertain her Great-Aunt Pip. His face cleared. He prepared to rise.

Pip had been watching him closely – this sandy-haired, pinkly plump little man with the penetrating blue eyes and colourless lashes – pleased to have him to herself; for any man, apart from her brothers, was better than no man at all. A man's company was so cheering, so invigorating; it took a man to thoroughly appreciate her larky good nature. And then she saw that Henry was gathering himself. 'Stay,' she cried, rising, stumbling, falling on top of him. 'I want to talk to you.' But the jolt of their collision had jarred her arthritic hands. 'Oh, oh,' she wailed. 'Just look at them, Henry.'

He had no alternative. Her hands, raised to within inches of his eyes were deformed, the knuckles grossly swollen, the fingers turned under and outwards like impotent claws.

'They throb, and throb. And they are utterly . . . *useless.*'

As she got out the last word a piece of spittle flew from her lips and settled on his. He was hotly aware of it during her catalogue of woe – her difficulty with dressing and undressing, with using a knife and fork, the crossness of Charlotte, the roughness of the nurse who came twice a week and brushed her hair so hard that her scalp ached for hours . . . He longed to push a discreet hand across his mouth, but she was sitting on one of his hands and the other was grasping her forearm to prevent her toppling against him.

Despairingly, she put her hands away, one into the back of the sofa, the other, to Henry's increased consternation, into the soft flesh of his spreading thigh. 'And to think, Henry,' she mourned, 'I was once such a nimble-fingered gel. You should have seen me doing my nursing – I was so very . . . *dexterous*.'

Another shower. This time Henry threw politeness to the winds and wiped his face frankly on his shoulder.

Pip was not offended. She gazed at him kindly. 'You are . . .'

(He was learning. She had a useful way of pausing and wrinkling her nose before giving a word explosive emphasis. He ducked.)

'. . . *nice*, Henry,' she confided. 'I want you to speak to Meg for me. She'll listen to you.'

'Of course, anything I can do . . .' Speaking to Meg must surely secure his release from this terrible proximity . . . (Henry dreaded all physical contact. Even the bed business with Meg was something to be got over with as briskly as possible. In the early days of their marriage it had been more easily accomplished, roused as he was by all their delicious chat about his exciting prospects. Now it was a distasteful chore; for his part, having procreated, he would prefer to let it die and preserve dignity. Meg had other ideas. When his excuses mounted she began to cast aspersions on his manhood. Henry did his duty, but how

66

he loathed alien breath across his nostrils, alien hands invading the privacy of his body.) 'And what would you like me to tell her?' he prompted urgently.

'Tell her Charlotte . . . *steals*. She steals my letters — my lovely old letters from the boys in the war. Oh, such darling letters, and some of them so naughty! How you'd laugh, Henry. Shall I show you? If you come up to my room . . .'

'Later, perhaps. But some of them have gone, you say?'

'Charlotte has . . . *stolen* them. She's always been jealous, you see, because I was such a popular gel. Can you imagine me in my uniform, Henry, with my bright red hair? Full of life, fun . . . *esprit!*'

'But the letters . . .'

'Are vanishing. One by one. Charlotte sneaks into my room and takes them. And when I tackle her with it she pretends she can't hear. Oh, it breaks my heart! I'm so . . . *sad* to be without them; they remind me of such marvellous times. I want you to ask Meg to have it out with Charlotte. Meg knows how to handle her; they are so alike, you see. Will you do it for me, dear Henry?' she asked piteously.

'Certainly. Right away. Now, if you'll just allow me . . .' Firmly, now that he had a reason to leave her, he disentangled their bodies and put her away from him. He almost bounded from the room and down the hall and up the wide, turning staircase. With authority, he rapped on Miss Ludbury's bedroom door.

Meg opened it. 'What do you want?' she frowned, seeing that it was he.

'You'd better come down at once and speak to your Aunt Pip. Without . . .' he hissed and nodded towards the interior of the room, '. . . her. It would appear there has been some unpleasantness.'

'Unpleasantness?' Meg repeated suspiciously.

'You'd better come down and sort it out. I've had enough. I'm going to stretch my legs.'

'Back in a moment,' Meg yelled at Aunt Charlotte and hurried away to the drawing-room.

Charlotte observed Sally, who was squatting on the floor and turning the pages of an old photograph album. Then she rose and went to the window. Presently, Meg came out on to the gravel path with Pip hanging on to her arm. They walked slowly over the lawn towards the monkey-puzzle tree. Charlotte knew very well what was being said, and she was unperturbed. Meg had always understood that the strong-minded members of the family must shoulder an awesome burden, that certain weaker vessels required constant vigilance. She went to the bed and sat down to await Meg's return.

But at that moment Louisa whacked the dinner gong.

'You've *burned* them? Whatever possessed you?'

'They were indecent. Depraved. Utter *filth*.'

'Hush!' Meg hurried to the door. But the landing was safely deserted. She reclosed the door and returned to Charlotte's side. 'Pip's always been a bit off' — Meg's expression was the sort used to greet a bad smell — 'but what possible harm can it do now, after all these years?'

'A great deal. We are reaching the end of our lives,' Charlotte pointed out with some solemnity. 'When we are gone, *people*' — she pronounced the word with disdain, for it included those unrelated to the Ludbury family — 'will come and sort through our things. It happened to poor Ada when she was widowed (she referred to her long time friend and patron, Mrs Ada Skedgemore) and there was a great deal of nastiness. *Things* were found . . .'

'What things?' Meg asked, interested.

But Charlotte had never been clear on this. She recalled with clarity, however, the unpleasant whispering and innuendo among the Skedgemore set.

'Well I'm sure no-one is going to be the slightest bit interested in poor Aunt Pip's correspondence. When the time comes it'll just be disposed of. In the meantime those letters are important to her. You really must not go helping yourself and setting fire to people's property, Aunt Charlotte. Promise me you won't do it again.'

Charlotte pressed her lips into a stubborn line.

'If you don't, I shall advise her to get a lock put on her door.'

'She couldn't turn the key with those crippled hands,' Charlotte observed spitefully.

Meg became thoroughly angry. 'I've a good mind to tell them about this at Willow Dasset. I think, if they knew how unhappy you've made her, stealing and burning her letters, they'd insist on her going to live with them.'

'No! Don't say a word at Willow Dasset,' Charlotte cried in alarm.

'Very well. Then give me your promise.'

Charlotte turned away. She was bitterly hurt. That it should come to this, she marvelled, now, in the evening of her years – all her striving in the family's interest to be set at naught! It seemed she was expected to stand back and allow the revelations that can occur at death to wipe out her life's work. And that Meg should be so blind, so uncaring, so irresponsible! Without Meg's support she doubted she had the strength to go on. The family would have to take its chance. She, Charlotte, was at the end of her tether. 'If that is your wish,' she conceded, sinking heavily into a chair.

*

The girls were exploring. They had discovered the nether region of the house, a series of dim cavernous rooms crammed with abandoned and forgotten treasure: stone jars, cobwebby bottles, a cider press, lead weights, a wicker trunk, a bulging attaché case, ancient boots, misshapen tennis racquets, dusty croquet mallets, a shotgun, a torn parasol, the brush of a long-dead fox . . .

A distant, rhythmical rumbling disturbed their delving. They climbed the back stairs in search of its source. By the time they reached Great-Aunt Louisa's sewing-room the noise was loud and near at hand. 'Is it snoring?' Anne wondered. But Sally shook her head. No human frame could sustain the throes of such strenuous resonance – ribs would surely split, lungs burst, eye-balls spurt from sockets; it was the work of some machine.

'It's in there.' Anne, who had led the way, came to a halt by a closed door. They remained there for a moment, suffering the noise. Sally placed her hand on the doorknob to see if it vibrated in sympathy with the massive sound. Anne misinterpreted the gesture. 'Yes, go in. Let's see.'

Trembling a little, Sally turned the knob. At once the door swung open. She hurried after it to forestall a crash of door on wall.

'It *is* snoring,' said Anne, approaching the sagging, iron-framed bed.

Great-Uncle Edward lay on his back. His boots lolled outwards and quivered at each snore's peak.

'Isn't he . . . horrible?' Anne said at last.

Great-Uncle Edward's horribleness was profound. Food droppings spotted his waistcoat (Sally had taken note of his poor style at the dinner table), his trousers were unbuttoned at the waist and his shirt gaped to reveal a triangle of dingy underclothing. Mercifully, his piggy eyes were closed, but his huge, pitted, purple nose glistened, his open mouth trembled, and his blue chin and upper lip had sprouted beads of moisture.

'Really, really horrible,' Anne marvelled, and added, 'smelly, too.'

'But I wonder why wicked?' Sally recalled their mother's injunction to keep away from Uncle Edward because he's a nasty, wicked man.

'He must do wicked things.'

'Murder's wicked.'

'Gosh!' They looked at one another, wide-eyed.

'Perhaps,' Sally hissed, 'he kills little girls.'

'And eats 'em,' embellished Anne.

Suddenly, Great-Uncle Edward missed a beat. He lay still and silent. Then, with a shout and a great flinging of arms and legs, he snorted his way back into the swing of things.

The girls, who had suffered a temporary paralysis, recovered the use of larynx and then of leg. Two banshees tore from the room, along the passage, through a doorway and on to the main landing.

Their screams woke Edward. He sat up, took note of the open door, swung his legs over the bed and scrambled beneath it. 'Never touched her,' he moaned. ''S all lies.'

Meg was on the landing. 'What in heaven's name?' she asked, and then, losing patience with their white-faced, tongue-tied shiftiness: 'Oh, very well. But as you're here, you, Anne, go downstairs and find Aunt Louisa – one of us ought to give the poor thing some attention; and you, Sally, go to Aunt Charlotte's room – talk to her, occupy her.' Her daughters disposed of, she rapped on Aunt Pip's door.

Pip was hunched in a chair. When Meg came in she rose too eagerly, and was obliged to catch hold of a chair arm to steady herself. 'You managed it? You got them back?'

71

'No – not exactly. Sit down Aunt.'

But Pip was full of agitation. 'My . . . *precious* letters!'

'I'm afraid, Aunt, they have been destroyed. Burned, to be exact.'

It took some time for this news to sink in. Then Pip's eyes filled with tears which soon spilled over the bony promontories of her face.

For the first time in her life Meg was moved by her, felt tremendous pity for her. She put an arm across Pip's narrow back and gripped a shoulder. The little body was a bag of bones. 'Poor Auntie Pip,' she said gently. 'Come.' She led her to the chair and sat her down, and from her jacket pocket fished out a handkerchief. 'There. Have a good blow. And listen – because it's not all bad. I made her promise faithfully never to do it again. I don't think she will because I threatened to tell them about it at Willow Dasset.'

'Oh, but you mustn't worry Rebecca.'

'It won't come to that. But if you do have any more trouble tell Jim when he comes, and he and I will put our heads together. Now, you still have some letters? Well, show me where you keep them, and we'll think of other hiding places.'

Louisa was walking sadly in the kitchen garden. Her silly heart had begun to ache again – she was quite cross with it, for it was all nonsense – *nonsense*. Meg would find time for her soon. She might even visit her Aunt Louisa's room, for she had always liked to do that, had even, one summer long ago, preferred it as a sleeping place to her Aunt Charlotte's spacious bedroom. Oh, such wonderful, far-off days! And there had been Sally, then – Sally Edmunds, her dearest friend who had died, oh, so many years ago. Sally . . . It had been the name, too, of the poor little niece who had died; and now it was Meg's daughter's name. It was a very *dear* name, Louisa decided, stooping to pinch a leaf of marjoram, then sniffing her fingers.

A brown hen in search of an illicit nest ran with a great flutter from a nearby rubbish heap. 'Shoo!' cried Louisa, lumbering after it.

'Shoo!' cried Anne, arriving to do her mother's bidding.

'Oh, Anne! How nice! And just when I was starting to be silly . . .'

They chased the hen back to its quarters.

Louisa was breathless. Tiredness caught her unawares, these days. 'Shall we go up to my room and look at my things?' she gasped, holding her side where a sharp stitch had come.

'All right,' Anne said, kindly.

'Shall I take the photograph now?' Henry boomed, standing alone in the hall with his Brownie camera. Time, he was pleased to note, was getting on nicely; it would be a shame to allow any hold-ups.

They emerged from different parts of the house, calling to one another, becoming excited.

'Where's Edward? Oh, we can't have it taken without Edward.'

The girls, dispatched to discover their great-uncle, ran everywhere but to the place where they had last set eyes upon him. 'He's nowhere,' they panted, returning, spreading their arms to reveal emptiness.

'Never mind,' Meg said, briskly. 'We'll have to get on without him.'

The three aunts were arranged on the long, slatted

garden seat, and Sally and Anne instructed to perch between them. Meg, straight-backed, hands clasped at her waist, stood on guard behind, ready to keep order and tell them when to smile.

'We're ready,' she called to her husband, who was swinging the camera from side to side and shielding the view-finder.

'Hang on a minute. Can they squeeze up?'

Meg squeezed them up. 'Now,' she called, 'get on with it.'

'They take snaps of us to look at when we're dead,' explained Pip loudly. 'So they can laugh and say: What funny old things. Which won't be long now,' she added thoughtfully.

Meg sucked in her breath. That was just the distasteful sort of remark one had come to expect of Aunt Pip. 'Smile!' she ordered.

'Say cheese,' called Henry, and pressed the button.

Louisa's heart was pounding; but pleasantly, for she was giddy with the importance of Meg and Sally in her room. Henry had looked at his watch and mentioned setting off. It had galvanized her. She had seized Meg's arm. 'Do, do come to my room before you go. And bring Sally.'

Meg had agreed, feeling that she had failed to share herself equitably on this occasion. 'Just for a minute, then.'

Louisa regarded her visitors with moist eyes – Meg sitting on the edge of her bed, Sally at her dressing table running a finger along the teeth of a tortoiseshell comb to make them sing. 'I think it's so nice that you called her Sally,' she confided, nodding in the direction of her great-niece. 'You named her after your little sister, I expect.'

'Well – yes. I thought it would please Mama.'

'Of course, it was my dear friend's name, too; but I don't suppose you had that in mind.' Flustered by her silliness, she hurried on: 'I'd like Sally to have . . . You see, I've been getting rather tired lately; sometimes I feel quite . . . And I've decided that Sally should have my silver-lidded jars. You remember . . .' A summer, long and hot; Meg, twelve years old, scheming to share Louisa's room in preference to Charlotte's; Louisa, overcome with pleasure, throwing caution to the winds, showing Meg her hidden treasure – gifts from Sally Edmunds, her beloved friend. What a wild, daring moment it had been! – a moment more alive for Louisa than the faded present, for the small glass jars had never emerged from their hiding place, had never sparkled bravely on her dressing table; that one showing had remained their single chance to shine. The thought saddened her, and she hastened to reassure herself: it could not have been otherwise; difficulties were made about so many things in those days; no, concealment had been the safest, the only course. But how right she had been to trust dear Meg. She reached out and took Meg's hand. It was a solemn moment, Louisa felt.

Meg bit her lip. What the dickens was Aunt Louisa rambling on about? Downstairs, Henry would be getting impatient.

Louisa went to kneel by a chest of drawers. She pulled a drawer open, drew out a parcel and removed some paper wrappings. Three rather plain glass jars with thin silver lids were placed on the carpet. 'Sally . . .'

'Yes,' said Sally, promptly.

'I want *you* to have them.'

'Oh! Look, Mummy; aren't they *sweet*? Thank you very much, Aunt Louisa.'

A great lump rose in Louisa's throat preventing her

response. And there were so many things she longed to say. Never mind, she told herself as Meg ushered Sally to the door; her darling silver-lidded jars were in safe hands. If she were to . . . Well, whatever happened, Charlotte and Pip could not, now, discover their existence.

As the car rolled down the drive, Sally, who had been thinking, reached out and jabbed her mother's shoulder. 'I say, did you have another sister, Mummy?'

'Yes.' Meg was very tired.

'What happened to her?'

'She died.'

'What?' cried Anne, stirring.

Meg sighed. 'I had a little sister called Sally who died when she was quite young – five years old.'

'My name's Sally,' Sally pointed out coyly. When her mother failed to comment, she continued: 'Did you call me that because I look like her?'

'Good heavens, no. There's a superficial resemblance, I suppose – you've got her dark hair. But she was a pretty, dainty, little thing.'

'Oh,' said Sally, hurt.

'You did all right for yourself,' Meg remarked, recalling an unpleasant acquisitiveness about her daughter regarding Aunt Louisa's glass jars. And where were the blessed things to go, she'd like to know. More darn dust traps. Perhaps the Christmas bazaar . . .

Sally hugged her trophies. 'Aunt Louisa wanted me to have them,' she said virtuously; and the feeling grew in her that she had earned them. 'Anyway, I talked to Aunt Charlotte for you for hours and hours. And to Aunt Pip . . . She showed me her autograph book. It was jolly funny. There was a drawing of a man and a lady, and the lady had fallen off her bicycle and her skirt . . .'

'Never mind that,' Meg interrupted, hoping that the road claimed Henry's undivided attention. 'Anne was very nice to Aunt Louisa, but she didn't get any glass jars. Hardly fair.'

Anne felt it was safe to own up. From under her skirt she withdrew a china pig. 'Aunt Louisa gave me this.'

'Oh, that nice pig! It's rather good — Staffordshire, I believe. Aunt Louisa won it years ago at the County Show, I seem to remember. For her pork pie.'

'I love it,' Anne said.

Meg settled back comfortably. The visit had gone rather well. Furthermore, no repetition would be required until this time next year.

Beneath the portico the handkerchiefs were no longer waving. Though the car's noise had faded some moments ago, no-one had moved away, not a word had been spoken. Louisa had crumpled her handkerchief into a ball; her hands worked on it as if kneading a dumpling. Pip had made several attempts to poke hers into her pocket, but a large portion still trailed obstinately. 'Drat the thing!' Pip said, looking hopefully at Louisa. But Louisa was not attending; the stitch in her side still persisted: she rubbed at it vaguely with the handkerchief ball, then lurched down the steps, across the front of the house and round the side towards the kitchen garden.

Charlotte looked about her and sighed. A handkerchief still drooped from hands clasped beneath her bosom. Presently, she turned and walked aimlessly through the chilly, dim hall.

When she was quite alone, Pip struck the nearest pillar

with her walking stick. Plaster pieces fell softly on to the step. 'The house is rotting,' she muttered, pushing her stick into the pillar to dislodge a large, loose flake. And then she added bleakly: 'Like the poor devils who live in it.'

6

When the rain stopped and a watery sun came out, Sally put on her Wellington boots and went outside. The pasture behind the rickyard was sodden; she walked across it with a swinging stride, watching water spurt from her shiny black toes – a shooting jet with every forward thrust. When she came near the tied cottage she paused. Aunt Bunny would be inside with Mrs Gurney, Benjamin's wife. Mrs Gurney helped Aunt Bunny with the washing and cleaning. Today they were 'giving the cottage a do'; for new occupants were expected: a man to help with the harvest, plus a wife to help Aunt Bunny while Mrs Gurney was away visiting her sister, plus two small girls. 'About your age,' Grandad Ludbury had announced.

This shocking news had unnerved the sisters. The thought of two other small girls making free with Willow Dasset was too fearful to discuss. Sally and Anne took care to avoid one another.

'That is, if we ever do start harvesting this year,' their grandfather had added gloomily.

It was too depressing for words: the rain, the postponement of the harvest, the threat posed by interlopers, and the fact that their holiday at Willow Dasset had but a few more days to run.

By tea time a few hours of steady sunshine had put Grandad Ludbury in a brighter frame of mind. 'Reckon we'll be harvesting after all, if this keeps up. Shame, though, that the girls have to go home on Saturday.

Should've thought you could leave 'em for a couple of weeks. They'd be all right with their grandad. Wouldn't you Sal? Eh, little Annie?'

Such a thing had never been mooted before. They were astounded, overcome. While they pleaded, their parents calculated. Meg thought of all she could achieve in two weeks without the children. Henry totted up the cost of the extra journeys and set it against the saving on two weeks' food — not forgetting, of course, a second opportunity to fill the car boot with provender.

'It's exceedingly kind of Father, but it would mean a great deal of extra work for Bunny,' Henry said, demurring considerately towards the teapot.

Meg turned to her silent mother. 'What about you, Mama? I don't suppose you're keen to put up with two great girls charging about the place any longer than you have to.'

Rebecca smiled dreamily at her abandoned slice of bread and butter. 'I enjoy the thought of them here.'

'Well, if you're sure you don't mind, Bunny? Thank you Daddy. I know how disappointed they were to think of missing the harvest.'

'There!' George grinned, proud of his achievement.

Later, they were too excited to sleep. They talked and talked, speculating on their glorious two weeks, promising to be fair to one another in the matter of choice harvesting jobs, plotting to snub and exclude the newcomers. When moonlight glinted strongly through the curtain cracks, Sally was still awake, but Anne, irritatingly, had fallen unconscious in the middle of Sally's prescription for a satisfactory harvest tea (strawberry jam sandwiches and chocolate cake, with smokey tea from a billycan). She shuffled into a sitting position, for a noise she could not identify had interrupted her busy thoughts. It came again. It was not mice scuttling in the walls, nor wind rattling the window. It came from the yard. She slipped from her bed to investigate. Outside, in the driving seat of Uncle Harry's Riley, shone a small red glow. (Uncle Harry had arrived after tea. Her mother had been dying to talk to him, but had been thwarted by Aunt Bunny. 'Hello, what are you two up to?' Aunt Bunny had asked suspiciously, coming in with her nieces from shutting up the hens. Mummy and Uncle Harry had sprung guiltily from their perch on the scullery table.) Now, it appeared, they were having their talk in Uncle Harry's car.

Sally climbed on to the window seat and put her ear to the half-open window. Uncle Harry had wound down the car window to tap out his pipe. Now he was relighting it. 'Can't' – puff – 'get a word' – puff – 'out of her. Mind you, she's an ill old woman, I suppose she can do as she likes. No,' – puff – 'it's Jim who annoys me. He'll never do anything with that place. I've a shrewd suspicion the old man's had to bail him out once or twice. As Dora says, it's not fair on the rest of us. Now, if my advice had been taken, they'd have expanded here – bought that five hundred acres on the other side of the road . . .'

Grumble, grumble, grumble. It was time Uncle Harry went home to Aunt Dora, Sally thought disgustedly, removing her ear from the window and leaning back against the wall at the side of the window seat. Willow Dasset by moonlight was a tiny, self-contained world. From her bedroom window at home, she looked out on to a row of houses exactly like her own – dingy terraced villas with small squares of garden; and at night, lorries from the docks swished ceaselessly along the nearby main road. Here, in fluid navy and gold – only the deep, staunch shelter of house and barns, the yielding flow of willows, the minimal shiver of high trees by the garden wall, the

81

deserted track leading to infinite space, and the sudden, jarring screech of a night creature – was completeness, an entity, a place to just be. Grandma Ludbury had the right idea.

Yawning her head off, thinking that if she had the chance she would do as her grandmother did, Sally returned to bed.

Rebecca had kept to her room all day. 'She's poorly. We must all be quiet as mice,' Bunny had said. Meg had bristled. It riled her when Bunny assumed authority. It riled her, too, that her mother was getting away with it. 'It's an excuse,' she told Henry who was not listening. 'An excuse to keep out of our way. We've been here a fortnight and she's had enough of us.' After tea, when Bunny and the girls had gone to shut up the hens for the night, Meg went to her mother's room.

Rebecca looked like a queen on her high snowy pillows – that was Meg's impression as she entered the room – aloof, smug, and grandly waited-upon. But drawing close to the bed, a brisk comment ready on her lips, Meg changed her mind. Mama really did look poorly.

Rebecca's eyes followed Meg, but her head, as if intolerably weighty, remained still; her lips and eye-sockets were bruised-looking, her hands lay abandoned on the counterpane.

'Not too grand, today,' Meg commented kindly.

Rebecca said nothing.

As the silence lengthened, Meg's churning indignation returned – that she should stifle it, not give way to it in a sick-room, she well understood; even so, she could not tear her mind from her grievance. Mama might indeed be ill, but this was not always the case. And it was not improbable that her self-imposed decline had contributed to her present weakness. Meg pressed her lips together, determined to hold her tongue. However, she would permit herself one, mild suggestion.

She began gently: 'I would appreciate it, Mama, if one day you would explain things to me. I know you are ill today, but you're not always like this. So I'd just like to know why you do it. Why *do* you do it, Mama?' Damn. In her frustration, she had rather moved on from 'one day'. But it was said now, and could not be unsaid. With impatience she awaited an answer.

None came. It seemed her mother was set against speech.

'You do know what I'm talking about? – Your cutting yourself off from us. It's been going on for years, ever since you came to this place, more or less . . .'

'I've been so happy at Willow Dasset,' Rebecca said in a surprised, far-away voice.

This was beside the point. 'We're not here to be happy,' Meg admonished sternly. 'We're here to do some good in the world, to think of others beside ourselves.'

'I often think of others.'

Her mother seemed to be talking to herself – *complimenting* herself. Meg became violent with the urge to dispel her complacency. 'And what *good* does it do them, may I ask?'

There was a long pause. Her mother was too crushed, perhaps, to reply. But then in a small voice, at last it came: 'Well, at least it doesn't do them any harm.'

And what, Meg asked herself, did she mean by that? The suspicion crossed her mind that her mother was imputing something unpleasant to her. That she was an interfering busybody? That by trying to do good she did harm? If this was so, her mother had a darn cheek – we couldn't all lie back and let the world go to pot. 'What,' she demanded ringingly, 'do you imagine it can be like for poor Daddy with no-one to talk to but that empty-headed Bunny, and a wife who never addresses a single word in his direction . . . ?'

'We ran out of words long ago, your father and I.'

'Indeed? More shame on you! Daddy has plenty to say when he gets the chance. Thank goodness he's got Henry and me to have a sensible conversation with now and then, because he needs the stimulation of alert minds. He's just read the most interesting book about Winston Churchill – Henry's reading it now. You should have heard them at tea time. They were full of it.'

'But I don't think,' Rebecca said mildly, 'that I've anything to say about Winston Churchill.'

'Because you're out of touch,' Meg cried triumphantly. 'Take the war. Everything was going on around you – from the yard steps you could see Coventry burning; and there was the time those prisoners of war escaped and hid in the barn by the brook; and the night they bombed the aluminium factory . . . But not a flicker of interest from you; you just went on with your weeding, or your sewing, or shut yourself up in your room. I call that quite disgraceful . . .' But here she paused, for her mother had closed her eyes. In a less vehement tone, she added: 'It's just that I don't understand it. You used to be so lively, Mama. If only you'd explain.'

Meg grew uneasy. Her mother's face had turned grey. 'Are you all right, Mama?' She racked her brain for something conciliatory to say.

'You're going home soon?' a strained voice asked from the pillows.

'Yes. Tomorrow.'

'Good.'

Meg rose in a huff.

84

'I meant only' – the words came with difficulty – 'that you'll be glad to get back. You're at a loose end here. Doesn't suit you.'

A lump rose in Meg's throat. Her mother, she recalled, had been so understanding in the old days, had never clung or tried to prevent her doing as she wished; unlike some others – her father, her Aunt Charlotte. 'I'm sorry I went on, Mama,' she mumbled.

Rebecca smiled, but her eyes remained closed.

'Is there anything I can do?'

'Just . . . when you go . . . close the door properly.'

Mr Grieve – or Bill, as George Ludbury decreed he should be known – was the first of the cottage family to be seen. This was appropriate, for he was the first to be speculated upon. News of Mr Grieve had preceded his arrival. Benjamin and Arthur, on learning the identity of the man taken on for the harvest, lost no time in acquainting the Guv'nor with the man's fame as a Methodist lay preacher. Such was his popularity that several chapels contributed to the Grieves' upkeep. Mr and Mrs Grieve took paid employment when it was available, so long as God's work went unhindered.

George was taken aback. Last summer there had been a spot of bother over a landgirl, and when Grieve called at the door in search of temporary work and accommodation (there had been a delay over the allocation of a council house), George saw the obvious solution to his staffing problem. With Benjamin's lad and the two old fellows who always gave him a hand with the harvest, Grieve would complete the summer team. But if there was one thing that made George thoroughly uncomfortable it was religiosity. Tentatively, he explored his fear at the tea table, taking care to disguise it with sneering banter.

His son-in-law, who abominated nonconformism, leapt in with a full heart and launched upon an amusing description of The Protestant Squat; which caused George, who had never risked his dignity by kneeling, to narrow his eyes. Then Henry grew warm over the nonconforminst mode of addressing the Almighty – a crude and insulting mode lacking the intercession of Cranmer's hallowed tone. Worst of all (and at this point a vein at the side of Henry's temple became alarmingly engorged) was the presumption of the artisan preacher – an ill-educated, unqualified fellow, with traces of oil under his finger-nails or coal-dust in his hair. It was nothing short of blasphemy . . .

In something of a difficulty, George observed his spluttering son-in-law. It seemed churlish to point out his own feeling on the matter, that religion, of whatever flavour, was a bad thing unless kept firmly in check. He decided to lighten the tone with a reminiscence about his wife's late brother-in-law, one Samuel Biggins, who had given up the drink to become an authority on hell-fire. (Whereupon Rebecca sighed and retired to her room.)

William Grieve was seen at milking on the first Monday morning of the girls' bonus fortnight. They watched him talking to John, the cowman. He was a short, stocky, solemn-looking man, and it seemed unlikely that the name Bill would stick. John, the girls noted, had preferred Mr Grieve. 'Call me William,' the new man had cordially invited. He did not look promising, the girls decided; more of a Benjamin than an Arthur.

Later on, they came across Mrs Grieve in the wash-house. They paused in the doorway, but did not speak; it was not the custom at Willow Dasset to speak to the cleaner – Aunt Bunny spoke shortly to Mrs Gurney, and Mrs Gurney similarly to Aunt Bunny, and that was the limit of communication between cleaner and residents.

'Hello,' said Mrs Grieve surprisingly. She was winding a sheet through the mangle, producing a stiff, steaming arc. She was a large, dark, untidy-looking woman and she smelt distinctly, but not unpleasantly, of armpit.

'Hello,' they replied doubtfully.

'And who are you?'

'Sally and,' Sally pointed, 'Anne.'

'Mr Ludbury's granddaughters? Aren't you lucky to be here for the harvest? I shouldn't think there could be a nicer place for a holiday.'

Sally saw how it was. Mrs Grieve was not as Mrs Gurney; rather she was as Mrs Mackie, her mother's school cleaner and occasional saviour of the Robinson household. Mrs Mackie was also her mother's best friend and confidante. 'Whatever would I do without you, Mrs Mack?' her mother would cry; or: 'Oh, Mrs Mack, dear, *would* you pop home and do something about the bathroom? Henry was complaining again this morning. And I upset the frying pan over the stove . . .' Her mother chatting with Mrs Mackie, as the two of them sat and spread their knees over the dying embers of the staffroom fire, was the cosiest thing imaginable. And Mrs Mackie felt herself free to advise and bully the Robinson children. 'Never seen so much rubbish on a girl's bedroom floor. If I was your Mam I'd open the window and chuck the lot out.' But the girls were always pleased to see her and hear the latest gossipy tales or shocking story. So, thought Sally, brightening, here was a cleaner in the Mackie mould. 'Yes,' she cried gladly, 'we love being here more than anything, specially at harvest.' And she proceeded to enlarge upon the amenities of Willow Dasset.

'I dare say you'll bump into my two sooner or later – Miriam and Ruth.'

'That'll be nice,' Sally said cautiously. 'We might show them our jumps.'

It was during a description of the Dutch barn facility that Aunt Bunny's shadow darkened the doorway. 'Whatever are you doing?' she cried angrily, looking towards the girls but somehow directing the enquiry at Mrs Grieve.

'Getting to know one another,' said that lady cheerfully.

'Orff with you!' Aunt Bunny's neck, as she drove at them, became suffused with a raspberry-coloured spottiness – like newly plucked fowl's skin, thought Sally, who always associated Aunt Bunny with poultry. Evidently their Aunt did not comprehend the sort of cleaner she had on her hands. The girls retreated smartly but, Sally considered, with dignity.

Sally had been mistaken, she discovered after further, covert observation of Mrs Grieve. She was quite unlike garrulous, bustling Mrs Mackie. Mrs Grieve was stately, almost queen-like, as she processed along the garden path with an overflowing linen basket and listened with grave attention to her employer's curt instruction. On her way home, when the girls ran deliberately across her path from their hiding place in the willows, her demeanour was friendly but serious. There was something tremendously impressive about Mrs Grieve, Sally felt, watching her statuesque progress up the steep slope of the track before she disappeared in the dip on her way to the cottage.

That afternoon, Arthur and Mr Grieve began to overhaul the threshing machine. The girls watched this activity for a while, then wandered off to the Dutch barn where they climbed to the topmost bales and lay on their stomachs to keep watch over the cottage garden. A cold draught watered their eyes – it was almost always cold in the rickyard – but at length their vigilance was rewarded: two girls came dancing down the garden path. Dancing seemed the best word to describe their ambulation; they pranced, skipped and twirled, caught one another's hands and sprang apart, drew nearer the gate and receded.

'Do you think they'll ever come out?' Anne wondered.

It was hard to say. But at last they arrived simultaneously at the garden gate, paused, looked about, then ventured into the rickyard.

'Get ready,' Sally warned; and then, as the strangers approached: 'Now!'

The Robinsons wriggled swiftly towards their staggered jumping bales, and leapt in swift succession through the air to land in the hay at the startled intruders' feet. Rising, adopting an implacable stance, they presented a daunting obstacle – two heavily breathing, red-faced creatures with gleaming eyes, uncompromising pigtails and prodigious lengths of sturdy bare leg – to the newcomers, who turned to one another with frightened expressions, shrugged and pressed their hands together beneath their chins.

At last the elder girl spoke. 'Erwer Dad works here.' It was not a challenge, but an explanation.

'And our grandfather owns it,' said Sally, adopting the proprietorial expression the sisters assumed on Wednesday afternoons at their mother's school (four and a half days a week being sufficient tuition for the privately educated child). There was a long silence while the Grieves grimaced at one another in nervous embarrassment, and the Robinsons gazed unflinchingly at the Grieves.

'Are you Miriam?' Sally asked the elder girl.

Miriam agreed that she was.

'And you're Ruth,' Anne told the smaller one, who was too shy to admit it.

Miriam and Ruth were stunning. They had an abundance of freely flowing, thick auburn hair which clung to their freckled faces and fell beyond their shoulders; their eyes were dark and soft and their lips rosy-red. Their over-long skirts and demure manners gave them a strangely old-fashioned air.

'Would you like a go on our jumps?' Sally asked them.

But Miriam and Ruth were unsure.

'You can start with easy ones,' Anne said. 'We did, then worked up to the higher ones. We'll show you.'

They demonstrated; and discovered that Miriam and Ruth were easily amused – a landing with a skirt blown over the head, or in some other undignified posture, provoked squeals of shocked laughter. The Robinsons encouraged the hilarity with a show of great derring-do and rudery. At last, thoroughly disarmed, the Grieves were emboldened to join in. The cold wind whipped them as they hurtled through the air, screaming with terror at their daring. It was a rapturous afternoon.

That night, in their bumpy double bed, Sally and Anne lay on their backs and stared into a darkness inhabited by the enchanting, laughing ones. Now and then, each broke into the other's reverie as the urge overtook them to confess besottedness. Miriam and Ruth, they agreed, were their favourite friends in the whole world; all previous attachments paled. It was impossible to say, when each pressed the other in delicious deliberation, which of the two they liked best. Ruth's gold-streaked hair was the prettiest ever seen, but Miriam's dark eyes were devastating. Really, it was as a pair that Miriam and Ruth shone.

This year, the harvest field was less of a draw. The matter was never discussed, but by some instinctive osmosis all four girls understood that Sally and Anne might go freely where Miriam and Ruth might not. Mrs Grieve was never put out when they burst into the cottage and raced up the bare staircase to bang about or whisper in her daughters' bedroom. But she was exceptional: all other adults were treated with caution.

Hence, the harvest field was spasmodically spied upon, but never entered with a view to getting on tractors or taking other liberties. Harvest tea was awkward because Aunt Bunny invariably included supplies for two children but not four. Sally and Anne overcame the difficulty by sharing with Miriam and Ruth, and filling up afterwards at the cottage. But there were secret delights to share at Willow Dasset: building dens in the barn, dangling legs in the brook, thrusting bare arms into sacks of grain that had been wickedly untied, banks to roll on, trees to swing from, and an unlimited number of hiding places. One day they smuggled Miriam and Ruth through the window over the back stairs and crept shoeless about the farmhouse – four terrified, giggly girls, in search of nothing but the thrill of complicity and the vague enjoyment of wielding hidden power.

Ruth's birthday was to fall a few days before Anne and Sally were due to go home, and Mrs Grieve invited them to a birthday tea. Words were inadequate to describe the treat in store; Miriam and Ruth gasped, spread their hands, widened their eyes; Sally and Anne learned in particular that there would be red jelly, and in general that they should anticipate an occasion more wonderful than their wildest dreams.

On the day of the party it became clear that Mrs Grieve understood that the Robinsons had sought and obtained their aunt's permission. Sally, unable to come down from her high cloud of expectation for a single second, airily – and misleadingly – confirmed that this was so. Later, the sisters became anxious, recalling their aunt's tight-lipped expression whenever they mentioned their friends.

'I expect she'll say yes,' Anne said. 'After all, we're always going there. And sometimes we do have tea.'

'But she doesn't *know* that,' Sally pointed out. And they lapsed into gloomy silence.

'P'r'aps it'd be better to just go.'

'Without telling her, you mean?'

'We could sneak upstairs after dinner to change, and then nip off when she's not looking. I mean, how's she to know we're not doing ordinary things?'

This was sufficiently unanswerable to be reassuring. They cheered up. Sally decided she would wear her new frock with the red spots. Anne, who had only one best frock, wondered whether the jam on it would show.

It is possible that the next day, while polishing the Willow Dasset silver, Mrs Grieve touched upon the subject of the birthday tea. By whatever means, it became evident that Aunt Bunny was in the know. 'Stay where you are,' she said sweetly, when Grandad Ludbury, who had been strangely silent during dinner, rose abruptly and left the room. 'I thought,' she continued confidingly, 'we'd have a nice time stringing the currants this afternoon, and then we can make a tart for Grandad's tea.'

They looked at one another in disbelief. 'But we never do that,' Sally cried – meaning things domestic. 'And anyway, we're going out . . . to play.'

'Not this afternoon.' Aunt Bunny's tone was unnaturally light-hearted. 'This afternoon you're to stay in and help me. Grandad wishes it.'

'Grandad?' Sally would not believe that he had a hand in this.

'Grandad wishes you to stay indoors this afternoon.'

'But *why*?'

'Little girls shouldn't ask questions,' Aunt Bunny said infuriatingly. 'Come along. We'll clear the table and wash up, then we can start on the currants. I picked some lovely ones this morning. Come on,' she insisted, as the girls remained, horror-struck, in their chairs.

'Aunt Bunny, we can't,' Sally blurted, seeing that cards must be put on the table. 'It's Ruth's birthday, and we're invited to tea.'

'I don't recall your mentioning it.'

'We forgot. We're sorry. But it doesn't matter, 'cos we always play with them.'

'Not this afternoon.'

'We've got to,' Anne cried wildly. 'We said yes.'

'Never mind. I don't suppose Mrs Grieve expects you.'

'She does.'

'Then she has no business to. Mrs Grieve should know better. Now, let's get on, shall we?'

They watched miserably as Aunt Bunny scraped the pudding plates and piled them on to a tray.

'Please, Aunt Bunny,' wheedled Anne, aware of her status as preferred niece. 'Mummy'd let us go.'

'But Mummy,' Aunt Bunny pointed out triumphantly, 'isn't here.' And she took up the tray and marched off through the hall towards kitchen and scullery. Her feet went briskly, making the loose linoleum smack resoundingly on the stone flags beneath.

Sally was suddenly galvanized. She chased after her. 'You knew all along, didn't you? And you decided to stop us. Why? It's stupid. There's no reason.'

Her aunt, tray in hand, turned. Her neck had that plucked fowl's skin look again. She spoke fiercely. 'There *is* a reason, Sally, and it's a pity it has to be explained to you. Little girls from *the house* do not go to tea at *the cottage*. Do you understand? As this is your grandfather's house, and not your mother's, you will behave as he wishes.'

'As *you* wish, you mean. Gosh, you're a snob! That's what it is. You're a nasty snob!' (Aunt Bunny was evidently flattered by the term, for a pleased smile crept over her face.) 'You don't care how upset they'll be – that they've been planning it for days, been to a lot of trouble, been looking forward . . .'

'That, I'm afraid is their misfortune. Their mother is at fault. She had no right to propose it.'

'You're cruel! You *want* us to be miserable, you beastly old . . .' (She cast frantically through her meagre repertoire for a sufficiently vile epithet. A recent Bible class came to her aid.) '*harlot!*'

Bunny, in one flowing movement, put the tray on the scullery table, turned, and smartly boxed her niece's ears.

Sometimes Sally's mother caught hold of her with her strong arms, swung her over a knee and thoroughly slapped her bottom. 'There!' her cleared face seemed to imply as she returned her daughter to the vertical, 'I feel much better for that; now, perhaps, we can behave reasonably to one another.' There was nothing malicious about her mother's occasional intemperance, only the sudden snapping of well tried patience. But malice now shone in Aunt Bunny's eyes as dazzling and brilliant as sun on a frosty day. It was Anne, though, who burst into tears.

'Don't be silly, dear. I'm not cross with you. It wasn't you who was rude.'

When the shock-waves in ear and bone subsided, Sally put a hand to her burning cheek. It was plain that they could not go to the party. How, then, to alleviate the feelings of their kind hosts? 'We can't just not turn up,' she moaned, half to herself. 'Imagine them waiting . . . We ought, at least, to say sorry.'

'Very well. Go and say it. But on the doorstep. You're not to go in.'

'Anne too.'

'I don't really want to,' wailed Anne.

'Quite right, dear. If Sally thinks it is necessary, Sally can go — alone.'

At once, leaving no chance for permission to be withdrawn or for her own courage to evaporate, Sally rushed through the open door and across the yard to the steps. She ran along the track, down into the dip by the willow-pond, then up the slope — puffing, feeling heavier — until the cottage came in sight. The way became easier as the track wound down to the point where a narrow path led off to the cottage gate. She fumbled with the latch, burst through, and charged up the garden path. The front door opened.

Mrs Grieve stood in the doorway looking grave. Unaccountably, Miriam and Ruth were not smiling in welcome, nor dancing with excitement. They peeped at her from behind their mother's back, their faces sombre, their hands clasped beneath their chins. Through the open parlour doorway Sally caught sight of a festive table.

'We can't come,' she blurted.

Miriam and Ruth seemed to shudder and retreat further behind their mother.

'No.' Mrs Grieve spoke without surprise. 'I'm very sorry.'

'So are we. We wanted to come so much. It was Aunt Bunny. She's hateful. She's a *snob*.'

Mrs Grieve turned to her daughters and spoke quietly. They went into the parlour and closed the door. 'I'm sorry you and Anne have been disappointed, Sally, but you had better go straight back to your aunt.'

Somehow Sally removed herself from the cottage step

and arrived at the gate. At some point she heard the door to the cottage close. Her legs trembled violently and her terrible words sounded again and again: She's a snob . . . a snob . . . a snob. 'Oh, oh, oh!' she moaned aloud, her voice rising. 'How *could* I?' She had compounded the insult. Her shame would last for ever.

When she arrived back at the house she found she could not speak.

'Was it . . . ? Were they . . . ?' asked Anne from the kitchen table, already well stained with currant juice.

'Have you something to say to me?' Aunt Bunny demanded.

Sally shook her head.

'Then go to your room and stay there till you have.'

On leaden legs, Sally climbed the stairs.

The house soothed her. It was so quiet, so constant. Intermittently, sounds of activity reached the room; but far way, very far away. Even milking, it seemed, was going on behind a thick curtain. The only wide awake noise came when Benjamin's lad called at the yard door for the harvest teas. Then panic rose from the kitchen – evidently the making of a fruit tart had proved absorbing. Apart from that one brief flurry, nothing disturbed the easy, sun-speckled, floating airiness of a house lulled by birdsong and the unwavering, resonant beat of a grandfather clock downstairs by the garden door.

Nothing mattered really. Being here was the thing, hearing, breathing, feeling Willow Dasset. People didn't matter – no-one – not Grandad, not Arthur. And Miriam and Ruth were destined to fade to a charming, half-remembered dream. She knew it, and it didn't matter.

'Why, Sally!' Grandma Ludbury cried, catching sight of

the rumpled child on the bed. 'How you startled me!' She paused in her progress towards the bathroom, then, seeming to make up her mind, came towards the bed. 'My dear, what are you doing here?'

'I've been sent.'

'Are you ill?'

'No.'

Grandma Ludbury ran a finger along the lace border of a runner on the dressing table near the bed. 'Well . . . I thought I'd have tea downstairs today. I'm feeling better. Will you be there?'

'Don't think I'm allowed. I haven't said sorry. 'Cos I'm not.'

'Sorry?'

'For calling Aunt Bunny a harlot.'

Grandma Ludbury seized a hairbrush and examined it minutely. (How Sally wished she had combed out the dead hairs.) Then the brush was dropped, and her grandmother turned with a shout of laughter. 'Not a very apposite name,' she remarked when she could control herself.

'It just came to me,' Sally said gruffly, doubt setting in – she could have sworn Father Timms had said it meant wicked woman.

'But why did you wish to insult your poor aunt?'

'Because we were invited to tea at the cottage – it's Ruth's birthday today – she and Miriam are our best friends – but Aunt Bunny wouldn't let us go. She said house children couldn't have tea with cottage children. Mrs Grieve had made us a lovely tea, and Miriam and Ruth and Anne and me were' – her voice faltered – '*yearning* for it – it was going to be such a party . . . I had to go and tell them we couldn't come. It was awful. I think I hurt their feelings . . .'

Grandma Ludbury lowered herself carefully on to the

bed – Sally thought that she was very light because the bed didn't sag as much as it did under other people's weight – and took her granddaughter's hand. She studied it, turned it over, patted it. 'Well . . .' – it was a long sigh – 'I don't think I shall bother with tea after all – such a sticky little meal. Have you got a good book to read?'

Sally nodded.

'Much the best thing. It's so difficult when one is powerless . . . But soon you will go home where I expect you have a great many friends, and where people, I feel sure, are not quite so . . . petty.'

Sally waited, feeling her grandmother would speak again. But no, she relinquished Sally's hand and pushed her own into the bed to lever herself to her feet. Then she craned forward and peered at herself in the looking glass above the dressing table. 'But you are quite right, Sally, to be upset. Hurting people for no good reason is inexcusable.'

For the first time that afternoon tears welled in Sally's eyes. Soon they overflowed and ran in rivers down her cheeks. She cried and cried, loving the release, hoping that it would go on and on. Grandma's unexpected sympathy was so good, it would be nice to have more. She searched through her remembered ills for a heart-rending enormity, and, almost at once, hit upon the case of her ruined friendship with Sheila Crib.

(Mr Crib had been sent to prison for embezzlement; and other parents – notably Henry Robinson – were urgent that Sheila be removed from the school. Argument raged in the Robinson household, for Sheila was Sally's best friend and a frequent visitor to the house. Meg was of the opinion that any possible danger had disappeared with Mr Crib's incarceration – besides, if all the children with felonious fathers were removed from Corporation

Street Elementary, it would make quite a dent in the register. Which just went to prove Henry's point – private education was supposed to safeguard one's children from that sort of contamination. Besides, the man had appeared before the court, *Henry's* court; and Henry must consider his reputation. Meg, who had more important things on her mind, gave in.)

'They stopped me being friends with Sheila Crib,' Sally choked, as heartbroken as if it had happened yesterday. 'And she was my best friend. Just because her dad got sent to prison . . . They wouldn't let her come and play with me anymore, and when she asked me to her house I had to say no. It's *always* happening.' She almost believed it.

'Always?'

'Over and over. Whenever I'm friends with anyone.' But here her imagination gave up. She fell back, exhausted, against her pillow.

'Oh . . . dear!'

It was such a sad whisper that Sally opened her eyes, but her view was distorted by her sodden lashes.

'I must think about this. I must think . . .'

The voice fading, the figure receding – 'Grandma?' – she had gone.

Anne was shaking her. 'Wake up. Aunt Bunny says if you come down now and say sorry, you can have tea and Grandad needn't know.'

Oh, it was tempting, for the thought of Grandad hearing sour tales about her from Aunt Bunny was not at all pleasant. 'I can't,' she said, reclosing her eyes.

'Please, Sal . . . You might starve.'

Indeed she might. She moaned in anticipation.

'Won't you, Sally?' As there was no reply, Anne went dubiously to the door. 'I'll try and bring you something.'

When tea was underway, Sally crept from her room and crouched on the top stair, straining her ears to hear what was being said in the dining-room. Words rumbled indistinctly. She could not make them out, so she invented them, making her grandfather say with a sorrowful shake of the head: 'Never would've thought it of Sal.' Misery bit into her and a nervy weakness attacked her joints. She keeled over, then crawled and slithered like a baby over the polished boards, carelessly rucking up rugs in her path, until she could haul herself back into bed.

It was a lump of cake that Anne brought her, compressed crumbs in a handkerchief. Sally put it on her knees and lowered her face so that she could scoop pinchfuls into her mouth without waste.

Anne watched. 'Grandad did know,' she said conversationally. 'At tea he said: "You put a stop to that business, I take it?" And Aunt Bunny said: "Yes, but Sally wouldn't take it with a good grace." So you see, he *did* know.'

'Liar.' Sally said nastily through a laden mouth.

'Cross my heart.'

When every crumb had been eaten Sally thrust the handkerchief at her sister. 'That was disgusting. I need a drink to take away the taste.'

'Well, I'll try . . .'

Morning asserted itself as beguilingly as ever. Sally lay very still, listening, not thinking. Beside her, Anne stirred, then, with a gasp, hurled herself from the bed and began to pull on clothing. Every now and then Sally caught a word or two of her rapid muttering: 'John . . . just going to . . . 'cos I won't . . . silly thing . . .' Without pausing to visit the bathroom, Anne pounded down the back stairs, leaving Sally marvelling at the nature of her sister's bladder – an unreliable organ during hours of enforced tedium, but a thing of iron when lively matters were at hand. Soon her grandfather could be heard going about his morning tea duties. Insidiously, in spite of her determination to suppress it, yesterday's stale emotion crept over her, unattractive and shameful in the light of a new day. She paid fierce attention to her grandfather's progress – up the front stairs, along the landing with Grandma's special tea, back again to Aunt Bunny's room at the head of the stairs, and now, she supposed, he would go down again. But no – she held her breath – he was approaching her room.

'Cup of tea,' he announced, putting it on the table beside her. 'Drink up while it's hot. And then, m'lady, I'll expect you downstairs ready to eat a hearty breakfast. That's what all landgirls need inside 'em when they've a day's harvesting to do.'

Struggling into her clothes, determined to be gone from the room before her aunt passed through it, nothing in the world seemed as enticing as a day's harvesting.

They were going home. Added to that sorrow was an uneasy suspicion that she had earned her mother's wrath.

'Come and say goodbye to Grandma. And' – Sally felt her mother's strong hands upon her shoulders – 'without any dramatics from *you*.'

Anne and Sally went with their mother along the landing.

Grandma Ludbury was smiling at a rose in a vase on the dressing table. She waved a hand towards it when they came in, inviting their admiration.

'We've come to say goodbye, Mama,' Meg said, pushing her daughters forward.

They kissed gravely, first Sally, then Anne.

'And what else?' murmured their mother.

'Thank you for having us,' they chorused foolishly, feeling it was an inappropriate thing to say to their grandmother. Perhaps she agreed with them, for her smile widened.

'Goodbye, Mama,' Meg said, kissing her. 'See you at Christmas, probably. If not then, at Easter. Come along, girls; Daddy's waiting.'

Passing the foot of the bed, Sally paused to stare through the iron bars of the bedstead. Grandma Ludbury gazed back. In her travelling clothes, Sally felt already gone from Willow Dasset, a mere passer-by peering enviously through railings at the resident in possession. How content her grandmother looked, how lazily amused by the spy at her gates.

'Sally!' her mother called angrily from the stairs.

She went to the doorway, but before going through, turned towards the bed for one last, lingering look.

'Well, I hope you're satisfied!' Meg exploded a little later, as the car rolled along the drive.

They were passing the tied cottage, and Sally and Anne were trying to look at it without turning their heads. Sally, to whom the outburst was directed, felt her stomach turn. 'Why?'

'You know perfectly well why. How dare you upset your grandmother with a pack of lies? – Complaining that we stop you being friends with people, that you're miserable at home.'

'What's this?' Henry asked sharply.

But a contribution from her husband could not be borne, Meg felt, not after that scene with Mama. 'Oh, she's been dramatizing herself again,' she said in an off-hand way. 'But,' – she turned again towards the back seat – 'it beats me how you could upset her like that when she could have a heart attack at *any moment*.'

'I thought you said there was nothing really wrong with her.'

'Don't try and be clever with me, miss! All I'm saying is: if anything happens to your grandmother in the immediate future we'll know whom to blame.' She turned her head towards the front of the car and addressed Henry. 'Honestly, I've never seen Mother so roused by anything – not for years, anyway. That girl's getting to be a nasty little trouble-maker.'

''Spect the old man's been spoiling them. She'll sober down soon enough once she's home.'

And Sally, gazing out at the widening divide between herself and Willow Dasset, thought how apt were the words 'sober down'.

8

In October Louisa died. Charlotte telephoned Meg with the news and told her that the funeral would take place three days hence.

'Well, I can't possibly come.' Corporation Street Elementary School was undergoing an inspection, and although a glowing report was a foregone conclusion, not for anything would Meg leave her deputy in charge at such a time.

'On Thursday, that is,' Aunt Charlotte bellowed confidently.

'I said I can't, Aunt.'

'At three o'clock. And stay with us afterwards. I've a great deal to say to you.' With which she hung up.

'Damn,' said Meg. She'd telephone Jim – he would be sure to go over there. But Jim, his housekeeper reported, had already set off for The Grange. A couple of hours later Meg tried again.

'Hello. Who's there?' yelled Pip.

'Meg,' said Meg, jerking the receiver further from her ear.

'Oh, you. Jim was here, but he's gone to see the undertaker.'

'Look, I tried to explain to Aunt Charlotte but she didn't seem to take it in. I can't possibly come. It's too sudden.'

'Sudden? Nonsense. I've known for months.'

'Known?'

'Her eyeballs were yellow as mustard, and she was forever rubbing her side.'

It took Meg a moment or two to adjust to this. 'You mean, you knew Aunt Louisa was ill?'

'Of course I did, you silly girl.'

'Then why on earth didn't you tell us? We could have done something for her.'

'Put her in hospital, you mean, so she'd die all alone in a strange place missing her garden and her hens? No, no. She was better off here. I kept an eye on her. When she got bad I made her nice and comfy and sent Edward to fetch me some whisky. She complained of the tea tasting nasty, but it did the trick – the pain eased off, she was lovely and drowsy. Kept her like that for days. Of course, my tablets helped, too. She just dozed away on the *chaise-longue* by the window. Chucky, chucky, chuck, she said just before the end – poor girl thought she was chasing the blasted hens . . .'

The time signal interrupted her.

'The pips!' shrieked Pip, and dropped the suddenly scalding receiver.

The front door slammed (a slack, wobbly sound; sooner or later its leaded squares of brown and green glass would surely fall out) and Meg came into the hall.

'You're late,' Henry called accusingly from the dining-room where he was supervising tea. 'Bunny phoned.'

'Bunny?' This was surprising; no-one made trunk calls before six in the evening.

'It's your mother. She's had a bad do, apparently. The doctor says it's just a matter of time.'

Meg dropped her bags in the doorway and stood up. 'How much time?' she asked, feeling threatened. In advance of enlightenment she pledged herself that nothing, nothing whatsoever, would be allowed to inter-fere with her many commitments. Good grief! – it was getting on for Christmas – didn't they understand?

'A matter of days, I think. You'd better ring her back.'

'Later. I need a cup of tea. I've just had a very difficult meeting.'

'You might as well get it over. Then we'll know where we stand.'

Meg reached into her capacious handbag and drew out her diary. She marched with it into the hall and put it on the table next to the telephone, propping it open at the last week in November. Those scrawled in engagements – the nativity play rehearsal, the choir practice, the staff meeting, the meeting with the mothers who were organizing the school parties, the luncheon with the Townswomen's Guild at which she was to be the guest speaker – would stiffen her resolve. 'Hello, Bunny. What's all this I hear?'

At the dining-room table, Henry, listening with his daughters to the one-sided conversation in the hall, motioned that they were to get on with their tea. Sally continued to gnaw her knuckles.

'What's the matter?' Anne hissed.

'Shush!' said Henry.

When her mother hung up and came slowly back into the room, Sally felt she would faint.

'I'll have to go. Seems there's no doubt about it. I just hope' – Meg sank wearily into a chair – 'she gets on with it.'

'Here's your tea,' Henry said, pouring her a cup. 'It's certainly come at an awkward time for you.'

That was kind of him, thought Meg. She had expected him to list the many inconveniences to himself. 'You'll manage all right with the girls? I expect Mrs Mack'll put something in the oven.'

'Of course.'

'Is Daddy going to look after us?' Anne asked. And then, as her mother nodded: 'Can we do each other's plaits? Daddy pulls our hair out – he doesn't unpick the knots – just yanks. It's terrible.'

'Yes, yes,' Meg said impatiently.

Anne looked with relief at her sister, but Sally was not attending.

Meg spread bloater paste over a slice of bread and butter. 'I've got a busy night ahead of me. I can put off one or two things, I suppose, but I'll have to write instructions for the others. I wonder if it'll be over by Friday – you know – in time for the Townswomen's lunch. Have we got a train timetable? I'll go late morning – better go into school first thing . . .'

'Mummy,' Sally put in hurriedly, 'was it me? Was it 'cos I upset her?'

They looked at her blankly. Meg, recalling that time was of the essence, took a large bite of bloatered bread. 'Oh!' she spluttered. 'She means that business at the end of the summer holiday. Good heavens, child, that was months ago! Trust you, though, to push yourself into the limelight. If she can't be the heroine,' she commented to her husband, 'she'll settle for the villian's part – so long as it's a starring role . . .'

'I did think at the time,' Henry put in mildly, 'that you were a bit strong.'

'I've no patience with her. Now, you girls, clear up properly because Daddy and I have a great deal to do.'

'My turn to wash up. Yours to dry,' Anne said hastily to Sally.

'All right,' Sally said without argument – which led

Anne to conclude that something really was up with Sal.

Meg caught the train with barely a minute to spare. As she battled into a compartment – hair trailing, suitcase refusing to turn neatly lengthwise through the doorway – a man in the corridor raised his hat. 'Good morning, Mrs Robinson. What an unexpected pleasure! Don't tell me I've caught you playing truant!'

Meg, who could not make out who the man was, bared her teeth in what she took to be a smile, and flopped down in a corner seat. The man moved on, thinking, perhaps, that the striking, but rather scatty Mrs Robinson was in no mood for company. Meg's short-sighted frown was always daunting, and spectacles, because she forgot to clean them, often made matters worse; hindered by a build up of spots and smears, she glared out at the world more fiercely than ever. And the vigour of her thoughts compounded the fearsomeness of her expression; the inner workings of her mind often took precedent over happenings around her, so that she stared fixedly but unseeingly, causing discomfort to strangers and offence to unrecognized acquaintances.

Now, her last minute instructions to the school staff absorbed her. She went over them again and imagined them put into practice, looking out for pitfalls. But as the train rocked on and on, its rhythm took hold of her; her thoughts became feeble and began to fade. Through the window she watched slag heaps loom, and her mind's eye turned them into grassy banks. One black, grainy mountain she clothed in buttercups and scabious and long wind-blown grasses. It was so pretty that she looked up and smiled at the woman opposite to whom she gave her mother's face. At least, thought Meg, Mama and I had that in common – our love of flowers and growing things. She recalled their flower-hunting expeditions – one specimen only plucked for the scrap book – and all the country flower names her mother knew: eggs and bacon, lady's slipper, love lies bleeding . . . Such pleasure they had shared . . . Of course, it had always been Meg and Daddy, for she and he were so alike, the busy doers, the problem-solvers, sometimes uncomfortably aware of the other's thoughts and fears. Mama had been outside their special closeness – apart – a lovely stranger. But Meg had loved her; she could recall how, coming upon her mother sitting alone and dreamy in the lamplight, she would be obliged to blurt: 'I do love you, Mama.'

The train was slowing. Here came Sheffield and the moment to change trains, to hurry to platform two.

'Mrs Robinson – your case!'

It was that man again – where on earth had she seen him before? 'Oh, thank you. I was thinking of something else, I'm afraid.'

Indeed she was, the travellers nearby confirmed to themselves, observing a tear crawl from under each side of her spectacles.

Meg grabbed her case and marched off in search of platform two, resolving that as soon as she could put down case and bag she would blow her nose, for the sharp wind had made her eyes water.

At her journey's end she found Jim waiting with their father's car. 'What are you doing here? I told Bunny I'd get a taxi.'

He took her luggage and put it in the boot. 'Henry rang to tell us the time of the train you were catching.'

'Well, he shouldn't have. I might have missed it.' As they drove from the station yard, she asked: 'How's Mama?'

''Bout the same.'

Then they were silent for some time until Jim, taking his pipe from his mouth and holding it against the steering wheel, suddenly said: 'I wondered whether to fetch Aunt Pip.'

'Whatever for? Her nursing days are long gone.'

'Not that. I thought Mama'd like it.'

'Has she asked for her?'

'She hasn't asked for anyone. Don't think I've heard her utter more than a half-dozen words. Is the clematis in flower? That's all she's said in my hearing.'

'Her mind must be wandering – clematis at this time of year!'

'The sun was pouring in at the time.'

They thought about this, then Meg said: 'Well, if I were you I'd forget all about Aunt Pip. It'd only cause fuss and bother. What does Bunny think?'

'Same as you.'

'There you are then.' And Meg shuffled in her seat to indicate the end of the matter.

Dusk had fallen over Willow Dasset. Climbing the steps to the yard, Meg felt suddenly weary. Bunny was waiting for her by the kitchen door. They spoke tenderly to one another – 'Oh, Bun . . .' – 'Meg, dear . . .' – and held each other in a long embrace.

'Well?'

'Come and see.'

There was still sufficient light for them to go without a candle, but the way was shadowy-dim and the uncurtained landing window breathed coldly over the stairwell. Rebecca's room glowed with firelight. Bunny drew the curtains and lit the lamp, then went to lean over her mother. 'Mama?' But when Bunny smiled up at Meg across the bed it was plain that she had expected no answer. 'Isn't she peaceful?' she marvelled softly.

Meg nodded.

Jim came into the room.

'Come on, tea's laid,' Bunny whispered, moving round the bed to take her sister's arm. 'Jim'll stay here.'

George was already waiting at the table. He remained seated when his daughters came in, managed a feeble acknowledgement – 'How do, Megs?' – allowed her to kiss the side of his face, then became resolutely silent. Meg recalled his retreat into silence all those years ago when her little sister had died.

'Tea, Daddy.' Bunny passed a cup of tea to Meg, who set it beside her father.

As they expected, he said nothing.

'Bread and butter? Jam?'

He took the offerings without a word.

'You're looking tired, Bun. Have you managed to get any sleep?'

'Oh yes. Jim and I take turns.'

'And Harry?'

Bunny pulled a face and indicated their father.

Meg nodded to show that she understood. Harry, like his father, would be frightened by the situation and seek to avoid it; beneath their manly bluster George and Harry were full of fear.

'He pops in every day, but he's no use. Jim's wonderful, of course. Nothing upsets him. He was so good to them at The Grange when Louisa . . .' But perhaps they would talk more easily later on, away from their father's brooding presence.

Thank heaven for Jim, Meg thought. But later, sitting with Jim at the kitchen table, while he consumed sufficient food to account for a delayed tea and an early supper, she suppressed the appreciative words that sprang to her lips, fearing a dose of his pantheism: 'Death's nothing to get excited about – just nature's way of making room for new life. It's a wonderful thing, when you come to think about it . . .' No, Meg was too tired tonight to bear Jim's comfortable philosophizing. 'You go home,' she told him. 'Get a decent night's sleep. I'll sit up with Mama so that Bunny can do the same.'

He munched for a while, then drank lengthily from a glass of beer. 'I'll come back directly after morning milking, then.'

Bunny, settling Meg in the basket chair beside their mother's bed with a hot water bottle, blankets and a cup of tea, demanded to be woken at five o'clock sharp. 'Then *you* can have some sleep. We must guard against getting too tired. This may go on.' And with that alarming suggestion she crept towards the door, pausing before leaving to whisper: 'Wake me, of course, if there's any change.'

Alone with the comatose creature on the bed, Meg could summon none of the emotion she had experienced earlier on the train. Then, she had felt her mother's presence quite distinctly, had been warmed and moved by it. But this still form, its face rapt as if all effort were devoted exclusively to the single act of breathing – which went on laboriously through slightly parted lips – seemed not to be her mother; for her mother's spirit would surely disdain a preoccupation with the purposeless mechanics of prolonging life. In the small hours the breathing became rasping and Meg wondered whether the moment had come to rouse Bunny. Then, in the midst of her indecision, her mother sighed – clearly and deeply – and began to breathe as if newly come to sleep. Clinging to the easy sound, Meg breathed in sympathy.

It was Bunny who roused Meg.

'Meg! You must have dropped off. Go and get into bed. I'll watch now.'

'What's the time?'

'Just after five.'

Meg lurched stiffly from the room in search of Bunny's warm bed.

Sleep: and a dream about Mama in a scarlet cloak – billowing, swirling, the silken folds ablaze, almost blinding . . . Meg sat bolt upright in the bed and blinked furiously against the flooding sunlight. Whatever was the time? But it was not too disgraceful – only half past eight.

She hurried to the bathroom and back again to dress, then went to the head of the landing. The door to the room where her father had been sleeping – the room used during the holidays by Henry and herself – was open. Daddy had gone. She pictured him stalking angrily about the farm, looking for a quarrel to pick with one of the men. She opened the door to her mother's room.

'See what we have here!' Bunny invited softly in the idiot tone of a manipulative nursery-school teacher.

Meg was so astounded that she responded like a compliant child, gasping, clasping hands to her chin, and grinning foolishly at her mother who was sitting up in bed and allowing Bunny to draw a brush – slowly, oh so carefully – through her hair. The hair flew over the pillow, live and lustrous, white silk over snowy linen.

'Meg!' Rebecca, said, sounding pleased.

'Isn't this nice?' Bunny encouraged.

'Wonderful!' But Meg's smile became fixed as a small knot of fury formed in the secret pit of her emotions. What did this mean? Had the wretched doctor misread the signs? Or was this the pattern of a long drawn out departure? Dear Lord – and she had a job to do! This week

114

had been totally wrecked, she could not allow another week to suffer similarly . . .

'I've brought you away from your work,' Rebecca said sorrowfully.

In her confusion, Meg rushed to look out of the garden window. 'Nonsense Mama, I wanted to come.'

'I wonder . . .' Bunny mused, her head tilted artfully to one side, 'whether we could manage a few sips of our special tea?'

'Perhaps,' murmured Rebecca, and then, more positively: 'Meg, is the winter jasmine in flower, can you see?'

Meg pressed her face to the window to peer down at the wall of the house. 'I'm not sure. Shall I go and look? Would you like me to bring you a sprig?'

'Oh, I *would*.'

'Right-oh. Shan't be a sec.'

'And I'll go and make that tea.'

So, thought Meg grimly as she stomped down the stairs, Mama has recovered her sense of season. It is winter jasmine she enquires after, not clematis. She took secateurs from a cabinet by the garden door and went outside. Squinting up, she selected a piece of blossom and snipped. It lay in her palm, one moon-coloured flower among tight creamy buds on a stem of jutting greenery. About to take it upstairs, she hesitated, and went instead along the half passage to the kitchen. 'Shall I take this up, or would it be nicer on her tray, do you think?'

'Bring it here. Look – the tea you gave her, cream and green; it matches the jasmine exactly. And I've put it on one of her nicest tray clothes – just look at the work, Meg – isn't it *fine*? Mama was so clever!'

Meg placed the jasmine sprig on the tray cloth. 'There?'

'Yes. Perfect.'

As pleased with themselves as two good girls can be, they bore away their handiwork to their mother's room.

Rebecca, it appeared, had fallen into a doze. She was exactly as they had left her – the white light of her hair, the curving abandonment of her hands, a hint of a lazy smile – except that her eyes had closed.

'Mama?'

'Mama, dear?'

She was utterly still.

'Bunny, I think she's gone.'

'I'll just put this down. Let me see. Ah . . . Oh, Meg!'

They moved towards one another and each sank a head on the other's shoulder. Then Meg reached out for the piece of jasmine on the tray. She gave it to Bunny, who turned and placed it on the pillow beside Rebecca's hair.

9

They were to spend Christmas at Willow Dasset.

This was by no means a foregone conclusion, for Henry preferred to worship at St Luke's on the major Feast Days. But the Robinson larder had developed bare patches (the result, not of financial collapse, but of neglect during this busy time), and the thought of Bunny's prime roasted fowl prompted Henry to consider it his Christian duty to divert the widower from his grief this Christmas.

Meg readily agreed. She was always glad to let someone else do the cooking. And her spirits were high, she was game for anything, for in spite of the calamitous loss of a week's work at the end of November, the term had ended in triumph. The school nativity play had received flattering notices in the local press, and had been applauded by a bishop, no less. A few days later Meg had been appointed to the national body of the Church's Advisory Service for Schools. The Townswomen's Guild, whose luncheon had coincided with the day of Rebecca's funeral, had forgiven her and allowed her to address them the following week. This, too, had been a success, and their President, who was also a member of the more august Ladies' Forum, had volunteered to sponsor Meg's entrée into that more selective little band. But this honour Meg had declined.

Henry was put out. 'Mrs Massingbird-Formby belongs to the Ladies' Forum,' he protested. 'It's an honour to be asked. You can't turn them down.'

'Well, I have. I'm not sure that I've any patience with them.' And that, of course, had been that, for it was well understood that those with whom Meg had no patience were well and truly done for.

After her mother's funeral, Meg had returned in a softer frame of mind, prepared to deal patiently with her children's anxious questioning. The suggestion that Sally had hastened her grandmother's death was finally scotched. 'If that little upset had affected her, she would have had a heart attack back then in the summer, not three months later.'

'Mummy,' Anne had ventured, 'was it all . . . blood?'

'Blood?'

'When she died. Was there ever so much blood?'

'Whatever gave you that idea? No, it wasn't like that. It was very peaceful.'

'What did it look like, then?' Anne persisted, trying to hide her disappointment over the lack of gore.

'She just closed her eyes . . . and slipped away.'

'You mean vanished?'

'No, silly! Died. But gently. Just closed her eyes and died.'

'Like falling asleep?'

'Yes. Exactly like falling asleep.'

Sally, who had listened carefully to this exchange, wondered whether falling asleep would ever seem such an innocent pastime again. Both girls rallied, however, when they learned they were to spend Christmas at Willow Dasset cheering up poor old Grandad.

If their grandfather required saving from his grief, it was not immediately apparent. The girls, he declared, greeting them on the doorstep, had grown so large that he could scarcely lift them – this as they were swung into the air, one on each arm, and clapped to his great hard chest. How delighted he was to pull their pigtails, to tip up their chins and wink at their solemn, wide-eyed staring, to pinch their firm, fat cheeks, to see his own two girls again – his dear little, *nice* little girls.

The house was decked with holly. Every picture (the hunting and racing prints), every clock, every curtain rail, sprouted sprigs of prickly green stuff. And on the dining-room sideboard lay a box of crackers. ('Crackers!' exclaimed the children. 'Don't suppose they'll be up to much,' warned the grown-ups, rightly suspicious of all post-war manufacturers.) Bunny ushered Meg into the pantry to inspect the naked fowl, the crumbed ham, the well-hung sirloin. It all looked most promising, Meg was able to report to Henry over the unpacking in their bedroom. Encouraged by the news, Henry burst into song: 'Good Christian men rejoi-oi-oice . . .'

At the other end of the landing, Anne and Sally paused in their unpacking. 'Go and close it,' Sally commanded, indicating the door. Anne hurried to obey, thus preserving them from the raucous, skidding, rising fifth of the carol's penultimate line.

'Thank goodness for that,' Sally murmured as the bellowing was reduced to the faintness of a bull in distant pasture; and they continued their unpacking with a view to changing as soon as possible into farming clothes. One holiday they had rushed out on arrival without changing, and had returned to the house reeking of silage, their school gaberdines fatally impregnated. 'Ruined!' Meg had cried, beating each daughter soundly in turn. So it was with care that they put away decent clothes and withdrew old holey jumpers, skirts too short and mud-coloured socks. Wellington boots and old coats were discovered in the scullery. Virtuously shabby, they raced over the yard to reclaim their favourite haunts.

119

Seasonal change preoccupied them. They spent some time in thoughtful silence sinking booted feet into a ridge of soft mud (so recently an impregnable rock) and withdrawing, feeling the sucking resistance, enjoying the plop and splat. In the farmyard they climbed on to a fence and gazed at the huddled creatures deprived for the winter of their freedom in the fields. The cattle, standing knee-deep in steaming, blackened straw, gazed back and nudged one another aside to secure an improved perspective. Arthur, the girls discovered, had knotted a muffler at his throat in deference to the season. There would be endless opportunities for sitting on tractor mudguards, the girls learned, for the ploughing had to be completed before the hard frosts came, and the imprisoned cattle required the tractor to be forever arriving with clean straw and fresh hay and departing with muck to enrich the distant fields. Winter, it seemed, had cast its own distinctive charm upon life at Willow Dasset.

Farming was forbidden the girls on Christmas Day. They were to remain in best frocks and stay clean and tidy. Christmas Day, Anne considered, when the excitement of exploring her filled stocking subsided, was in danger of turning into a Sunday, for church was to follow hard upon breakfast. But for Sally, who at ten years of age still held to her belief in Father Christmas, the filled stockings lying at the foot of the bed like knobbly worms that had over-eaten themselves, had lent a magic to the morning that would not easily be dispelled. It was different for Anne. Having a practical turn of mind she had discovered the truth of the matter three years ago at the age of five. 'I knew it was you,' she had called – a vindicated spy squatting on a chamber pot in the dark. The jerry had seemed a bright idea, affording an opportunity to claim sudden, innocent wakefulness; but her mother had not been deceived. As Henry hesitated in the bedroom doorway, wondering whether to proceed with the exchange of empty old sock for filled old sock, Meg swooped on her daughter intending to deliver a smart smack. The long vigil, however, had resulted in a fusion of pot and skin, and the pain suffered during their separation was considered punishment enough. Anne was forgiven on condition that she refrain absolutely from destroying her sister's faith. This had proved tiresome, for the gaining of years did not, in Sally's case, result in the gaining of worldly wisdom. It was mortifying to own a sister in the *top class* who still clung to childish myths. And scoffing friends, enlarging upon the impossibility of the Christmas Eve task for one overweight, elderly gentleman, made no impression; Sally would admit no difficulty. She could imagine – rather, she could *feel* – that Father Christmas might encompass the whole world in a single tender instant by the sheer force of his generous spirit. After all, if God and the angels, why not Father Christmas and the reindeer? (Overhearing this line of reasoning, Meg had suffered a momentary qualm.) So it was with tarnished joy that Anne beheld her filled stocking, for the sight of it revived memories of recent encounters in the playground. Sally, squeezing her father's straining sock in the unreal half-light of early morning, was full of awe. She lay back in bed, clutching the mystery to her chest, disdaining, for the present, to examine its contents. Anne got on with it. She shook out puzzles, trinkets, crayons, a whistle, a little car, a little book; and totted up her parents' score. Overall she was not impressed, but consoled herself with the thought that proper presents were still to come.

Returning from church, the Robinsons entered a house suffused with the perfume of roasting fowl, herbs and sausage-spices. The fragrant assault threw Henry into a lather of excitement. His voice, throbbing with the certainty of virtue soon to be rewarded, boomed out a carol in the cloakroom under the stairs. The girls rushed to find their grandfather. He was discovered in the dining-room reclining in his tall armchair, his legs twined together in a long, straight line over the hearth rug.

'Back from church,' he observed.

They nodded.

'Vicar have a lot to say for himself?'

They pulled faces to indicate that the sermon had indeed been protracted.

'Always used to time the blighters, meself. A nice short sermon and I'd give the fellow a good tip. A long-winded one and he'd be lucky to find sixpence on the plate from George Ludbury.'

This view of The Offertory widened their large eyes.

'Come here. Give Grandad a kiss.' He caught them to him, an arm around each as they moved to his side. He smelled deliciously of Coal Tar soap and starched linen. 'Grandad's good girls,' he murmured contentedly.

Henry strode into the room. 'Good morning, Father! No,' – he broke off to examine his wrist watch – 'I tell a lie! Good *afternoon*!' He had planned this little sally as a neat way of calling attention to the swift passage of time. It would be heart-breaking if dinner were late.

George relinquished his granddaughters and drew out his fob watch. ''Pon my word, time's getting on. Wonder how they're doin' in the kitchen. Glass of sherry, Henry?'

'I might venture a small one,' Henry conceded, distrustful of alcoholic liquor, but mindful of its obligatory role in today's proceedings.

From a deep drawer of the sideboard, George took a

bottle and four glasses. He filled them and placed two on one side. 'For the ladies.'

'My pleasure!' Henry, seizing the opportunity to nudge things along in the kitchen, carefully bore the filled glasses to the turbulent end of the house.

'Put them over there,' Bunny cried crossly, pausing between range and table to remove hair from her eyes.

'What is it?' asked Meg, who could see very little through her steam-smeared spectacles. 'Oh! Good Lord! Is it that time already?'

'Might I be permitted to facilitate matters? Lay the table, perhaps?'

'I suppose so . . . But *shut the door*!' screamed Bunny before Henry had so much as returned a toe into the hall.

Outside, the dogs barked. The girls ran to welcome Uncle Jim and kiss him beneath the mistletoe in the hall. Henry was relieved; things were really moving now. 'I was rash enough to volunteer my services as a table-layer,' he confessed to his brother-in-law with the rueful expression of one who is too good for such things. Jim, who had declined sherry, and intended to pour himself a large glass of beer in the pantry, indicated that the task might safely be left to him.

At last all was ready. George carved and dismembered the roasted fowl with the ease of a practised butcher. George's daughters watched him with rapt admiration. Jim, who made it a point of honour never to admire anything his father did, whistled tunelessly under his breath. Henry experienced mounting irritation – Meg and Bunny seemed to equate well carved meat with the execution of a work of art, refusing to serve anyone so much as a brussel sprout until their father had reseated himself. Anne and Sally, passing meat-laden plates down the table, marvelled at the contrast between this peaceful, almost reverent operation and the tantrums which accompanied the carving of the Robinson weekend joint – their father cursing the butcher, cursing the knife; their mother hot and exasperated, gulping aspirins down with water, rapping clenched knuckles against the tablecloth.

The dinner was delicious. Henry's good spirits revived. When his immediate hunger pangs were quietened he recalled his duty to assist the jocularity of the occasion, and gave them an account of how, at a recent function in the town hall, an American guest had helped himself too liberally to the mustard. 'Apparently, American mustard is weak as ditch water,' he explained, 'and the fellow spread the stuff thick as jam all over his beef. Then he took a mouthful and . . .' But Henry's amusement, as he enlarged upon the unfortunate guest's near asphyxia, was so vast that the remainder of the story was unintelligible. Meg, who had in any case heard it before, looked coldly at Henry across the table, and resumed her discussion of the merits of various forcemeats with Bunny. Jim continued to amuse his nieces by making their chairs wobble and their spoons disappear. Only George paid prolonged attention to Henry. Observing his son-in-law's hilarity, he reflected that he had allowed the fellow one sherry too many. 'More meat, Henry?' he asked as Henry wiped his eyes; and searched the dish for a dark and, he sincerely trusted, chewy morsel. The arrival and serving of the Christmas pudding brought a lull, and George was able to tell them a tale of a Christmas long ago when he had been a lad; a tale they had all heard before, Henry, Meg and Jim longed to point out, but which Bunny, Sally and Anne still found utterly enchanting.

After dinner the table was cleared for present-giving. The men got socks, handkerchiefs and slippers, the women stockings, handkerchiefs and scent. Sally and Anne received, as well as socks and handkerchiefs, exactly what they had long and loudly hoped for; in Sally's case a fat book of school stories, in Anne's a garage for her collection of Dinky cars. Then the wireless was tuned up for the King's speech, and Henry embarrassed the company by standing to attention throughout. Afterwards they yawned and made up the fire and remarked on how lazy they felt. A brisk walk was mentioned. Anne was let off because she was about to help Bunny shut up the hens, but Sally was detailed to accompany Henry, while Meg and Jim made a start on the washing-up.

Henry was not a lover of the out-of-doors. His idea of fresh air was a lowered car window. Even he, however, felt the need for movement after such an ample dinner. He resolved to get it over with as quickly as possible. 'To the road and back again! Quick, march!'

Sally broke into a half-run to keep pace with him, and became miserable with the silliness of charging down the slope, round the pond, up again, then down the gentle incline beyond the path to the cottage and on to the road gate, as if they had a train to catch. On the return march she had a brainwave. At the junction with the cottage path she stopped and knelt down. 'I'll catch you up. I've got a stone in my shoe.'

If he heard her he gave no sign. Presently, the top of his sandy-coloured head bobbed out of sight below the high point of the track.

'I am very much afraid that we cannot come to tea this afternoon,' Sally apparently told the brown, blistered, closed front door of the cottage. But her mind's eye had banished the door and replaced it with Mrs Grieve, who stood listening with grave attention. 'It is entirely my fault.

I did not ask Aunt Bunny if it would be convenient, and unfortunately she has arranged for us to string currants this afternoon and make a tart for our grandfather's tea. It is most regrettable. I am very sorry.'

So far, so good. She had conveyed that they would not come, she had taken the blame upon herself, and she had managed it without giving offence. Now perhaps, with a little skill, she could present the matter in a way that would flatter, rather than hurt her would-be hosts. 'The reason why I did not ask Aunt Bunny was that I have been so looking forward to the party that I couldn't quite come down to earth. Do you see?' She peered anxiously upwards, and was relieved to see a faint smile play upon the face of Mrs Grieve. 'Anne and I are dreadfully disappointed. We send Ruth our best wishes for a happy birthday.' At this point Ruth and Miriam peeped out from behind their mother's back. They smiled – sadly, but forgivingly. But Miriam and Ruth were not her prime concern; she craved their mother's good opinion. Mrs Grieve's dark eyes bore into her own with intelligent comprehension; slowly, with great dignity, she inclined her head in acknowledgement of a task gracefully accomplished.

It began to rain.

When her hands had rubbed clear her blurred vision, the cottage door was back in place. She went to the window of the little parlour and peered in. There had been a table in the middle of the room, spread with a birthday feast, she recalled. And against the wall there had been a lumpy sofa where she and Miriam had sat to share a book. Now the room was bare. There was nothing to suggest such things had ever been. Walking up the garden path, she pictured the parlour of the Grieves' new council house home. There would be a

Christmas tree with tinsel, and the fairy on the top would be nowhere near as pretty as Miriam or Ruth. Miriam and Ruth would scarcely remember the Robinson girls; their mother would have seen to that – for the Robinson girls had hurt them, and their mother was a woman of imagination and strength.

Chilled, in need of physical comfort, Sally trudged back to the house.

Light glowed from the scullery window. Approaching cautiously, Sally saw Aunt Bunny at the sink, and behind her, sitting on the edge of the table, her mother, talking vigorously. She crept along the yard and let herself into the house at the hall door. A faint cry of 'Snap!' came from the little-used parlour. Soundlessly, Sally turned the door handle and looked in. A fire and lamp had been lit. By the fire sat Daddy and Uncle Jim and Anne. Daddy had his eyes closed and his mouth open. Evidently he was 'out'. Uncle Jim and Anne were slapping cards on to a pouffe. 'Snap!' cried Uncle Jim fractionally before Anne. But Anne had cried louder and pounced on the pile of cards. Uncle Jim protested mildly and applied a match to his pipe. 'No, I was first,' Anne said. 'But next time I'll give you a chance.' Carefully Sally closed the door.

Grandad was in the dining-room, fast asleep in his high-backed chair. The only light came from the fire and the last of the gloomy daylight. She sat down on the hearthrug beside his shiny boots and ran her eyes along the great length of him, admiring the long, neat line of his trousers (no big stomach bulge at the top like Daddy's and Uncle Jim's), and the elegance of the fob chain across the waistcoat and the corner of dark red silk protruding from the jacket's breast pocket. The romance of the high Edwardian shirt collar and narrow tie struck her next. And then she studied his face, so bony and fine — the hooded eyelids, the wispy curls above his ears, the faint red tracery on his cheeks, the blue shadow on his chin. Finally, the hands. These hung over the armrests, large, well-used and wrinkled, the nails showing half-moons and scrupulously clean — dear, lovely hands. There was no-one on earth to touch Grandad, he was the loveliest, kindest . . . But here a denial stole into her mind. She steeled herself to face it. He was not always kind — she had seen with her own eyes that he could treat his men curtly, sneeringly. And she knew in her heart that her sister had reported the truth: he had indeed had a hand in the shabby treatment of the cottage children. Yet she had never known a warmth to match Grandad's. As she struggled with the conundrum, pain swelled the glands of her neck so that sadness seemed about to choke her. She clutched her throat and gasped.

His eyes opened suddenly and looked down directly into hers. He thought for a moment or two, then said: 'Sal.'

'Hello, Grandad.'

'I've been asleep.'

'I know.'

'You've been sitting there watching me?'

'Yes.'

'Well, well. I don't know. You're a rum 'un.'

'I love you, Grandad.'

'And I love you, my little dear.'

The door opened. 'Good gracious me! Whatever are you two doing in the dark? The lamp not lit, the curtains not drawn. And look how low you've let the fire get! Really, Daddy . . .' Aunt Bunny bustled and soon had them blinking with the brightness.

Henry came hurrying. 'Did someone call tea?'

'No, but . . .'

'Then I beg your pardon!'

'We're just going to lay the table. Come on Sally, you can put out the crackers.'

Henry rushed back to the parlour, crying, 'Yes, it's tea time. Hurry and finish the game.'

Crackers! thought Sally, and suddenly Christmas Day was magical again.

The novelties in the crackers confirmed the worst fears of Meg and Bunny. 'Rubbish,' they agreed. 'Terrible waste of money.'

But the girls were delighted. The high spot for Sally came when she pulled a cracker with George and the motto said: 'You are my lucky star.' She read this out doubtfully, unsure as to who was whose lucky star, and whether the sentiment would be considered trashy.

George endorsed it with pleasure. 'It's a true saying,' he cried. 'For that's what you are, Sal – my lucky star.'

Sally put the precious motto under her handkerchief in her pocket.

In winter, beds were found by candlelight at Willow Dasset. When bedtime came on Christmas night, the girls assembled with their aunt in the scullery. Candles were lit and the procession – through the kitchen, up the back stairs, along the passage to bathroom and bedroom – began. But tonight Sally felt reckless. As Bunny raised the latch to the staircase door, she scampered away, calling that she would go through the front of the house, alone.

'You'll be scared,' warned Anne.

'Mind you don't spill any grease,' Bunny called.

Low voices murmured in the dining-room, conjuring lamplight and firelight so that the closed door seemed to give out heat. The hallway grew cold as the reflection of the candle flame in a glass pane of the garden door jigged closer. A pale, indeterminate moon floated behind the flame; it loomed nearer and became her face. For a moment she confronted her suspended image, and the twin candle flames leant away from one another as chill air shimmered from the glass. On the stairs her monster shadow hung menacingly. The moving candle made it dart and swoop. Terror took hold of her, but she controlled it and walked with measured tread over the rugs and polished boards of the landing.

Anne and Aunt Bunny were in the bathroom. Sally took the motto from her pocket and smoothed it between pages of her prayer book. Later, lying in the dark, wishing to bring back the moment, she whispered the motto aloud.

'What?' Anne hissed.

Sally was silent. Her sister had been too engrossed in her own cracker-pulling to notice that Sally had been specially favoured. Luckily, before she could summon the strength to insist upon an answer, Anne had fallen asleep.

Although unmarked by grief, a small change in George was discernible, most evident in the subtle adjustment of the relationship between himself and Bunny. Sally had spotted it at once, a new tone in Aunt Bunny's voice, a silent acquiescence about her grandfather. 'Where are you going, Daddy?' (This, as George prepared to go outside.) 'No you are *not*. The vet will be here directly and if I have to traipse all over the farm looking for you, I shall be vexed.' Then, when George was smitten by a coughing fit at the dinner table: 'Who went out without a scarf?' And, turning to include the others: 'I shouted after him, but he wouldn't hear. He's such an obstinate man!' Of course, her mother had been too busy thinking of other things, and her father too intent upon his dinner, to notice the liberty, but Sally had been shocked, had turned pained eyes to her grandfather and observed his expression of bleak displeasure.

At breakfast on Boxing Day, Aunt Bunny's new presumption was plain for all to see. From George's bitter observations – that the day being cold and fine it was perfect hunting weather, that his horse, eating his head off in the stable, required exercise, and although young Nick Brownlow would ride him, he doubted whether the lad ever gave the horse his head, that it was a poor do when a fellow who had worked hard all his life was denied a bit of innocent sport – it emerged that Bunny had put a veto on hunting until a decent interval had elapsed, for Daddy had not yet been widowed two months and people might talk. Meg, who had never heard such tommyrot in all her life, took her father's part. It wasn't going to do poor Mama much good was it, if Daddy didn't go hunting?

The mistress of Willow Dasset grew cross. Her neck sprouted red pimples, her eyes blazed. 'I'm sorry, but I won't have it. There'll be a picture in the paper – there's always a photo of the Boxing Day meet. Daddy might be in it – as he was the year before last. Whatever would people think?'

The headmistress of Corporation Street Elementary became equally roused. 'I've no patience with what silly people think. If I know a thing's right, I just get on and do it.'

George, however, cared deeply for what people think. ('People' conjured the chaps he met every week in the cattle market, stout fellows all, and keen upholders of decent appearances.) Reluctantly, he conceded that his younger daughter was right. 'I shan't do it. Not for a while yet. Young Nick'll have to do his best for poor ol'

Red. Tell you what, though,' he cried, his face brightening, 'I might go after 'em in the motor. No harm in that, I take it?'

Bunny was sweetness in victory. 'Of course not, Daddy. I'll make you some Camp coffee in a Thermos.'

'I shouldn't bother,' George said, winking at his grand-daughters, thinking of other liquids, other flasks. 'You two rascals like to come too? How about it – spot of hunting with your old grandad?'

'Oh, *yes*,' they cried.

But Henry saw a difficulty. His father-in-law was the most terrifying driver it had ever been his misfortune to come across. He turned persuasively to his daughters. 'You know you don't like being cooped up in a car. Wouldn't you rather run about on the farm?'

'But we're going *hunting* . . .'

'With *Grandad*.'

Meg thrust out a long leg and kicked her husband's calf. 'Why not let Henry drive you, Daddy? Then you could concentrate on looking for the hunt.'

'No, no.' George had had enough of people attempting to take the reins – and now, it appeared, the steering wheel – out of his hands. 'I shall find 'em all right. No danger. And I'll drive m'self. You have to be quick off the mark once you spot 'em.'

Husband and wife exchanged meaningful looks across the breakfast table. 'You'd better go too,' Meg told Henry. 'The girls can sit in the back. You sit in the front, in case . . .'

Henry swallowed. 'That all right with you, Father? Room for one more?'

George sneered. 'If y'think y'll be interested.'

'Rather! Jolly good. Right-oh.'

Later, driving to the hunt's terrain, it occurred to Henry

that many years ago, in the course of giving George a few tips on how to handle a motor car, some bright spark had recommended braking before a bend and accelerating out of one, for George applied this procedure with inflexible dedication, jumping on the brake pedal whenever a bend loomed ahead and then accelerating so violently that it seemed the car would turn over. As for The Rules Of The Road, Henry, an innocent party to their flagrant dishonouring, felt heartbroken. He sat with an arm along the back of his seat, endeavouring to keep an eye on the situation in front and behind, mortified by the hooting and screeching tyres of other vehicles.

At last they turned on to a quiet lane, and after a few miles George pulled up. He opened the sun-roof, stood up on his seat and surveyed the country with a pair of field glasses. This scrutiny went on for some time, and it became bitterly cold in the Morris. Henry glanced at his watch. Back at Willow Dasset there would be sustaining cups of coffee with wrinkled skins on their surfaces, and rich tea biscuits in the saucers. Sally and Anne began to fidget and wondered whether they might get out for a while. Henry thought they had better all stay put. This was just as well, for the next moment George was scrambling into a sitting position and fumbling with the ignition switch. The car finally got the point of his frantic footwork and shot forward. 'Tally-ho!' cried George.

'Perhaps a change of gear,' Henry murmured, pained by the roaring of the engine, then winced as his advice was taken.

'Do you see them?' George yelled.

'Where?' The girls craned their necks to look, as their grandfather was looking, to the right.

'Over yonder. Coming down the slope from the copse.'

A stream of dogs, and horses with riders upholstered in

red or black, flowed towards the meadow by the side of the road. For some moments, hunt and car ran together, separated by a low hedge. Suddenly, at a point where the horses were obliged to leap a hedge into the next field, the lane veered to the left, but George was at one with the chase and kept the nose of the Morris pointing straight ahead. Spurred on by a cry of 'Hup!', the front wheels cleared the ditch and broke through the hedge but the car's hind quarters were sluggish and hit the bank on the far side. After a breathless, quivering moment, the car rolled back.

There was silence for a time. At some point, it was not clear when, the engine had died.

'Out! Quickly!' Henry cried, fearing an explosion. He and the girls made haste to jump from the car. George followed their example at a leisurely pace, looking dazed. 'You . . . fool!' Henry shouted. 'You should be banned. I shall make it my business to report you.' Then, seeing that the car was unlikely to explode, he gave it a prod and a shove. 'Not a hope. It'll take a lorry with lifting gear to shift this. Any idea where we are, for Pete's sake?'

Still in a daze, George offered the proximity of Fawley Wood and the back end of Bestwick Farm.

'The nearest garage – that's what I'm after. I'd better walk back to that crossroads we shot over just now; see where the nearest village is.' But then came the sound of an approaching car and Henry dashed into the road, ready to throw himself beneath its wheels rather than expose himself to a long and possibly fruitless walk. The car slowed and stopped.

''Fraid the silly old fool lost control,' they heard Henry tell the driver, who looked at the beached Morris, shook his head and advised Henry to hop in.

'Stay with Grandad,' Henry bellowed, winding down

134

the window as the car moved off. 'Keep right away from the car. Shan't be long . . .'

The world seemed empty when the car had gone. They were a sorry little group, Sally felt, Grandad at a loss, staring along the empty road, Anne snivelling, and she herself too embarrassed to move an inch from where her feet had taken root. For it had been a terrible thing, that rounding on Grandad, and by her father, of all people, whose oily deference hitherto had taught them that he was but a pygmy in their grandfather's presence.

George collected himself, recalled that he was a strong, well-built fellow. 'Let's see if I can't shift her.' He climbed down into the ditch, but his sudden vision of presenting Henry with a swiftly disappearing view of the car rear soon dissipated in the pain of useless exertion. 'It's no good. Blighter's stuck fast.' He took a silver flask from his pocket, unscrewed the cap and tipped the flask against his lips. The shivering children watched him in silence. 'Like to take a drop?' he asked them awkwardly. But they shook their heads. 'Run about a bit, then. Go on, let's see how fast you can go.'

They looked at one another. 'Race you to that gate and back?' Anne suggested.

'All right.'

They began half-heartedly, but soon, encouraged by grandfatherly cheers, they were bursting to show how fleet of foot they could be, how high, how far they could leap, how they could turn cartwheels, and run wheelbarrow fashion. When they were hot and puffed, George pulled a rug from the car.

'You see what it is with cars,' he invited, lowering himself on to the rug and patting the space on either side of him, 'when it comes to the crunch they ain't up to horses. Cars must have it all laid out for 'em – nice, smooth roads, nothing in the way. Come across a fallen tree, or a bit of a flood, and where are you? Stuck in the confounded car, that's where. A car ain't going to hop across tree trunks or wade through water. Now, you get yourself a good, strong horse and nothing's going to stop you. I'll tell you a tale, shall I – a true'un.' He slipped an arm around each granddaughter and pulled them close.

'Once I had a horse called Samson; a great black giant of a stallion; the truest horse I ever had. We'd come through a fair bit of trouble together, Samson and me. I'd rescued him from a foul-tempered fool who was too scared of him to do him justice, and I'd nursed him over a nasty injury. Well, one afternoon – 'bout November time – Samson and me were going back home after visiting a farm some twelve miles away where I'd been to look at some beef-cattle. A terrible thick fog came down – mist patches at first – but soon a fog so dense you could hardly breathe through it, never mind see. Well, I thought we were doin' all right, taking it nice and slow – I had a picture in m' mind of where we were. But suddenly Samson came to a dead halt; wouldn't budge another inch. Maybe you know something I don't, old fellow, I thought, and I slipped off his back and groped for a stone. I chucked the stone forward and heard it drop. Then it dropped again; down, down, down; until the sound was muffled by the fog. You know where we were? Right on the edge of a quarry. Another couple of steps and we'd've been over it, hurtling to the bottom like the stone. 'Course, then I knew where we were – miles out of our way at Snareshill Quarry. Right, old fellow, I said, turning him round. You seem to know what you're about, which is a darn sight more than your master does. And I got back on him and let the reins go loose. It took us a couple of hours or more, but that horse found his way back to his stable without any help from me. Ay – that was Samson. Best horse a man ever had. Now what car'll do that for yer, eh? You tell me that.'

They stared up at him, at the tears standing in his eyes, struck by this glimpse of another time, and by the notion that what is now, is not, in every instance, progress.

When a breakdown lorry arrived and the Morris was restored to the road, George did not demur when Henry announced his intention to drive. He climbed with resignation into the passenger seat.

Henry, trusting that his elaborate courtesy to other drivers, his frequent recourse to the rear view mirror, his smooth way with gear stick and brake pedal, were providing his father-in-law with overdue instruction, drove like an angel. He did not curse other drivers or burn to overtake.

'Another month should do it,' George said.

'What's that, Father?' Henry asked, obeying a Give Way sign with ostentatious scrutiny of the T-junction.

'That'd make three months in all. Ought to satisfy 'em, I reckon.'

'Three months?'

'That's right. She died on November the twenty-fifth. Come February I shall tell Bunny: it doesn't do to overdo things – could look morbid, goin' on and on with it. Moderation in all things – that's what I always say. Ay, first meeting after the twenty-fifth of February, Red and me'll be there. After all, a man's got to consider his horse.'

A wild, grey day: wind, rain, sleet. By three o'clock, Bunny had lit the lamp in the dining-room, and those unwise enough to leave the fireside to slope about the house did so in the gloom of a premature close of day.

Sally was creeping down the attic stairs, away from the apple smell and the tense hush of small creatures waiting for danger to pass, on her way to the bathroom. The screen around the lavatory was one of her favourite things. It was covered in richly coloured pictures and small Victorian scraps, and lacquered over to a glossy shine. She peered at and fingered familiar images, the boy lying on his stomach to drink from a stream, the girl dangling a cherry above an infant's mouth, the farmyard animals, the posies, the pigeon-breasted ladies with bustled behinds, the moustached military men, the fat cherubs. Somewhere she would discover, as she always did, some gem that had previously escaped her notice.

After a time she went through the bedroom she shared with Anne to the landing. Here she used a rug to scoot over the polished boards. A collision with the tallboy gave her pause, but no-one came or called. Then, observing the door to Aunt Bunny's small room, it occurred to her that its interior had not been viewed for some time. Anne was often in the room, chatting while Aunt Bunny exchanged her work-a-day blouse, skirt and cardigan for the blouse, skirt and cardigan of the more dainty afternoons. But Sally always hovered in the doorway, unable to participate in their intimacy. Now was her chance to take a proper look.

The room, she discovered, smelled of Aunt Bunny. It did not smell of rose or lavender water or essence of Devonshire violets, as one might have supposed, bearing in mind certain Christmas presents. And there was no sign of these or any other gifts in the strictly utilitarian display upon the dressing table; the hinged looking glass presided over no articles of feminine mystery; all was mundane and predictable. There were hairnets – a thick one for night-time, a fine one for the days following a hair-do when it was prudent to make it last. In a china tray there were hair-curlers and pins. And – yes – if one raised the lid of the painted wooden bowl, there, indeed, were twists of dead hair – several days' worth of combings from the hairbrush. The brush – a Mason & Pearson, its hard, black bristles embedded in a nasty pink, spongy cushion – lay quietly beside a tortoiseshell comb. Nothing else. The rest was naked wood. There was no clue here to the essence of Aunt Bunny, no hint to explain the dislike in her eyes when she viewed her elder niece.

The top drawer opened grudgingly. In a corner was a carton of yellow-pink face powder and a dingy puff. Beside it were handkerchiefs, brown lisle stockings and pink suspender buttons. There were layers of underwear in tea-rose interlock, cream flannel nightdresses and crêpe silk petticoats. In the middle drawer were piles of blouses and cardigans, all in blue-green, green-blue, or green-green.

It was not easy to pull open the bottom drawer. It got stuck on the right side, then on the left side, and required much dexterous encouragement to reveal its contents. But these, when examined, were astounding. Still in their half-open wrappings, years and years of Christmas presents lay jumbled on top of one another. Many bore labels: To Bunny from Mama; To Bunny from Jim; Happy Christmas to Aunt Bunny from Sally and Anne. Boxes of handkerchiefs, packets of stockings, bottles of scent and bath crystals, a pair of gloves, a pair of slippers, a sponge bag, a cardigan (in neither blue-green nor green-blue, but shell pink), a hot water bottle cover, a leather purse; all unused, all discarded.

Sally sat back on her heels and breathed hard. Here, she soon concluded, was nothing so simple as a drawerful of unacceptable presents, here was the clue to that look in

139

Aunt Bunny's eyes. She imagined the presents thrown into the drawer, the drawer closed with a violent shove; long, thin arms hanging loose, at a loss . . . Her imagination roamed, but she could not fathom a meaning.

'Can we come again at Easter?' Anne asked as they drove away from Willow Dasset.

'I shouldn't think so. We'll come back in the summer.'

'Personally, I find two helpings a year of your inestimable relatives a more than generous sufficiency,' Henry said cleverly, pleased to be hitting the road.

'And I dare say they've had quite enough of you to be going on with.'

'But, Mummy, Daddy,' protested Anne. 'Remember what you said about cheering Grandad up.'

'Yes, 'cos of Grandma,' Sally recalled.

And then they fell silent, as each became struck by the thought that there had been no sense of someone missing at Willow Dasset this Christmas.

10

Perfect summer.

Ever after, Perfect Summer was the name she gave to those weeks of constantly fine weather following her twelfth birthday. It was a milestone in her memory. It was the climax of all that had gone before, for this time nothing was able to mar the perfection of being at Willow Dasset; and it was the end of an era, for never again would she remain unconcerned for the consequences of the past, or the requirements of the future; never again would she be totally content with *now*.

So much richness. Harvesting from dawn till dusk, and anyone, everyone, welcome to lend a hand. The sailing, reaping progress through the corn, the flying dust, the racket in the rickyard as a belt conveyed life from tractor to binder. The lazy tea times under a shady tree, the teasing laughter, the tall stories, the sun-induced silences. The evening procession home with full wagons, the soft close-of-day singing, the sound of departing workers calling to one another through the fragrant, dewy gloom.

Endless, unblemished, summer.

The harvest made everyone shine. Arthur, dark and glistening, was more handsome than ever in his sun-kissed state; and Joyce, the landgirl, gorgeous in jodhpurs and straining shirt, with her straw-coloured hair and red, red lips, was as luscious as any film star. Arthur and

Joyce were the harvest's king and queen. Their romance heightened the atmosphere, provoked wittier repartee and saucier leg-pulling, inspired foolish grins and tactful turnings away. Their romance crowned every day and made wistful every dusk; it was felt that, because of it, this was a precious time.

Even dour Benjamin was seen to smile and to encourage the baiting of Barry, his thirteen-year-old son. And Barry, although generally detested, had his uses. His trying, guttersnipe cheek rendered him a legitimate target for trickery, and those who discomfited him were rewarded with mirth and congratulation. Benjamin's elder two sons swelled the work-force in the evenings and all day on Sundays. John came to the harvest field whenever the requirements of his bovine charges would allow, and after tea he was sometimes prevailed upon to sing 'I'll take you home again, Kathleen' in its entirety, and to follow up with 'I'll walk beside you' and 'The Londonderry air'. Mad old Lou (Loopy Lou, the girls unkindly called him), an itinerant hedger and ditcher by profession, lent charm to the scene with his grimy face, his toothless grin and his stories told in a dialect so rich that, though their subject matter remained obscure, their telling was a growling, chortling music, a rumbling from long ago. A tall, thin, wild-eyed fellow with a battered straw hat was an occasional toiler in the field. This was Martin, a feckless, wandering, posh-voiced toff (disowned by his family, it was rumoured), who exchanged his labour for the privilege of shooting the rabbits that scuttled from a shrinking rectangle of unharvested corn.

'Ever seen one of these?' enquired Barry, who, having come across the girls on the track between an exuberant summer hedgerow and a steep grassy bank, had thrown himself to the ground and now lay motionless on his back, squinting up at them.

'One of what?' Sally required to know.

'One of *these*.'

But she could see only Barry on the track amid tufts of plantain and pineapple weed. She stepped nearer.

Behind her, Anne gasped. 'Come back! He's being rude!'

Sally's eyes travelled to that portion of Barry where rudeness might occur. Sure enough, there was a thin, pink, pencil-like protrusion – a sickening naked thing. 'Urgh!' she said in disgust.

'Come *on*.' Anne seized her sister's hand.

Red-faced, long legs pounding, they raced away. When the privacy of their den in the Dutch barn was achieved, they flung themselves down and groaned. It was altogether horrible – the way he had tricked them into viewing his part, but so very like him, for he was a nasty little tyke.

'I bet we could get him banned.'

'From Willow Dasset?'

'Yes. 'Cos Grandad wouldn't like it at all.'

Their eyes brightened at the prospect. Barry's proprietorial swagger about the sacred grounds had often grieved them. An encounter at dusk one early Easter had been particularly galling. Their father had been despatched to summon them in to bed, and as they accompanied him homeward along the track, Benjamin and Barry came towards them.

'I see you're all set to make a night of it, Benjamin,' Henry said, nodding at their luggage – shotgun, waterproofs, blankets, and a linen-covered basket.

'I shall 'ave that vixen t'night. 'Er shan't take another lamb.'

While Henry enquired politely about the fox menace, Barry took in the girls' envious faces. 'Arff to yer beds, are yer?' he sneered. 'I'm up all noight. Know what's in 'ere?' He indicated the covered basket. 'Plum duff 'n custard – all *roight*!'

'Plum duff 'n custard – all *roight*!' became a catchphrase between the girls, a private vehicle for a snigger. But they were consumed by jealousy of Barry's privilege to be abroad while they were confined to bed. Now, they considered whether he had handed them the means of securing his own downfall. But after a time they sighed and shook their heads. It was unthinkable that such a subject should be broached – they had both independently concluded – by Grandad's nice little girls.

'I'm going to give you something, Arthur,' Sally cried above the tractor's roar. She was obliged to say something, love was bursting out of her. Passion for Arthur had become an uncontainable force this summer. 'I think I'll marry Arthur,' she had said thoughtfully, a day or so after their arrival at the farm.

Hearing her, Henry had put on his clever look. 'I think you'll discover that Arthur – and a certain young woman of undeniable charm - may be somewhat opposed to that idea.'

He meant Joyce, Sally had understood at once. Thereafter she had paid particular attention to the courtship in the harvest field, and discovered, rather to her surprise, that she was not in the least bit jealous. Joyce *deserved* Arthur, she truly did. Joyce was magnificent, whereas she herself, at twelve years old, was straight as a stick and plain of well-scrubbed face. It was beyond her to do Arthur justice.

Bouncing about on the tractor, the sun beating, the

engine throbbing, it suddenly became urgent that she find another means of expressing her emotion, given that living happily ever after with Arthur was inappropriate. She found herself in some difficulty – attempting to set foot in a territory unexplored by storybooks. And so – rather feebly – came that blurted promise to give him something.

'What?' sneered Barry, who was standing on the tractor step below her.

'Something,' she said vaguely.

'Yuh! 'Er doesn't know, does 'er, Arthur?'

'Yes I do. It's going to be something . . . marvellous.'

'Bet it ain't. When yer goin' t'give it 'im, anyway?'

'This afternoon.'

'Bet yer don't.'

While Barry cast doubt, and Anne worried that her elder sister was about to make them look foolish, Arthur smiled. It was an understanding smile, directed briefly at Sally and then through the shimmering exhaust fumes at the way ahead.

When the tractor arrived in its shed, Sally leapt to the ground and ran swiftly to the house. In her room she ransacked the chest of drawers and the shallow drawer of the dressing table. Then she searched them again, more slowly, more thoroughly. Obstinately, Arthur's present refused to be made manifest.

Henry bustled in. 'What are you doing? Didn't you hear? Grandad's waiting to carve.'

During dinner, her confidence waned alarmingly. Anne's stern gaze promised eternal enmity if she failed to produce some face-saving offering. Anxiety drove her into a trance. If only she could travel further into the hollow at the back of her mind she would light on the object she sought. Then, stealthily, it appeared, came floating towards her through space; a thing of exquisite delicacy and charm. She studied it closely.

'Are you all right, Sally?' asked Bunny, noticing that the child had closed her eyes and had gone remarkably pale.

All eyes were upon her, she found, returning to every day consciousness.

'Are you all right?'

'Yes. Well . . . As a matter of fact, I'd like to be excused. Please may I leave the table?'

'I suppose she may, mayn't she?' Meg said to Bunny, eager to resume their discussion about the garden.

Bunny agreed, and Sally fled; out of the house, across the yard and along the track past the paddock. Approaching the stubble and stooks and ever-reducing patch of standing wheat in Bailey's Field, she slowed to a walk. All was peaceful; birdsong the only sound, a bee the only toiler. She began to pull from the hedgerow long, trailing stems of convulvulus. When she had gathered an armful, she crouched in a shady spot beneath a beech tree and set to work, weaving the long stems into a circlet until she had a wreath of soft green arrow heads and sweet-pink trumpets. So wrapped up was she in admiration of her masterpiece, that she failed to hear the noise of the tractor. Looking up, shading her eyes, she was startled by its arrival through the open gateway. Arthur, Barry and Anne turned their heads to look across at her. She rose, and with an exhilaration of delight, ran towards them, brandishing the ringlet high above her head. 'Arthur, Arthur . . .'

He brought the tractor to a halt.

'Look, look what I've made for you.'

'Is thart it?' cried Barry in disbelief.

Anne stuffed a fist into her mouth.

'It's for you, Arthur.'

146

Arthur leant down and received his crown.

'It's weeds. It ain't nothin' but weeds. What a present, oh moi! Bet you'm roight pleased with thart, Arthur.'

'It's beautaful,' Arthur declared. 'And I know just where t'put it.' He stood and reached forward and slipped the flowery ring over the tractor's chimney. It slid down and came to rest on the tractor's nose, accomplishing a neat coronation.

During this perfect summer, Henry sometimes ventured into the harvest field. It was Joyce who lured him there and exposed him to the danger of having a pitchfork thrust into his hand. His admiration for her was strong, so strong that he was unable to resist mentioning it at the tea table. But this he did with tasteful restraint. 'What a charming young woman that landgirl is – Joyce, I believe? Quite so. I was lending a hand in the harvest field this afternoon, and, I must say, I found her engaging manner most refreshing. Arthur is a fortunate young man.'

Harry, who had called in after work to eat his tea and to labour for an hour or two at the goddess's side before returning home to his wife, leered knowingly at Henry and winked. Even George, who always inspected his work force from the saddle, was moved to reminisce approvingly. 'Splendid young filly, no doubt about it. Speaks up when she's spoke to. Looks up at you straight in the eye. And she's not afraid of the horse getting near her, like some of these silly young women.'

Evidently, Henry had hit upon common ground. 'Exactly my experience,' he enthused. 'Guileless, fearless and unspoilt. A perfect example of healthy, outdoor beauty.'

A less than perfect example of indoor beauty, who, in spite of an impatience with personal vanity, nevertheless considered herself the owner of certain physical charms,

147

narrowed her eyes and addressed her husband with some scorn. 'It's news to me you're so keen on farming. I was under the impression you'd run a mile from a bit of sweaty work. Still, one lives and learns, I suppose. Maybe I'll stroll up to the field later on, and take a look. Watch you hard at it – that'll be something to see!'

Meanwhile, the labourers – and they included Anne and Sally – were taking their ease beneath the beech tree. Lou had concluded a rambling tale that had lulled them into a doze. Joyce arched her back over a bale of straw, stretched her arms over her head and yawned. Eyes slid towards her, to the damp stains under her sleeves and the mounds of her breasts and the way her shirt had pulled from the top of her trousers to reveal a glimpse of navel. Arthur stirred and shifted himself, remarking: 'Thart were some tea, thart were.' They chorused their agreement and watched him settle so that his knee came to rest against her thigh.

'Don't say the tea's all garn,' complained Barry, examining every billy-can. 'I 'opes us is gettin' some coider t'night.'

'Us is, you en't,' quipped Benjamin, quick as a flash. And while Barry whined, the others chortled.

'Arthur, are we gathering sheaves tonight?' Sally asked.

'I dare say. When us 'as cut the larst of the corn.'

Hearing this, Martin, who had been cleaning his gun, stood up.

'Ay. 'Tis time t'make a move,' Arthur confirmed.

''Cos, if we do, can I drive the tractor between the stooks?'

'I don't see why nart.'

And so it turned out. Sally, under the envious eyes of Barry and Anne, drove sedately from stook to stook, anticipating every Whoa! and Move arn!, even turning unaided at the bottom of the field to bring the hitched wagon cleanly round into the next row. They worked late that evening, determined to clear Bailey's Field.

'Like t'ride up alarft?' Arthur asked Sally, as the homeward procession assembled.

'You mean up there?' she asked, looking up at a laden wagon – an old hay cart, brought out of retirement for this exceptional harvest, its horse-shaped shafts adapted to a tractor's requirements.

'I loved it when I was a lad. Flat arn me back, gazin' up at the stars.'

'Oh, yes,' she breathed.

He climbed on to the wing above the wagon wheel and hauled her up. Then he pushed and she scrambled. 'Lie still, mind,' he instructed, before leaping to the ground and getting on to the tractor.

If a sprig of time could be relived, she would ride again on that deep high mattress, going with the lurch and sway, hearing only the faintest, intermittent murmur of a far-away engine and the groan of an old cart's joints as it moves over a rutted track. Above her, the endless, starry canopy of sky. By her side, a passing tree-top, black and thickly drooping. On and on she would journey, adrift, undulating, wrapped in the damp, scented hush of Willow Dasset at night . . .

Part Two

DISINTEGRATION

1

Something was wrong. She knew it the moment they turned in at the gate. It was hard to be precise, but Willow Dasset had shrunk, become dull-looking, almost mean. Having applied these words to the scene, she at once withdrew them. Shrunk, dull, mean, overstated the case. The change in Willow Dasset was diffuse. But it was there, and it was alarming.

A year had passed since the Robinsons were last at Willow Dasset. There was a reason for this. It had come to Henry's notice – due to Meg's carelessness – that his wife had deceived him. She had participated in a financial arrangement with her father, and she had kept this fact from Henry. Gratifying though it was to learn that hand-outs no longer depended upon application in person, Henry was shaken. She had offended against one of his most cherished principles – that there should be total honesty between husband and wife. Nothing, it appeared for several succeeding weeks, could assuage his indignation or restore his marital confidence.

It occurred to Meg that she could not have been more thoroughly denounced if she had taken a lover; but she kept this thought to herself. Her one aim was to pacify Henry as rapidly as possible. (Peace, and the smooth running with the minimum attention of the Robinson household, were high on her list of priorities. Any domestic disruption – illness, accidents, rows – came as a threat to her professional life. Her way with the sick was more effective than medicine; she would stand at the foot of a sick-bed and declare that she had no patience with the malingerer, who was succumbing to weakness, or possibly shamming, and should, in any case, pull herself together, get up and go to school.) When hints were dropped that a new car might win the peace, she conceded at once. Anything – a Rolls Royce, even – if Henry would only shut up.

In the event, Henry acquired a second-hand Rover. Christmas had gone by; Easter was approaching. Meg felt she was not quite ready to turn up at Willow Dasset in the Rover. Perhaps, as she and Henry were both so busy, they would wait until the summer. The postponement had suited Henry very well.

When the car drew up, Sally was not astounded by the fresh beauty of the house and farm buildings as she had been on every previous arrival. This time, she detected an air of weary predictability. And Grandad Ludbury seemed distracted, his mind elsewhere, as he received their kisses, patted their heads, and gazed out across the yard to where their parents were pulling belongings from the Rover's boot. Rather crestfallen, the girls wandered into the house.

Aunt Bunny's welcome was the same as ever, Sally decided, evaluating it closely – kindly towards herself, for she had only just arrived and had had no chance to annoy – affectionately conspiratorial towards Anne. But the house? She ran through it, looked into every room, peered through the glass in the garden door, raced up the front staircase to survey the landing, then went slowly into her bedroom. Anne and Aunt Bunny were already there, having sensibly taken the direct route up the back stairs, and were engaged in an animated conversation.

154

'Do you think everywhere's gone a bit dull?' she interrupted them, compelled to voice her misgivings.

Bunny looked at her, and felt the stirring of a familiar irritation. 'It's a dull day,' she confirmed.

'Oh, you mean the weather.' Sally rushed to the window. 'Yes, I see what you mean. It's very overcast. Perhaps that's what it is.'

Bunny sighed and turned away. 'Oh, Annie! Look at your knee! However did you get that enormous scab?' she cried, admiringly.

Anne embarked upon an account of how, flying downhill on her bicycle, she had been let down by the brakes.

Sally went into the bathroom to see whether the screen around the lavatory still had power to charm.

At the dinner table, the feeling that things were out of joint persisted. Grandad, for instance, did not engage in the special jocularity that usually characterized their first meal. He was strangely silent. If he attended to their father's enthusiasm for the smoothness of the Rover's gears, its formidable acceleration, its astounding economy (this last, somewhat unexpected, feature was due, of course, to Henry's cunning carmanship), he gave no sign.

Unexpectedly, and rather off the point, their mother put in a word about the car. 'It's not a new one, you know. It's four years old.'

Towards the end of the meal, a tractor engine was heard.

'Arthur!' cried Anne, stuffing blancmange into her mouth.

'Not Arthur,' said George. 'Mick.'

There was an uncomprehending silence.

Bunny provided enlightenment. 'Arthur has left us. He

works for Moxons, the grain merchants in town. His bride thought Daddy didn't pay him enough.'

'Would that be the charming Joyce?' Henry asked carefully.

'The landgirl,' George confirmed. 'Spent all last summer making up to him, then, as soon as she caught him, began to rearrange his life. Poor blighter! I was shocked to see him when I called at Moxons the other day. Gone to seed. Fat as a porker.'

'Sign of a happy man, perhaps,' Henry suggested.

'He's as unhappy a fellow as I ever saw. "This work's too soft for you, Arthur. It don't suit you," I told him. "I dare say, Guv'nor, but the missus likes the size of me pay packet." Money, money, money. That's all they think of, nowadays.'

'But you found a satisfactory replacement?'

'Mick. Polish or somesuch. The "displaced persons" people asked me to take him on. We've quite a few of 'em working on the farms around here. He'll do, I suppose, I can't fault him; but the man's got a look in his eyes that I don't much care for.'

'Indeed?'

'Shouldn't wonder if the fellow weren't a bit bolshie. Something about him . . .'

'It's because he's a *foreigner*, Daddy,' Bunny said loudly, as if her father's hearing, or understanding, might not be capable of coping with the information. 'I've told you before. Foreigners have funny ways. It doesn't *mean* anything.'

'Mick doesn't sound particularly Polish,' Henry mused.

'Oh, it's not. His real name's *frightful* – quite impossible. Daddy said he'd better be called Mick because his name begins with M.'

'One thing I'll say for the fellow: he's certainly got a

way with machinery. I don't know how we'd manage the combine without him. Jim can't seem to get the hang of it.'

'Now be *fair*, Daddy. Poor Jim didn't get a chance.' Bunny turned to her sister. 'He sliced off the end of his thumb. You should have seen the blood! We had to drive him to hospital.'

'Whatever happened?'

'He was trying to tighten a bolt on the front of the combine. It's a lethal thing. You girls, by the way, had better keep right away from it.'

'What is it?' Anne asked fearfully.

'An enormous harvesting machine that does everything in one go – cuts the corn, thrashes it, even puts the grain into sacks and shoots them on to the ground.'

'Saves time. Saves money. Harry put me on to it. He's got me thinking about a milking machine, too, since we've been put on the electricity.'

'The wonderful thing is, we don't have to take on all those people at harvest time.'

'That's right. No need for all those scoundrels and tramps, or flighty landgirls, or Benjamin's blessed relatives.'

Perhaps, after all, there was a small consolation. 'So Barry doesn't come here anymore, Grandad?' Sally asked.

'Oh, Barry's here often enough. But he's only a lad. And he's pleased as Punch with five bob now and then. No, I meant those factory-working sons and brothers of Benjamin's, coming round here after work to lie in the straw drinking my cider, and expecting to be paid for the privilege.'

With heavy hearts, the girls went to their room to change into farming clothes.

'Anne,' Sally began tentatively, 'do you feel everything's changed?'

'Of course I do, you lunatic. Arthur's gone, there's a horrible new man, and it sounds as if harvesting's ruined.'

'No, more than that. Underneath. Willow Dasset itself.'

'Don't be silly. Come on – might as well go and see what he's like.'

They found him ministering to a silver monster at one end of the Dutch barn. For a time they watched him in silence. He was large, larger than Arthur, with fair hair, light eyes and a red face. 'Hello,' he said presently, without looking up.

'Hello,' they replied.

'You are visiting?'

The word displeased them; it conveyed transience.

'We stay here for weeks and weeks.'

'Every year. Usually twice a year.'

He worked on in silence.

'Are you,' Sally ventured, 'Mick?'

'If you like.'

'Arthur, who used to work here, let us ride on the tractor. In fact, he allowed us to drive it sometimes, didn't he, Anne?'

'He did. He let us do lots of things. He was our friend.'

Mick raised his head for the first time, and studied them. 'And you wish that I, too, be your friend?'

'Yes, we do. Don't we, Sal?'

'We can be jolly useful. We can open gates and put the pin in the trailer. And we can drive the tractor slowly while the men do the loading.'

'You are permitted to do those things?'

'Oh, yes, we are.'

'This,' he brought his fist down with a bang on to the machine's pointed wing, 'you will not go near. It is dangerous. Understand? But at the back . . . Come!' He climbed an attached ladder at the rear of the harvester, and called to them from a platform. 'Up!'

They required no urging.

'Through these flaps will come grain. We catch it in sacks, we tie the sacks and we push them down here. You would like to slide down the chute?'

Indeed they would, they demonstrated.

'I suppose the sacks have to be put in a cart,' Sally said thoughtfully, reclimbing the ladder. 'I could drive the tractor for the loading.'

'And I bet I could help up here. I could watch out for when the sacks are full.'

'Why not?' he agreed.

Overjoyed with this fine attitude, they began to feel that there was hope for them, after all. When 'I'll take you home again, Kathleen' rang from the cowshed, they excused themselves politely, and hurried away to discuss the matter with John.

Meg was turning things over. Something would have to be said. It was a pity something had not been said sooner – at once – the moment they had bought the blessed car. She should have mentioned it on the phone, or in a letter. Damn, damn, damn! Nothing but footling, distracting trouble! Trying to avoid trouble, she had hurt Daddy. And Daddy had been so good . . .

From her vantage point at the dining-room window, she saw George come out into the yard, go to the kennel to release the dog, and turn towards the farmyard to begin his evening tour of inspection. She opened the dining-room door with the intention of setting after him. In the hall she half-saw Sally hovering by the hat stand. She hurried by.

'Mummy!'

The girl had caught her arm. 'What is it?'

'Oh . . . nothing.'

She was plagued by attempts to distract her, she thought grimly, almost running from the house for fear of meeting Henry or Bunny.

By the barn she caught up with him. 'Can I come, too, Daddy?' She slipped her arm through his on the side of him not extended by a walking stick. They walked in silence, she considering how best to broach the subject, he wondering how she would set about it. Meg had never been devious, he reflected. Strong willed, sure of herself, quick to challenge opposition, but not devious. She would be having a hard time of it, now.

'Look, Megs . . .'

'Look, Daddy . . .'

As if responding to a signal, their simultaneous appeals broke the silence with clean precision. They smiled at one another in a sheepish, Ludbury way.

Soon they found a gate to lean against.

'How long have you had it?'

'Oh . . . couple of months,' she lied.

'That all? I thought, maybe, the reason you've stayed away so long was that you and Henry had helped yourselves to a car and didn't care to face me.'

'Daddy! What a thing to say! Look, he found out about the account. We always have the dickens of a row when we go over our affairs, and I suppose I let something slip in the heat of the moment. So he went through my drawer in the bureau – I don't lock it, of course . . .'

'The scoundrel!'

160

'Oh, no. *I* was the scoundrel. You should have heard him! I told you he wouldn't like it if he ever found out.' She paused here, recalling that this was not the line she had decided to take. 'The thing is, Daddy, the car – the old one, that is – kept breaking down. It needed quite a sum of money spending on it. It made sense to spend that money on a new one, one that would last. So I gave Henry the money from the account, and month by month I've – we've – been paying it back. So, you see, it'll all come right in the end.'

George considered this. 'So long as it's there when you need it for the girls.'

'It will be – is, almost. And things are much easier now. The grammar school's free, you know.'

His face became twisted, took on a crafty appearance, as it always did when he was embarrassed or had something difficult to say. 'I had me suspicions – I can't say I didn't – when you didn't come home for Easter.'

'But I explained on the phone – I was busy. Honestly, Daddy, what with one thing and another I'm sometimes too busy to think. But I'll try not to let such a long time go by again.'

'Thing is, I miss yer, Megs. And the little girls. A couple a days'd do – you don't have to stay for ever. I just like to see yer now and then – hear how yer doin'.'

'I know. I'll remember.'

They grinned ruefully at one another, linked arms and strolled on.

Later, turning into the farmyard, they were in time to see Henry streak across the house-yard, go down the dip by the pond and disappear behind the willows. He was not quite running, but his walk was suggestive of pursuit, or fear of pursuit.

'Whatever's up with the fellow?' George wondered.

'Taking exercise,' Meg explained. 'He's had several boils on his neck – because his blood is sluggish, according to the doctor. He's supposed to take vigorous exercise. He remembers now and then, usually when he can feel another boil coming.'

'Why doesn't he do something sensible? Not much point in charging about, is there? Might as well do something useful – chop a few logs, turn some hay.'

Meg sighed. Her father had voiced her own opinion. Oh, for a surplus of energy over tasks remaining to be done! How Henry could squander himself so wastefully when there were shelves to be put up, a shed roof in need of repair, a hedge requiring regular clipping, was beyond her comprehension. He might even clean the house occasionally, instead of falling asleep over a book every evening, while his wife laboured over registers and reports as a diligent headteacher must. And she recalled another form of vigorous exercise that had once been to Henry's taste. This he had neglected of late; and Meg had been feeling, quite urgently for some time, that he ought to employ it now and then.

'The trouble is, he ain't up to you, Megs. Can't think why you married the fellow.'

She flushed violently.

'I shouldn't have said that, old girl,' he said, seeing her discomfort. They had come to a halt by the great barn. George lowered his bottom on to the ledge across the wide doorway. After a brief hesitation, she perched beside him. 'But you'll forgive your old Dad, I dare say, because we've always been able to speak our minds to one another.' He took her hand and squeezed it. When he spoke again his voice was hoarse. 'I can talk to you, Megs, without the fear of it being used against me. Bunny's forever tripping me up. Can't open me mouth these days without gettin' a tickin' off. And Jim never says a word – puffs on his pipe, picks his nose, whistles through his teeth – I never know what the fellow's thinking. Harry, of course, blows up. Least thing, and he's storming off. You and me, though, Megs, can say what we like to one another. It's a rare thing, that.'

She smiled at him vaguely, imagining his horror if she were to say how she was feeling at this moment, had been feeling ever since that thought about Henry's neglect.

A blackbird hopped near to peck amongst the cobble-weeds for a late snack. They watched it companionably, pleased to have said all that needed to be said. George felt mellow, soothed. Meg thought she and Henry might have an early night.

From the window-seat in her bedroom, Sally – arms around ankles, chin on knee – had observed her father's rapid departure from the house. She watched until he vanished behind the swaying willows. A feeling of dislocation still disturbed her. Temporarily restored by the promise of the afternoon, evening had cast an air of dejection over the place, filling her with a sad ache. No-one else appeared conscious of the calamity, but, on reflection, this did not surprise her. No-one else would pause in their busy doings or suspend their all-consuming thoughts to look about and notice. Sally was lonely in her knowledge. If she could share it, explore it, an explanation might be found. She turned towards the room. It confronted her placidly, but with a hint of hopelessness. Feeling rather desperate, she jumped down, ran from the room and down the stairs, across the kitchen and out through the open doorway.

Henry had reached the gate to the road. With a smart, military, forward-across thrust of his arm, he consulted

163

his wristwatch; his aim was to wage war on the boils in the shortest possible time, and then, with shining virtue, sink into a chair, release the top button of his trousers behind a convenient library book, and think comfortable, somnolent thoughts.

Sally reached the path that led down to the cottage gate and waited, watching the flip-flap of approaching trouser bottoms against sock-covered toes jutting from ancient sandals. As he drew level, she stepped forward. 'Daddy!'

He frowned. His unwavering stride told her that he would not stray from duty.

'I want to ask you something.' She broke into a half-run at his side. 'Daddy,' she persisted, 'do you think Willow Dasset's changed at all? Because I do. I wish you'd look around and see, because it really seems different to me. And it makes me feel sad.'

To descend the slope, Henry leaned back on his heels. Rounding the pond, he was confronted by the steepest climb of all; but he took heart, for the house was in sight. Resolute as a flagellant, and with a similar fanaticism, he thrust forward his unwilling flesh, while his eyes dwelt on the yard wall above as if it were the gate to Salvation.

'Daddy, I do wish you'd say . . .'

At the top of the house-yard steps, Henry seized a stone pillar and clung to it. 'What's . . . the matter with you?' he asked, blowing hard.

She looked at him doubtfully, at his beetroot face and bulging eyes. He did not appear ready for introspection, but in another moment a book would claim him. 'Something's happened to Willow Dasset. It's changed.'

Henry reached into his trouser pocket, drew out a handkerchief and wiped his brow. 'Phew! Nothing like a brisk walk for toning the system. No,' he said, having considered her statement, 'Willow Dasset hasn't changed. You have. You've shot up since we were last here. Grown four or five inches, I should think. Better watch out, or you'll end up a beanpole like your mother.'

Sally remained in the yard for a long time after he had gone. She sat on the wall beside a cat, idly exploring the furry hollow between the sharp cliffs of its shoulder blades, oblivious of the profound concentration her careless fingers inspired. People came and went. Her mother and grandfather, who had been sitting on the ledge across the barn doorway, came strolling across the farmyard. Her grandfather leant down to tether the sheepdog, then picked up the terrier and dropped it over a stable door for the night. 'Day-dreaming?' he called kindly to Sally, before following his daughter into the house. Then – the sound of her chatter preceding her – Anne came into the farmyard, hopping and skipping at Aunt Bunny's side. They paused to deposit the pails that had contained chicken-feed in the barn doorway, then came on slowly, Aunt Bunny holding a bowl of eggs, Anne ceaselessly chattering.

Anne ran straight into the house, but Bunny hesitated and looked across the yard. 'What are you doing?'

'Thinking.'

'Thinking never finished the job.'

'What job?'

Bunny wondered whether this was insolence. 'Aren't you coming in?'

'Soon.'

'Is anything the matter?'

'I feel sad.'

'Well!' Affronted, Bunny took herself indoors, and switched on the electric light.

Sally observed the steady gleam at the windows – lamplit evenings, candlelit bedtimes had slipped into the past. Her father's explanation, that it was she who had grown, not Willow Dasset that had shrunk, had, at first, given her hope. But now she saw that it was a desolate explanation. If growth had clouded her vision, she might never see the shining, glowing expansiveness of Willow Dasset again. Willow Dasset would join the gloomy streets, the stained pavements, the woebegone trees and endless stretch of houses that made up her northern home, in unrelieved ordinariness. There would be no escape, nothing to aspire to.

Aunt Bunny's voice sounded crossly through the open scullery window. 'Your elder daughter informs me she is sad.'

'Oh, *Sally*,' her mother's voice answered witheringly. 'That girl can be an irritating little pest.'

If she didn't pull herself together, Sally saw, she would soon bring trouble upon herself. And, really, Willow Dasset *must* be better than home. Faded or not, it was still the place where she had glimpsed perfection.

2

Meg lay in the big feather bed, awaiting Henry. An inadequate sixty-watt bulb, shaded by parchment, hung from the centre of the ceiling. It was operated by a switch at the door or by a cord over the bed. (This last feature, common to every bedroom in the house, was a facility in which Bunny took enormous pride.) The far corners of the room were dim; the door in one corner was invisible, and in the other, only reflected light in a looking glass betrayed the presence of a dressing table. Nearer at hand, a great mahogany wardrobe with a mirrored door appeared particularly massive under steady illumination, and on the other side of the bed, a marble-topped wash-stand bearing white china gleamed with a novel chill. Directly under the light, the brass bedstead bore witness to the efficacy of Brasso. Meg idly surveyed the adjusted appearance of the familiar room, then turned her mind to the more pressing matter of the pros and cons of removing, or keeping on, her nightdress.

If she had only her own inclinations to consider, she would remove it, never having been one to beat about the bush. She could also conceive of a partner who might welcome a frank approach. But not Henry. Henry liked to pretend that such an event happened without any conscious decision, and afterwards he liked to pretend that it had never happened at all. She warned herself that there must be no over-eagerness; if Henry was to be persuaded back on to the path of love she must mask her urgency, be crafty, take her time.

Henry bustled into the room, removed his dressing gown and tossed it on to a basket chair, stepped out of his slippers and climbed into bed. 'This is more like it, I must say,' he said, pulling the cord to extinguish the light. 'Beats creeping around the place with a candle.'

'Yes, doesn't it,' Meg agreed. And then, with particular pleasantness: 'I had a word with Daddy about the car, by the way. I made him see the sense of buying the Rover. You must take him for a run in it while we're here, I'm sure he'll be impressed.'

'Mmm, I will,' said Henry, who was always ready to be seduced into showing off in a car.

'I'm glad you're so pleased with it, darling.' She snuggled a little nearer.

'Went like a bird on the way down, didn't she? Of course, a powerful car like that demands more than a modicum of skill, but I don't think I flatter myself if I claim some expertise in that department.'

'Of course you don't, darling. You've always been a wonderful driver.' She slipped her hand into his.

Henry, staring into the dark, seeing himself at the wheel, with the sun-roof open and his fair hair flying, was hardly aware of his hand's capture. 'I expect you'll want to be driven here and there this holiday – to see the aunts, to Stratford for the day, or Warwick.'

'That'll be nice . . . Henry?'

'You know, I'm not sure that I haven't underestimated the miles per gallon. I forgot about the jam we were caught up in outside Leicester. That ought to be taken into account – all that stopping and starting and crawling along in bottom gear . . .'

'Henry . . . darling . . . give me a little kiss.'

For a moment Henry lay in stiff silence, his happy thoughts flown. Then he turned his neck – becoming mindful of an incipient boil – and pecked her cheek. 'There! Goodnight, dear.'

'Henry, you do love me, don't you?'

'Of course; you know I do.'

'And I love you.' She pressed closer to his side and raised her free hand to that spot behind his right ear lobe which had once rendered good results. This was an unintelligent move, for she merely succeeded in signalling her base intent. Henry pulled her hand away and returned it to her own vicinity. 'Don't start fooling about. I want to get some sleep.'

Becoming desperate, Meg flung an arm over his chest. 'Henry, I'm your wife!'

'Then kindly behave with decorum,' he retorted, attempting to remove the encumbrance.

'But I love you! You said you love me. You've become so cold lately. Why? I haven't changed. I'm still the same. Oh, Henry!' She threw herself bodily on top of him, driving him into a deep valley between mounds of feather mattress.

Fearing suffocation, Henry put up a struggle, and was at last free to leap from the bed. 'If you're going to behave like a trollop, I'm going downstairs for the night.'

'No, Henry, wait!' She knelt up in bed and groped for the cord. Finding it, she prepared to give it a mighty tug. 'Look at me!' she cried, producing light. 'Once you told me I was beautiful!' She gathered up her nightdress and pulled it over her head.

Henry, who had been standing by the bed gripping the top of his pyjama bottoms, backed away. Keeping wary eyes upon her, he felt for his dressing gown, but having found it, he hesitated to remove a hand from his pyjamas in order to put it on.

'What's the *matter*?' she demanded, scrambling towards him over the bed.

He fled to the door and stood there, hurriedly pulling on the gown.

His flight caused Meg to take stock. Slowly, she moved back across the bed, climbed down and presented herself to the long mirror on the wardrobe door. She peered closely, for she had not examined herself for a long time. She discovered no blemish, no hideous fault; the same long, lithe body confronted her, none the worse for wear. If fault there was, it lay in Henry. What had her father said earlier? Henry wasn't up to her. Well, he wasn't. Marriage to Henry was all give and no get. More fool her for putting up with it! She turned and reached over the bed ro retrieve her nightdress. Pulling it on, climbing back into bed, rearranging the bedclothes, rebellious thoughts took shape. She lay quietly, ignoring Henry's cautious return, turning her back on him as he put out the light. In the darkness she vowed to herself that she would do all sorts of things. She allowed herself full reign, in the knowledge at the back of her mind that wicked plans wither in the clear light of day.

In a single instant, Anne awoke, flung herself from the bed, seized a handful of clothing and began her first soliloquy of the day, thereby nudging her sister into a slow see-saw of consciousness in which a dream gave way to the mightier claims of arousal. Soon, Anne's footsteps sounded outside in the yard. Sally opened her eyes and watched the gleam and fade of a quavery sun against the curtains. She got out of bed and climbed on to the window-seat. Sunlight, however uncertain, improved

170

matters, but Willow Dasset still disdained to rekindle her former sense of wonder. The scene was affectionately familiar, more than that she could not say. She would dress herself and go outside – perhaps into the garden – and test the ambience there.

The garden was wet. Thin sunlight glanced over, but could not vaporize, the lingering dew. And it was cold; goose pimples rose on her bare arms. The sound of her feet on the gravel – a measured tread, for she was intent on every sensation – made her recall her grandmother. She scrutinized the low, hummocky plants – sedum, harebell, dianthus – and the tall exuberance of plants in the herbaceous border with her grandmother's eyes, and found everything in place, nothing there that should not be there under Aunt Bunny's stewardship. Her mother would share the labour during their stay at Willow Dasset, ensuring that the garden continued as its creator had ordained. Even the Ludbury men liked to walk here and be assured of its abiding glory. Sally ran to the bottom of the sloping lawn where she paused to examine the reptilian bark of a horse chestnut tree and the way its roots sank into the steep bank like giant, mailed toes. Her own toes, she saw, were sodden. Cautiously, she returned to the house and ran upstairs to change her shoes.

Breakfast was already underway when she arrived in the kitchen. 'An egg?' offered Bunny. 'Slice of ham?' George enquired. But Sally, sliding along the bench to her place beside Anne, thought toast would do very well. Meg speared a slice of toast with a bread knife and presented it across the table. Bunny stood and reached over with a cup of tea. Then, the two women exchanged a look of some significance. They have been talking about me, Sally concluded uneasily. And when she had finished her meal, was not surprised to learn that her mother wished to have a word with her. Upstairs. Alone.

'I'll wait for you in the yard,' Anne told her, pulling a face of commiseration.

Sally followed her mother up the back stairs.

Entering the room, Meg turned quickly. 'Have you got another top you can wear?'

'Why? You said this one would do for the farm.'

'Did I?' Meg peered at her daughter's chest. 'Well, your aunt thinks it's too small for you. Though why it should cause her such agitation . . . What else have you got?'

Sally became hot. A glance in the looking glass revealed that her face was red; revealed, too, the cause of her aunt's complaint. She fell to her knees and busied herself in a drawer. 'There's this old school blouse,' she mumbled, holding it up, but not raising her head.

'Try it on.' Meg perched on the window-seat and waited.

Sally waited, too.

'Oh, good Lord!' The child had become shy all of a sudden. 'I'll be in my room. When you've put it on, come and show me.'

In her room, Meg sat down on the bed, but something – a sight of herself in the wardrobe mirror, a memory of herself in the night? – propelled her to her feet and thence to the window. It was ridiculous of Bunny to be offended by the sight of an immature bosom. Ridiculous, but somehow predictable; for if the girls were becoming young women, where did that leave Bunny? Meg closed her eyes. It was to be hoped that here was not further potential for trouble.

Sally came into the room with an uncharacteristic slouch.

'Come over to the light. Stand up straight, or how can

I tell? Yes, that'll do. I can't see anything to complain about, now.'

As the girl hurried away, Meg experienced a surge of tension. Suddenly, she, too, felt threatened by usurpation. It was as if her daughter's tumescence signalled the waning of her own vitality. Of course, there was a standpoint from which the idea appeared rooted in logic – and Meg, staring bleakly out of the window, was momentarily able to assume disinterest – for she had married late and then delayed before becoming a mother. Logic be blowed! she muttered, allowing the return of her customary conviction; how she *felt* was the crux of the matter, and she had never felt more urgently vital. Waning might suit Henry, but she, Meg, was not ready for it, not yet, not for some considerable time. Tentatively, she recovered one or two of the night's wild resolutions, and discovered, rather to her surprise, that they lost less by submission to daylight than she had anticipated.

In the yard, a bored Anne was glad to see Sally come through the kitchen doorway, but was amazed by her choice of attire. 'Urgh! Why've you put that thing on?'

'Told to,' Sally said, rushing past.

'Wait on! Was the other one ripped?'

'Yes,' Sally lied, after a pause.

3

Pip stood alone on the steps beneath the portico. 'Charlotte, you ninny! They're here!' she screamed, jerking her stick in the air.

Henry had his eyes on her as he turned off the engine. 'Now, remember what your mother said,' he urged his daughters.

(Their mother had said: Girls, if Aunt Charlotte leads me away for a private word – which I dare say she will – you are to stick close to your father. He may need your protection should Aunt Pip leap on top of him.

There is no need to be vulgar, their father had said.)

Charlotte came running. 'Why didn't you call me? Oh, my dears . . .'

'Deaf as a post! I started screeching like a cockerel the moment I saw the car. Oh, *isn't* this nice? *Isn't* this wonderful? But, you naughty girls, you've shot way past your poor old Aunt Pip! Aren't they wicked, unkind girls, Henry?' Pip, shrivelled and bent, caught Henry's arm and hung on it heavily as they hobbled and lurched indoors.

Charlotte was shouting in Meg's ear. 'Deceitful. Sly. Hides things; creeps about the house. Such a worry to me, Meg. I shouldn't put it past her to burn us alive in our beds . . .'

'What nonsense, Aunt! She's a frail little thing.'

'. . . or put poison in our food. She's got all those pills and medicines, you know . . .'

'Come on, Aunt Charlotte. Let's go in.'

In the drawing-room, Pip flopped against Henry on a settee. 'I'm *frightened* of her. She bullies me so. I'm not very nimble on my pins, nowadays, and she will come too close – towers over me – it's quite menacing. And when I need some help' – she briefly raised her crippled hands – 'she's rough. Sometimes she leaves me half-dressed in a tangle of clothes and says: That'll keep you out of mischief for a while. And, of course, I can't make her hear . . . Oh, Henry; what sort of mischief does she suppose I can get up to? Mind you, when I was a gel . . .'

'How are you getting on with the new cook?' Meg, having pushed Charlotte into a chair and seated herself, loudly interrupted Pip.

'What?' Charlotte asked.

'The new cook. Meg asks, how are we getting on.'

'Oh, the cook. Better than the one before. But we do miss Louisa. What's the woman's name, Pip?'

'Beckett. Mrs Beckett. Such a dear.'

'Yes . . .' Charlotte said vaguely.

'She's very obliging,' Pip said. 'This morning I went into the kitchen and said: Mrs Beckett, dear, give my back a good scratch. Poke your wooden spoon down underneath my vest. Scratch hard, Mrs Beckett, there's a good girl. And busy as she was, she gave it a good do. Oh,' Pip shuddered pleasurably, 'it was such a relief. My back's always itchy, and I can't get at it for the life of me.'

'I wonder what's for dinner?' Henry said gloomily, hoping that the wooden spoon had not played a prominent role in its creation.

'Let's go and see,' cried Pip, pushing herself against him in her effort to stand. 'Let's all go and see Mrs Beckett.'

'Where are we going?' Charlotte asked.

175

'To meet the cook.'

'Oh, the cook. Mrs . . . How is it, Pip?'

Mrs Beckett was basting the joint. She shot her eyes towards the ceiling when the crowd trooped in and found herself unable, for the moment, to shake hands.

'How do you do, Mrs Beckett,' Meg said in the bright tone that served her so well on parents' evenings at school. 'That looks good.'

'Mmm. Well, I just hope the butcher gets his money for it one of these days.'

'Oh, dear. Like that, is it?'

Meg indicated to Henry that they should retreat. Pip went off happily with the girls, but Charlotte was more difficult to budge.

'Shall we look at the garden?' Henry bellowed in her ear.

'Yes,' Meg urged, flapping her arms. 'Go with Henry.' Then she turned to the cook. 'Things in a bit of a pickle?'

'Pickle? Well, now: Mrs Edge as does the cleaning — been doing it for years, else I reckon her'd give it up — hasn't had her wages for weeks. I get mine. I don't start work of a Monday without I've been paid of a Friday. But there's talk in the village. Some say they should be put in a home.'

'I'll have a word with my brother. He tries to keep an eye on things. But it was Miss Louisa who kept the place running — though they treated her as if she were a simpleton.'

'I heard. And I know your brother comes when he can . . .'

'Don't worry, Mrs Beckett. And tell Mrs Edge we'll make it all right. I'll have a word with my brother as soon as I get back. The family is most grateful,' she said vaguely, wondering how best to encourage the workforce.

At the dinner table, the demeanour of the head of the house deepened Meg's anxiety. Words seemed beyond Edward, vowels shorn of consonants his only mode. 'Oi ... er,' he offered in response to polite enquiry, and saliva coursed freely from the corners of his mouth.

'Edward prefers me to carve,' Charlotte announced, in case anyone should wonder.

Later, it emerged that Mrs Beckett was not the only person with liquidity on her mind. Charlotte seized Meg's arm and drew her upstairs. In her bedroom she pulled open a wardrobe door and took from a shelf an ancient fox. 'I'd like you to have my fur,' she said urgently. 'For ten pounds.'

Meg was indignant. 'That horrid thing! Catch me wearing a dead animal round my neck! If you're short of money though, Aunt, I'll lend you some.'

'What?'

'Lend you some.'

'Oh,' said Charlotte, visibly crestfallen.

'Give you some, then. Hang on.' She hurried to the stairs, and when she was half-way down, called: 'Sally! Come here. Fetch my handbag, will you? I think I left it in the drawing-room.'

Seeing the departure of the handbag, Henry became agitated. When Sally returned from her mission, he asked lightly: 'What did Mummy want her handbag for?'

'To give Aunt Charlotte some money.'

The news alarmed him. It was the first thing he mentioned when the Rover set off down the drive. 'Have you been giving them money?'

Meg ignored the query. Her mind was grappling with the problem of how to organize The Grange from a distance. 'They do seem to be in a muddle – it must be that – they can't really be broke. We'll have to have a family conference.'

'Can't that younger brother help them? He's well off, isn't he? Owns several pubs, according to Jim.'

'Uncle Freddy? He's a trouble-maker. He and Edward once took shotguns to one another. And it's his wife who owns the pubs. Don't suppose she'll want to help them. And it wouldn't do her any good if she did.'

'Why ever not?'

'Because she's never received at The Grange. According to Aunt Charlotte, she's common.'

The house had returned to its customary gloom. Pip wobbled up the stairs and went to her room. With difficulty, she opened a drawer and began to sort through her pill box. 'Running low,' she murmured. 'But Doctor Paul will come tomorrow. I want a lot more of *these*.' She selected a small white tablet. 'The yellow ones are no darn good.'

She closed the drawer and raised her eyes to the looking glass. 'Useless, useless,' she chided her reflection. 'If you'd any sense, you old hag, you'd swallow the lot and be done with it.'

4

Harvest got underway. The problem of what to do about The Grange was, of necessity, suspended. In any case, Jim was of the opinion that there was little to be done; visitors to The Grange should understand that they merely witnessed decay – a painful phenomenon to observe, perhaps, but less painful to those who understood the wise ways of Nature. The kindest course was to keep interference to the minimum, for any imposed diversion, such as the selling of The Grange and the placing of its inhabitants in an hotel or nursing home, would be sure to either hasten death or extend painful, bewildering life. No, decay was not a thing to get steamed up about; it was a thing to welcome as part of the natural process – necessary, satisfactory, even beautiful in its way – for who had not been charmed by the sight of a crumbling oak, a tumbledown cottage or a wild, monastic ruin? Since it was upon Jim's shoulders that they chose to place this particular burden – he it was who sorted through the bills, interviewed the farm manager and the family solicitor – no counter argument was forcefully raised. And they were all agreed that the harvest, like time and tide in general, would wait not even upon Ludbury concerns.

The weather – the sun feeble and frequently overcast – was by no means perfect, but by ten in the morning, conditions were generally dry enough for the combine to be put to work. The grain merchant's lorry called regularly to take away sacks of grain to store on drying platforms.

Harry was trying to persuade his father to install his own drying platform in the barn, but George thought he'd wait and measure the profitability of the projected milking machine before considering further sophistication. Jim was sceptical about all these improvements, but he had agreed to operate the combine at Willow Dasset in return for the assistance, later on, of Mick and the combine with his own harvest at Horley-in-the-Hedges.

This year's harvest was not as the girls thought of harvest. A new institution was inaugurated. This consisted of Uncle Jim, begoggled, overalled and hatted, hunched over the wheel high up at the front of the combine; Benjamin in charge of sacking the grain on the platform at the rear; Mick with tractor and cart gathering straw for baling and sacks for the merchant's lorry, and always ready with tools when – as not infrequently happened – the combine broke down; and John and the children – Sally, Anne and Barry – available for supporting roles. Tea was brought to the harvest field, but it was taken in comparative silence; there were no star-turns, no tales or songs or elaborate, teasing tricks.

Anne, who was much taken with the sacking operation, stuck fast to Benjamin, exercising reliable judgement as to the moment when, a sack being full, it was time to seal off the grain, and the moment to depress the lever on the chute so that sacks arrived on the ground in easily collectable groups. Barry was set to work with a pitchfork. Sally clung to the tractor, waiting for her chance to take the wheel and enable Mick to devote his strength to loading.

Mick was given to moodiness; he was sometimes sullen, at other times confiding. One confidential afternoon, Sally learnt that he was to move into the tied cottage, and, because of this, his wife would soon be allowed to join him. He planned to work on the cottage during every spare moment, so that by the end of the year, when his wife would arrive, it would be a comfortable, charming home. He would distemper the walls, paint the woodwork, dig and plant in the garden. He would collect wood this autumn so that the winter fires burned brightly. By next summer – and here his face became dreamy, his voice soft – there would be roses by the door and in the back garden a handsome crop of vegetables.

'Hollyhocks would be nice by the wall,' Sally called to him one evening, having paused at the cottage gate to watch him dig the front garden.

'Hollyhocks,' he repeated, as if memorizing the name.

'And marigolds along the path.'

'Marigolds.'

'And something blue near the marigolds . . . Scabious. I love scabious; they're sort of misty because of their beaded centres. There are a lot of scabious in Grandma's garden.' She looked at the bare strip of dug-over earth and thought how a plant here and there would never be missed from the house garden. 'I could bring you some,' she offered, unable to resist the fairness of the supposition, but daunted, immediately afterwards, by her rashness.

He looked at her, considering the suggestion. 'You could,' he said – not as a statement, not as a question, but as something in between. Then he pushed his foot down hard upon the spade, reattending to his work.

She went slowly along the track, unhappy, but somehow committed. The offer could be forgotten, she supposed; if he referred to it she could say it had slipped her mind. But it might become an issue between them, and undo her patient work; for she had learned to

181

take account of his moods, to hold back when his face was grim and wait for the return of his expansiveness when it was easy to insert herself helpfully into the tractor's driving seat. Thinking of this, she decided that she must keep her word. And that being so, there was no time like the present.

Looking about her, she let herself in through the high, seldom-used gate at the bottom of the garden near the willow-pond. The gate whined protestingly, and when she had closed it behind her, she stood for some moments, listening in the shrubbery. But the only noise was the call of a bird and the thudding of her own heart. She crossed the garden, keeping to the trees at the bottom of the bank. To reach the herbaceous border she must run up the bank of lawn beside the tall hedge separating flower from vegetable garden. Before leaving the trees' shelter, she studied every window of the house, every faintly rippled pane; but there was no movement against the glass, no lurking, moon-faced watcher. She ran until she could crouch beside the border.

The scabious clumps were no longer in flower, but she knew their greyish-grassy foliage, and chose likely specimens from which to wrench her spoils. She had decided to work with bare hands, and afterwards, to carry the plants in her arms against her skirt; for soil-encrusted hands and clothes were the result of many a past escapade, whereas possession of trowel or fork or newspaper parcel would be hard to explain away. The plants, however, were more firmly rooted than she had supposed, and the operation became messy and damaging. Guilt, like fearful indigestion, lodged in her throat. She felt herself observed, not by mortals who would soon come shrieking vengeance, but by sorrowful spirits, her grandmother, and perhaps God. Calming herself with stern reason, she recalled that it was good gardening practice to divide plants after flowering: but not like this, insisted a small voice in her head.

When she had several plantable pieces, she did her best to smooth down the battered remains. An animal would be blamed, of course; a fox or a rat or some scrabbling night-time creature. She thought of this as she turned her back on her vandalism and darted for the trees with her trophies, but it did not make her altogether comfortable.

He was still in the cottage garden, and seemed not surprised by her return.

'Scabious are taller than marigolds, so set them further in,' she said, employing a bossy tone to disguise her sudden embarrassment. 'About here.' She made a mark with her heel, then laid the plants on the ground and turned to go.

He stepped quickly in front of her. 'You must come inside and wash.'

'Oh, no. No need for that.'

'But they will see your hands. They will ask, why are they dirty? You must wash them before you go.'

The discovery that they were conspiring together was so alarming that she lost her ability to think. She swallowed, and found that she had allowed him to draw her into the cottage. Inside the doorway, she looked up at him, unable to do other than obey.

'Through there,' he pointed.

Of course, she knew where the scullery was, but the place, now, was sinister and alien. He turned on the tap and she took a piece of soap in her hands.

'Use the brush. Scrub under the nails.'

She scrubbed diligently, wishing to remove every trace of an excuse he might use to detain her. He unhooked a towel from behind the back door, and stood leaning against the side of the open doorway, watching her. 'Here. Show me,' he commanded, when she turned off the tap.

Holding her hands before her, she went to him.

'It will do,' he said, handing her the towel, but before she could use it, he grasped her forearms and looked down. 'Your skirt . . .'

'Oh, don't worry about that. It's always getting filthy. They won't think anything about that,' she gabbled.

He drew her close, closer than was reasonable, and his tightening grip hurt her arms.

She knew, although not how, that she was in grave danger. She removed her eyes from his face and turned her head to look through the cottage towards the front door. 'I must go now. They expect me,' she said through a dry mouth. And then, surprising herself with her cunning: 'I told Anne I was coming here.'

He seemed disgusted, and threw away her arms. 'You fool! She will tell them.'

'No, no, she won't do that,' she cried, running to the front door, and on to the garden gate.

Her legs were leaden: she willed them to pound faster along the track. When the house was in sight, she slowed to a walk, panting, squeezing a stitch in her side, thinking of how she would never sit with him on the tractor again.

Meg was approaching the rickyard. A beastly, squashy sensation in the pit of her stomach had propelled her, yet again from the house. Every evening for the past week, she had been obliged to take violent exercise. This evening had been particularly grim: if Bunny had whispered once more – as if to mention such things in a normal voice were indecent – that they must go through Mama's things in the morning; or if Henry had dozed off

184

again behind his library book, to jerk awake and cry: 'I do beg everyone's pardon', it was certain that she would have clouted them. Much better, she had concluded, that she walk out into the evening air. As her legs swung forward, she found some relief in stretching and pushing her stride. Enforced idleness was the problem, she reflected. These violent tensions she had experienced before – many times during the past few months – but her busy life afforded many outlets and distractions. Here, it was difficult to busy oneself for five minutes before Bunny came along to interfere; to complain that she was cutting back the forsythia too vigorously, or sorting the laundry on to the wrong shelves. She had bitten her tongue many times today, but such petty irritations were as nothing compared to the nerve-wracking tension with which her body now teemed. 'Walk, walk, *walk*,' she muttered fiercely, accompanying each word with a stride, almost stamping her feet to the ground, willing the discomfort to pass.

Then she saw him. He was standing in the cottage back doorway. He was looking at her. He was – she ran her tongue nervously over her lips – waiting for her.

This was surprising, but not altogether unexpected. The first time their paths had crossed – she coming out of the wash-house, he going to open the gate to the cowshed yard – she had seen that she interested him. 'Good morning,' she had called as she would have called to Arthur. His failure to at once reply caused her to turn and look back. She saw that he was making quite a study of her. 'Good morning,' he said at last, challengingly. In the kitchen doorway she had taken her turn to watch him – jumping down from the tractor, swinging spadefuls of cow dung into the trailer. He was no mere farm hand, she decided; the misfortunes of war had placed him in his present position. His discerning interest in herself gave weight to this theory. Later, she had walked up to the harvest field on purpose to watch him, and as her eyes dwelt on his glistening strength, she told herself that she detected strength of character.

And now he was waiting for her in his cottage doorway. She made up her mind quickly – it would be natural and friendly to go over to him, to call out a greeting, to enquire about his background and how he had come to be displaced by the war. While her justifying thoughts ran on, her heart began to beat quickly and her tension focused on a sharp anticipation of pleasure. She stumbled forward in her short-sighted way, beginning to smile, stretching a hand towards the gate at the end of the back garden. She saw, then, that he was not looking at her after all. He was looking across at someone in the scullery, and now he was speaking. 'Here,' he said. 'Show me.' Someone joined him in the doorway. She heard their voices but only caught 'skirt'. Suddenly, the scene in the doorway became the coming together of two people. It was *his* form, massive and arresting, that had engaged her attention, but now she concentrated on the other, the small figure.

It was Sally. It couldn't be. But it was.

In swift succession, both figures vanished from the doorway. She hung on to the gate as emotion coursed through her, contradictory and confusing. Then, with no clear purpose in her mind, she turned and set off for the house.

Sally, in her knickers and blouse, was leaning over an open drawer.

Meg came softly into the room. 'What are you doing?'

Sally shot up her head. 'Oh! Looking for a clean skirt. I got soil on the other one.'

'Put it back on.'

'What?'

'Put it back on – the one you took off.'

'Why, Mummy? It's dirty, I . . .'

'Put it on. At once.'

Sally took a rolled-up skirt from a corner of the drawer, shook it out, and stepped into it.

Meg paid close attention.

When she had fastened the button at the waist, Sally dropped her hands.

'Turn around.'

Sally turned a slow, full circle.

Meg, expecting a surge of relief, experienced a curious stab of disappointment. 'It's down the front,' she said flatly, observing the dirty mark. 'And there's more on the front of your blouse.'

'Is there?' Sally looked down. 'Oh, yes. Sorry. I'll put clean ones on, shall I?'

'Not much point. It's almost bedtime.'

Sally saw that the crisis – if that was what it had been – was over. Her mother had lost interest, and was moving away to the window. The matter seemed unlikely to attract further investigation. 'I'll stay as I am, then, and put clean clothes on in the morning. I think I'll go down for a bit,' she said hopefully, longing for solitude to soothe away the evening's trauma.

'I saw you in the cottage,' Meg said suddenly, swinging round.

Her mother's eyes, Sally saw, were peculiarly dark.

'I saw you with that man,' Meg continued, telling herself that it was her duty to enquire, and that she must do it carefully. But inside her, in the pit of her stomach, in her wrists and elbows and knees, her nerve-ends screeched. 'Tell me what happened,' she wheedled. 'I shan't be cross.'

A gross eagerness shone in her mother's face. Sally backed, and Meg came forward. Sally became trapped against the foot of the bed: for the second time that evening, an adult pressed too close.

'Tell me what he did to you. Go on, you can tell me,' Meg spoke hurriedly, exhaling hot breath.

Suddenly, it was only from this that Sally wished to escape – not from discovery and retribution in the matter of the stolen plants – only from this horrifying encounter. She ducked and dived and ran. In the safety of the doorway, she turned back. 'I stole some plants from the garden and took them to the cottage. He's trying to make the place nice for his wife. I wanted to help. He didn't ask me to. I just did it.'

Meg struggled with herself; with relief and anti-climax, with the knowledge of her daughter's innocence and of her unwitting guilt. For the girl had attracted the man – that was the nub of the matter, the magnet drawing to itself all Meg's pent-up feeling. 'I see that your aunt is quite right about you. She says you hang around the men, and that Grandad doesn't like it. It's time you learned to behave more responsibly.'

'Hang around the men?' Sally repeated in disbelief. 'But I don't. We don't. We go farming, Anne and I.'

'We go farming,' Meg mocked in a baby's voice. 'For heaven's sake, grow up! It's all very well for Anne, but you – you're *developing*.'

At once, Sally hunched her shoulders. 'I don't want to hear what you say. I think you're horrible . . . disgusting.' And she ran on to the landing and down the stairs, and let herself into the garden.

5

'Why didn't you come?' Anne demanded, having run into their room from a morning devoted to the combine harvester.

Sally was perched on the side of the bed. She did not turn round. 'Couldn't be bothered.'

This was not to be believed. 'Were you stopped? Are they cross with you?'

'No,' Sally said, turning with a fierce frown.

'Gosh! You look horrible.'

Sally craned towards the looking glass to see. She looked pasty and dull. While mooching disconsolately about the house, she had pulled lank strands of hair from her plaits. She was untidy in an unwholesome way, unlike her glowing, wind-ruffled sister. 'That's because I *am* horrible.'

Anne was embarrassed. 'I don't mean you *are*, just that you look it. Anyway, you'll come to the field this afternoon, won't you, Sal?'

'Shouldn't think so.'

'But *why*?'

'I don't like being on the tractor anymore.'

More unbelievable nonsense. 'I suppose you don't like Mick.'

'Well, I don't, really.'

'I'll let you come on the back of the combine, if you like,' Anne said generously. 'Benjamin's a misery, too, but I don't take any notice. It's really good when the grain

189

comes gushing out – you can put your arms into the sack and it comes right up them – feels lovely.'

'Oh, all right, then,' Sally said, feeling, as she imagined the effect described by her sister, the safe tug of childhood.

The afternoon was surprisingly enjoyable. The sun shone steadily, and as the dust flew and the grain ran and the platform juddered beneath her feet, Sally's confusion, which this morning had seemed so unassailable, melted away. She and her sister were simply busy, bossy girls, finding fun in unlikely places, supremely confident in the roles they invented for themselves. They waved cheerily to Mick and to John, exchanged insults with Barry, and sometimes crept cautiously to the front of the combine to grab the rail and stand by their uncle's shoulder.

It was when her grandfather rode into the field on his chestnut-coloured hunter and paused by the hedge to watch the workers, that she grew uncomfortable. Was he watching her? Was he thinking, seeing her holding a sack for Benjamin to tie, that she was hanging around the men? This bewildering accusation had worried her all morning, and now rang again in her head. For safety's sake, she moved to the front of the combine and made herself inconspicuous by squatting on the floor. Jim glanced at her quickly, took in her lowered head and her finger tracing a pattern in spilled ears of wheat on the floor. 'All right?' he bellowed.

She called: 'Yes,' and was pleased to see him smile as he leaned forward to check the combine's scissor action. Evidently, she did not inspire universal distaste. She half rose so that her mouth was close to his ear. 'You don't mind me being here, do you, Uncle?'

'Not if you stay back there and hold tight.'

She searched his answers for hints of encouragement or repulsion.

He looked round again, and perhaps glimpsed her anxiety. 'It's not every farmer has a nice young lady to keep him company on the combine,' he shouted ahead to the unsuspecting corn.

His grin, quite definitely, signalled satisfaction.

'Sal, your sack's nearly full,' Anne yelled.

'You can do it. I'm staying here for a bit.'

Later, at the tea table, Henry proposed a family excursion to Stratford. If they made an early start in the morning, they might get tickets for the matinée in the afternoon.

Anne objected, pointing out that a start on the harvesting of Bailey's Field was forecast for the morning.

But Sally was relieved by the prospect of a day away from the farm, and hastened to remind the company of her love of the theatre, a love so great that, when she was grown up, she intended to become an actress.

At this Bunny looked up at the ceiling, and Meg expressed surprise that her daughter was not already embarked upon that career.

'Now, now,' said Henry, feeling that they were being unfair to the one person who had been good enough to welcome his proposal. 'How about it? The sights in the morning, a picnic lunch by the river, and the theatre in the afternoon.'

'Might as well,' Meg agreed. 'It's good for their school work, I suppose.'

At Willow Dasset, Stratford meant the cattle market, and the market stalls by The Fountain where the autumn mop fair was held; it was where one shopped and took lunch at The White Horse. There was never a mention of the theatre — unless a visiting Robinson mentioned it, and then Ludbury voices trailed away and eyes became veiled with embarrassment. To Meg and Henry, Stratford was a handy place to imbibe a little culture which might be exhibited during conversations back home. And the theatre's exclusive devotion to Shakespeare preserved it from raffish or disreputable connotations; a visit there might be mentioned with confidence in staffroom, vestry or town hall. Sometimes during a performance, Henry was dismayed by unseemly gestures or lewd tones, but he put these down to actorishness (clearly at variance with the bard's intentions), and was able to emerge, blinking into the daylight, feeling he had been done considerable good. Meg had always been a great one for Shakespeare, particularly for the passages she had learnt by heart at school; she was prepared to endure stretches of tedium for the pleasure of pricking up her ears when familiar lines reached their turn. But their chief motive in motoring early to queue for tickets to join the sweaty afternoon throng, was to obtain value: a brush with Shakespeare, they had supposed, could only enhance their daughters' prospects in the eleven-plus examination, and when that obstacle was safely overcome, they looked for a similar benefit with regard to the School Certificate.

Sally was aware of these several views of Stratford. She was aware, too, of the one held by Anne — that it threatened a boring intrusion into the joys of farming. And she had her own view of Stratford — a liberating place, gaudy with flags and flowers, dazzling with light and water, lazy with lawns and swans; a place where one might encounter a stetson or a sari, overhear excitable foreign talk, sniff cosmopolitan smells. Above all, it was the place where she heard *that voice* — the thrilling sound that seemed to issue on an unending stream of breath

192

from a deep and resonant cavern to declaim the passions of Viola, Portia or Rosalind. It was, she considered, the only voice suitable for the expression of significant emotion. She sometimes practised it in her room, and when seriously misunderstood at home or at school, had been known to employ it, at least to temporary effect. Now, on tenterhooks lest the last tickets be sold before they reached the head of the queue, she groaned and clasped her hands.'If we don't get tickets, I shall *die*.'

'Don't be ridiculous. And keep your voice down,' Meg urged, hoping that they were not about to witness the resurrection of the Stratford effect. (Still fresh in her mind was the occasion following a performance of *The Merchant of Venice* when Sally, finding herself thwarted in some unmemorable matter, had given a fair imitation of Portia's advocatory skills to the amazement of the crowd in Sheep Street.) 'Just be patient. It's nearly our turn.'

But the suspense was hard to bear. The queue was longer than Sally had ever known it. Disappointment over this rare and wonderful treat would be insupportable coming so soon after the pain and confusion that had come upon her at Willow Dasset. When they reached the box office, only two seats in the upper circle remained. There were, however, for purchase, two returned tickets for the stalls. Meg and Henry hurriedly consulted one another – while Sally thought she would swoon – and decided in favour of extravagance. Meg and Anne would sit in the upper circle until the interval, when they would exchange their seats for Henry's and Sally's in the stalls.

When the tickets were safe, Sally relaxed. Walking through the town, looking in small, stuffy shops, paying homage outside the Birthplace, the Grammar School and Hall's Croft (the interiors of which had been inspected on

193

previous occasions and did not require further examination), she was the perfect, taken-about child – not just because it was certain that *A Midsummer-Night's Dream* would not pass by without her, but that the snatches of life through which they wandered were vivid and absorbing. Anne was less obliging, requiring an ice-cream, then the lavatory, wishing to know whether it was time to eat: as Meg remarked to her husband, if it wasn't one child, it was the other. In Holy Trinity they bowed their heads over the grave in the chancel, and watched a man taking a rubbing from a brass. Then – the time having been parcelled out neatly – they went back to the car for the picnic basket, and searched for a suitable spot to sit down.

The sandwiches were delicious. This was not always the case. On a journey, the Robinson picnic was an unpleasant affair. Henry was reluctant to stray from the car; he preferred to keep an eye on the traffic rather than the scenery, and was keen to ensure a minimum delay. So it was often to the accompaniment of exhaust fumes and the smell of hot rubber that they ate sandwiches filled with slices of damp tomato and sulphurous hard-boiled egg. Here, sitting opposite the theatre on warm grass dotted with similarly engaged groups, it was pleasant to eat and laze and throw crusts to swans that came gliding and fanning their tail-feathers. Several rowing-boats passed by. Anne watched them, enviously. Meg saw her strained face, and recalled that a sedentary afternoon lay ahead. She turned to Henry. 'Shall we take a boat? There's plenty of time.'

Henry, who had been watching a red-faced man with a knotted handkerchief on his head heaving a boat-load of females through the water, did not care for the suggestion. 'I'd be grateful for the opportunity of allowing my luncheon to settle, if that's quite all right with you.'

194

Meg hesitated, then rose. 'I'll row, then. You stay here and snooze.'

'Sit down,' Henry commanded. 'You know what you're like – blind as a bat and completely uncoordinated. You'd drown them; and everyone else on the river. Let's have a bit a peace, for Heaven's sake.'

Meg looked about her. 'We'll go for a walk, then. Are you coming, Sally, or will you stay with your father?'

Sally, who was following a wonderful piece of gossip being shared by a trio of neighbouring ladies, thought she'd stay where she was.

'Right-oh. Come on, Anne.'

'Keep an eye on the time,' Henry warned.

'We'll be back in half an hour.'

On the other side of the bridge they found the hut where there were boats for hire. Stepping firmly from the landing plank, they almost upset the boat, and Meg took a quantity of water on board in her attempt to propel them away from the mooring. A helpful youth with a long pole set them off, in the direction, Meg was careful to establish, that led them away from Henry. Several times on their meandering journey they made contact with the bank, and once with another craft, which led to a cheery discussion with a laughing man as to who should pull which oar.

'People are jolly friendly here,' Anne called to her mother, who was looking young and gay and rather nice. 'That man was so funny, and you had made him awfully wet.'

'A very nice man,' Meg confirmed happily. 'I think I'm getting the hang of this, now.'

'Twelve and half minutes late!' Henry announced, when they returned to the site of the picnic. 'And you're wet! Did you fall in the river, or what?'

'We got splashed by a passing boat,' Meg said airily.

'You really missed something,' Anne hissed in Sally's ear as they returned the basket to the car. 'I'll tell you about it later.'

'I say, this is comfortable,' Meg remarked, as she and Anne sank into the superior seats in the stalls.

'I don't think it's as good as upstairs. I don't think I shall be able to see.'

'You will when it begins.'

'But what about that big man? I won't see anything with him in the way.'

The man, seated three rows ahead, was indeed tall. 'Change over,' Meg suggested; and when they had re-seated themselves: 'Better?'

'Maybe,' Anne said gloomily.

Meg glanced at her, and wondered whether the play was a total failure so far as this daughter was concerned. During the interval just now, Anne had seemed happy enough, seizing the opportunity to poke through souvenirs in the foyer. It was Sally who had been subdued. But thinking back, Meg did not doubt her elder daughter's enjoyment. Sally seemed not to have left the auditorium. 'I know a bank whereon the wild thyme grows,' she had quoted suddenly, musingly, apropos of nothing. 'Is wild thyme like garden thyme? Does it smell the same?'

'Wild thyme grew on Astly Hill – near where we lived as children,' Meg recalled. 'It attracted hordes of small bees. Their humming was sometimes quite deafening. And, yes, it smells just as good – probably stronger.'

'I should like to go there,' Sally said, thinking not especially of Astly Hill, but of a secret tree-lined bank, of oxlips, violets, woodbine.

Now, Meg suspected that Anne's frantic exploration of

the foyer had masked a desperate boredom. 'Don't you like it really – the performance, the play?'

'Well,' Anne began cautiously, 'I'm not all that keen on fairies.'

'Ah. Well, what about Bottom and his friends? You'll like the next bit, I should think, when Bottom has an ass's head.'

'If that man keeps leaning over, I don't suppose I shall see it.'

'He's listening to his companion. He has to lean over because she's much smaller than he is. When the curtain rises they'll stop talking.'

Meg kept her eyes on the man, waiting for him to sit upright. The feeling grew that he was familiar, and then, with a sudden stabbing pain, that he had once been beloved. It can't be him, she silently protested. Karl's hair had been darkish brown, whereas this man's hair was totally white. And what if it were? She hadn't really *loved* him, just felt a superficial attraction. She stirred irritably in her seat, as if trying to get things straight. But when the curtain rose, and stillness became obligatory, the past was persistent, and the present enactment a mere backdrop on her thoughts. The truth was that she had been strongly attracted to him, she now sadly confessed, but had been unwilling to accommodate his views and attitudes. Rather than compromise, she had renounced him. And how right she had been; for along had come Henry – the embodiment of her ideals – a convinced and passionate churchman, requiring only the tempering her skills and energy would provide! She raised a fist to her mouth and bit on it to stifle a snort of derision. What had life with Henry become if not one of compromise? She tried to look at herself objectively, and saw that it was the feeling of time running out that was leading her into unaccustomed, and probably unfruitful, reflection. And the thought of life escaping her compressed her stomach muscles in a way that had become horribly familiar. Not that, she prayed. How can I cope with the rest of the day if I start feeling like that already? For the tension did not usually arrive until evening, when it was possible to remove herself from company, endure in privacy, look forward to a couple of codeine tablets to hasten blessed oblivion.

She made up her mind. When the lights came on at the end of the play, she and Anne would remain in their seats; for it would take Henry and Sally some time to descend the many flights of stairs from the upper circle, and she was determined to avoid being discovered hanging about in the foyer by Karl. When others rose, she kept her head low, motioned to Anne to stay still, assumed an interest in the programme notes. But it had always irked Meg to bide her time – the passage of a few seconds stretched like pulled elastic when she was required to pass them in patience – and soon, an irresistible peep revealed Karl and his companion still firmly attached to their seats.

She might have known it, she fumed, thrusting her startled daughter to the end of the row and into the gangway throng; the man had always been perverse; you could place your last shilling on his doing differently to everyone else. When they reached the spot designated by Henry as their meeting place, she turned her back on passers-by and directed her own and Anne's attention to a photographic display on the wall. The crowd thinned; stragglers passed leisurely; Henry did not come. Then she heard Karl's voice – not loud or dominant, but unmissable for its eccentric discursive manner. She held her breath until she could no longer make it out, and then, because she felt herself safe, indulged in sentimental regret and turned to look after him. For some reason he chose that moment to look back, but seemed not to take her in. She returned at once to the photographs, her heart drumming in her ears.

'Meg, is it not? My dear! What a very great pleasure! Betty come here! Meg, this lady is my wife, Betty. And my dear – is this not too wonderful? – Meg, you see, is dear Ronald's niece . . .'

'Aunt Gussie's niece, actually,' said Meg, who liked to be correct about these things.

'Alas, poor Gussie died – did you know? But Ronald is very much alive; in fact, we share the house with him in Maitland Square. When he retired he wished me to carry on the practice. But look – am I to believe my eyes? You are utterly unchanged. You are still the marvellous girl I remember. When Meg was a student in Chelsea,' he told his wife, 'she was crowned Queen of the May in what was surely the most provocative ceremony any innocent young man has been called upon to witness . . .'

As he explained her extravagantly to his wife, a soft warmth flowed over her. She saw herself as he described her, and became elated by the vision. 'You haven't changed much, either,' she cried laughingly, too dazzled by her own image to see any longer the startling white of his hair.

'Oh, but my dear,' he reproved her softly. 'I think that I have. And now I see, after all, there is something new about you.'

'Oh?' she cried in sharp alarm.

'Your spectacles. Of course! You are short-sighted. It gave you a deliciously vague appearance, I recall. No – do *not*!' he caught hold of the over-eager hand that had flown upwards to remove the impediment. 'They are not unbecoming . . .' And he drew her hand slowly to his lips.

'Karl, you are an old rogue,' said Betty.

Meanwhile, Henry and Sally at last reached the bottom of the concrete stairway and stepped into the open air at the side of the theatre. Now they must walk against the crowd pouring from the front. Henry gripped Sally's shoulders and steered her as he would the Rover; but the child seemed dazed, oblivious of spaces that occurred. 'Now. Turn. Go on,' Henry snapped impatiently from time to time in her ear; then, colliding with a stranger, hastily sweetening his tone: 'I *do* beg your pardon.' When they entered the foyer, the bulk of the crowd had gone. Only a few chatterers remained, and among these Henry spotted his wife. She looked flushed and had a silly expression on her face. The very tall man she was attending to was wearing a deeply upsetting bow tie.

'Hello, my dear,' Henry intoned in the voice for which he was treasured at Saint Luke's.

'Oh,' Meg said, turning. 'This is Henry.' She spoke in an offhand, almost pitying way. 'Henry, meet Doctor and Mrs Karl Bruchstein.'

Shaking hands, producing the children, Henry wondered what had come over her. The sooner he got her away, the better. 'I don't wish to hurry you, my dear . . .'

But Karl, it appeared, had something very particular to say to Meg. He took her arm and turned her intimately to one side.

Betty took note of this and diplomatically engaged Henry's attention.

'You must come to London and visit us,' Karl was urging. 'It would delight your uncle.'

'Perhaps I shall,' Meg said gaily, feeling that she might do anything. 'When I can fit it in. I'm tremendously busy these days. I'm a headmistress, and on dozens of committees and governing bodies . . .'

'You imperious creature! I can imagine it, dearest Meg. You rule sternly, brook no nonsense, exact a *merciless* discipline . . .'

'Are you an actor?' enquired Sally, suddenly coming to.

Karl contemplated her earnest, upturned face. 'What an astute child! She has known me for precisely one minute and already she has found me out.'

'I thought so. I could tell. When I'm grown up I'm going to be an actress.'

'Of course she isn't,' Meg put in hastily. 'She's a very clever girl. She'll go to university. Really, Sally, you shouldn't say such ridiculous things! And Karl is teasing you. He's a very clever doctor.'

Still unsteady with tears pricked by Puck's sweetly apologetic farewell, Sally clutched her throat and looked wildly about. What was happening? Everyone seemed set on misrepresenting her this holiday – that awful business about her hanging around the men, now this wicked denial of her long-standing, clearly-stated ambition. It was as if she was not to be herself but must become some creature of other people's devising. Well, she *was* her own self, and they'd better understand it. Helena's recent complaint sprang to mind ('Wherefore was I to this keen mockery born?'). She took in breath, flung out her arms, and set the foyer reverberating with her closely argued grievance.

'My . . . dear . . . child,' cried Karl, clasping Sally's arms when at last she ran out of words. 'Rest assured, we are all of us satisfied that you are destined for the stage. If we – and these several others who have gathered here – do not now break into rapturous applause, it is because we are too deeply moved . . .'

'Karl,' Betty said firmly. 'Do, please, recall that we

201

promised to collect Mummy from the Bensons' at half past five.'

Drat the girl! I shall kill her, Meg vowed, casting wildly about in her mind for a means of restoring his attention to herself; for it had seemed, in some vaguely delightful way, to have been leading her somewhere.

Too late. Karl at once took heed of his wife, and the party – amid polite regrets, insincere invitations and promises – broke, step by small step, into two eternally separate parts. Walking to the car, Meg wondered what on earth had precipitated her sudden excitement, what on earth – with such gathering elation – she had begun to expect.

'You didn't tell me you had a blue-stocking friend,' Henry remarked, as he drove from the car park.

'Didn't I?' Meg asked cautiously.

'You needn't have been ashamed of her. She's not at all the sort one expects a university woman to be – you know – shaved head and moustache. On the contrary, she's a very nice looking woman. Pity about her old man.'

'What do you mean?'

'Well . . . Rather a bounder, didn't you think? I thought he was getting you a bit flustered, until that wretched child broke in and showed us up.'

'Huh.' She stole a look at him, then allowed herself a wry smile. Trust Henry to get the wrong end of the stick, to assume that the woman was her friend. Why, in heaven's name, had she saddled herself with such an idiot? To suffer all this – years of irritation and interference – because of a temporary weakness for a pair of flashing blue eyes and a masterful way with a processional cross! And it was not as if she had been new to temptation. Once, she had very nearly settled for a dead-end job in a village school for the sake of being near to Karl. And then there had been the presumptuous clergyman . . . So why, having survived these trials, had she succumbed to Henry? Unattached, she would have moved on – perhaps to London, perhaps to an important position in her old college. There was no telling what she might have become, unburdened by Henry. Slyly, she watched his hands on the steering wheel – pink, veiny, covered in faint gold hairs. In the pit of her stomach the squashy sensation stirred. Dear Lord, she must have been mad. Why had she done it, *why*?

You know darn well, *why*, she told herself, as if putting straight a guileful child. You know darn well what the trouble is – always has been – and over Henry it got the better of you. But Meg had a forgiving nature towards herself, and she made haste to tot up points in mitigation. It was not her fault if she had been born with a stronger drive than most women – She recalled Mrs Mack, the school caretaker, hinting – with much rolling of the eyes – at Mr Mack's demanding nature, and the wave of sympathy that had gone round the staffroom. 'Men!' the married women present had said to one another through gritted teeth. And over the years, several wretched mothers had leant wearily against the school gate and confided to her the insatiability of their husbands' appetites. The world, Meg had come to understand, was full of reluctant women and rampant men. Her failure to coincide with the prevailing feminine view did not surprise her, for she was not as most women are in any respect. She was Margaret Charlotte Ludbury, capable of just about anything, given the chance. It was just wretched bad luck to have tied herself to such an untypical man. And she was now thoroughly satisfied that it was in Henry, not herself, that fault lay. There was nothing wrong with *her*, she told herself stoutly, recalling Karl's flattering manner.

Karl was still on Henry's mind. 'Can't stand that clever-dick type,' he mused. 'I had his number the moment I clapped eyes on his tie. Ought to be banned from the public gaze, that sort of neck-wear; I can think of certain places where it would cause a breach of the peace. 'Course, it's all put on, that arty-farty stuff. Sheer affectation. Can't believe a word he says, a chap like that. And talk about poor judgement! I mean, fancy leading on an overwrought child!'

Meg's stomach buckled. Deep inside her, her demon leapt. Yes! That was it! *Now* she knew where she had been heading! She had been at the point of exorcism; in another moment Karl would have made a proposal that would have set her free from her bedevilment. But the girl's interruption had ruined her chance, had drawn away the healing force. 'I thought she behaved abominably,' she snarled, turning to serve the occupant of the right hand side of the back seat a vicious look. 'Just . . . you . . . wait . . . madam,' she growled as her body teemed and her temple throbbed. 'Don't imagine you've got away with it.'

Sally was silent, gripped by a new and altogether more frightening interpretation of recent events. Could it be, not that she was misunderstood, but that things were going on around her that were beyond her understanding? A dark mist made up of other people's unfathomable emotions swirled in her mind, engulfed her.

'I do wish you'd stop that,' Henry said.

'Stop what?' Meg asked.

'Tapping your feet. Tap, tap, tap. We won't get there any quicker, and you might make a hole in the carpet.'

Meg sank her teeth into her tongue. She was so swollen with tension that she longed for a collision – a head-on crash into that looming oak, perhaps; or an overshoot of the bend on Sunrising Hill. Yes, she would relish that – falling back, hurtling down, turning over and over, smashing, splintering, shattering in smithereens over the valley.

When at last the car came safely to rest in the yard below the farmhouse, Meg rushed to free herself, leap to the ground, turn and seize the one upon whom she intended to wreak vengeance.

'No! Let me go! You frighten me!' Sally shook off the grasping hand and ran off.

Meg tore after her.

'Stop. Come back,' cried Henry. 'Whatever's got into you?'

Anne began to whimper.

'We'd better go in. I expect they'll come back in a minute.'

Her mother cornered her in the barn. They had raced over the farmyard, the rickyard, the paddock, and back again to the farmyard. By the barn, her mother got a hand to her, but Sally leapt over the ledge across the barn doorway and left her mother floundering. She hid herself inadequately behind the sacks of grain. 'You can come out. I know you're there,' her mother's voice called across the vaulted gloom. In despair, Sally raised her head. It was inevitable that she would not escape; she, too, had a strong pair of legs, but she would never match her mother's will. 'I think you want to kill me,' she wailed.

Kill – yes! Meg thought. She wanted to kill, all right. Kill, crush, obliterate. The object of her lust was not specific; but it was at hand – though not quite within her grasp. 'I shan't hurt you,' she called sweetly. 'Come here. Come.'

'You do! You really do want to murder me!' Her mother's unreal voice made it certain. 'Help me, someone,' she cried, and heard her own voice gone unnaturally thin and high.

'I shan't hurt you. Just come. Here. Come.'

'Mummy, no. Please Mummy, no.'

'Got you!' Meg screamed as she pounced. 'Got you, got you!' And she put her hands around the girl's neck and began to shake.

'That'll do!' George roared from the doorway. His walking stick, dropped in his hasty climb over the ledge, clattered alarmingly on the cobbles. He paused and looked at them. Then he held out his arms. 'Megs!'

'Daddy!' She ran to him and fell against his chest. 'Help me, Daddy! I think I've gone off my head!'

He rocked her in his arms, murmuring, stroking.

Sally watched them. She felt that she did not exist. As there was no source of comfort, she wrapped her own arms around her body and hugged herself tight. Then she crept on tiptoe to the doorway. Before leaving the scene, she picked up the walking stick and hooked it over the plank so that Grandad would retrieve it easily on his way out.

The others were in the dining-room taking a belated tea. Sally walked towards the sound, but on reaching the door, crept by, and went up the front stairs. On the landing she paused – no thought in her head, no desire in her heart, she was without will or direction. Her feet took her to the head of the landing, and when she arrived at the oak chest beneath the window, she climbed on to it and gazed down into the garden. Help me, someone! Her forlorn cry seemed to sound again, but she had not uttered it.

A peacock butterfly flew from flower to flower along the border. A tabby cat on a sun-baked staddlestone, uncurled, stretched, jumped down and stalked away. A flash of mauve silk brushed the side of the rosemary bush; Grandma Ludbury stepped on to the path.

She carried her gardening trug, and every now and then, paused to examine a plant or pull a small weed. The white light of her hair was so dazzling that Sally's eyes hurt to watch. Presently, Grandma Ludbury looked up at the landing window. She smiled a dreamy, knowing smile: Thus life goes on, it seemed to say. Then she turned and went slowly down the slope by the side of the rose trellis. Down, down, down, went her shiny, pointed, button-strap shoes, and the silk of her skirt bounced softly with every step. At the holly bush there was one last shiny glint, then she was gone.

Sally climbed down from the chest, went to her room, and crawled beneath the eiderdown on her bed.

6

'*What* a pair of sleepy heads!'

Aunt Bunny was standing at the foot of the bed. 'Stratford does seem to have taken its toll! We had to undress you and put you to bed last night,' she went on, speaking to Sally.

Anne flung herself from the bed. 'Bailey's Field, Bailey's Field,' she muttered from time to time, getting dressed. Later, taking her place at the breakfast table, she asked her uncle anxiously: 'You didn't finish Bailey's Field yesterday?'

'No. Might today, though, if all goes well.'

When Sally arrived in the kitchen, Anne and Jim had gone. 'Just toast,' she mumbled, sliding along the bench.

'Just toast *please*,' corrected Henry.

George had finished eating. His fingertips were drumming a gallop on the table top. Sally ate her toast and watched him closely; Grandad was turning something over in his mind.

'Thought you and I might go for a spin, Megs,' he said eventually. 'There's a big sale at Greycot Manor today – we might pick up a bargain, you never know; and you always enjoyed a good sale. 'Spect they'll lay on a decent dinner at The Swan – it's bound to attract a crowd.'

'That'd be nice, Daddy,' Meg said, brightening.

Henry coughed discreetly against his knuckles. 'Might I be permitted to drive you in the Rover?'

'No. Me and Meg'll manage on our own. Be like

old times, eh Meg? Remember when we bid for the barometer? What a bargain we had! At Donnington Hall, weren't it? Go and put on a nice frock, and we'll be off.'

'But, Daddy,' Bunny, who had seemed in danger of choking on her bacon, now got out. 'I should enjoy that, too. If you'd *told* me . . . As it is, I could probably put out a cold dinner and do something about the men's teas if you can wait half an hour.'

'No. You stay here.'

The redness on Bunny's neck rose higher and suffused her face. 'Well, I don't think you *ought*. Not today. The egg man's coming, and I asked you to have a word with him. You said yourself he's diddling me . . .'

In the middle of her stricture, George had risen. Now he walked to the door, saying: 'Make haste then, Megs.'

'Well!' Bunny said, turning in appeal to her sister. But Meg brushed her napkin against her mouth, threw it down and hurried away.

'Well!' Bunny said again, seeing the unrolled napkin and the general disorder they had left. '*I* had better get on.'

Henry saw that the day would be trying. 'I'd make myself scarce if I were you,' he said out of the side of his mouth to Sally when Bunny had stamped into the scullery. 'Might a mere male lighten the load?' he called mellifluously, making, nevertheless, for the hall door.

'I shouldn't think so,' Bunny said in a clipped voice, returning to bang crocks on to a tray. She had no wish for a lightened load; let her load be never so heavy, let it wear her down so that when the gadabouts returned they would be ashamed.

Henry slipped away, murmuring: 'Do call if there's anything . . .' and was not seen again until dinner time.

When he had gone, Sally went along the hall passage

209

to the parlour. She closed the door, and selected *The Scarlet Pimpernel* from the bookcase, then curled up on the damp, rough settee and escaped gratefully to the horrors of revolutionary Paris.

Dinner – such as it was – was served without comment in the kitchen. The diners were left to wonder whether, in the absence of George and Meg, they failed to merit proper consideration in the dining-room, or whether Bunny was too overburdened to carry the boiled potatoes – the only hot item – beyond the kitchen.

Jim and Anne came to the table with tragic news. The combine harvester had broken down. Jim and Mick had a difficult afternoon ahead of them with hammer and oil, bolts and screws. There was one bright spot, however: Benjamin had decreed that the remainder of the workforce should wage war on the Willow Dasset rats.

'Ratting,' breathed Anne ecstatically. 'We've never had a go at that before. You will come, Sal? It sounds marvellous fun.'

'I don't know about ratting, but I should get some fresh air if I were you,' Henry urged his elder daughter. 'You look peaky. I myself will read in the garden this afternoon – unless Aunt Bunny has plans for me, of course,' he added hurriedly.

Bunny said nothing.

'A deck chair, I think. Like to join me, Sally?'

The garden. It might be interesting to lie about in the garden. Daddy would fall asleep, and if she kept quiet and still . . . 'Daddy, do you believe in ghosts?'

Henry cleared his throat and sat up straight – and Anne kicked her sister's shins under the table.

'I believe in the *Holy Ghost*,' Henry announced stoutly.

'I didn't mean that sort,' Sally said quickly, seeing her

mistake. 'It doesn't matter. It was just something I read in a book.'

'What book?' asked Henry, narrowing his eyes.

'A book at school. Ages ago. There was a ghost in the garden – I just remembered it.'

'Ratting might be a good idea,' Henry said.

But when the time came, Sally let Anne run ahead. Then she returned to collect *The Scarlet Pimpernel* from under a cushion in the parlour and set off for the Dutch barn. Soon, she had made herself comfortable on a pile of hay at the foot of some bales.

Later, she could not understand why she had chosen that place – the Dutch barn – any barn, come to that – and why, when the first shouts rang out, she had not taken alarm. As it was, she did not raise her head from her book until a pitchfork flew past her and came to land with a vicious thud near her feet. She regarded it with some surprise as it quivered but remained upright, then she peered forward to examine the prongs. A large white rat lay pinned to the straw-covered ground. Almost at once, Barry was beside her, hot and damp with triumph. 'Got the bugger,' he cried. He placed a boot over the rat and pulled free his fork. They watched the rat in silence for a while, he standing, she sitting on the ground. The rat rapped its string-like tail, jerked, thrashed, but could not rise. Its whiteness grew less immaculate as blood welled, then oozed from wounds made by the prongs. Suddenly there was other movement, and Barry rushed away. Out of her sight, she heard him kill another, then another, while she remained still and unmoved, her eyes on the quivering rat.

The shouting came closer and a dog rushed by.

''Ere they come. It'll be bedlam 'ere in a minute.' He came towards her curiously. 'Can't take yer eyes arf it,

211

can yer?' And he raised a foot and smashed it down into the rat's body.

She rose urgently.

He grinned and came close. She saw that he had grown, sensed that he had become strong.

Then the rickyard was full of men, dogs, darting rats, flying forks; shouts, barks, small shrieks. Anne pounded by, red-faced. 'We killed millions in the barn. You should've seen.'

Looking about her, Sally saw that each image – a small twitching body, a boot, the jutting rear of a thrusting terrier, a piece of straw, her own hand – was separate from every other image, and each was brilliantly lit, unnaturally defined. She wandered through the dream landscape – 'Mind out!' – 'Out of the way!' – and found herself, after a hollow hole of time, on the path leading into the farmyard. Carefully – to forestall vomiting – she walked over the cobbles to the house, over the clacking lino on the kitchen floor and up the dull thud, thud of the back stairs.

In the looking glass on her dressing table she examined herself. Ugly, ugly, she thought, staring at the bare face, the scraped-back hair, the pigtails on her shoulders. She jerked her head to make the tails jump and flick. They disgusted her. The longer she contemplated herself, the more keenly she understood that she was alone; no other reacted to *her* pain; hers was quite distinct, as each image had been distinct in the rickyard. Armed by her separateness, she made a stately descent of the front stairs, and took a pair of gardening scissors from the cabinet by the garden door. Then she returned to her room, not thinking, looking straight ahead. Standing before the looking glass, she began to slice through her hair.

*

Bunny discovered time on her hands. The egg man had departed, duly chastened. Jim had returned to the house to telephone Massey Ferguson for a part for the combine; there would be no more harvesting until it arrived, and harvest teas would not be required until further notice. The unexpected gap in her afternoon put Bunny at a loss. Then she recalled the mending and the scalding of milk pans, but decided to attend to these later with an audience. Now, she would take a bath while the house was quiet.

She went to her room to collect dressing gown and towel, then proceeded through the girls' bedroom towards the bathroom. With her hand on the bathroom doorknob, she paused, thought for a second, then retraced her last dozen steps. Presently the house, the yard, the garden, rang with her appalled screams.

Hair, Henry found, arriving out of breath, was everywhere. Two severed plaits lay on the lino beneath the dressing table, and furry clumps clung to the rug and the eiderdown. Henry felt ill. He wished he could think. He wished Bunny would be quiet. 'Where is she – any idea?'

Bunny shook her head violently. A terrible thought occurred to her and she gave a new shriek. 'What if she's wandering about . . . *shorn*? Daddy might come back at any moment. If he caught sight of her he'd have a heart attack. We must find her. At once.'

'Right. I'll go and look for her. You clear this up – if you don't mind,' he amended.

Bunny shuddered; she crossed her arms over her chest and hid her hands under her armpits – hands that wrung chickens' necks, plunged into gory innards, drowned new-born kittens in a bucket of water; hands that had now met their match. 'I couldn't. I'm sorry, Henry, I just . . . couldn't.'

'Understood. I'll get this up. You go and search for her. Brush and dustpan in the scullery?'

'Yes, and newspaper in the dairy.'

'Bring her up here if you find her.' But when Henry returned with a dustpan and brush, and bent low to clear up the mess, he caught sight of a sandal and ankle-sock beneath the bed. 'Come out. I said: *come out.*'

Her reluctance was understandable, for she was a shocking sight.

An awe-struck silence prevailed. Then: 'Whatever's your mother going to say? Whatever's your grandfather . . .' There was no end to the list of people whose future sayings alarmed Henry. Cover her up, he thought vaguely, and said: 'I think you'd better get into bed.'

He removed as much hair as he could from furniture and floor, and wrapped it in a newspaper parcel. Footsteps on the stairs made him anticipate further to-do – quite simply, he couldn't stand it.

'I'll head off Aunt Bunny. You change into your nightdress and get into bed. And for Heaven's sake, pull up the covers and stay put,' he implored, making for the door.

'It's all right, Bunny,' he called in a soothing tone. 'She's here. But she's getting into bed. No; we'll leave her,' he said, barring the way. 'She's not . . . up to much. Her mother'll deal with her.'

'Poor Daddy,' moaned Bunny, staggering back down the stairs. 'What a terrible, terrible shock. He was so fond of their hair. I can see him now, pulling their pigtails . . . Oh, Henry! It'll break his heart.'

'Quite so. Mmm. Dear, dear. I think we should perhaps keep it under our hat, so to speak, until Meg has had a chance to think about it.'

Bunny recalled that it was she, not Meg, who was

214

mistress of Willow Dasset. 'I will not allow this to undermine Daddy's health.'

'We must certainly seek to avoid that. So let us keep calm until we've had a chance to think.'

'Why did you do it?' Meg demanded, sitting heavily on the side of the bed, feeling her carefree day menaced by the lapping swell of evening.

'Don't know.' This was not altogether true. She had groped towards an explanation, had come up with something along the lines that, since she was no longer a nice little girl she had hastened towards grown-up nastiness, but lacked confidence in her ability to express it.

'Whatever happens,' Bunny declared from the foot of the bed, 'we can't let Daddy see her like this.'

'I think we'd better go home. Straight after breakfast tomorrow.'

'We could smuggle her into the car with a coat over her head.'

'But what'll we tell him?'

'That she's got something catching. And that it could give him shingles.'

'All right.'

'And you'll all have to stay away from Willow Dasset until it grows again.'

'Don't be foolish, Bun. It took years to grow those plaits. But I suppose, after six months or so, it won't look so bad.'

Their eyes were not on one another, but on the object of their discussion.

'That's settled, then. Better get the tea.'

One last bleak look, and aunt and mother departed.

Anne came in to stare at her. At first she was speechless, then she volunteered her opinion. 'I think you're hateful.

We've got to go home tomorrow 'cos of you. I hope you die.'

'Hop it!' said Henry to his younger daughter as he came in with a tray for Sally. 'She's supposed to be infectious.'

Some time later, Sally put aside the tray, got out of bed and went on to the landing. The murmur and chink of tea time drifted up the stairwell. She went to the head of the landing and began to climb on the chest beneath the window, but changed her mind. Softly, she opened the door to Grandad's room and walked to the foot of the great high bed.

'Hello, Grandma,' she said, taking hold of the rungs of the bedstead.

Grandma Ludbury, propped up on a pile of snowy pillows, smiled her dreamy smile.

'I think,' Sally said, 'that I want to be like you.' In her mind was Grandma Ludbury's cool detachment, her being so at one with her surroundings and high above the fray. And her clear, fine beauty – that was something to aspire to. 'If I could just try very hard to be like you, I think everything would be all right. And it wouldn't matter so much if it weren't.'

Grandma Ludbury appeared to agree. Her smile broadened, she raised a light hand to her breast and inclined her head.

'Oh, Grandma! I can't come back to Willow Dasset for ages.'

This was sad. Grandma Ludbury's hand slipped from her breast on to the eiderdown; she sighed and closed her eyes.

Quietly, so as not to disturb her, Sally crept from the room.

Part Three

DEPARTURES

1

The following winter, Meg and George suffered unrelated minor accidents. They did not suffer permanent harm, although neither emerged from their experience in quite their former condition.

Bicycling to school one frosty January morning, a patch of ice caused her wheels to slide and Meg to fall to the ground. The driver of a following car managed to avoid her, but was unable to prevent his car from mounting the rear wheel of her bicycle. He ran to her in great alarm. Meg, briefly stunned, revived to find herself being manhandled. 'I'm all right,' she insisted, shrugging him off, scrambling to her feet, falling again on the ice.

'It's Mrs Robinson,' the man exclaimed as others hurried to help. 'The headmistress of Corporation Street Elementary School. Let's get her into the car.'

'No need for that. No need at all,' Meg protested, but was put into the front seat, nevertheless, and tucked up in a blanket.

'Put her bike in the boot.'

'It's my glasses I'm worried about,' Meg called, blinking at the shadowiness of her surroundings. 'Can you find them?'

The spectacles were recovered, but a lens was found to have become dislodged from its frame.

'Shouldn't be a difficult job. Who's your optician?'

'Bates in the market place.'

'I'll take them round there. If they're ready, I'll get them

219

back to you by four o'clock. And I'll see what can be done about the bike. First, we'd better get you to a doctor.'

'Absolutely not. I'm a bit bruised, that's all. And none of this is your responsibility. I slipped on the ice. If you'd just drop me at a bus stop . . .'

'My dear Mrs Robinson, I wouldn't dream of it. If you're quite sure you don't require a doctor, I'll drive you to school.'

'Perfectly sure. Thanks. It's awfully kind of you.'

After a time, she began to reflect upon the fact that he appeared to know her. Perhaps he had seen her photograph in the local paper, or attended a meeting she had addressed. Then she recalled her famous blindness and wondered whether she ought to know him. 'Have we met?' she asked timidly, fearing to learn that she had been discourteous.

The man uttered a sound indicating the possibility. 'The Strategy for the Eleven-Plus meetings? I was in the chair.'

'Good heavens! Councillor Fairbrother! I do beg your pardon. I can't see a thing without my glasses.'

'And we met once on a train.' This seemed to cause him private amusement.

'On a train?'

'You were somewhat preoccupied. When you got out at Sheffield you left your case behind. I called out and handed it to you, if you recall.'

Memory stirred. 'Was that you? Good Lord! The truth is, I was on my way to see my mother, who was dying, who did in fact die . . .'

'I'm so sorry . . .'

'Quite all right. Oh, here we are! Now, you mustn't bother about my glasses . . .'

'No trouble. I'll call back when I've made progress.'

Members of staff, discovering her lack of spectacles and a large hole in her stocking, and learning that she was without a bicycle for the time being, were amazed by her blithe unconcern.

'Anyone going home for dinner?' Meg asked, surveying the staffroom, and her eyes came to rest upon lively, young Miss Knight. 'How about you, Miss Knight? Could you go to a shop and buy me a pair of stockings? A pair similar to your own would do very well. Hang on, I'll get my purse.'

'But I could pop out for you during the morning,' objected Mrs Mack from the sink where she was scrubbing out yesterday's unwashed tea cups.

'You've got enough to do, Mrs Mack,' Meg said firmly, thinking of the thick, sagging lisle covering the caretaker's legs.

When she had gone, Mrs Mack shook her head. 'I'n't she a marvel? Nothing stops her. A shock like that'd leave most folk right upset.'

'A marvel,' agreed Meg's loyal staff.

On and off during her busy day, Meg found her thoughts turning to Mr Fairbrother. She recalled that he was a fruiterer; Fairbrothers was a prominent name in local retailing. And since he was a member of the Education Committee on the County Council, their paths had crossed many times. How annoying that she had taken so little notice of him, that she had only the vaguest memories to feed her curiosity!

It was not until the school was virtually deserted that Mr Fairbrother returned. 'Put the kettle on, Mrs Mack,' Meg shouted into the corridor when his car drew up outside.

He was exactly the same height as herself, she noted – and then gave him an extra inch to allow for her heels being higher than his. And he had a nice face – frank, friendly, a twinkle in his eyes. Mr Fairbrother, whose presence hitherto had merited no more than cursory acknowledgement, now became subject to the single-minded concentration Meg applied to all matters occupying her mind. For the moment he replaced the fourth years' reading list, the fierce letter she must compose about the boys' lavatories, and what she proposed to say to the music adviser tomorrow when he called to promote his airy-fairy ideas. She decided she rather liked Mr Fairbrother.

'I'm sorry,' Mrs Mack hissed in a stage whisper as she entered with two cups of tea on a tray, 'but I shall 'ave to go. It's Mr Mack's Legion night, and I 'ave to get us teas early.'

'Of course, Mrs Mack. I'll lock up.' Taking the tray, she thought how cheerless her little room seemed with the single bar electric fire and the hard seats on either side of the desk. 'Shall we take our tea into the staffroom? There are some easy chairs in there, and I expect the fire'll revive with a bit of a poke.'

'Good idea,' he said, and followed her.

'I'm so glad to have my glasses back, I can't tell you . . .' She poked the fire and created a small blaze.

They sat in chairs drawn close to the hearth, sipped their tea and watched one another. She decided to draw him out with questions about the fruiterers' business. It emerged that he made regular visits to Covent Garden, which prompted her to think of the flower market. 'I go to London myself now and then,' she said, 'every other month to attend meetings of the Church's Advisory Service for Schools. One of these days I must get up early and go to Covent Garden; I should love to see the flowers.'

He took this up at once. 'Perhaps, if our visits there should coincide, I might show you round.'

'I say, that'd be nice,' she said brightly, picturing herself on his arm amid a hundred different blooms.

He smiled at her enthusiasm.

Their eyes met. Her face fell, for it came to her with a thump that she did not merely like Mr Fairbrother – oh no, her feelings for him went a great deal further than that. Flustered, she drank rapidly, and replaced the cup noisily on the saucer.

'Is something the matter?'

'No, no . . .'

'You seemed suddenly . . . Perhaps you feel stiff from your accident. I say, what an awful bruise!'

Smartly, she crossed her legs so that an unblemished leg covered the bruised one. 'It'll soon fade.'

'It would be a tragedy if it didn't.'

His eyes were on her silk-stockinged legs. In his voice she detected admiration. He feels the same! she told herself exultingly, and her heart began knocking.

'I wonder . . .'

'Yes?'

'These occasions in London. Do you have a very busy schedule?'

'Why?' Meg asked hoarsely, with her customary directness.

'Because I would enjoy taking you to dinner – if your evenings are ever free.'

'I am free in the evenings, as a matter of fact. We finish business in time for Evensong, then we're done until the following morning. The men – mostly clergy – go to their beastly clubs. I used to dine with Miss Butts . . .' Her voice trailed away and she frowned at the memory, for Miss Butts was the sort of woman – masculine, nearly

223

as broad as she was long, hair severely shaved into the nape of her neck, a smouldering cigarette jammed into a corner of her hairy mouth – with whom Meg hated to be associated. Dining with her made Meg feel degraded in the eyes of other diners. And in the morning it amused their male colleagues to pretend they had imagined the two women spending a riotous evening. Whenever she could, Meg preferred to dine at her old college; and in the morning, when her male colleagues asked with patronizing grins: 'And what did you two get up to last night?' it was very satisfying to be able to answer: 'I don't know about Miss Butts – or about you men in your fusty old clubs – but *I* had a very good dinner in Chelsea.' *That* had wiped the grins from their faces. *That* had shut them up and earned their silent respect.

'Usually, I either eat alone, or dine at Saint Ursula's, my old college,' Meg went on to explain.

'Then perhaps you would do me the honour?'

'Oh, yes.'

'It remains, then, to discover whether we are ever to be in London at the same time.'

She got to her feet unsteadily. 'I'll go and fetch my diary.'

In her study, she took issue with herself. Not on the grounds of right and wrong, for Meg had always known that she, blessed with Common Sense and a specially intimate relationship with the Almighty (in which it was as appropriate for her to advise Him as for Him to influence her), might sin with impunity where others, those who for safety's sake must be confined to the straight and narrow, might not. It was propriety that concerned her. She was a well-known headmistress, she reminded herself, a member of the Diocesan Board, not to mention the Church's

Advisory Service for Schools: she had a reputation to safeguard.

But so, insisted an eager voice in her head, had he. He was an important man of the town; he could not afford to be indiscreet. Futhermore, a Mrs Fairbrother probably inhabited the background; a wife would put him on the same footing as herself. And let her not get things out of proportion – he proposed dinner, not an orgy. This last consideration was disappointing, and even as she returned to him, stiffened with the resolve to be prudent, the promise afforded by a hotel bedroom flickered at the back of her mind.

'I expect Mrs Fairbrother likes to take the opportunity to visit the London shops,' she remarked blushing at her obviousness.

'I'm afraid not. Mrs Fairbrother is very much a home-body. My wife likes to preserve herself from all forms of excitement – the least disturbance brings on her migraine.'

'What a shame,' Meg said insincerely.

'And Mr Robinson? Does he ever accompany you to London?'

'Certainly not. My business in London is nothing to do with him.'

Having settled that, they consulted their diaries.

'The next conference is on the fourth of February,' Meg reported.

'Well, well! That fits in with Covent Garden, exactly. Shall we say dinner on the fourth, and an early morning excursion to the market on the fifth?'

Meg agreed. They made a note of the arrangement, and Meg felt her legs go weak. 'I must lock up now, then go for a bus.'

'But I shall run you home, of course. And tomorrow I hope to deliver your repaired bicycle.'

225

Accepting his kindness calmly, she walked on shaky legs to lock up the various doors. He took her bulging, work-crammed bag and placed it in the boot of his car. Then – lingeringly – he handed her into the front seat. The touch of his hand at her waist and elbow burned on when he relinquished her. She imagined touching him, and clasped her hands and stretched her long legs in luxurious anticipation. It was the rush hour, but his sidelong looks at her and his courtesies made her feel that nothing could mar his pleasure in driving her home. How different this was to Henry at the wheel, who would be grumbling, drumming impatient fingers and blaming her lateness for getting them caught up in the traffic. Then, because she was capable of realism, she acknowledged the probability of Mr Fairbrother – Charles – behaving with a similar lack of solicitousness to *his* wife. For that was the way of the world, she reflected comfortably. Bad luck, Mrs Fairbrother!

Towards the end of February, George had a hunting accident. He had prepared to jump a hedge, was sailing over it, when a wide, steep-banked ditch loomed deceitfully on the far side. The horse was wrong-footed. 'It weren't the horse, it were me; I put him wrong,' George told ambulance men, nurses, doctors, visitors, anyone who would listen, during the following shocked hours of pain. During their struggle to right themselves, the horse had trod off a sizeable portion of his master's left ear. The bleeding was staunched, the ear stitched and a transfusion given; but George was a terrible patient, and after three days in hospital it was agreed that his recovery should continue at home.

When the news reached her, Meg, who was feeling relaxed and optimistic about life these days, saw no reason why she should not take a Friday off school and spend a weekend cheering up her father at Willow Dasset.

'Megs! What a sight for sore eyes!' George cried when Meg arrived at his bedside.

'That's more than I can say for you! You look like something out of one of those wartime photographs with your head bandaged up like that.'

'It's nothing much,' George said gruffly. 'But you should have heard the fuss. Bunny's the worst. She treats me like a baby. No, it's the horse that bothers me. He should have been ridden regular after a tumble like that, instead of which he's been shut up in his stable ever since. Do you remember Fred Emberton – fellow who used to break horses for me? He came to see me the other day, promised to exercise Red for me tomorrow – it is Saturday tomorrow? Well, keep an eye out for him, will yer? I'm frightened Bunny'll put him off. Tell him I'd like a word afterwards. I want to hear how he gets on.'

''Course I will, Daddy. Stop worrying.'

Later that evening, Harry arrived. Jim had remained at Willow Dasset after bringing Meg there from the station. Harry, Jim and Bunny seated themselves with some solemnity at the dining table.

'What's this? Family confab?' Meg asked, joining them.

'We thought we should discuss Daddy,' Bunny announced.

'His horse,' Harry corrected her.

'Is something wrong with the horse? Daddy never said.'

'We think it should be got rid of,' Bunny said primly.

'Why?'

Harry raised a warning hand and turned to address Meg. 'It's quite plain the brute's got too much for him.

He should stick to the mare – if he's fit enough to ride again after this accident. But no more hunting – he's not up to it anymore. Next time he could break his neck.'

'Well!' Meg looked from one to the other. Bunny, pale, eager, seemed almost to smile in anticipation of extending her control over Daddy. Harry, always calculating what would come to him, always looking for advantage, studied his finger nails with shifty eyes. But Jim . . . 'I'm surprised at *you*,' she told Jim. 'I thought you'd be the last one to interfere. Live and let live – that's what you always preach.'

Jim smiled his philosophical smile, and the hearts of those watching, sank. 'It depends what you mean by live and let live,' he began, reaching into his pocket for his pipe. 'I'm all for the Guv'nor doin' what suits him, as long as it doesn't upset anyone else. But look at the worry and work this has caused Bunny.' He paused to stuff tobacco into the pipe's bowl. There were two further, more pertinent considerations at the back of his mind: firstly, depriving George of his hunter would herald the downfall of a father who had always undervalued him; secondly, if George were indeed to break his neck, he, Jim, would be saddled with Bunny, and the vision of his sister upsetting his easy-going life was sufficiently alarming to make the preservation of his father's life an urgent priority.

'Mmm,' Meg said, rightly unconvinced by what she had heard. 'If you want my opinion, you've all got a darned cheek. As for Daddy breaking his neck – he knows the risks, he's not an imbecile, so it's up to him. I'll tell you this: without a horse he'd be nothing – he'd just lose heart.'

Bunny and Harry exchanged a glance. 'We may as well tell you,' Harry said, 'that we've decided to talk it over with the doctor. We want him to know how worried we are . . .'

'Count me out!'

'He may be able to tell us how to go about it. I expect he's used to dealing with awkward old people . . .'

Meg got to her feet. 'I'm not going to sit here discussing Daddy like this. I think it's outrageous. I'm going upstairs to sit with him.'

But her father was sleeping, she discovered. Not wishing to face the others until her temper had cooled, she went into her bedroom to read.

When Fred Emberton arrived the next day, Meg swept past a suspicious Bunny and waylaid him in the yard. She secured his promise to report on the horse's condition, then went to reassure her father.

George was out of bed and standing by the bedroom window.

'Good girl. I saw you go after him.'

'Ought you to be out of bed?'

'I'm waiting for Red to come out. I want to see the old fellow. I want to watch him go off.'

'Put this on, then,' she said, holding out a dressing gown. 'Look,' – she pulled a basket chair to the window – 'sit in this. When they come out you can stand up for a better view.'

Watching the yard, she could feel his eagerness. 'Right, here he comes,' she said presently.

George rose. He studied his horse in silence.

Nothing will escape him, thought Meg. He will take in every detail, and afterwards he will know precisely what state his horse is in. For her father had the keenest eye in the business; there was no-one to touch him when it came to judging a horse. She stole a glance at him, and saw that dressing gown and bandages could not diminish his stature. How *dare* they belittle him, she fumed, thinking of her sister and brothers. How *dare* they try to close a chapter of his life without so much as a by-your-leave. Then, suddenly, she understood that Henry had attempted to do exactly that to *her*. 'That,' he had implied (meaning sex), 'is over, done with, finished.' He had assumed the power to cut her down. No wonder she had gone wild! And it could not be supposed that her present peace resulted from anything so fleeting as her trips to bed with Charles Fairbrother – delightful though these had been. No, no. It was proving Henry wrong, gathering her life into her own hands, *going on*, that had earned her peace of mind.

Horse and rider disappeared from view. George relaxed, turned towards the bed, then changed his mind. 'I'll sit in the chair for a bit. Why, what's the matter, Meg? Seen a ghost?'

She sat on the bed, smiled, shook her head. We are alike, he and I, she told herself. We allow nothing, no-one to thwart us. Our strength makes others resent us and try to pull us down. But we fight back; we'll die fighting back. 'I'm going to tell you something,' she said.

As he listened, his eyes grew cold. For a while he was silent. Then: 'I suppose they think I've got one foot in the grave,' he suggested with an embarrassed sneer.

'It's beastly when people behave like that,' she said, sympathetically.

'I shall put 'em right – don't you fret.'

'Good. It'd make my blood boil if anyone tried such a trick on me.'

His face softened. 'You're a good girl, Megs. Always have been. Remember when you were a little 'un, mindin' the horse on the delivery cart while I was in the kitchen of some great house coaxin' an order out of the cook?'

'I remember, Daddy.'

'What was it your Mama used to say? You and Meg — what a pair! She was right. We are a pair. We won't be bested.'

'Just what I was thinking, Daddy.' She rose and went to kiss him. 'I'll go down now, to make sure Mr Emberton gets a welcome when he calls. I'll bring him straight up to you.'

He caught her hand and laid his cheek against it.

She was smiling to herself when she walked to the door.

The bed was strewn with articles of clothing.

'Whatever's going on?' Meg asked, coming into the room.

George, sitting on the bed in his pyjamas, shook his head. 'Thought I'd get dressed, but now I've found me clothes, I don't know whether I've the strength to put 'em on.'

'I'm not surprised. Let's put them away, quick, before Bunny comes in and has a fit.' She bustled between bed, wardrobe and chest-of-drawers.

'I'm going downstairs,' George warned her. 'I'm not going to deal with 'em lyin' in bed.'

'All right; I'll give you a hand when you're ready. But I can't see that a dressing gown's going to alter things. You're more than a match for them, anyway.'

'You're right,' he acknowledged, allowing her to help him into the woolly gown. 'You're off this morning, I take it?'

'Jim's going to run me to the station in half an hour.'

George sat down. 'When will I see you again? Easter?'

'July, more likely. That reminds me . . .' She sat beside him on the bed. 'Look Daddy; there's something I've been meaning to say. The girls are growing up. Sally is almost a young woman. I know how you love their long hair, but Sally's too old for pigtails, now. If she'd kept them any longer she'd have been teased at school. So she's had her hair cut short – not too short – she wears it in an Alice band, rather like the Princesses had their hair at her age – do you remember?'

He nodded, watching her closely.

'You'll tell her how nice she looks, won't you, Daddy? Girls need reassurance when they're growing up.'

'So you and Sal are gettin' along better, now?'

'Of course! That business in the summer was nothing to do with Sally – not really. I told you how worked up I was feeling,' she reminded him. 'Well, I'm over that now.'

His eyes were anxious. If only I could tell him that I was in the same boat then, as he is in now, she thought, wondering if she could explain the situation without mentioning sex. The memory of his bewildered loyalty last summer brought a lump to her throat. But she contented herself by taking his hand and repeating: 'Yes, I'm completely over that. I just thought I'd mention Sally's hair so that you won't be shocked. Now,' – she rose – 'want an arm?'

'So little Sal's nearly grown up,' he said, thinking it over as they walked slowly, arm in arm, along the landing.

Bunny heard them on the stairs. 'What are you thinking of?' she shouted angrily. 'Meg! Take Daddy back at once.'

Ignoring her, they continued on their way.

Bunny followed them into the dining-room. 'I shall telephone for the doctor. We'll see what he's got to say.'

'While you're at it, telephone your younger brother. Tell him, if he knows what's good for him, he'll get over here sharpish.'

'Dora won't let him come till after dinner,' Meg said softly, when Bunny had gone. 'Do you want me to catch a later train?' she offered, holding her breath.

'There's no need for that.'

She sighed softly with relief.

On the way to the station in Jim's battered car, Meg reflected that Charles Fairbrother would, at this very moment, be setting out to drive to Sheffield, where they had arranged to meet.

'Got to change at Sheffield?' Jim asked, thereby throwing her into confusion.

'Oh . . . yes . . . believe so.'

Her vagueness prompted him to study the timetable while she fumbled for her ticket.

'I say, you'll have two hours to wait in Sheffield if you catch this one. Why don't you go this afternoon on the three ten? Then you'll only have to wait fifteen minutes.'

Meg wished he would mind his own business. She wished, too, that he would go. 'I'm here now, so I'll catch it. Look, no need to hang about. Daddy wants a word with you.'

'Does Henry know what time to pick you up? I could give him a ring.'

'Don't you dare! He's always busy on a Sunday, and tonight there's a magic lantern show after Evensong. I told him I'd get the bus – to expect me when he sees me. You're not to bother him – do you hear?'

'All right. Shan't.' He pecked her cheek. 'Cheerio, then.'

'Cheerio, Jim.'

She watched him go, then took up her bag and went towards the barrier.

2

Sally walked cautiously across the yard. Ahead of her, Anne leapt into Grandad's arms, was swung up, enthused over. She waited until Anne shot indoors. Then she placed her hands on his forearms and stood on tiptoe to press her lips into his whiskery cheek. 'Hello, Grandad.'

'Hello, Sal,' he said shyly. 'Well, let's have a look at you. My, what a smart young lady!'

She smiled, stepped past him and went into the kitchen.

Anne was talking nineteen to the dozen to Aunt Bunny. A small frown grew between Aunt Bunny's eyes as Sally drew near.

'Hello, Aunt Bunny.'

'Hello, Sally,' Aunt Bunny said reprovingly, jutting a chin towards a niece's dutiful peck.

Sally continued through the house.

At the garden door she paused and stared through the glass panes. The view is better from the landing window, she told herself, and went upstairs. Kneeling on the chest beneath the window, her eyes searched the garden paths and lingered over the rosemary and holly bushes. Then voices rang out below – 'Terrible journey; lorries nose to tail between Newark and Leicester' – 'Usual rooms, I suppose, Bun? Anne, do help your father!' She decided it would be prudent to go and assist with the unloading. 'Later,' she whispered, allowing for the possibility of being overheard, and returned downstairs to the living.

234

'Did you see it?' Anne asked as they pulled belongings from the car boot.

'See what?'

'Grandad's ear. It's really sickening,' she reported with relish.

'Oh, no. I forgot to look.'

At dinner, seated at her grandfather's left hand, Sally found ample opportunity to appraise the ear. She discovered that it could be viewed in two ways. Examined closely, to the exclusion of other considerations, it was an ugly object, jutting inwards where it ought to curve out, lumpen, corrugated, angry-red at its depleted extremity. But viewed as part of a whole, its significance shrank; indeed, on sitting to table she had found it necessary to seek the blemish out, so unlikely did a blemish seem. The ear, however horrible as an ear, was of no real consequence to the dear, fine-featured whole.

'Nasty looking thing, ain't it?' Grandad Ludbury asked slyly.

She blushed and stammered, and on the other side of the table Anne flushed in sympathy and avoided her sister's eyes.

Towards the end of the meal the sound of a tractor reached the dining-room. Anne hastily cleared her pudding plate. 'Please may we go?'

Aunt Bunny consented, and Anne fled.

'Not going with her?' Meg asked her elder daughter.

'No, I don't think I'll bother,' Sally said carelessly, then wondered whether she imagined their faint stirring of relief; certainly, they had waited intently for her reply and now resumed their animated conversation.

She did not leave the house until early evening. Then she slipped out alone and sped over the cobbles by the side of the barn, turned to race up the steep slope by the tractor sheds and into the paddock. Here the unmown grasses were long, their seed heads dwarfed thousands of intermingling buttercup and clover flowers. A strong breeze sent waves of silver and mauve scudding through, as the grasses bowed and rose.

The hedgerow along the track to Bailey's Field was dense and wild. Bramble flowers and dog roses bloomed here and there, paper-frail in the tough, thorny tangle. Lower down, clumps of cow parsley and scabious clouded the thicket, and long stems of convolvulus trailed trumpets over the bank. Near to the gateway a patch of poppies blazed; there were poppies, too, in the yellowing wheat, she observed, climbing over the gate: Grandad would be cross about that.

Dew was rising by the time she entered the garden. Birds called and bees hummed with a last-fling-of-the-day urgency. The glossy shrubbery, the path beside the rose-trellis, the flower-backed lawn, were all deserted. As she stepped on to the main path bordered by small alpine plants, headed by staddle stones, leading to the garden door, she raised her eyes. There, at her bedroom window, Grandma Ludbury stood perfectly still, watching her garden. The white light of her hair shone behind the wavy glass. Satisfied, Sally walked slowly towards the house and went indoors.

'She embarrasses her uncles,' Aunt Bunny shouted insistently.

'Hush!' her mother admonished. 'You do say some ridiculous things, Bunny.'

In the kitchen, Sally came to a halt.

Behind the closed scullery door, Aunt Bunny's voice rose higher, but Sally could no longer take it in; her heart's beating deafened her. She crept silently to the back stairs and squatted on a stair half-way up, to think.

It was Sunday afternoon. They had been a large party at dinner, for Uncles Jim and Harry, and Harry's wife, Dora, were spending the day at Willow Dasset. After dinner, Aunt Dora, who was heavily pregnant, had gone upstairs to lie down on Aunt Bunny's bed. Anne had disappeared, Henry had excused himself, and Grandad had fallen asleep in his tall, fireside chair. Her uncles had remained at the table to continue an argument. Sally had stayed there, too, hearing conflicting points of view she had never considered before. By the time her mother and Aunt Bunny had finished the washing up and returned to the dining-room, Uncle Jim and Uncle Harry were hot.

'Now come on, you two. You know you'll never agree,' her mother said lightly.

But there was no stopping them. Their disagreement centred on the future of agriculture. Sally had never imagined that farming might be done differently; often, she had listened to Uncle Jim praising the beauty of crop rotation and working with, rather than against Nature; she had assumed that these truths must stand for ever. But Uncle Harry proposed confining animals in close quarters, and using fertilizers to make it unnecessary for a field to lie fallow every four years; cheap food for the masses, and farming run as a business to maximize return, were the twin planks of his case. Uncle Jim prophesied that Nature, thus abused, would wreak a terrible revenge. Sally was enthralled. From time to time she questioned the protagonists, and each became determined to win this representative of the new generation to his side.

Aunt Bunny lost her temper and pressed her fists on the table. 'Will you boys *stop*? I'm sure Daddy isn't enjoying this. Now stop this minute, do you hear?'

Uncle Jim got up, felt for his pipe and strolled from the room. Harry went to the window, observed aloud, but apparently to himself, that those who turned their backs on progress never prospered, and that, in any case, Jim had always been a fool; then he suggested to his father that they go to the milking shed to inspect the working of the new machinery.

Now, alone on the back stairs with her head in her hands, Sally went over every word, searching for clues to explain what Aunt Bunny had meant. So engrossed was she that her mother's sudden opening of the staircase door took her by surprise.

'Why are you sitting there?'

Sally, for the moment, could not answer.

'Is something wrong? What is it?'

'I heard Aunt Bunny say that I embarrass my uncles,' she blurted.

'Oh – Good Lord! She didn't like it because they noticed you. I should forget it, if I were you. It's just her way. You should hear what she says about me, or about your father, even.'

'But she must have meant *something*. It sounded . . . horrid.'

'She doesn't know what she means half the time. She just feels jealous or spiteful and says the first thing that comes into her head. And it's always rubbish – take it from me.'

The door to the boxroom opened and Jim came to the head of the stairs.

'Hello,' Meg called. 'I was just coming up for a chat.'

Sally scrambled to the bottom of the stairs and fled through the kitchen.

'Something the matter with Sal?'

'Oh – Bunny. Bunny's always had a down on Sally, and

now Sally's growing up she's worse than ever. It makes life rather difficult.'

'Why not let her go back with me? She can stay at Horley-in-the-Hedges for a few days – as long as she likes – there's always plenty to do.'

'Won't Mrs Flower mind?'

'Not her. She takes things as they come. I dare say she'd enjoy a bit of female company.'

'Well – thanks, Jim. That'd solve a ticklish problem.'

Her departure was a triumph. Afterwards she recalled every detail. She had gone upstairs to pack, and to change into her best princess line jacket and skirt. The case, though crammed with old clothes and novels, nevertheless looked pretty dashing, she considered, studying herself in the tilted-down looking glass. Then she had gone down to the kitchen where people were standing about, and a bored Aunt Dora sat painting her nails blood red at the kitchen table. 'I say, you do look nice,' Aunt Dora had remarked with lazy surprise. 'That costume shows off your nice little figure a treat. Can't wait to get my waistline back.'

Aunt Bunny had turned purple with wrath.

They had all trooped out into the yard to watch them go. Uncle Jim took her case and tossed it into the back of the Land Rover. Then she climbed in, and he, with a friendly wink, climbed in on the other side. As they started up the hill she waved her hand out of the window and continued to wave until she knew the bend had cut them off from view.

Life went on differently at Horley-in-the-Hedges. Glebe Farm was a village farm, the house right on the village street. And unlike her grandfather, Uncle Jim worked on his farm and employed only two farmhands – John Flower, husband of Mrs Flower the housekeeper, and a lad, Colin. Mr and Mrs Flower and Colin lived in the farmhouse. Unless visitors requiring some ceremony were expected, life was conducted informally in the commodious kitchen.

Sally found plenty to do. Her farming activities were no longer largely play; she was given tasks to perform according to her capabilities. Particularly, she was useful to Jim with the dairy herd, for generally Jim had no assistance with the cows. After a few mornings when Sally had shown herself reliably ready to accompany him to the fields, Jim judged that she might collect the cows on her own and he lie in bed for an extra twenty minutes. Early morning and mid afternoon, this became her task. At other times her ability to drive a tractor was appreciated. When there was nothing for her to do on the farm, Mrs Flower was always grateful for a gossip and an extra pair of hands to shell peas or collect necessities from the village shop. Villagers called constantly at Glebe Farm, and Sally and Mrs Flower visited most of the houses and cottages. Young people abounded; besides Colin, there were Mrs Flower's nieces and the teenage sons of Uncle Jim's friend. Life was rich, and Sally found herself in no hurry to return to Willow Dasset.

Sometimes, she and Uncle Jim sat on in the kitchen with cups of cocoa after the others had gone up to bed. It was then that she heard new sides to old stories.

'When I've been here to tea, with Mummy and Daddy and Aunt Bunny and Grandad, it was never like this, never so friendly,' she reflected on one of these occasions. 'We always ate in the dining-room and Mrs Flower served us.'

'Yes, well, it doesn't do to upset people.'

'I suppose it would upset them to eat with everyone else in the kitchen.'

'It suits me. But it wouldn't suit everyone – your Aunt Bunny, for instance.'

'Nor Grandad.'

This was agreed silently between them. After a while Sally said: 'I think it's very snobbish of them, though.'

'I dare say. But people have to live according to their lights.'

'You change *your* lights whenever the rest of the family come.'

Jim, having finished his cocoa, decided to allow himself one last pipe. 'You see,' – he paused to puff – 'I take a tip from your grandmother. She found she was out of step with the rest of the family. As far as they were concerned they already knew all there was to know. Now, this was hard on her because she liked to keep an open mind. When there were great events – such as the two World Wars, or when people such as poor old Aunt Pip told her about their terrible experiences, or when she read an interesting book – and your grandmother was a great reader – she was prepared to look at things in a new light. This wouldn't have done for the rest of them, of course; they'd have been most offended. So she learned to keep her thoughts to herself. She'd talk to me because she knew I'd stay cool: but apart from me and Pip I don't think she ever really talked to anyone in her later years. Pip told me an interesting thing soon after your grandmother died. Did you know your Great-Aunt Pip won the Royal Red Cross medal in the First World War? Well, the family was pleased as Punch to think she was a heroine, but the only person who wanted to know what it actually meant to be a nurse at the front, was your grandmother.'

The pipe had gone out. He poked at it with a match-stick, then applied a flame. 'Of course,' he went on between puffs, 'things change. It'll be different for you. You'll get away, make a life to suit yourself . . .'

'You could have,' Sally pointed out.

He grinned. 'Well, I'm a lazy sort of chap. I tend to take the easy way. I thought about going to Canada once . . .'

'Poor Grandma,' Sally said after a thoughtful pause. 'She must have been lonely. I say, Uncle, do you believe in ghosts?'

'Ghosts? Let me think, now. Ah, yes: I'll tell you a story about a ghost.'

Hardly daring to breathe, Sally hunched nearer to him.

'It was when we were living at Priors Grendon – all of us except your mother who was away at college. One winter's night I was walking home after a dance in the village. As I went up the lane I heard footsteps behind me. I stopped. Whoever it was stopped too. So I looked behind – there was a full moon – but the lane was empty; there was nobody there but me. I went on again. So did the footsteps. Suddenly my blood ran cold, and I ran until I could dart in against the side of a barn. The footsteps came up the lane. They went by. But whoever was making them was totally invisible, for I watched as the footsteps passed and there was no-one to be seen. Then I thought, I'm not having this, and I jumped out to chase after the sound. Know what I found?'

She bit her knuckles and shook her head.

'A leaf. A single leaf blown up the lane by the wind. Straight as anything it went, turning over and over: Tap, tap, tap.'

'Oh!' she gasped, trying to hide her disappointment, deciding after all, to abandon the subject of ghosts.

Uncle Jim thought it would be a good idea if she spent the final days of the holiday at Willow Dasset. It would be a pity to hurt people's feelings, and an even greater pity to make it difficult for her to stay again at Horley-in-the-Hedges. Sally agreed fervently with this second consideration; all the same, she bit her lip and looked doubtful.

'You've always loved Willow Dasset,' he encouraged.

'It's not Willow Dasset – it's *people*.'

'What about 'em?'

'I don't think they like me now; not as I am.'

They were walking back to the house after evening milking. Jim decided on a diversion and went to lean against a paddock gate. Sally trudged after him.

'You see,' he said, after much thought, 'it's like what you said about me changing my ways whenever they visit me from Willow Dasset. Sometimes it's best to be tactful . . . discreet. Your grandfather's an old man. In his day, young ladies like you didn't go charging about the fields with the men.'

'Mummy used to – she told me. When she got back from school she had to go straight out and help Grandad.'

'Help her *father*. Like you help me. And it's different here. Here we all mix together, free and easy. You've seen what your grandfather's like with his men? It's not like me with John and Colin, is it?'

She shook her head.

'You can't expect an old man to change his idea of how things should be.'

'I know. But it's Aunt Bunny, too. She says things about me . . .'

'I expect your growing up has made her feel she's not a young woman anymore.'

'Hardly my fault.'

'No. But if you understand, you can be sensible about it.'

'I 'spose I can.'

He put out a hand and squeezed her shoulder. 'Of course you can. Things usually sort out when you think 'em over.'

Harvest, she discovered, was in full swing at Willow Dasset. Mick was now in charge of the combine harvester (Uncle Jim had declined to have any more to do with it, and intended to rely on the good old binder to accomplish his own harvest.) Sally sometimes watched from the edge of the field, but took herself off whenever she was noticed. Mostly, she read – lying on her stomach on the lawn or on the settee in the musty parlour.

On the final afternoon she became restless. She roamed the house, eventually stole into her grandfather's bedroom. The white counterpane lay smooth and flat over the high bed. The garden, too, was empty, and though she gazed out of the window until she grew giddy, no-one stepped out from behind the rosemary bush. Almost despairing, she went downstairs. As she passed the garden door, a flash of mauve caught her eye. She looked quickly. Grandma Ludbury in her shiny dress was kneeling on the path beside the harebells. Sally let out a long sigh. Minutes passed. Then Aunt Bunny came from the hall with a brisk, cross step, on her way to her room to change for tea.

3

The front door slammed.

Sally, sitting on the floor in her underclothes, paused in her reading and was, for a second, disorientated. She was in two places at once: a church tower where, Miss Dorothy L Sayers led her to believe, a murder was about to occur; and the squalid bedroom of a fifteen-year-old – a towel lying damply in the open doorway, the bed unmade, clothes, books, pieces of paper everywhere, even the curtains not fully drawn.

'Anyone at home?' her mother enquired loudly from the bottom of the stairs.

Reality, like the clap of doom, engulfed her. Downstairs, the washing-up remained undone: in another moment this fact would be discovered. She, Sally, was to have completed the chore before going off to spend the morning with her friend, Valerie Burnet. Unluckily, while crawling over the floor in search of a sock, a book under a chair had drawn attention to itself, with the usual consequences. She now noticed how stiff and cold she had become; she had been reading for two or three hours. Apart from Sally, the house had been empty all morning. Although it was the Christmas holiday, Anne had returned to school for a netball practice; her father was at work in the town hall; and her mother had been at Saint Luke's, showing The Young Wives how to make The Three Kings out of old stockings and party frocks to augment The Crib for Epiphany.

Her mother's next utterance surprised her. It made no mention of the washing-up, nor was it couched in angry terms. 'Hello, it's me,' her mother said – it must be presumed – into the telephone, and her tone was light, intimate, as if conferring a treat. 'All right?' she went on to enquire. 'Good-oh!' There was a pause, then a laugh – and it was not a motherly laugh.

Sally slithered in her socks over the lino to the gaping door, anxious to miss not a word.

'It doesn't matter. I know what she's like. Don't worry about it, Charles. Thursday? I should think so. I can't think of an excuse off-hand, but I'll come up with something. What? Well, we rather like The White Lion, don't we?' (Again, that startling peal of laughter.) 'No, I'll get the train – it's safest. You meet me there. Same time, I suppose? Fine.' There was a pause; then an emphatic: 'Me, too! Like anything! Yes. Bye for now. Byee.'

It was astounding, amazing; it left Sally floundering for the sense of it. Meanwhile, from the scullery, there came a sound of roughly handled crockery. She put her foot on the towel, scooted it out of the doorway, closed the door carefully without a sound, and began to hunt for her clothes.

'By the way, I have arranged to spend Thursday with Kitty Shepherd,' Meg announced during tea. 'We're going to spend the day looking at reading schemes. Kitty will drive me to Browne's.'

'It's the first I've heard of it,' said Henry.

'That's because I've only just made the arrangement. I'm telling you now so that you can arrange to eat in town on Thursday. I'll leave something for the girls. And don't wait tea for me – we shall probably make a long day of it.'

'What's the matter with *you*?' Henry demanded of his elder daughter who had been listening with her mouth open and her brow furrowed.

'Nothing,' Sally mumbled, thinking that she could not possibly have mistaken Charles for Kitty. Besides, Kitty Shepherd her mother's deputy, was a fearful old battleaxe, and her mother's manner to her was unfailingly matter-of-fact. There could be only one explanation: her mother had come up with something, as she had promised the mysterious Charles.

'Aunt Bunny phoned. Twice,' Anne reported as Henry came through the front door.

Henry put his briefcase on the floor and removed a bunch of keys from between his teeth. 'Twice?' he repeated, impressed. 'What'd she want?'

'Wouldn't say – except that it's important.'

'Must be.' Henry checked his wrist watch. 'Twenty past five. Browne's shut at half-past. But I expect they're back at Kitty Shepherd's already – they wouldn't risk getting caught in the rush hour. I'll give her a ring.'

'I shouldn't,' Sally said from the dining-room doorway.

'Shouldn't what?' Henry, hunting for Kitty Shepherd's telephone number, paid her no real attention. He dialled and waited. 'Ah, Kitty! Henry Robinson here!' he announced ringingly. 'Sorry to interrupt the good work, but a brief word with my lady wife, if you would be so kind. Beg pardon? But I could have sworn she said Thursday. Something to do with the jolly reading scheme . . .'

The watching Sally observed a deep flush mount the bulge of her father's neck above his starched, white collar.

'Obviously I misunderstood. No, no. Not at all. Of course. Goodbye.'

'Tea's ready,' Sally said nervously.

Tea was taken in silence. Henry ate savagely, drank noisily.

'What's up?' Anne hissed, when Henry dashed to the wireless to switch on the six o'clock news.

Sally pulled down the corners of her mouth to indicate a gathering storm.

At five past six, Bunny telephoned again. Henry was reassuring: he would personally see to it that Meg returned her call the moment she arrived home. Meanwhile, he trusted there was nothing untoward. Edward? Great Scott! When? Well, yes, there would certainly be much to discuss.

It was seven twenty-two precisely when Meg's key was heard in the lock. Henry was certain of this because he was checking his watch at the time. 'Upstairs, you girls,' he ordered.

'Oh, Dad . . .'

'Come on,' Sally urged, tugging her sister's sleeve.

As Meg listened carefully, her eyes darted, and the feeling grew that he had a darn cheek. Well, let him bellow, let him get it all out – dot every i, cross every t. It would be all the better for her, for she intended to bamboozle him, to protect an area of her life for which he had shown disdain.

'Have you finished?' she enquired when he paused in search of a new tack.

He was enjoying venting his feelings and was not yet ready to abandon the floor. 'And another thing,' he cried, lighting on the further sin of her having made him appear foolish in the eyes of Kitty Shepherd.

Meg sat down. By the time his appearance in Kitty Shepherd's eyes had been thoroughly examined, she had him in her sights.

'Well, I'm waiting,' he cried, at last.

She began coolly. 'As you have discovered, I have not spent the day with Kitty Shepherd. I have spent it about my own business. As a matter of fact, were you not so self-opinionated, so fond of the sound of your own voice, I might have mentioned how I intended to spend the day. As it is . . .' She shrugged.

'Well, what have you been doing?' he asked, and she was pleased to hear a note of uncertainty enter his voice.

'I have been doing a thing that you often do. I have been on a retreat – a day of fasting, reading and prayer.'

'I didn't know there was a retreat arranged for today,' he put in suspiciously.

'There is more than one church in this town. There is more than one priest, more than one congregation . . .'

'Ahah!' He spotted her guilt at once. 'You've been with the Prots – a Low Church do! Been doing a spot of Bible study?' he asked jeeringly.

'There are times, Henry, when it doesn't matter a jot whether things are High or Low. In any case, it's none of your business.'

'Look, you could have told me . . .'

'And been catechized for my pains? No thanks. And now' – she got to her feet – 'I'd better phone Bunny. When did Edward die, exactly?'

'Early this morning. Wait a minute, Meg.' In spite of his indignation, he had begun to suspect that she had a case. 'I'm sorry if I seem to interfere. I suppose I do get a bit heated about . . . standards. But in future I'll keep my mouth shut. If you want to go on another retreat, just say; I promise not to ask questions.'

This might prove useful in the future, she saw. 'All right, Henry. I'll bear that in mind if I decide to go

again. Meanwhile, make me a cup of tea, there's a
good man.'

'I thought you were fasting.'

'After all that fuss, I *need* one.'

'Go and phone her, then, and I'll bring it to you.'

Meg, squinting through the gloom, was relieved to see,
as she paid off her taxi, that the door to The Grange
was ajar. It was early evening, and apart from a crack
of light between curtains drawn across the dining-room
windows, the place was in darkness. It was also Monday:
tomorrow was the start of the new term. How typical of
Uncle Edward, Meg had thought, to die at a moment
which entailed his funeral coinciding with the first day
of term – although it was doubtful whether Edward had
done a sensible thing in his life. Meg's first reaction had
been to refuse the summons, but Aunt Charlotte had
been so distraught – she had made Bunny, and then Jim,
telephone to beg her to come – that Meg had relented.
After all, the death of Edward would now precipitate
the selling of The Grange (and not a moment too soon,
Jim had warned, having gone over their affairs); it was
no wonder that Charlotte urgently wished to unburden
herself to Meg, her god-daughter and favourite niece. Pip,
too, had sounded agitated on the telephone. 'I *couldn't*
live with Charlotte. You will make them understand that,
Meg? Jim and Bunny were talking about us both sharing
a room at Fairlawns in Droitwich. I couldn't stand it. I'd
rather be dead.'

Meg had bowed to fate, had spent the weekend and
this morning chivvying Kitty Shepherd, Mrs Mack and
the rest of the staff, and now intended to sort matters
out briskly at The Grange to facilitate a return to work
no later than Thursday morning.

The hall was black. Meg swept a hand over the wall, but failed to locate a light switch. From memory, she went on cautiously until, on her left, a cold draught cut the air where the hall widened towards the staircase and a line of light showed beneath a door.

'What a dim pair!' she called, entering the dining-room. 'You might have left a light on in the hall.'

With distracted cries, the sisters rose from chairs drawn close to the hearth.

'And what a mean little fire,' Meg remarked when she was free of their reaching arms. She took a shovelful of coal from the coal box and threw it into the grate.

They watched without comment, then reseated themselves.

Meg seized a hard chair from the side of the table, drew it to the fire and sat down.

The aunts sighed.

Suddenly, Meg was ravenous. She had eaten lunch standing over a desk spread with class timetables. She had hoped for a cup of tea and a bun at Sheffield, but for once there had been no time to wait between trains. 'Have you had supper?'

'What?'

'She asks, have we had supper.' Pip turned to Meg and lowered her voice. 'No, we haven't. We don't have anything after our tea.'

'Well, I didn't get any tea,' Meg shouted for the benefit of her senior aunt. 'So I'm starving. I'll go and see what I can find in the kitchen, if you don't mind.'

This casual way of putting it masked her expectation that Mrs Beckett, having learned of her imminent arrival, would have left her a plateful of something satisfying. But the kitchen table, Meg found, bore no napkin-covered plate or laid-out tray. In the pantry, she discovered a hunk of stale-looking bread in the bread bin and, on raising an upturned pudding bowl from a saucer, a square of hard, cracked cheese. Anger and incredulity spurred her to make a more thorough, more enterprising search. This produced three damp water biscuits, a cup of furry dripping, and a saucer-covered jug containing sour-smelling milk. Meg slapped the bread and the cheese on to a plate and marched with it into the dining-room. 'Am I expected to make do with *this* for my supper?'

In spite of Meg's raised voice, Charlotte seemed unable to comprehend, and the despised food could not draw her attention. 'It was such a shock,' she mourned. 'Such a cruel, bitter shock.'

'Nonsense!' Pip told her sister. 'You knew perfectly well he'd never get out of bed again. Jolly good riddance, too.' She turned to Meg to elaborate further. 'I said to the doctor: Do give him something to hurry things up, there's a dear boy. All this shoutin' and creatin' makes my poor head hurt. I don't know whether he did, but I wouldn't be surprised – he's such a considerate fellow. It was all very well for Charlotte because she couldn't hear . . .'

'What's that?'

'I said, it was all right for you because you couldn't hear Edward's din . . .'

Meg, still holding the plate, sat down. 'Aunt Pip,' she interrupted, striving to keep calm, 'please tell me: is this the only food in the house?'

Pip gazed sorrowfully at the plate. 'I can't say. It might be. Charlotte keeps me out of the kitchen because I'm too friendly with Mrs Beckett.' Then, brightening, she looked towards the sideboard at the far end of the room. 'There are some Marie biscuits in the biscuit barrel . . . oh, but' – her voice faltered, her face fell – 'I may have eaten them. Yes, I think perhaps I did.'

'What's Mrs Beckett thinking about? There's nothing in the larder.'

'She walked out. On Friday was it? Or Thursday? – I lose track of time. Charlotte accused her of stealing Edward's things.'

Charlotte craned forward.

'I shall kill Jim and Bunny,' Meg promised. 'They could have warned me. . .'

'I don't suppose they know; Charlotte's cagey, and I can't remember things – if no-one asked me, I'd have forgotten to mention it.'

'What does she say?' cried Charlotte.

'I understood Jim was keeping an eye on everything,' Meg said.

'Charlotte thinks he steals from us, too. She hides whatever money she can get her hands on – in her drawers, in her desk, stuffed into her shoes in the wardrobe – under her mattress, I shouldn't be surprised.'

'Why are you whispering? Speak up! And don't believe a word she says. She's a liar, a disgrace to the family. I warned Mama about her over and over again. But Mama wouldn't listen . . .'

Meg rose, banged the plate on to the table, and went off in search of something to drink.

There was a tea caddy on the dresser. Raising the lid, sniffing the contents, Meg decided to have tea – black tea, she amended, recalling the milk in the milk jug. The kitchen range was cold, but an electric cooker proved to be in working order. She filled a saucepan with water and while waiting for it to boil, set out a tray. When the tea was made she carried the tray to the dining-room.

Pip watched as Meg sipped gingerly from her cup and cut into the middle of the cheese in search of a palatable portion. 'I've got a bottle of brandy in my bedroom,' she called softly. 'Bring yourself a glass and join me, after we've gone up to bed.'

Charlotte, who had been uttering small groans, wringing her hands and heaving her breast, was now sufficiently worked up to deliver herself: 'What *are* we to do about Freddy? The worry of it is driving me to distraction! It's been on my mind for days.'

'What about Freddy?' Meg asked.

'About what he'll do tomorrow. It was bad enough at Louisa's funeral when he turned up at the church with that woman. But tomorrow, as it's Edward's funeral, I'm so afraid he might bring her to the house. We must prevent him. Think of something, Meg. I spoke to George about it on the telephone, but we were cut off. When I rang back, Bunny said – or rather, she shouted – that girl can be very rude – that George had gone up to the fields. And Jim's useless, of course; just mumbles to himself. I can't get any of them to see the gravity of the situation. That is why, dearest Meg, I am so thankful you have come. *You* will understand. *You* will do your duty. I know I can rely on you.'

Meg gave up the cheese as a bad job. She ate the last of the bread and drained her cup. 'Well, Aunt,' she said, wiping her mouth on the back of her hand, 'I can't think what you expect me to do about it. This was Freddy's home. Edward was his brother. I should expect him to come – and bring his wife, too.'

Charlotte clutched the arm of her chair. 'Think of your poor grandmother,' she urged. 'Would *she* have received such a person in her drawing-room? She would not! I beg you, to support me, Meg. Telephone Freddy first thing tomorrow and tell him he must come alone.'

'I can't, Aunt. Sorry, but there it is. I dare say the woman's perfectly all right. Daddy's met her, you know.

He said there's no harm in her – not our sort, but quite a jolly type. And she's got pots of money, so you needn't think she'll be after any of this mouldy old stuff.' Meg waved an arm airily to indicate the room's furnishings.

'You know, I bet she could tell a tale or two,' Pip put in thoughtfully. 'Living in a pub's bound to be an eye-opener. I was always disappointed Freddy didn't bring her here; not that I really expected him to; that boy was always a coward.'

Charlotte closed her eyes. She was weary of her ungrateful family, sick and tired of them . . .

'Oh, Aunt Charlotte!' Meg, guessing her thoughts, reached out and took her hand. 'You will agitate yourself over other people, and it never does any good; in the end they go their own sweet way. That's why it's best to just please yourself. After all, yours is the only life you're responsible for. Give it up, Aunt, do!'

Charlotte opened her eyes and observed her niece coldly.

Might as well tell a fish to stop swimming, thought Meg, withdrawing her hand. She got up and took the tray to the kitchen.

There was a weighty atmosphere in the room when Meg returned. Her aunts were glaring across the hearth, as if sizing one another up.

'We must go to bed now,' Charlotte declared, her eyes still on Pip.

'Shan't,' said Pip.

'But it's only just gone nine,' Meg protested.

'We always go early.'

'Shan't budge until you've done my hot water bottle.'

There was a tense silence.

'You know that I mean what I say,' Pip warned. 'Nurse said you must do it for me, and so you must.'

'I'll fill your hot water bottle, Aunt Pip,' Meg offered hesitantly, fearing to intrude into a private quarrel.

'No. *She* must,' Pip cried. 'Every night I have to fight her for it. She's cruel. She hopes I'll freeze. She's pleased I can't do things for myself because she likes to make me suffer. But I've got a hold over her, she wants us to go to bed so that the fire can go out – she likes to save the coal and the light – but I won't go until she's done my hot water bottle.' Pip made a show of settling back in her chair.

With hatred in her eyes, Charlotte rose.

'See?' Pip cried out in triumph. 'She has to give in.' And her eyes gleamed as they followed Charlotte's progress to the door.

'Well, she'll be disappointed if she thinks I'm going up yet,' Meg said. 'Where am I sleeping, by the way?'

'I don't know. Ask her.' After her triumph, Pip seemed suddenly deflated.

Meg knelt by the hearth and made up the fire.

When Charlotte returned she was holding a hot water bottle. 'Come now,' she commanded from the doorway.

'Not me, Aunt. I never turn in before eleven. But you'd better tell me which room I'm in.'

There was a pause. Then: 'Louisa's,' Charlotte said shortly, and the sisters exchanged a sharp look.

'Well,' Pip sighed, 'it's nothing to do with me. In any case, I'm too tired to bother. Oh, I'm so stiff, my hips hurt . . .'

Meg hurried to help her.

At the door to Pip's room, Charlotte handed Meg the hot water bottle and went off without a word.

Meg put the bottle between Pip's dingy sheets.

'There's a bottle of brandy in the commode. Put me a thimbleful in that.' Pip said, pointing a gnarled finger at a tumbler on the table beside her bed. 'And pass me a pill.'

256

Meg handed her the glass, noting as she did so how sticky it felt, then took a pill from a box on the table. 'One of these?'

Pip nodded, put the pill on her tongue and swallowed the brandy in a single gulp. 'You can take the bottle. Bring it back in the morning. Now go. Go on, I'm too tired to bear another word.'

'Can't I help you in to bed?'

'Just go. Goodnight.'

'Goodnight, Aunt Pip,' Meg said, taking the bottle. 'Goodnight, Aunt Charlotte,' she bellowed outside that lady's door.

There was no reply.

What a cantankerous pair, Meg thought, going down stairs, one hand clutching the brandy bottle, the other pushing ahead on the balustrade. On the bottom step she paused, and squinted beyond the patch of light in the dining-room doorway to the thick shadow of the wide hall, feeling a chill bloom upon her face and the tacky damp of the newel post beneath her hand. The pungency of mould and rot, of dust crusting undisturbed corners, stung her nostrils as the cold air moved. This was the habitation of decay – impossible to imagine life fostered here. With an effort she cast back in time, heard feet pounding the stairs, doors slam, a polka played on the piano, a clear treble declaim Grandma Ludbury's verse, and Charlotte and Pip screaming venom at one another then imploring their mother to take their side. How treacherous of fate to lock these two together in hopeless, helpless old age.

She went to the dining-room, took a glass from the sideboard cupboard, and poured herself a stiff drink. Aunt Louisa's bed awaited her, she reflected, leaning her arm along the mantelpiece and gazing down into the fire. As a child, she had shared that sad, good soul's bed, and now felt reluctant to lie there again. She considered the *chaise-longue* against the dining-room wall – perhaps she should camp on that. But no, it would be a long day tomorrow; she had better pull herself together, finish her brandy, then go up and get a good night's rest.

A strange odour pervaded Aunt Louisa's room. Meg glanced around, unable to place it. Hoping that the bed was aired, she drew back the bedclothes and pressed her hands to the bottom sheet. A dark stain caught her eye; further examination revealed a spattering of spots and a large smear. The truth hit her like a blow. Almost reeling, she backed away, turned, pulled open the door and fled along the landing. Hysteria mounted inside her, but by the time she reached Aunt Charlotte's room she had gathered her sense of self-preservation, and pure, hard anger burst forth. 'How dare you!' she stormed, switching on the light and charging the bed.

Charlotte, propped on high pillows with her shoulders swathed in cardigans, opened her eyes and blinked.

'Edward was in that bed, wasn't he? Go on, admit it.'

'Edward?'

'In Aunt Louisa's bed.'

'Easier for the doctor and nurse,' Charlotte mumbled.

'And the sheets haven't been changed. He died in them, didn't he? *Didn't he?*'

'I . . . that is, Mrs Beckett . . .'

'Don't give me Mrs Beckett. *You* asked me here, begged me to come, and you didn't even see to it that I had clean sheets. It's outrageous! What are you going to do about it?'

Charlotte shrank into her wrappings.

'Right! I'll have *this*' – she pulled a pillow from the bottom of the pile supporting Charlotte – 'and *this*' –

and the eiderdown from the top of the bed. Bundling pillow and eiderdown in her arms, she marched out of the room and down the stairs to the dining-room and the *chaise-longue*.

In the morning, Meg washed in the kitchen, dressed, and went to the telephone. 'Bunny!'

'Hello!' Bunny responded, surprised.

'Look, things here are appalling. You'd never imagine what happened to me last night: I was expected to sleep in Edward's sheets – the ones he'd died in!'

Bunny gave a cry.

'What's more, the place is filthy – stinks – and there isn't a crust to eat . . .'

'Be *quiet*!' screamed Bunny; and Meg recalled Bunny's belief that the world at large would stop at nothing to gain news of the Ludburys, particularly news showing them in a poor light.

'Oh, very well; I'll tell you later. The thing is, The Grange is uninhabitable; the aunts can't stay here another night. I suggest, after the funeral, you take Charlotte back with you to Willow Dasset, and Jim takes Pip to Horley-in-the-Hedges. It'd be better for everyone if they're separated.'

'But we can't just . . .'

'We *must*. If outsiders get wind of the conditions here . . .'

Bunny became agitated. 'You don't think . . .?'

'Well, you know what people are like. So get a bed ready for Aunt Charlotte – and put me in the girls' room tonight. I'll phone Jim, now, about Pip. Oh, and Bunny – bring some sandwiches in case people want to eat after the funeral. And some milk. I'll go and light some fires so that Daddy doesn't catch pneumonia. See you later.'

Meg rang off, called the operator back, and prepared to address Jim or Mrs Flower.

Jim was the first to arrive, followed closely by Harry and Dora. Then, hearing a cry from Aunt Charlotte and her heavy feet ascending the stairs, Meg hurried to the door to receive Uncle Freddy and meet – for the first time – Aunt Gladys, licensee of The Green Man.

'Bad do, ain't it, Meg? Good Lord – if it ain't poor old Pip!' cried Freddy, who seemed rather unsteady on his feet.

'Freddy, you rascal! Pooh! You stink of whisky. Now why haven't you brought your wife here before? I've been longing to meet you,' Pip told the bejewelled, startlingly rouged, well-upholstered publican.

Gladys beamed. 'What a lovely old placé! Quaint! I'm a terror for quaintness, aren't I, Freddy? – though, I must say, I like things nice and cosy, too.'

Meg ran upstairs and discovered Aunt Charlotte lurking, knuckle in mouth, on the landing. 'Come down, you silly woman. Daddy'll be here in a minute, and we don't want any unpleasantness.'

She took her aunt's trembling arm and drew her downstairs.

Charlotte stood stiffly in the hall and waited, with terror in her eyes, to receive her sister-in-law.

Gladys spared herself nothing in putting the poor lady at her ease. Her sympathy, her knowledge of Charlotte's anguish following her sad loss, were feelingly expressed, and in future, Gladys promised, she intended to keep a close, sisterly eye on the Ludbury ladies.

This news provoked a general and thoughtful hush. Then Dora, who enjoyed an evening out, and had not yet had the pleasure of acquainting herself with the facilities at The Green Man, stepped forward and steered Gladys to an intimate corner.

When George arrived, Meg saw that he had changed. He lifted his legs stiffly from the car and set them down on the gravel. Bunny rushed round the car with his stick. As he rose, his clothes seemed to hang on him. His face was unusually pale, transparent almost, so that blue veins showed prominently on his forehead. He passed through the throng with a faint leer – his habitual expression when ill at ease – and perched on an arm of a chair in the drawing-room, his stick between his knees. He was greeted and kissed, claimed tearfully by Charlotte and noisily by Pip, but Meg guessed that he took little of it in. She stood protectively close to his side.

When the hearse arrived, everyone rose. As others moved forward, George went to the back of the room.

'All right, Daddy?' Meg asked, joining him.

He looked at her pleadingly. 'I don't know about you, Megs, but I don't care for this funeral lark. Truth to tell, I'd rather stay here.'

'Then why don't you, Daddy?' she asked impulsively. 'And I'll stay with you.'

His face became cunning. 'They'll kick up a fuss. And Bunny won't like it.'

This was true. But now she came to think about it, she wasn't too keen to spend time on her knees on Uncle Edward's behalf, either. Once, when Meg had stayed at The Grange as a girl, she had been obliged to fight off the indecent attentions of that disgusting man. 'I'll say you're not up to it. Come on, let's slip into the dining-room, then I'll go and break the news.'

Bunny did not like it one bit, and neither did Charlotte. Pip hoped she, too, might be excused. But they were none of them a match for a fully resolute Meg, and soon hearse and mourners had departed leaving only George and Meg in possession of The Grange.

They sat over the fire with glasses of whisky poured from George's flask, and reminisced cosily while healthy colour stole into their cheeks. Father reminded daughter of the discomfort now being endured by the rest of the family – cold church, hard seats, doleful hymns, windy parson. Daughter laughed and held out her glass for more. 'Good health!' each toasted the other. They sipped appreciatively and chuckled to think how well they had done for themselves.

Six weeks later, as Meg hurried to get ready for school, Bunny rang.

'Bunny! Whatever . . .?'

'I've just had the matron of Fairlawns on the line. Pip's dead. They found her this morning.'

'Good Lord! But they'd only just settled in. What was the matter with her, do they know?'

'Well, you know how forgetful Pip had become? – Matron said she had seemed quite scatty from the moment they arrived . . .'

'Yes?'

'She took all her pills. The whole bottle. Absent-mindedly, of course. Matron says she probably took a couple, then forgot she'd had them, then took some more . . .'

'Blast!' said Meg, and hung up.

In frantic haste, she dialled Jim's number. 'Good morning, Mrs Flower. Meg Robinson here. May I speak to my brother?'

'Yes, yes. I'll go and get him. We've just heard the sad news . . .'

'Hello?'

'Look here, Jim. You did do as I said? – put them in separate rooms. You didn't put Pip in with Charlotte?'

'The money wouldn't stand it, Meg. They could have gone on for years – specially Charlotte. The doctor said she's strong as an ox.'

'Well, Pip won't be going on, apparently.'

'Matron said it was an accident. Pip was scatty, didn't know what she was doing . . .'

'You're a blithering idiot, Jim.' With which, Meg slammed down the receiver, grabbed bag and briefcase, and rushed off to work.

4

Sally, hearing her name called from the hall below, opened her door with sluggish reluctance.

'Hurry. It's Uncle Jim on the phone.'

Galvanized, she tore along the landing and down the stairs to seize the telephone receiver from her mother's hand. 'Uncle Jim!'

'Hello, there! Broken up from school?'

'Yes, thank goodness. Wish I'd left.'

'You don't really. You'll be sorry as anything this time next year.'

'Another year to get through!'

'You make the best of it. In the meantime, I suppose you've some time on your hands. Want a job?'

'A job? Where? Do you mean at Horley-in-the-Hedges?'

'Mrs Flower's hurt her leg. She's got it all strapped up. She ought to keep off it as much as possible for the next few weeks. Like to come and help us out?'

'Oh, I *would*. But poor Mrs Flower! I'll come tomorrow. Did you ask Mum if I could?'

'She thought it was a good idea.'

'I'll find out about a train, then, and let you know what time to meet me. Thanks ever so, Uncle.'

'You're coming to *work* for us, my girl.'

'Oh, I am. I will. But isn't it lovely?'

From among the rows of parked vehicles on the station forecourt, her eyes instantly selected the Land Rover. He was leaning against the bonnet, one foot crossed over the other, hands in pockets, pipe in mouth. A hat put his face in shadow, but his stance told her that it had not irked him to wait for her delayed arrival, that he had been perfectly content to stand for twenty minutes in the sun. When he noticed her, he took the pipe from his mouth – she could imagine that he would make none but this minimal gesture should he be presented with sudden catastrophe or amazing good fortune – but she did not doubt his pleasure. His smile broadened as she drew near.

'Well, hello . . .'

She embraced him warmly. 'Sorry the train was so late.'

He took her case. 'Good journey?'

As they drove away she chattered about her travelling companions, but soon lapsed into happy silence as landmarks along the road to Horley-in-the-Hedges caught her eye.

He stole a glance at her, then whistled tunelessly through his teeth before making up his mind to observe: 'You've got lipstick on. And stuff round your eyes.'

She looked at him and grinned. 'I put it on on the train.'

'They don't approve, then – your parents?'

'I haven't really asked them . . . Usually, I put make-up on in other girl's houses, or in the Ladies' at the bus station. Once, when I'd been to the pictures with Valerie Burnet, I forgot to rub it off before I went home; but they didn't seem to notice. Mind you, I'd probably licked off the lipstick when I ate a choc ice, and the eye stuff might have got smudged – the film was dreadfully sad . . . Why, Uncle? If you don't like it, I'll take it off.'

'No,' he said equably. 'I was just wondering why you looked so much older.'

'I'm seventeen,' she cried. ' I was only sixteen when you saw me at Christmas.'

'That accounts for it, then.' He grinned at her, noting that, in the absence of a demure Alice band, her dark curls fell charmingly about her face and shoulders.

'Valerie Burnet's left school to work in a bank. You should see her now – absolutely plastered in make-up.'

'I shouldn't like that,' he said, considering. 'No, I reckon you've got it just about right.'

How reasonable he was, she thought; it was this quality that set him apart from every other adult of her acquaintance. He did not bolster his judgements with intimations of immorality, failure and doom; if something displeased him he said so, but did not go on to enlarge, in parental or teacherly fashion, upon the danger of her disappointing his hopes for her. And school friends could be as unreasonable as adults, pouncing upon and deriding any want of confidence, no doubt because it mirrored their own. Only in *his* company was it possible to be unguarded, voice an idea to discover how it might sound, adopt a position to gain a view from a new perspective. Unflustered, he considered merits and pitfalls, perhaps committed himself in a particular direction, but would never allow the exercise to colour his idea of *her*. The luxury of such intercourse lying in store for her over the next few weeks made her dizzy with a sense of good fortune. She was about to express this when she remembered that it was to happen as a result of another's poor luck. 'Tell me about Mrs Flower,' she demanded, steadying herself.

'Fell over a cat. She was carrying a great pail of swill across the yard, and the cats came running, of course. It was a very nasty fall – strained a ligament, bruised her black and blue.'

266

'The poor thing! Well, she needn't move an inch. I'll do everything.'

'I'm not sure she'd welcome that. It's the running about, the fetching and carrying. I expect you'll work it out between you.'

'Of course we will. I'll fit in with her.'

'That's the ticket.'

'Is the corn nearly ripe?' she asked, sizing up a passing field of wheat.

'Coming on. Not quite ready. I've got a new crop this year – something that'll interest you. There's quite a story behind it.'

'Yes?'

'Wait till you see it,' he said mysteriously, smiling to himself.

They found Mrs Flower stringing beans at the kitchen table. She was sitting in one Windsor chair and her injured leg lay over another.

When Sally had changed, she returned downstairs to join her.

'I'll help you with those.'

But Mrs Flower thought otherwise. 'Put the kettle on. We'll have a nice cup of tea,' she said, wrinkling her nose.

Over the teacups, Mrs Flower told, and Sally heard, all about the accident. The story had a polished feel, for it was already well rehearsed. Sally listened with comfortable half attention, putting in soft cooings and exclamations at suitable moments to convey rapport. It was no matter if she failed to take in every detail, for she knew there would be further opportunities. This knowledge gave her a feeling of security; nothing could embarrass life at Horley-in-the-Hedges into divergence from its own steady pattern. And Mrs Flower had no shame in endless repetition. Her confidence in the choicer anecdotes was transmitted to her audience who smiled at the start of each retelling as if greeting a friend.

'Yes,' – Mrs Flower broke off to address a black and white cat lying snug in the fireside chair – 'you know very well I'm talking about you. Look at her,' she invited Sally. 'I'd have to be hard-hearted to harbour a grudge. Mrs Twitten didn't mean it, did oos den?'

Sally leant over to rub the base of the cat's ear with a finger. The cat leant against the pressure and purred.

'She's enjoying that,' Mrs Flower said, pleased.

After a while Sally asked what she might do to be useful.

Mrs Flower pulled in her small pointed chin so that her massive under-chin swelled. 'There is one thing,' she said primly, 'but I hardly like to ask.'

'Oh please do – that's why I'm here.'

'Well, people have been very kind – my sister, Pat and Dottie,' (they were her nieces) 'Mrs Hugget, even Mrs Boyer from Holly House – but they all think they know best what wants doing and it's very awkward trying to get them to do anything else. It's the flags.' She waved a plump arm at the floor. 'You know what the men are – trampling in and out however much you shout "Boots!" I do like the scullery and kitchen floors to have a regular scrubbing, just for my own piece of mind.'

Sally sprang to her feet. 'I'll get on with it right away.'

'That *is* a kind girl.'

'Know what it is?' Jim asked, looking over the field.

It was the hour between the completion of farm work and the getting of supper. Jim had suggested that he and Sally drive up the farm road in the Land Rover, then walk across the fields to inspect the new crop.

'It's a grass,' Sally said, stooping to look closely.

'It's cocksfoot. See?' He pulled a stem and pressed the three-pronged, outward pointing seed heads against his palm to demonstrate the name's likely origin. 'I read an article by a scientist at Cambridge about how they're growing all sorts of grasses and crossing them, trying to improve varieties of wheat and barley and make them more disease resistant – maybe breed new grains that'll grow on poor soil in other countries. So I wrote and told him how interested I'd be to help.'

'That's marvellous, Uncle.'

'They came and took samples of the soil, then asked me to grow a field of cocksfoot. Some of the farmers around here think it's no end of a joke. And you should hear your Uncle Harry – couldn't see this sort of thing making a profit. The point is, though, *this*' – he waved his pipe at the field – 'is working with Nature. I'm not poisoning the land or doing unnatural things to animals. No, what I like about Doctor Roe (a very interesting man – he'll be down here again soon to judge when to harvest it), what I like about him is that he's keen as the next man on progress, but by working *with* Nature, not against her. 'Course, Harry just wants to see the balance sheet . . .'

'But think of the interest, the satisfaction . . . !'

'That's it. That's just what it is – the satisfaction.'

Mrs Flower's niece, Dottie, was a plump, dark, red-faced girl, two years older than Sally. For a living she worked in a greengrocery in the nearby town, but her concerns were all with the village. The hours between catching the ten past eight bus in the morning and the five-forty bus in the evening were limbo hours, hours spent doing as little as possible and doing it grudgingly with a vacant expression. On the homeward journey Dottie came alive

269

again, chatting with other villagers who were obliged to get their living in the town's shops, offices and factories. Her ambition was to become like her mother and aunt, a village woman in a village dwelling with the consequent feeling of counting for something. (For high or low, every member of an old village family can claim consideration and interest, if not always respect.) In order to obtain her rightful place in life, it was necessary for Dottie to become Mrs Somebody-or-other. The precise name was not important, so long as it belonged to a man whose roots – and right to a cottage or council house – were firmly in Horley-in-the-Hedges. It was felt at Glebe Farm, and even more strongly at Rose Cottage where Dottie lived with her mother and father and younger sister, that Colin who worked for Mr Jim Ludbury would do as well as any.

Sally, to whom Mrs Flower had confided that Dottie was sweet on Colin, was aware of the plans for him, and observation led her to believe that Colin would present no serious opposition. He blushed furiously in Dottie's presence and was unable to suppress the daft smile that prevented his lips from getting around any words he might say for himself.

At this moment, as the residents of Glebe Farm were eating their supper, Dottie was lounging against the kitchen door frame, a basket of freshly laundered linen at her feet. Having been thanked for her kindness and bidden to convey thanks to her mother for attending to the Glebe Farm laundry, she seemed in no hurry to go, but embarked upon a torrent of teasing banter designed to encourage Colin to take her to a village dance on the forthcoming Saturday evening. Her delivery was loud enough to reach anyone passing by in the village street, and she did not deign to look in Colin's direction, but addressed, instead, the others at the table, or the table itself, or the cat in the fireside chair. (There was no feeling that this was an intrusion. Supper at Glebe Farm was always protracted – except at the weekend when other activities might follow. The supper table was where the residents took their ease after completion of a day's work, and any callers would find them there and might suit themselves whether to draw up a chair and join in, or hold forth, like Dottie, from the kitchen doorway.) Now and then Mrs Flower assisted her niece with an encouraging comment, and Jim and Mr Flower made one or two unhelpful asides to demonstrate ineffectual male solidarity. Colin, flushed and tongue-tied, looked moderately pleased with this attention.

'Go on, Colin,' Mrs Flower wheedled when her niece had departed with the matter still undecided. 'You take her and enjoy yourself.'

'Make a fool of meself, more like,' Colin said bitterly. 'I can't dance, can I?' It was asked scoffingly, but, Sally felt, with an undertone of despair.

'I'll teach you if you like,' she offered. 'That's how I learned – from girls at school. You'd soon pick it up.'

'There now!' exclaimed Mrs Flower, thrilled.

Jim and Mr Flower were both tickled by this proposal. Their amusement was rewarded with Mrs Flower's decree that they should do the washing up. Sally shooed the cat and helped Mrs Flower into the fireside chair, then began to push table and chairs to the wall.

'Help her, you great lummox!' Mrs Flower cried; and Colin, looking apprehensive, did as he was told.

'We'll do the waltz tonight,' Sally decided. 'Then the foxtrot tomorrow and the quickstep on Friday.'

The dancing lesson began. As the sounds of Mrs Flowers mirth and Sally's increasingly exasperated 'One two three, one two three', penetrated the scullery, Mr Flower and Jim

271

could not wash and dry fast enough, and soon it was to an audience of three that Sally pulled Colin over the kitchen floor, one hand grasping his, the other clutching a fistful of shirt, and the top of her head rammed into his chest the better to observe his footwork. Her occasional yelp of pain as their feet collided and her cross cry of '*Left* foot, you idiot!' caused tears to flow down the watchers' cheeks, and when things became so desperate that she relinquished his shirt and seized an errant leg, the seated ones almost fell from their chairs.

At last Sally detected some improvement in her pupil's performance and decided it was time for musical accompaniment. While Colin moaned and caught his breath, she turned the knobs on the wireless in search of Radio Luxembourg. 'I think he's getting it,' she confided, precipitating further paroxysms.

'Oh dearie me,' sobbed Mrs Flower. 'Just wait till I tell our Molly.'

And Sally, tapping her feet to a rumba while she waited for a waltz, understood that she was creating history. An account of 'That time when Mr Ludbury's niece, Sally, taught our Colin to dance. (Laugh? I nearly split me sides!)' would be recounted over and over again until it became a standard village tale.

The following evening, '*One* two three, *one* two three' became 'slow, slow, quick, quick, slow'. On Friday evening Sally pronounced Colin a fit partner for any girl with a modicum of patience, and Jim and Mr and Mrs Flower saw that their fine entertainment was concluded.

Supper on a Saturday was always taken an hour earlier than on a weekday. Colin was late coming to the table. As the others passed the cold ham, Mrs Flower observed his empty chair and appeared anxious, but her face cleared when he came shyly into the room wearing a dark suit and white shirt and daringly narrow tie. His face shone from recent scrubbing and his thick, fair hair was liberally greased. Jim and Mr Flower exchanged jests about his appearance, mostly to the effect that he had plucked and trussed himself nicely for Dottie's culinary convenience.

'Well, I think he looks nice,' said Sally. And Mrs Flower sent her a look of conspiratorial gratitude.

The following Wednesday, Colin was late for supper once again.

Jim looked down the table at Mrs Flower. 'Where's Colin? I should've thought he'd be hungry after shifting that hay.'

'He'll be in directly. He's in the yard having a word with Dottie. They seem to have a lot to say to one another.'

'Ah. It was a success, then – Saturday night.'

'I rather think it was. Help yourself to vegetables, everyone.'

For a time they ate in silence.

'You heard the weather this evening, Mr Ludbury?' asked Mr Flower.

'Didn't sound too bright, John.'

'Then we shan't get on with the wheat.'

'Not for a day or two yet, I reckon.'

Mrs Flower cleared her throat. 'Mr Ludbury,' she said coyly, 'I wonder you don't say anything about the pie.'

'Why? It's up to your usual standard, wouldn't you say?'

Mrs Flower looked at Sally who was gazing bashfully at her plate. 'I wonder,' she insisted, winking and nodding at her employer, 'if you don't find this one a bit extra special.'

'Well . . . Now you come to mention it, there is something unusually tasty about it.'

273

'Sally made it,' Mrs Flower confessed unnecessarily. 'She put herbs in it, didn't you Sally.' (Herbs were mentioned with awe.)

'Marjoram,' said Sally.

'Very nice, too.'

'She's got a light hand with the pastry — I'll say that for her,' Mr Flower volunteered.

Blushing, Sally changed the subject. 'It's a shame you can't get on with the harvest, Uncle. I hope it doesn't spoil.'

'We can't order the weather. Wouldn't do us any good if we could, for we'd never stop arguing about it. I say, Mrs Flower, do you reckon you could manage without her tomorrow afternoon and evening?'

'I dare say . . . It's early closing in town tomorrow. I'm sure Dottie'd be pleased to come and give me a hand.'

'Good. It's time I visited my aunt. Like to come with me, Sally? We'll spend the afternoon at Fairlawns with Aunt Charlotte then go somewhere nice for dinner.'

'You mean *evening* dinner?' Sally asked.

'I reckon she deserves a treat.'

'I should jolly well think she does,' Mrs Flower declared.

'Right! Wear your best frock. I'll book us a table at The Swan's Nest.'

'Gosh! Thanks, Uncle.'

'Push it again, Jim,' Charlotte Ludbury said, imperious in her high-backed armchair.

At Fairlawns, refuge for elderly gentlewomen, home for Charlotte since the selling of The Grange, they were sitting in a trio of chairs by the side of a fireplace in the great drawing-room. Charlotte had greeted Jim with a brief flurry of tremulous emotion. She had bravely borne

274

the news that the young person in the cornflower-blue frock with white piping at neck and armholes (the frock was sleeveless) and circular skirt that swished with every sandalled stride, was her great-niece, Sally. Sally, suffering her great-aunt's scrutiny, wished she had forgone lipstick and eye-shadow, but Mrs Flower had been so certain of their propriety. (Of course, put some on, dear; you do it so nicely. After all, your uncle is taking you *out*. Out of Horley-in-the-Hedges, Mrs Flower had meant – an exodus evidentally calling for the highest degree of personal presentation.)

Shortly, Sally had begun to relax, noting how Aunt Charlotte's air of jaded distraction, of faint disappointment even, sharpened to one of intense interest as small happenings occurred in other areas of the room. She became particularly rapt when a tall, military-looking man was escorted by a maid to the side of a frail-looking lady sitting in the bay. The appearance of the newcomer, Sally saw, caught the attention of every other lady currently entertaining tedious visitors.

'Lady Markham's nephew and heir,' Aunt Charlotte confided in a penetrating hiss. 'What a fine, upstanding man! Carries himself so proudly, I always think.' Then, as if fearing that the arrival of Lady Markham's guest might put her own requirements in the shade, she had indicated the push-button at the side of the fireplace. 'I can't think what has happened to tea. Push it again, Jim.'

Jim rose reluctantly and gave the button a swift prod.

'Did it ring?' Charlotte demanded loudly of her great-niece. 'I didn't hear it.'

At last the tea-tray arrived. 'Here we are,' announced a cheery maid. 'Who's going to be mother?'

Jim indicated that the honour belonged to the lady apparently frozen in her chair.

Charlotte waited for the maid to turn away (but not for her to be gone from earshot), and remarked: 'Dretful creature. This place is not what it was. As a matter of fact,' she went on, lifting the lid of the teapot and stirring the contents with a spoon, 'the person sitting alone by the piano – do you see? – dowdy little thing pretending to read a book – keeping her head down and I'm not at all surprised – was a gentleman's *housekeeper* before she came here. Mrs Durbridge found out about it. She complained to matron, but no action has been taken, as you can see. I think you ought to say something, Jim,' she said, handing her nephew a cup of tea. 'See matron before you go. If they allow a woman in her position to live here, who knows where it may lead? It's the slippery slope.'

'Not to mention the thin edge of the wedge,' Sally muttered.

Jim reached for a plate on which reposed three garibaldi biscuits. 'Like one?' he asked his niece with a wink.

'Thanks.' She sank back in her chair and nibbled a biscuit while her eyes roamed the room. Other visitors, too, were sitting edgily in their chairs; many were throwing desperate looks to one another, and visibly racking their brains for something to say; now and then they craned forward, shouting reports of the doings of absent relatives in tones of false heartiness. All to no avail; the resident ladies were unimpressed. Their eyes drifted to other encampments, noting details, weighing up, evaluating, storing titbits for picking over later; for their curiosity centred on one another, their day to day companions. At one point, becoming conscious of the frank stare of a lady whose guest had fallen asleep, Sally wondered whether her cornflower-blue frock might be detrimental to her great-aunt's standing. The thought came to her that Aunt Bunny's tweedy skirts and blue-green blouses and cardigans were more likely to strike the right note in the Fairlawns drawing-room. But Great-Aunt Charlotte seemed to have forgotten Sally's existence, being thoroughly taken up with a group on the other side of the fireplace engaged in the passing of photographs amid loud and complicated explanations as to the parentage of various children. ('No, Aunt Tilly, that's Veronica, Richard's eldest. You remember – she married the youngest Simmonds boy.')

'I think we should be getting along, Aunt,' Jim said at last. 'Don't bother to see us off, we'll find our own way.'

Charlotte, loath to miss further details of Miss Mathilda Evans' family connections, made no move to accompany her own relatives to the door, but, 'Mind you say something to matron,' she remembered to call.

Jim moved with uncharacteristic haste through the corridor and hall.

Having escaped safely, they climbed with relief into the Land Rover.

'What a beastly old woman!'

'It's just that she knows what's best,' he said wryly. 'She doesn't have to think about it, she *knows*. Some folks do, it seems.' And he added as an unguarded afterthought: 'Your mother's one of 'em.'

A shiver shook Sally.

'I should put your coat on; it's turned chilly.'

'It's not that. It's just . . .'

'Yes?'

'I expect it's my fault, but sometimes . . .'

He waited.

'She gives me the creeps.'

'Who? Your mother?'

Unable to say another word, she nodded vigorously,

277

wishing unsaid the words already uttered, for although they described the truth, hot shame always followed hard upon the wave of fear and dislike occasioned by close contact with her mother. Until this moment, words to describe her emotions had never clearly come to mind. And now she found herself unready to explore further. One day, perhaps. But not now, not yet.

'I used to feel a bit like that about your grandfather, I seem to remember.'

So her feelings were not unique – oh, the relief!

'I shouldn't worry about it. Time usually sorts out that sort of thing. Let's see now . . . This time next year you'll be getting ready to go away to university. So I dare say that by this time the year after, you'll have forgotten all about it – or at least, it'll seem pretty unimportant.'

'Do you really think so?'

'Bet you.'

After a while, he said: 'We'll have over an hour to kill in Stratford before dinner. What shall we do? Go and gawp at the theatre-goers? Take a stroll by the river if the rain holds off?'

'We'll do both.'

Sally was at an age when a new glimpse of life was a delight and wonder. Now and then, such a glimpse was deliberately sought out. One Sunday evening she and Valerie Burnet had slipped into Vespers at a Roman Catholic church. They had sat at the back covertly watching people who would not have merited a second glance in the street outside, taking part in a strange rite. It had been shocking to recognize the everyday face of one of the school dinner ladies – and shaming, too, to be caught in the act of spying. And one Saturday evening she had gone with Moira McAvennie into the cocktail lounge of The Dolphin on the seafront. (Moira McAvennie was the most advanced girl in Sally's class. Sally did not class herself as Moira's friend, for Moira, being entirely taken up with matters intellectual, had no taste for schoolgirl friendships; all the same, when Moira felt a need for company, it was Sally's she chose to tolerate.) 'Look bored,' Moira had instructed as Sally followed her through the swing glazed doors into The Dolphin's cocktail lounge; and Sally had duly disguised her panicky excitement with a vast yawn behind a languid hand. 'Two glasses of green chartreuse,' Moira had demanded of the satisfactorily bored-looking barmaid. ('You what?' 'Green chartreuse — it's there, behind you, with the twig in the bottle.') 'It's the strongest liqueur you can get,' she had explained, setting a glass before her companion. This information had seemed surprising in the warmth and glow of the cocktail lounge where couples sipped pre-dance drinks, and a group of men by the bar told jokes and waved hands cupping lighted cigarettes, and the muffled voice of an invisible crooner promised tantalizingly: 'Some enchanted evening, you will see a stranger, across a crowded room.' Later, battling through the freezing air blowing off the North Sea, Sally had acknowledged the undoubted potency of green chartreuse, and had been thankful when their perilous return to Moira's home and the difficult ascent to Moira's bedroom were safely accomplished. But hectic dreams and nausea had not diminished the memory. Saturday evening at The Dolphin remained as vivid and exotic a snatch of life as Sunday evening at Saint Ignatius'.

Dinner at The Swan's Nest with Uncle Jim afforded her another novel view, but this time as a participant rather than a voyeur. She was welcomed with grave respect, led down a thickly carpeted corridor, relieved of her coat, helped to a chair. The oak-beamed dining-room blazed red, white and gold – red carpet, curtains, napkins; white linen; gold candelabra. Sally, taking her cue from the grateful manner of those who waited upon her, the quick interest of other diners, the shining pleasure on her uncle's face, knew that she enhanced the scene. She was not overwhelmed as other girls in her position might have been, nor overcome with the sudden doubts that had attacked her in the Fairlawns drawing-room; on the contrary, she felt herself to be a vision of grace in her cornflower-blue frock and white sandals. 'This place,' she told her uncle, leaning confidingly over the table, 'is simply lovely. I never imagined anywhere so nice.'

Jim smiled broadly, not just at her eagerness, but as a badge of his own, for he had only recently discovered the pleasure of dining out in the evening. According to Ludbury tradition, eating out referred to luncheon at an hotel or afternoon tea at a café. But the younger members of the farming fraternity, encouraged by the example of Midland businessmen – particularly executives of the motor industry whose very brows shone with a patina of wealth and who knew how to do themselves well – were learning new ways, and Jim, who loved good food, availed himself of this treat whenever funds and opportunity permitted.

The menu was examined and discussed, expert advice sought and given. A wine was chosen, thoughtfully tasted, enthusiastically accepted. Curled, frangible pieces of toast arrived in a napkin-covered basket. They devoured the toast and speculated upon their own and other diners' choices of dish. Jim's pâté, followed by *boeuf en croûte* proved profoundly satisfying. Sally thought her watercress soup, followed by *sole Normande* were concoctions of the gods.

'Is that a pudding?' she inquired of a waiter, pointing

280

towards a dish of blue flames reposing on a burner drawn up to a neighbouring table.

'A dessert, Madam. *Crêpes Suzette*.'

'I'll have that.'

'For me, too.'

'Thank you, Madam . . . Sir.'

I must remember every detail, she thought, watching the waiter baste flaming pancakes with a spoon held in a napkin. She must allow for the possibility that this scene, marvellous though it was, might not loom large in her future life. At this moment she rather hoped it would (just as she had been sure that Saturday night at The Dolphin and Sunday evening at Saint Ignatius' would not). But even in the midst of her heady enjoyment she was reluctant to hold her future self hostage to present inclinations, sensing that as she grew in experience, her idea of the delightful would change; sensing the myriad choices before her, not all of which would entail eating out in glamorous dining-rooms. For the moment she would taste and savour, but always with that faint reservation.

'Tonight was one of the best times of my life,' she told her uncle later, as they drove home in the Land Rover. They exchanged warm looks, then fell dreamily silent. The headlights revealed tree-trunks, hedgerows and overhanging branches with selective, eerie luminosity. Insects darted. Draughts of night air blew in through the cracks between metal and canvas. Rocking and rattling, the jeep sped them endlessly along the winding, milky road.

'I've something to show you,' Jim said shyly, taking a photograph from a drawer of his desk.

The others had gone to bed. Jim and Sally, on returning from Stratford, had made themselves cups of cocoa which they did not require except as an excuse to prolong their pleasant evening. 'What do you think of her?'

She studied the face of a young woman made up in the style of ten or so years ago. A scrawled inscription across the corner of the photograph announced: To my darling Jim. Love for ever, XXX

'Very nice,' she said politely. 'Who is she?'

'Someone I expected to marry.'

'Uncle! Why didn't you?'

'She changed her mind. Married my best friend instead.' He took a second photograph from the drawer. 'Here they are.'

It was a wedding scene – a bride in white satin clinging to an airman's arm, flanked by a smiling Jim and a bespectacled bridesmaid.

'How awful of her!' Sally said indignantly.

'Oh, I don't know. Bob was a handsome looking chap, specially in his uniform. No, I reckon it turned out for the best.'

Sally found this hard to believe.

'About a year after the wedding she wrote to me saying she'd made a terrible mistake; that it was me she should've married.'

Sally caught her breath. 'Oh, how sad! But was it really too late? I mean, surely . . .'

'I thought about it, long and hard. But I came to the conclusion that which ever one of us she'd married, as soon as the novelty had worn off, she'd start to wonder whether she'd made the right choice. It was human nature to start hankering for the one she hadn't got and could've had.'

'But if she'd discovered she loved you best after all . . .'

'No. It was a case of the grass on the other side of the fence being greener . . .' He searched for another photograph. 'Now, here they are a few years later with their lad, Jim. Named him after me. Nice of them, wasn't it?'

A balding man in a nondescript suit sat, smiling thinly, by the side of a woman with hard eyes. At their feet, a boy of two or three played with a toy train.

She passed back the photographs.

'I admit it cost me a deal of heartache when she broke off our engagement. But thinking it over, I'm glad I'm the one she didn't have a chance to get tired of.' He returned the photographs to the drawer, then drew out his pipe and settled back in his chair. 'Yes, all in all, I reckon I probably had the best of it.'

After a while: ''Spose we ought to be going up,' he remarked, showing no inclination to stir.

Sally, lying sprawled on the hearthrug, stared into the empty grate and agreed absently. Cold air from the hall drifted in under the door and lapped her fingers; she dug them deeper into the woolly, faintly sticky pile. 'You kept her photograph, though – the one with the message.'

But he was deep in the balm of reflection and did not hear.

Outside, a mindless moth battered itself against the window, hot with ambition to reach a pernicious light.

Some weeks later, Meg telephoned from Willow Dasset.

'Your mother,' hissed Mrs Flower, her hand over the mouthpiece.

A familiar sense of apprehension seized her. 'Hello, Mum,' she said weakly.

'Hello. How're things? Mrs Flower's better, I understand.'

'Oh – much better, thank you.' She watched Mrs Flower move briskly from corner-cupboard to table carrying a large stack of plates. Mrs Flower's leg had been fully operational for over a week, since when Sally had spent most of her time helping her uncle in the harvest field.

'Well, we've been at Willow Dasset a few days, now. I think it's about time you joined us. Grandad's been asking for you.'

'Has he?'

'"Where's Sal?" he says. "Don't seem the same without both little girls."'

Her sudden joy on hearing that he had asked for her dissipated. 'Little girls?' she repeated doubtfully.

'You know what he means . . . Anyway, your father'll come for you tomorrow.'

'Oh, no, not tomorrow. We're starting on the cocksfoot tomorrow, and the people from Cambridge are coming. They're going to take photographs for a magazine.'

'Oh.'

Her mother sounded unimpressed.

'Well, I suppose one more day won't hurt. We'll say Thursday morning. And don't keep your father hanging about.'

'All right. Goodbye, Mum.'

She wandered into the hall and sat on the settle. On the warmest of days this was a chilly spot. Cold seeped from the flagstone floor and bit into the thin soles of her sandals; draughts from gaps under garden and street doors made her arms prickle and her forehead clammy.

Jim found her some minutes later. 'Dinner's ready. Your mother rang, I hear.'

'Yes. I've to join them at Willow Dasset on Thursday. Dad's coming for me.'

He stood, thinking, for some moments, jiggling the contents of his trouser pockets. 'Back to being a young lady, then. You'd better put the farm clothes to the bottom of your suitcase. Got plenty of reading?'

She nodded. 'I've been sitting here thinking how I'd hate to miss Willow Dasset – that it'd be terrible for summer to pass and not have been there.'

'Well, you've been a great help to us, Sal. I don't know how we'd have got on without you. Mrs Flower's going to miss you. So am I.' He reached deeper into a pocket and pulled out some tightly folded notes. 'You must take your wages,' he said awkwardly.

She was horrified. 'I can't. I don't want to. I've loved it here; it was like being part of a specially nice family. I'd help you out any time, Uncle.'

He hesitated, then returned the money to his pocket. 'And that goes for me, too. Don't forget – you're always welcome here.'

Even Mrs Flower had come to the cocksfoot field. One or two neighbouring farmers were there, and several villagers. The men from Cambridge expressed satisfaction with the crop. Mr Flower lined up the reaper, and Jim stood before it, fondling his pipe and grinning sheepishly.

'You ready?' Doctor Roe asked the photographer.

'Ready.'

The scientist advanced on the farmer with outstretched hand. 'We'll shake hands for the camera, shall we, Mr Ludbury?'

'Hold it there.'

Sally's heart swelled. Beside the waving cocksfoot, watched by his workforce, friends and neighbours, clasping his associate by the hand, stood dear Uncle Jim in battered hat and overall. His bony Ludbury face, beaten red by the Warwickshire wind, wore a smile signalling pleasure, honest pride, and a little embarrassment. It was more than a job well done, she thought; it was a job done with integrity, with faith, for a vision. 'It's the satisfaction,' she heard him say as the camera clicked and printed the scene for ever in her mind.

5

Time, during Meg's late forties and early fifties, seemed unable to convey her in the usual direction. While her contemporaries settled comfortably into middle age, spreading, fading, blurring at the edges, Meg's tall rangi-ness and the vigorous freedom of her movements became more clearly, more youthfully defined. The guiding hand behind this renaissance belonged to Charles Fairbrother.

It began with his casual observation that a frock in the window of the best outfitter's in town would become her stunningly.

'Navy?' she had objected. 'But green's my colour.'

'Navy with a white collar, and white undersides to the pleats which, I imagine, would flash as you walk and show off your legs.'

She had thought about it. A visit to the shop would bring him near, would be an extra treat, for they rationed their time together carefully, and adhered to a strict formality when their paths crossed professionally or by accident, determined to protect their liaison and make it last. It was an urge to see what had caught his eye that propelled her to the shop window, and pleasure that he had pictured her in such a jaunty garment that persuaded her to go in and try it on.

'Oh!' the sales lady gasped, when Meg stepped from the cubicle to consult the long looking glass. 'That's just how it ought to look. It's a gorgeous style, but hopeless on anyone who isn't tall and slim. Irene!' she called her assistant, 'doesn't Madam look lovely?'

'Madam can wear it,' Irene agreed in awe-struck tones.

Meg walked up and down, squinting at her reflection, noting the way the pleats flicked and the dropped waist-band slid provocatively against her hips. 'I'll take it,' she declared.

Henry had thought she was mad. He watched her pull it over her head as she prepared for an evening meeting. 'Whatever possessed you to buy that? It's not you at all.'

Meg said nothing, just tidied her hair, grabbed her bag and ran from the house and down the street to the bus-stop.

Her colleagues did not share Henry's reaction. Meg caused such a shock of admiration that several acquaintances were unable to hold back. 'Oh, you *do* look nice,' it was said repeatedly. Charles, presiding over the meeting, acknowledged her with his customary gravity, but with appreciative eyes.

Frocks progressed to suits, to coats, to shoes. One day, with great daring, Charles voiced the thought that it was a shame Meg dragged her exuberant curls into a bun at the nape of her neck. How more beautifully would a bob, skilfully cut, frame her face.

Meg's new look was well established when the Director of Education, making a visit to her school, confided that an application from herself for the position of County Advisor to Primary Schools would be welcomed. After consulting her old college, Meg applied for the post and was appointed.

Their new wealth and enhanced position seemed to indicate a move to a more congenial area, Henry considered; though not, of course, to the county town, for Henry must stay close to his work in their present

288

borough, he (being a he and by definition the bread-winner) was quick to add. Meg forbore to draw attention to the fact that it was her salary, and not his, that had augmented their fortune. Besides, she rather enjoyed the half-hour train ride to the county town, and her work, in any case, involved travel. Henry had always hankered for a house on The Park where the best townspeople lived. His imagination had not been equal to one of the mansions on the west side of The Park, but a tall semi-detached house with a conservatory and a garage at the head of the drive had seemed a fitting destiny. In due course, the Robinsons exchanged their dingy terraced house with garage in the alley at the back, for the very home of Henry's aspiration.

Its spaciousness might have become an embarrassment when the girls left home – Sally to attend a northern university, and Anne, two years later, a London medi-cal school – had not a new force entered the house, furnishing it with light, sound, and matters of absorbing interest. Nothing in Henry's life, hitherto, had proved so utterly captivating as the television. He gave himself to it unstintingly.

Every evening after tea a most cultivated class of person entered the sitting-room, with manners so polite and con-fiding that Henry was deeply moved. Here was the sort of company it befitted him to keep: the television announcer in evening dress and bright smile, outlining the evening's entertainment, recommending this, dropping a warning about that, showing such care, such consideration – Henry felt he received his due at last. Scrupulous not to take advantage of being invisible to his guests, he sat up straight in his town hall suit and arranged his features pleasantly, conscious of being just the man a television announcer hoped to address. When a favourite performer made a jocularity, Henry was charmed and looked quickly to see whether the gem had been noted elsewhere. Finding himself alone in the room, he stored the witticism in his mind to repeat later like a fond parent reporting the sayings of a precocious child. Of course, not every programme found favour. *The Brains Trust*, which allowed long-haired socialists and atheists to give their views, was particularly offensive, and Henry felt for the poor announcers obliged to give house room to these fellows. But generally, he experienced deep satisfaction, developing a catholic taste and a devotion even to *The Interlude*.

Henry was watching a Western when the telephone rang. He frowned and craned nearer to the set, but his wife, in some other part of the house, failed to do the decent thing. With a sigh he went into the hall and took up the receiver. 'Hello? What? Oh – yes.' He clapped a hand over the mouthpiece and yelled vindictively: 'It's for you – a reverse charge call – must be one of the girls. Come on!' And he stretched the receiver towards her as she hurried downstairs.

'For heaven's sake!' she protested, 'I was in the lavatory.'

'And I'm watching a programme,' he retorted, scurrying back to the front room.

'Hello?' ventured Meg.

'Hello, Mum.'

'Oh – Sally. What is it?'

'Can I come home?'

'Why? You've got finals in a few weeks.'

'I know. The thing is, I can't stay here.'

'What are you talking about?'

'I've been rusticated.'

'What?'

290

'It means I've got to clear off. They'll let me come back to sit the exams, but in the meantime I must make myself scarce.'

Meg, feeling a headache coming on, pulled up the hall chair and sat down.

'So can I come home, Mum?'

'*Why* have you been whatever-it-is? What have you done?'

There was a pause. Then: 'Got pregnant, actually.'

Meg presumed she could not have heard correctly.

But Sally enlarged upon her condition. 'It's started to show and they don't like it.'

'Oh, dear God! . . . Henry! Come here! Quickly! Your daughter announces that she is pregnant and it shows. The university is offended by the sight and she wishes to bring it here. Well, you can't,' she snapped nastily into the telephone. 'Why should we put up with it? We've got a position in this town. I can just imagine what the Ladies' Forum would make of it. And there's the Church and your father's work at the town hall . . . How could you, you wretch? – you stupid, messy little slut!'

'Here, let me speak to her,' Henry commanded, snatching the receiver. 'Sally?' But after a moment he put it down.

'What's the matter? What . . . ?'

'She blasphemed, then rang off.'

'Well!'

'You shouldn't have called her that.'

'It was the heat of the moment. Anyway, do you want her here, showing us up?'

'No, I don't,' Henry admitted. 'But there are ways of dealing with the situation and they have to be discussed. Now what are we to do?'

'Damnation!' cried Meg, thinking of the mountain of

work awaiting her on the dining-room table.

'I quite agree,' Henry said, hearing a cowboy whooping it up in the front room.

An idea came to her. 'I bet she'll try Jim.' With haste she dialled his number. 'Engaged! What did I tell you?'

'That's all right then. Let's leave it for a bit till we've calmed down.'

'You think he'll have her, then?'

'Bound to. He's soft where she's concerned.'

'Yes. And after all, he's only a farmer. I bet this sort of thing happens all the time in a village.'

'Villages are famous for it, I believe.'

'My goodness! What have you got in here?' Jim asked, lifting her overflowing canvas holdall and putting it into the back of the Land Rover.

'Books,' said Sally. 'I'm revising. But I'll take time off to help you with the cows, and I'll help Mrs Flower, too. I must earn my keep.'

'That's all right. You just get on with your studies.'

'You are *good*, Uncle Jim.'

He darted a look at her and grinned. 'Don't know about that, but at least I'm careful.'

'Oh!' She put a hand to her stomach and blushed.

'Goin' to marry the fellow?' he enquired after a while.

'No.'

'What's he think about it, then?'

'Doesn't know about it, actually.'

'Shouldn't he?'

'No, not really.'

'I see,' he said in a tone which admitted grave doubt.

'It's going to be all right, you know. Guess what my tutor told me the other day.'

'Go on.'

292

'He said I'm heading for an upper second at the very least. Probably a first.'

'That's good, is it?'

'Good?' She spread her hands in an attempt to convey its stupendousness. 'It's the most wonderful thing anyone has ever said to me in my whole life. It makes me feel like a lion – invincible.'

He frowned with an effort to comprehend.

'My tutor was warning me, you see, not to let this baby business put me off my work. I certainly won't. We – the baby and me – are going to be *all right*.'

Jim felt for his pipe, and although it was empty, jammed it between his teeth and sucked hard. 'Well, I'm here if you need me,' he said, more to comfort himself than reassure his niece.

'You are *good*, Uncle . . . Oh, hell!' She leaned across and noisily kissed his cheek. 'I knew you would be, but I didn't want to take advantage. That's why I rang the parents first.'

'One thing, though,' he said, as they turned in through the open yard gates. 'You'd better stay about the house and farm. You never know, some busybody might see you and bump into your aunt in the town. We don't want to cause upset at Willow Dasset.'

'Right-oh. Mrs Flower doesn't mind, does she?'

'Not her.'

'There she is! Oh Mrs Flower, Mrs Flower, it's lovely to see you!'

Sally went along the farm road in Mrs Flower's Wellington boots and her fat friend Katie's blouse and skirt. The sun shone on the wet grass. The early morning air was sweet and full of promise. Heady with joy, and because she had risen earlier than necessary, she allowed herself a few minutes' idleness before going to call the cows.

Life was bliss, bliss, she marvelled, stooping to pull long grasses. (She pulled gently, expertly, for only grasses that come away easily have stems of the desired milky succulence.) Nibbling a grass delicately, it came to her that once, in the old days at Willow Dasset before the first dread swellings of maturity had thrown everyone into a tizzy, she had felt like this before. As a straight, strong girl she had been sensible of her power; had conquered the Fordson Major, jumped from the highest bale, known without a shadow of doubt that ultimately she would triumph. But her power had dissipated in a fog of shame and confusion. And yet it had taken only a few words – 'You're heading for an upper second at the very least' – to send her spirits soaring, to bring her precious self-confidence back. She laughed out loud to think that it was a second swelling – a calamitous swelling – that had precipitated the reawakening of her former self.

'Come along, cows,' she yelled, pushing open a gate and striding into the field. 'Make haste, for I've work to do!'

Then, following the gentle creatures back along the road, watching their bony haunches and the long thin line of their bottoms so at odds with their swollen sides, the swish-swat of tails, the heads sometimes turned back to her so that great honest eyes gazed into her own and her nostrils caught their fragrant breath, she became tender with affection. 'I love you, my dears,' she assured her bovine friends. 'Come along, Missus,' she called to a straggler. 'Get on. Hup!' The cow lurched into a brief run to demonstrate good intentions, then dropped into a swaying walk. It was a particularly pretty creature, with a dark fringe of hair between its horns, a moist pink nose, and black rimmed eyes like a bull's on a Cretan vase. She rested her hand against its rump, and together they followed the herd.

Sally looked up from her book. A car had come into the yard. Going to the window, she saw her father get out of his car.

A scenario ran through her mind: her parents had hatched a plan, her father had come to lay it before her; they would brook no argument – this, they would say, is what she must do.

No, no . . . She gathered her books, took two apples from a bowl on the sideboard and fled – through the hall, through the garden door, through the gate in the garden wall and into the yard. The yard was unpeopled now; he had gone into the house; she could hear Mrs Flower exclaiming. Soundlessly in her plimsolls, she raced across the yard to the farm road. Here she slowed to a brisk walk.

As soon as Uncle Jim had agreed to take her in, she had seen what a good thing had been her mother's rejection. For at Glebe Farm she was allowed to work in peace. At home they would have insisted on relentless consideration of the future. Nothing, nothing, would deflect her from her purpose, she vowed, striding strongly on. When she came to a seldom-used barn on the farm's boundary, she went inside and made herself comfortable.

At six o'clock she discovered her father's car still in the yard. She turned her back on it and returned to her hiding place. By eight o'clock the car had gone. Cautiously, she entered the house.

'The wanderer returns,' Mrs Flower said. 'And just in time for supper.'

'Your father wanted to talk to you,' Uncle Jim reported from behind his newspaper.

'I'll talk to him later on; after finals. Sorry if it was a bother to you, though.'

'No bother. I told him you were quite all right,' Jim said calmly, turning a page.

Slowly, in bottom gear, Bunny manoeuvred the car into the yard. From pre-war days she had held a driver's licence, having been taught the basic skills by her brothers. But Daddy had always preferred to drive. These days, *she* took the wheel, for following a small accident, the doctor had insisted that George relinquish it. Bunny drove with excruciating care, never permitting her back to sink restfully against the seat, never finding occasion to move into top gear. Abruptly, she brought the car to rest before the farmhouse.

Mrs Flower caught sight of them from the scullery window and came running out in a fluster. 'Oh, Miss Ludbury, Mr Ludbury! Come in, do. Your brother is milking, Miss Ludbury, but he shouldn't be long. If you'll just step in, I'll pop down to the shed and warn – let him know you're here.'

'There's no need for that,' Bunny said loftily. 'We'll stroll down and let him know for ourselves. Or would you rather go in, Daddy?'

'No fear!' said George, who could never rest easy in another man's house.

'Oh but, oh dear!' Mrs Flower twisted her apron in her hands and hunted for inspiration. 'I'll run on ahead,' she cried. 'Let him know you're on your way.'

'Do no such thing, Mrs Flower,' Bunny said imperiously, infuriated by this evidence of her brother's lax way with servants. 'I suggest you get back to your work.'

Bunny's disdain, and George's refusal to even recognize

her existence, finished Mrs Flower. Moaning softly to herself, she returned indoors.

'Take that cow,' said Sally.

At the dim end of the cowshed, Jim and Sally contemplated the cow. The cow turned her head and stared back stoically; she chewed continuously and with vigour; she had recently been milked. Jim had set down the pail containing her milk, so that pantheism could the better find common cause with existentialism.

Sally leaned back against the side of the stall and eased the strain on her stomach by linking her hands beneath it. 'It is enough for her that she exists. Nothing leads her to doubt her existence. She eats, she pees, she *is*. We humans, on the other hand, need to know we live *meaningfully*.'

'And how do we go about it?' Jim asked, smiling with the pleasure of having someone with whom to philosophize.

She pulled lank hair from her eyes, thinking as she did so that it was about time she washed it – only stooping over a basin made her feel faint these days. 'It's fatal to put it into words. As soon as you start trying to define meaningfulness – which in any case may not be true for anyone else – you debase it. And if you outline methods of attaining it, you merely invent a set of hackneyed rules to be repeated by uncomprehending idiots. Like religion.'

'Ah, yes,' Jim said, brightening. The imperatives of religion had always filled him with despondency. 'That's an interesting thought. I suppose what you're saying is, we have to discover our own meaning, our own satisfaction as it were.'

'That's the beauty of it. You see, the craving for meaningfulness is the thing that sparks creativity; prompts the search for love. We should never, never abdicate responsibility for our own personal quest.'

This sounded to Jim like hard work. 'I wonder if the cow hasn't got the right idea,' he mused, and was about to enlarge upon this when George and Bunny entered the cowshed.

The quest for meaningfulness overwhelmed one and all. Each floundered in a sea of disbelief, horror, furious embarrassment.

George, standing in a pool of light in the doorway, peered into the gloom and saw . . . Becky: but his wife appeared as he had never seen her during her life – greasy, slatternly, swollen, lounging back against a wall like a brazen harlot. Giddiness shook the image and made it dance. Bunny's screams made his heart race, his stomach pitch and turn.

It had dawned slowly, oh so slowly, on Bunny. When at last the truth hit her, it tore from her throat the final shrieks of the damned.

'Oh, Christ!' said Sally.

Jim took his pipe from his overall pocket and sauntered towards his sister. 'I should calm down if I were you. It's only Sally.'

'Telephone, Mr Ludbury,' called Mrs Flower. Waiting for him to arrive, she put a hand over the mouthpiece and hissed to Sally who was sitting at the kitchen table: 'It's your aunt. She sounds most upset.'

Jim came in from the hall. 'Hello? A stroke? How do you know it was a stroke? Oh, I see.'

Sally caught her breath.

'Stuff and nonsense!' roared Jim. 'If anyone was to blame – and I don't see why anyone should be – he's an old man and about due for something like this – it was *you*, shrieking in his ear like a mad woman.'

(Oh, no, no.)

'All right. I'll come over straight away. But calm down, do you hear?'

(Did I cause it? Did I?)

Jim looked at her, seemed about to speak, but thought better of it and went into the scullery. 'Got to go to Willow Dasset,' he told his housekeeper. 'The Guv'nor's had a stroke. But I'll be back by dinner time.'

During the morning the telephone rang again.

'It's your mother,' Mrs Flower said nervously.

Sally took the receiver, and Mrs Flower went out of the room.

'Yes?'

'Well, you've certainly done it this time. Nearly killed your grandfather. You had to go and flaunt yourself, didn't you? Bunny feels properly vindicated, of course. I've just had her going on and on at me on the phone – apparently, she always knew you were wicked. And I must say, although I've stuck up for you over the years, I've had my doubts. Not that I ever dreamt you'd go as far as this . . .'

'You mean, not as far as you have?'

There was a pause. 'I beg your pardon?'

Sally waited. Into the silence she dropped a few quiet words with measured enunciation. 'Charles? The White Lion?'

When the silence became embarrassing, she gently returned the receiver to its cradle.

She left the house and walked along the farm road until she reached the gate to the field where the cattle grazed. Here she paused, seized the top of the gate and leaned away so that her back arched. Walking, she had had but one thought in her head: that for the second time in her life she had caused offence and threatened the well-being of her grandfather. Now, thought exploded into image. She saw a figure slouch and grovel near the ground, wearing shame like an iron collar. The figure was herself; her yolk was the perception of others.

She swung round, leaned back against the gate and closed her eyes. Slowly, deeply, sweet air filled her lungs. She let it out gently, resolving to return to the house and her work. This time they would not confine her. For she was her own self; she had the strength to reach beyond the dead weight of stricture; she had the power to soar.

Meg caught the next train to Willow Dasset.

It was a Saturday – a convenient day for a get-away. There was only Henry to consider, to advise about roasting the joint and paying the milkman.

'I say,' Henry said, getting up from his knees in front of the television. (He had not been praying, but taking advantage of the Test Card to make adjustments.) 'Cheer up! Bunny said he was going to be all right.'

Meg stared at him uncomprehendingly.

'Here,' – he pulled a handkerchief from his trouser pocket – 'wipe your eyes. Sit down for a minute.'

It dawned on Meg that she had been weeping, or rather, that tears were drying on her cheeks. Surprised, she sat down and removed her spectacles so that she could blot her eyes. Perhaps the news about her father had been more of a shock than she supposed. (In fact, her tears had been tears of fury and fear, and had not begun to flow until Sally threatened her – for that was how she interpreted her daughter naming her lover.)

'What did Bunny say? – That she's had the dickens of a job keeping him in bed?'

'Yes,' Meg responded eagerly. 'He wanted to get up and

go out! Isn't that just like him? The doctor said he didn't think there would be any lasting effect, because Daddy's such a fighter.' The phrase was invigorating. She repeated it to herself. Daddy's such a fighter. Of course he was! So why was she sitting here mopping her eyes? 'I must be off,' she said, getting to her feet. 'Oh, and don't forget the meeting tonight about the organ fund.'

Henry frowned. The coming of the television had changed his attitude to meetings. He had begun to feel that there were too many of them, and that their proliferation was due to people having too much time on their hands. 'Well, I hope it doesn't go on all night, that's all. Some people are such windbags.'

With no clear understanding of her emotions, Meg caught her train; and when she thought of Sally, she stared out at the flashing countryside and imagined a time before her daughter had grown too large for a thrashing.

The next day, she telephoned for a taxi and was driven to Horley-in-the-Hedges. She made the man put her down some yards away from the Glebe Farm gates, then slipped round to the back of the house, across the yard and through the open door. She swept past a startled Mrs Flower and went into the dining-room where she surprised Sally at the table.

'Oh,' said Sally.

Meg looked her over; the pregnancy certainly showed. She pulled a chair to the table and sat down. 'I want to talk to you.'

Sally laid down her pen. She looked her mother in the eye, saw her unquestioning certainty, her determination to let nothing, no-one escape her will. Her heart began to thump, and somewhere, far away, a thin voice shrieked: No! Please Mummy, no!

She took hold of herself. It was not she who was in

301

danger, but her child. She must resist. She *would* resist. She prepared to speak.

Meg, who had reached for a book, examined it and cast it aside.

'I want to explain. I want you to understand.'

She wants to talk about *herself* – justify herself, Sally understood with amazement. Back-tracking hastily in her thoughts, it was a moment or two before she caught the sense of her mother's words.

' . . . because my conscience is perfectly clear. It always has been. Charles and I are discreet; we know how to behave; we harm no-one. And most important of all, we're not depriving anyone of anything; the things we share are simply not wanted elsewhere. I suppose I might as well call a spade a spade: your father, many years ago, made it perfectly clear that he wished our sexual relationship to cease. As for Charles . . . the poor fellow hardly had a sexual relationship until I came on the scene. His wife has a permanent headache. Charles thinks she's allergic to him.'

'Wait a minute, Mother,' Sally put in nervously, but was overruled.

'I want to put you in the picture. Looking at it from an outsider's point of view, we're not hurting anyone; and looking at it from our own point of view – well . . . !' For a moment it appeared that the blessings beggared description.

Sally tried again. 'Mother, I don't really . . .'

'We're *good* for one another,' Meg cried. 'And I'm not just talking about sex – although, I must say . . .'

'Please don't,' begged Sally, feeling sick.

' . . . after your father, it's been an eye-opener. No, it's the easy-going comradeship, the *niceness* – none of that putting the other one down, none of that blasted

302

interference. Charles is supportive, but in an intelligent way. He's a very sensible man, rather a modest man – but powerful behind the scenes.' She smiled to herself.

Sally pushed back her chair. 'Why are you telling me this? Have you gone out of your mind? The door opens, you come marching in, and before I can collect my thoughts, you start sounding off about things best kept to yourself!'

Meg was dumbfounded. 'But you brought it up. You accused me . . . you *threatened* me.'

'I certainly didn't intend to. If it sounded like a threat, I'm sorry. But you pushed me, Mother; I was trying to defend myself.'

'How did you find out?' Meg asked curiously.

'Oh – I overheard you on the phone. Ages ago. Since then I've noticed one or two things – but don't worry, I'm sure no-one else has. And I'll never, ever mention it again. Now, can we please forget it?'

'Very well,' Meg said, vaguely dissatisfied.

'Look, I suggest you mind your business, and allow me to mind mine.' She rose. 'Shall we go out into the garden? I'll show you Mrs Flower's sweet peas; they're quite amazing and she's terribly proud of them. Then I'll made us some coffee.'

Later, on a conducted tour of the garden, Meg was sufficiently recovered to assume her natural authority. 'You'll have it adopted, of course,' she said, frowning at a bed of antirrhinums – 'an awful waste, I always think, these half-hardy annuals.'

'No.'

Meg straightened up and considered this. 'Well, if you're going to marry the fellow, I should get on with it,' she advised, having drawn her conclusions.

'I've no marriage plans, Mother.'

303

'In that case you'll *have* to have it adopted. It's no good going on in your airy-fairy way – plans have be made – arrangements . . . There are organizations dealing with this sort of thing. Perhaps your father and I can make some discreet enquiries . . .'

'Mum . . .'

'Yes?'

'I really hate having to say this, but it seems I've no alternative. One word – Charles.'

Ugly colour rose in Meg's face. Her eyes darted with disproportionate distaste over the antirrhinums.

'And make no mistake; if I have to say it again, and in front of others, then I shall. I'll do anything to protect myself and the baby. You see, I thought we'd reached an agreement back there to keep out of one another's affairs.'

'If that's your attitude . . .' Her eyebrows rose. 'All I can say is, don't think it's going to be a picnic. And don't come running to me, my girl . . .'

'Don't worry. I won't.'

304

6

At Willow Dasset the rain stopped and sunlight glanced across the dining-room table.

'There,' said Bunny, coming in with a pudding dish and setting it down awkwardly on a mat because it was hot. 'The sun – at last! Perhaps we'll get out for some fresh air this afternoon.' She cut into the solid rice pudding with a serving spoon and shook a dollop of it on to a plate, marched to the head of the table and put the plate in front of George. 'Oh, Daddy!' she cried, exasperated. His napkin had slipped again. 'You will fiddle with it!' She tucked it firmly inside his collar.

A childish memory of having had his neck pinched like this before stole over George and made him feel lost and tearful. He looked at his plate. 'No, I don't want this,' he declared, pushing it away.

Bunny was annoyed. 'But you *like* it,' she told him in a raised voice.

George could not remember whether or not this was so. 'Do I?' he asked dubiously.

'Yes, you *do*.'

And George found that it went down quite painlessly.

More than two years had passed since his first stroke. Five months ago he had suffered a second, more alarming apoplexy. Now he was inclined to drop things, to miss his mouth when feeding, to go outside with a purpose and discover himself a few minutes later bewildered in a barn or field. He had given in over the horses. His children and doctor had put forward a compromise: the stallion should go, and the fat old mare remain. George had promptly sold them both. Sometimes he looked in on the empty stables; usually he passed by without a glance. In his vigorous years he had despised quavery old age, had vowed that decay would never humble George Ludbury; rather, he would put a gun to his head, as he dispatched a faithful old dog whose time had come. But now that he was frail he clung to life with grim tenacity, directing the whole of his formidable will towards its continuation. If he slopped his night-time bread and milk laced with rum, or put on his boots when Bunny said slippers, he was not annoyed with himself, but with fate for having dealt him a devilish blow. Losing a grip on life was his only fear, but that fear was terrible; it haunted him, numbed his mind, choked him with inexpressible rage. He bore many irritations for the sake of self-preservation. Bunny was a particular bane, shouting at him as if he were half demented, telling him constantly what he might and might not do. Looking at her now across the table, he was full of hate.

'Oh, you've finished it,' she cried admiringly. 'Good! I told you you liked it. Tiny bit more?'

He shook his head.

'Very well,' she said, letting him off. 'Time for your medicine.' She went to fetch it.

When she had dosed him, measuring carefully into the spoon, putting the spoon into his mouth, mopping his chin with the end of his napkin, he felt the stuff warming his throat and constricted chest. Inside, he seemed to glow. The medicine was doing him a power of good, he told himself, clutching at straws; it was making a new man of him. He caught his daughter's hand. 'You're a good girl . . . Bunny,' he said, recalling her name in the nick of time.

At once she softened, leaned over and kissed the top of his head.

She was grateful. That was all right, then. No need for him to worry about being taken care of.

But sometimes George did worry. Mention of an old people's home – even of the genteel Fairlawns where Charlotte resided – or of visiting some poor old soul in hospital, filled him with terror. Let them not look at *him* and talk of 'homes' and hospitals.

'How about some nice fresh air while it's still fine? Come along, you've been gloomy all morning. Let's wrap you up and go outside.'

Scowling, he allowed her to shoo him into the hall and then to hand him garments, one by one. Under her stern gaze, he put them on.

'What are you doing that for?' George asked from the spare room doorway.

Bunny, turning the feather mattress, was hot, tired and irritated. 'I told you, Daddy. Meg and Henry are coming.' She spoke their names with emphasis.

'Meg and Henry,' he repeated. 'So you did. Meg and Henry,' and he added, because the familiarity of the phrase, like a line of the Lord's Prayer, was irresistible: 'and the little girls.'

'Daddy! Sally and Anne are grown women! Anne was here only a few weeks ago. Don't you remember? She checked your pulse and listened to your chest.'

Of course he did. Of course he remembered. Offended, he left her and went downstairs.

Hanging on the wall above his bureau in the dining-room was a framed photograph of the little girls as he preferred to remember them. The photograph was as essential a part of his life's furnishings as his favourite high-backed chair. The girls sat on a fur-covered table in a photographer's studio, wearing print frocks with Peter Pan collars. Their knees lolled slightly apart, their legs hung over the side of the table, white ankle sock crossing white ankle sock, and their feet in button-strap shoes. The lighting had cast a dazzling shine on their neat heads, and each had a pigtail brought forward over a shoulder so that its magnificence would be recorded for posterity. They dug their fists into the fur and held their backs stiffly. Anne's mouth widened upwards in response to the photographer's demand for a smile. But Sally, mindful of her father's instruction to keep her mouth closed over the gap where her two front teeth ought to be, maintained her lips in a straight, prim line. The eyes of both were unsmiling; they were wide and stern, for they were witnessing a style of behaviour on the part of the photographer – much waving of limp hands, much touching of crimped hair – that they had not encountered before.

George studied the photograph. 'There they are,' he told himself. 'The little girls. The nice, good, little girls.'

'His mind wanders,' Bunny confided over the washing up.

'You surprise me,' said Meg. Their father had deteriorated physically, but he appeared sensible enough.

'Oh, it does,' Bunny insisted. 'When I was making your bed up, do you know what he said? Meg and Henry and the little girls.'

Meg polished a tureen and reflected. 'Funny thing, isn't it? He never had any difficulty accepting that we four had grown up, and yet he's always clung to Sally and Anne as they were – socks and pigtails and tomboy ways.'

'Landgirls, he called them,' Bunny recalled fondly. 'Anne's still a bit of a tomboy. Fancy her riding a motorbike! She rang up last night, by the way. She hopes to be here on Friday evening if nothing crops up.'

'Oh, good.'

Then the sisters were silent, each thinking, but with different emotions, that Anne might be coming but Sally most certainly was not.

'Sally!' said George.

The train of thought leading to this remark was as follows. Meg had laughed in that hearty way of hers and cried, 'Good-oh!' It had filled him with such affectionate longing that whatever it was he had said and she had responded to, had gone clean out of his head. Megs, he had thought, dear, heart-warming Megs – the best of the bunch. She was his own, true girl. He had loved her more than the rest of them put together – Jim, Bunny, Harry . . . Then, with mounting panic, he recalled that there had been another child and that during her short life she had occupied a special place in his heart. Dimly, tenuously, the child returned to him; a tiny thing, dark and exquisite; a funny thing, given to day-dreaming, to telling herself stories and singing long, made-up songs. His panic intensified as he feared that his awakened memory of her might be as fleeting as her life now seemed. He had struggled to retain it, to utter her name. 'Sally!' he had said.

The others at the table, Meg, Henry and Bunny, looked at him.

Interest came into Meg's face. From the moment her grandson had become an accomplished fact she had taken a great interest in him, determined by encouragement and example to make a decent mother out of her hopeless daughter, for the little chap was full of character and reminded her strongly of her father and Harry. What a shame it would be, she had often thought, if her father should die never having known his great-grandson. 'Sally,' she repeated. 'Would you like to see her, Daddy? Would you like her to come here? She's not far away. I'm sure she'd come if she thought you wanted her to.'

He was bewildered; but her eagerness, he felt, required an answer in the affirmative.

'Oh good,' she cried. Then went on daringly: 'And what about Timmy – Sally's little boy. Shall he come, too? He's your great-grandson, your only great-grandchild. Shall I tell her to come and bring Timmy?'

Henry, seeing the alarming colour now flooding his sister-in-law's countenance, broke into a fit of nervous coughing.

George observed his daughters and saw that Meg was in favour of the proposal and Bunny hotly against. It was probably a good thing, he judged. 'Yes,' he declared. 'You tell her to bring him.'

'Fine,' Meg beamed. 'Good-oh! Wouldn't it be nice if she came at the weekend when Anne will be here? Then we'd all be together – like old times.'

'That's right,' George agreed. 'Like old times.'

'You took advantage – yes, you did. His mind was wandering again – he was probably thinking of when the girls were little – he's always harking back to those days – and you jumped in and manoeuvred him. He felt bound to agree; but didn't want to, I could tell. And now he's worried to death. You are *not* to ring up Sally – do you hear? If we don't say anything, he'll forget about it. Poor Daddy, I shouldn't wonder if her coming here with that . . . I shouldn't wonder if it brought on another stroke. I'm the one who looks after Daddy and I won't have it. Meg! *Meg!*'

Meg found the number in her diary and went downstairs to make the call.

'Sally!' she cried with relief when, after a succession of strange voices, the owner of one of them directed her daughter to the telephone. 'How are you?'

'Mum? Oh, fine, thanks.'

'Look, your grandfather has been asking for you. He wants to see you, here, at Willow Dasset.'

There was a pause. 'Heavens!' said Sally. 'What's brought this on? He's not about to turn up his toes?'

'No, no. He wants to see you, that's all. And little Timmy, too. I think it's struck him rather, that Timmy's his great-grandchild.'

'Well! What about Aunt Bunny?'

'Oh – that's all right,' Meg said vaguely, aware of Bunny marking every word on the other side of the door.

'I'm amazed. Dumbfounded.'

'Anne's coming up from London for the weekend. Why not come then?'

'Could do. But not Saturday – I've got something on. Could come Sunday I suppose.'

'Yes. Come on Sunday. We'll pick you up at the station.'

'No. I'll borrow a car. I'm only forty minutes drive away from Willow Dasset – I know because I drove past once, when Pete lent me a car for the day.'

'Pete?' Meg asked hopefully.

'A friend, Mother,' Sally said warningly.

'A jolly kind friend if he lets you borrow his car.'

'It's no big deal – he's got several old cars; they're his hobby.'

'That's nice, dear.' Tinkering about with cars conjured a reassuring image. 'You'll come early – make a day of it?'

'Right-oh. Got to go now, Mum.'

311

'See you on Sunday. Goodbye.'

It was the cue for doors at both ends of the hall to open. Bunny, opening the door from the kitchen a crack, saw Henry come through the baize door from the hall corridor. He bustled up to his wife, seized her by the elbow, and led her away, whispering urgently.

Bunny let them go. She had never thought much of Henry, but if he were now to take a firm line with his wife, he would rise dramatically in her estimation.

Henry, however, was exercised by a more immediate problem than the propriety of his elder daughter's proposed visit to Willow Dasset. George and he had been watching the television – or rather, he, Henry, had been watching, George had observed it with glazed half-attention. The time had come for the start of Henry's favourite serial, when George – without any reference to his guest – had leaned forward, said: 'That's quite enough of that!' and switched off the set. To add insult to injury, he had then closed his eyes and gone off to sleep.

'What do you expect me to do about it, you great booby? Listen, Henry – never mind your dreary old television – I've some interesting news. Sally's got a boyfriend. He's going to lend her his car on Sunday. What do you think of that?'

'I've given up trying to fathom Sally.'

'Don't be so defeatist. P'raps she'll marry him. Think of that. Then they'd be a nice little family.'

'P'raps,' Henry said gloomily. 'Couldn't *you* go in and pretend you want to see it. You're not to know he switched it off. You could say: "Oh, my programme's on. Do you mind?"'

'Don't be ridiculous, Henry. If you want it on, put it on. Why should I waste my evening?'

*

'Wotcher!' said Anne, as Sally got out of her car.

'Hello, Anne.'

'Nice old car. A '36 isn't it?'

'Haven't a clue. It isn't mine. A friend lent it to me. I hear you've bought a motorbike.'

'Yep. I'll give you a go on it later, if you like.'

'That'd be fun.' Sally opened a rear door to haul out her child.

There was a barrier of awkwardness between the sisters, arising from an inability to comprehend the other's life. Sally Robinson, MA – oh, Gawd! thought Anne, wincing at its forbidding stiffness. A medic! thought Sally in awed disbelief – impossible to imagine life and death in the hands of her young sister, and scenes from which Sally would run a mile, being the stuff of her everyday life.

'Wotcher, mate!' cried the aunt, as her small nephew struggled from his mother's grasp.

He evaded his aunt's embrace and ran unsteadily to the top of the steps where he spied his grandmother waiting.

'He's grown,' Anne commented.

'Yes, well, contrary to popular opinion, I do feed him now and then.' Sally watched her son hurl himself against her mother's legs.

'Timmy! Got a kiss for Grandma? What a nice boy! And who do you think this is?'

The child peeped past his grandmother towards the dour looking couple in the doorway.

'It's Great-Grandad and Great-Aunt Bunny.'

George stood his ground, but Bunny faded into the kitchen.

'Kiss Great-Grandad,' urged Meg.

George lowered his face gingerly. 'Well, well, well. What a nice little chap!'

313

'Good boy,' Meg said. 'Now we'll go and find Aunt Bunny and Grandad Robinson.'

'I see mother's taken over,' Anne commented.

'She's a professional, remember?'

The sisters exchanged a quick grin.

'Hello, Grandad,' Sally said shyly.

'Hello, stranger,' said George, feeling that here really was a stranger, for he could detect no resemblance to Sally of the photograph. She was familiar, though – put him in mind of someone . . . Becky! His heart jumped. She was a tousled, taller Becky.

'All right, Grandad?' asked Anne, grabbing his arm.

'Yes thank you, m'dear. Just a giddy turn.' He patted the steadying hand of his younger granddaughter who still bore a reassuring likeness to Anne of the photograph.

'Something the matter with Daddy?' Bunny, eager to be vindicated, hurried back to the doorway.

'Nothing's the matter,' Anne said firmly. 'Let's all go inside.'

For an hour before dinner, George enjoyed himself. It tickled him to watch the little chap's chubby hands explore new mysteries – the fire irons, the brass knobs on the fender, the spill box – and his fat little legs take him drunkenly over the lawn. He recoverd his old art for teasing, at which Bunny became quite excited. 'Isn't Great-Grandad a *one*?' she asked delightedly.

It was during dinner that George became unsettled. A lull in the talking was broken by a comment from Meg concerning Sally's job – lecturing, she called it. Lecturing? What sort of a job was that? It sounded nasty and officious, and not at all the sort of thing for a young miss like Sally. He corrected himself at once: his granddaughter was not a young miss, for here sat her son, tucking in like a good'un, to prove it. Then George grew agitated, unable for the

314

life of him to recall her husband, the little chap's father. When he remembered that she had no husband for him to recall, he let out a sigh of relief – his brain had not addled, after all. Relief was followed swiftly by indignation. He watched her slyly. She was explaining something, and moving her dessert spoon and fork about the table to emphasize a point. She was a cool customer. No-one would guess she was one of those fallen girls. Girls like . . . Rosie Parfitt. Rosie Parfitt! Fancy the name darting into his mind, clear as crystal after all these years! But Rosie Parfitt's case had made quite an impression on him, for the Parfitts were great pals of his Mama's and Rosie had often visited The Grange. Then, suddenly, she was never seen again, and any mention of her made Mama turn black. He had learned the reason for Rosie's disappearance from friends in the village. Rosie had fallen. Some reports had her incarcerated in an attic room of the Parfitt farmhouse, others placed her in some remote spot on the Cornish coast. He had come across other cases of the fallen during his life – that of Rosie had been his first, most striking encounter – and the consequences of falling had always been the same: the girl had disappeared from the sight of decent people. What the dickens, then, was this girl doing at his table – bold as brass – and her bastard beside her to boot? What was the world coming to, he would like to know; had everyone taken leave of their senses?

'None for me,' he declared as Bunny began to serve plums and custard.

'Oh!' Bunny cried, as if a catastrophe had occurred. 'You'll try a little custard,' she wheedled.

'That I will not,' George said with dignity, and he got up from the table and went to sit in his high-backed chair.

Bunny tightened her lips and breathed strenuously.

'It's the excitement,' Meg whispered. 'He's tired –

wants a little nap. And he did very well on the meat and vegetables.'

After dinner, Anne proposed that she and Sally put the motorbike through its paces.

Bunny, and Meg hanging on to Timmy, came out into the yard to see them go.

'Just look at them,' marvelled Bunny.

They went bumpily over the farmyard, Anne in her corduroy trousers, Sally's floral skirt bundled up in a knot between her legs. Sally's shrieks came back to the watchers over the engine's roar. When the bike shot up the incline past the tractor sheds, Meg and Bunny rushed through the kitchen to the window on the back stairs to watch machine and riders fly past the top of the paddock.

Anne opened the throttle. Sally screamed. 'Lean into it, or we'll come off,' Anne yelled over her shoulder, and their hair brushed the bank as they rounded the bend. Skidding, lurching, they rode the ruts, and tore on towards Bailey's Field. In the entrance to the field they turned and raced back, and continued on to the rickyard. Here they practised stunts: figures of eight, jumping the bike from the bank – from the shallow end at first, then from higher up.

'Better than leaping off bales!'

'Miles!'

It was not until they were back in the farmyard, trembling in the stunning silence of the engine's death, that Sally understood she had journeyed through hallowed ground. Bailey's Field, the paddock, the garlanded track; and the rickyard she had never thought to enter again, tormented in nightmares as she often was by the dying, thrashing white rat. She had returned in a whirlwind of desecration; whooping, yelping, shrieking. And it had been glorious. 'That was really fine,' she told her sister breathlessly.

'Yeah. Not bad.' Anne was parking the machine tenderly.

A voice rang out across the yard: 'I'll *take* you home *again*, Kathleen . . .'

'Milking. Come on – bring Timmy. Can't let old John down.' Anne strode away, whistling, her hands in her pockets.

Sally, watching, reflected that the embarrassing dawn of womanhood had not hindered her sister from doing as she pleased at Willow Dasset. She had managed to sprout discreetly; in fact, it was difficult to tell what Anne had got beneath the sloppy, bulky clothes she favoured. Anne had reached the stable door to the cowshed, the top half of which was open. She reached over the lower half and fumbled with the bolt. It appeared to resist, then to shoot back with an echoing clang. There had been no oiling of bolts, rehanging of doors, creosoting, or repointing, of late. The scene, steadfastly eternal, had about it a jaded air.

A tap on the dining-room window. It was Meg, smiling and pointing, warning that Timmy was on his way.

'Mummee . . .' He hurtled through the doorway towards her.

She opened her arms and caught him up. His legs went round her waist, his arms round her neck. 'Like to go and see how they do the milking at Willow Dasset? They don't do it like Uncle Jim. Here they use machines.' Over the yard they went, the child bouncing on her hips, her mouth against his cheek.

The machinery was startling. Timmy grasped a fistful of his mother's hair and thrust out his free arm to ward off any approach of jumpy nozzles and jittery tube clusters. Sally carried him down the shed to a cow that had already been milked. She put her hand into the silky hollow in

317

front of its jutting hip, and when she withdrew it, her son put his hand where hers had been. 'Cow,' he said. And the cow turned, slew-jawed, and gazed soulfully.

Anne and John were having a friendly argument. Sally took Timmy into the parlour to watch the milk pass through the cooler into the churns. Then she put him down and they wandered, hand in hand, over the cobbles of the yard, bending to sniff pineapple weed, pull pinches of sorrel beads, and twist indestructible plantain round their fingers.

'Dog,' said Timmy, when the sheep dog dragged its chain.

'Not that dog,' Sally decided, sensing canine ill-temper due to lack of regular exercise.

They drifted into the house.

George was in the kitchen, at a loss, propped against the table, his stick between his knees.

'Oh, hello, Grandad!' But there was something forbidding about him.

He grunted. He was unsmiling.

She went to lead her son on, but George put out his stick and barred their way. Instinctively, she drew Timmy back, close in against her legs.

George peered at the boy. After a while, he said: 'He's just beginning his life.'

'Yes.'

George raised his head. He looked her hard in the face. His mouth was twisted, his eyes burned with jealousy. 'And I'm at the end of mine.'

'Go on, darling,' Sally urged softly. She steered her son round the old man's stick, and when they were safely past, took his hand and led him to the garden door.

A curse had been laid upon them. She went in search of a blessing.

No jaded air wearied the garden. The garden glowed. The child scrunched his feet on the gravel and fingered mosses on the staddlestones.

I shall not look up at the window, Sally vowed, going slowly down the path. I trust her to be there. By the rosemary bush she knelt and circled the child in her arms. I am here, and I have my son.

If she raised her eyes she would see a benevolent face at the window, grave eyes wishing them well. But she would not look up.

The child broke free and ran to the flower-border with outstretched hands.

'It's a butterfly, Timmy,' she cried joyously, for she was here, at Willow Dasset, with her son.

'I suppose,' Bunny said, 'it went off rather well.'

'Of course it did,' said Meg. 'I told you it would be all right. And I think Daddy enjoyed having them.'

'Well, they certainly tired him out. He was more than ready for bed. But he went nice and calmly – no coughing fit when he got undressed, and he took his medicine without a fuss.'

'Sally was most impressed with the way you keep this up.' (They were strolling in the darkening garden.)

'I know. She said so.' Bunny's face brightened at the memory. 'She thinks it's as good as it's ever been.'

'It is, Bunny. You work wonders. If Mama could see it, she'd be so pleased.'

Bunny drew in a gulping breath. 'Oh, the orange blossom after a full day's sun!'

'I know.' Meg raised her head and sniffed. 'Gorgeous! It was nice, wasn't it, both the girls being here again?'

'Yes,' Bunny said with mild surprise. 'I suppose it was, rather.'

319

7

A roar of fury trailed into terror, ended in a heart-broken sob: 'Mama . . . !'

Those below in the dining-room caught every nuance. Every corner of the house received the cry, digested it, sent it on.

For a while Meg and Sally remained utterly still in chairs drawn close to the fire. Sally was aware of a furtive blankness abroad; there was no creaking, no groaning, no nervous shifting; Willow Dasset declined to be agitated by the master's terrible bellow. Even so, she detected an air of shame.

Meg sprang to her feet. 'Whatever's going on?' She went quickly from the room, up the stairs and along the landing.

Reluctantly, Sally followed her. In the doorway of her grandfather's room, she paused and looked towards the bed.

A baby lay there; an ancient baby with ruined eyes. Bewildered, disconsolate, it raised its head to the newcomers in search of pity. It was ignored.

Sally, unable to venture further into the room, saw that Aunt Bunny was lying across the suffering one, pinning him down and murmuring: 'There, darling, there. I'm here, I've got you. Never mind, my dearest, never mind . . .'

And Anne — Sally's heart began to thud as she understood the nature of her sister's occupation — was

320

manipulating an instrument in the area of their grandfather's genitals. And things were not going smoothly to
judge from Anne's tense, frowning expression.

'No, lie *still*, Daddy. Anne's only trying to help you,'
Bunny implored as George reared and roared.

'Oh, dear Lord!' muttered Meg, turning from the bed
to stare blankly through the window.

Sally returned softly to the dining-room.

The past two years had been full of new doings: she
had married Alex, a writer, and they had moved south
when she had been appointed to a better paid job; Timmy
had passed from babyhood to sturdy boyhood, Anne had
become a qualified doctor. But for Grandad Ludbury the
years brought only painful, undignified decline – and now
this new degradation . . .

She crouched over the fire, widening her eyes, willing
the heat to sear from them an impertinent image. But
her grandfather's helplessness was incombustible. And
when she closed her eyes the image grew from the
shadows. Going from the room, she found no solace
in the muffled, clothing-draped hall, nor in the hollow
clacking of her feet going aimlessly through kitchen
and scullery. But in the chilly parlour she switched
on the light and spied hope on the mantelpiece. She
advanced swiftly and carried the silver-framed photograph to the light. *There* he was – with his wife who
was holding an infant. The infant was herself, Sally
realized after some thought, for its tuft of hair was
dark, not fair as it would be if the baby were Anne. Here
stood the proud grandparents with their first grandchild.
Rebecca looked down at the child, amused, absorbed,
oblivious of the camera. At her side, George presented
himself; stood on straight, slightly parted legs, thrust
up chest and chin, grinned handsomely; a rogue of a

man, proud, a touch defiant, nicely turned out, king of his castle.

At the back of her mind the impertinent image trembled. Soon, soon, as she gazed and drank him in from the photograph it would be quite obliterated.

Footsteps sounded. Not wishing to be caught, she replaced the photograph, hurried to the door and switched off the light.

It was Meg on the stairs. Meg seemed not to care about Sally's doings; she passed her daughter wordlessly. Sally joined her by the dining-room fire.

For some moments mother and daughter sat in silence, listening to the faint whimpering from above.

'It's not working. If only he'd give in!' Meg blurted with sudden passion.

This was her mother giving in, Sally understood. For the past few years Meg had been unable to refer to her father without adding a fervent codicil: 'It's wonderful how he never gives in — he's a fighter; he won't be beat!' Now, Meg was giving in on her father's behalf, understanding at last that nothing of him remained beyond a blind will to go on.

Footsteps came wearily down the stairs. Anne looked in. 'It's no use. They'll have to operate. I'm going to phone Doctor Beardsley.'

When she had gone, Sally turned to Meg in horror. 'Surely they won't operate. It would be shocking.'

'If they can't get rid of his water, he'll die of agony I should think.'

'But Anne said earlier he'd never stand an operation.'

Meg put her face in her hands.

In the hall Anne's steady voice was explaining things calmly.

'*You* were supposed to phone Alex,' Meg recalled,

jumping gratefully at the opportunity to be taken up with the concerns of life and the living.

'I will when Anne's finished.'

'You should have done it earlier, before Timmy's bedtime,' Meg admonished, warming to a subject over which she could exert some control. 'Alex is so good to Timmy—couldn't be better if he was the boy's father; but you shouldn't take him for granted. You promised to ring at six o'clock.'

'It's only half past. And I expect they're still fooling about. Alex has no sense of time.'

Anne returned. 'The doctor's coming out now, to see.'

'Sit down,' cried Meg, rising. 'You look all in.'

'No, sit here.' Sally could not quite look her sister in the eye. 'I'm going to ring Alex; then I'll make us some tea.'

'Hello, Alex.'

'Sally! How are things?'

'Pretty bad. You sound breathless.'

'I am. There's a breathless game of skittles going on here.'

'Oh, lovely! You're getting on all right, then.'

'Of course. But things are bad there?'

'Oh, Alex . . . I don't know why I came. I'm useless. Anne's so clever . . . I can't take it in, somehow, that she's taken control of Grandad. Not that he seems quite like Grandad. The truth is, something like this shows me up for what I am: queasy, hopeless, inadequate.'

'Bloody nonsense, darling. It's just that you see more in things than most people do.'

'Mmm. Anyway, it sounds as if they'll have to operate, after all.'

'On a dying man? That's obscene! Poor old devil!'

'Well, the doctor's coming to take a look. But I shouldn't think he'd do any better than Anne. Oh –

hang on a minute, that might be him now.' Outside, a dog had grunted half-heartedly. But when the door opened it was Jim who came in. 'Oh!' She caught him to her and kissed him, then said into the phone: 'Alex, guess who's just walked in?'

'Jim?'

'Ask Alex how the book's coming,' Jim said, going on towards the stairs.

'He said: How's the book coming? What he really means is, when will it be finished so that we can all go and stay with them at Horley-in-the-Hedges?'

'About the middle of next month. Tell him I'm looking forward to the break.'

'Is Timmy there?' She heard him summon her son, and then the boy's breathy voice: 'Hello, Mummy.'

'Hello, darling. You and Alex are having a grand game, I hear.'

'Yes. Skittles. And we had sardines for tea. I painted a picture and Alex put it on the kitchen wall.'

'What was the picture of?'

'Can't 'member. But it was yellow and red. When are you coming home, Mummy?'

'Soon, my darling. In a day or so. Be a good boy for Alex. Goodnight, now.'

'Goodnight, Mummy.'

'I'll phone again tomorrow,' she promised her husband.

'Take care, love. Bye bye.'

When Sally returned to the dining-room carrying a tray, Meg looked up with a bright face. 'Everything all right?'

'Fine. They were playing skittles.'

'Skittles, eh?' Meg said approvingly.

Bunny trudged in. At once Anne and Meg offered her their seats, but Bunny turned a dining chair towards the fire and sat, with a temporary air, on its edge, hunching her body into a smaller edition of herself. Sally, passing her a cup of tea, saw that her eyes glittered. 'He's dozing,' Bunny reported in a whisper, as if louder mention of the respite might bring about its demise.

For a time no-one spoke. The fire rustled. Occasionally, cups rattled on saucers. The peace was broken when the dog in the yard spoke up resolutely.

'That sounds more like it. That'll be him.'

Anne rose and went to open the door to the doctor. Bunny darted a frightened look at the seated ones, then followed.

'Not going?' Sally asked the senior of George's children.

Meg shook her head. 'Let them sort it out.' Her bitter tone suggested that it was, in any case, a fool's errand.

Sally moved into the chair vacated by Anne and pondered on her mother's abdication. No use you marching upstairs and demanding of *this* lie-abed that he rise, dress and set about his business, she told her silently. This lie-abed is beyond your galvanizing willpower; for him the game is up. Was she shaken by her impotence? Was she brooding about it now? Was she even capable of reflection? Guessing that her mother was in the throes of an amorphous mass of emotion, she was suddenly full of pity. 'More tea, Mum?'

Meg seemed not to hear. Her head began to tremble, her lips moved crossly, her expression announced that she was thoroughly out of patience.

This was not surprising, for anything or anyone not susceptible to immediate comprehension was liable to put her mother out of patience. 'I've no patience with it.' The old defiant cry rang again in Sally's memory. It meant, of course, that she declined to waste time trying to understand the matter, for she was a creature of instinctive reaction, supremely confident of her innate wisdom. But there was one thing, surely, that had given her pause for thought. 'Mother?'

Meg dragged her eyes from the fire and fixed them sightlessly upon her daughter.

'Have you ever had to work things out? Had doubts, qualms? Your relationship with Charles, for instance; did it cause you a lot of heart-searching?'

Meg stared blankly. 'What are you on about?' she asked nastily.

'I'm interested.'

'Why?'

'Because it *is* interesting – how people come to terms and so on. After all, on the face of it, having an affair goes against everything you stand for.'

'You're calling me a hypocrite. Is that it?'

'No. I'm not calling you anything. Just trying to understand.'

'There's nothing *to* understand. And I thought we were never going to mention the subject again.'

'*Have* you had a struggle to reconcile it with your beliefs? Or can you keep things in separate compartments?'

Meg sat up straight and looked hard at Sally. Then she said pugnaciously: 'Look, it's none of your business, but if you must know, it was all perfectly straightforward. The chance cropped up. It seemed common sense not to let it go, especially as it was quite clear no-one else would suffer. You see, that's what I go on in life – common sense,' she explained with pride. 'When God gave me common sense, I suppose He expected me to use it. And if you don't mind my saying so, you'd do better to use a bit of common sense yourself, instead of brooding over everything.'

'But the Church says,' Sally put in timidly, and was interrupted.

'You mean, a lot of silly men say.'

'Silly or not, they speak for the Church, I take it?'

'That's hardly God's fault.'

'No . . . I suppose not.' She gave up, and toyed with a vision of God's great satisfaction on learning that Meg Robinson had taken charge of things.

'What is it?' Meg asked suspiciously, seeing a smile creep over her daughter's face.

'Just thinking.'

Meg breathed in sharply and returned her attention to the fire. It required stoking. She had leaned forward to grasp a log, when a wail from the room above stilled her hand. The wailing intensified. She drew back her lips and exposed gritted teeth.

Her mother's expression caused Sally's heart to sink – there was an element of cruelty in it – and she carried the look of vexed impatience back with her in an exploration of the years. Her mother's quick refusal to grant her pregnant daughter sanctuary came to mind. 'What would the Ladies' Forum make of it?' she had cried, uttering the most pressing thought to arrive in her head. But at once she took issue with herself: one could hardly bear grievance against such childlike honesty, and to call it hypocritical was to condemn a reflex action. Even so, there *was* a matter she would like her mother to address – had been for years – she had told herself repeatedly that one day . . . *Now*! She would ask her *now* – while death stalked the house threatening an end to chances. Craning forward, she said: 'Mother' – and her voice cracked on the word. 'Mother,' she said again more evenly, 'do you remember that time in the barn? When you tried to kill me?

327

'What?' The wailing had died to a whimper, but it played, still, in Meg's ears.

'Do you remember when you tried to kill me in the barn? – Would have if Grandad hadn't stopped you.'

'You must be mad! I never heard such nonsense . . .'

Sally closed her eyes and plunged on. 'I wish you'd tell me, because it's always worried me. What did I do that so revolted you that you wanted to throttle me? Because you were going to– *yes!*' She caught her mother's protesting hand and held on to it. 'You know you were, and not in temper but in cold desire. It had been building up, whatever it was, because you were pretty foul to me throughout that holiday. It was when all the fuss started about my bosom showing. Do you remember accusing me of something unspeakable to do with that man in the cottage? And then we went to Stratford and there were some friends of yours in the foyer. I seem to remember feeling hopelessly misunderstood. I threw a scene. I expect it was frightful – made you feel a fool – but was it really so appalling that it made you *murderous?* What was it all about, Mother. Tell me!'

Meg snatched back her hand and dropped to her knees to replenish the fire. Her actions were automatic; she did not know that she wrestled to free the log of her choice and upset the basket, that she righted it and gathered the spilled logs, built up the fire and swept the hearth. As she worked, images flashed through her mind's eye – the man in the cottage doorway – her friends in the foyer – her young daughter's burgeoning body. Aflame with old feeling, she all but cried: Sexual jealousy out of sexual frustration! How does that answer you, madam? But the passionate words were still-born as she tossed away the hearth brush. She sat back on her heels and surveyed her handiwork, and in the firelit moments of inactivity her emotion died, and with it the necessary abandon for a truthful outpouring. She knew she would not answer. It was years too late. 'You know your trouble?' she remarked, hauling herself back into her chair. 'An over-active imagination.'

She means I imagined it, Sally thought, sinking back in her chair. For a moment she wondered whether this was possible; then knew beyond doubt that it was not. Chance, time – perhaps her mother's nature? – had beaten her; she was condemned to remember and not understand.

They were silent for some time.

A shout of pain made them start to the edge of their seats. Feet rushed overhead, and a voice cried: 'Hold him!' Lowered voices mingled urgently. The cry went on, describing new heights of terror.

'Merciful Heaven!' Meg groaned. 'Let him die tonight!'

Footsteps, earnest voices in the hall.

The door opened and Bunny came in. 'Doctor's phoning the hospital. Daddy'll be all right, now, for tonight, but they'll have to do something about it tomorrow.'

'You mean operate?' Sally asked.

Bunny nodded.

'Then I hope,' Meg announced portentously, 'that he doesn't live to see the morning.'

Bunny flinched.

Sally hurried to steady her and draw her to a chair.

'I must go back to him . . .'

'Have a rest. Come. Sit down.' She pressed on her aunt's shoulder – Bunny crumpled like paper – and said: 'I'll go up and sit with them now.'

She found Jim sitting forward in a basket chair, arms resting on spread knees, hands clasped, staring down at the carpet.

George was propped up on his pillows. His eyes fastened on his granddaughter as she came in through the open doorway and went, touching Jim's shoulder briefly as she passed, to sit on a hard-backed chair.

'Hello, Grandad,' she said, looking nervously into filmy eyes.

He did not at once reply, but when he spoke it was with disconcerting clarity. 'Who's that black girl?'

Sally's hand flew to her hair.

Jim turned to Sally, and then to her father. 'You mean Sally? You know Sally.'

'Black . . . girl,' George protested fearfully.

'Do you mean her hair? It's not as black as Mother's used to be before she went white. Mama's hair was jet black. You remember Mama's jet black hair?'

'Never seen her before in me life.'

Sally rose.

George seized the counterpane. 'Don't let her come near me!'

'I'd better go.'

In her unlit room she climbed on to the window-seat and stared out into darkness. Soon her eyes adjusted and she saw the willows move against the sky and the pale track reach up and vanish behind the trees. Willow Dasset breathed evenly, oblivious of impending doom.

Was he disclaiming me, or his wife? she wondered. Both of us, she guessed, recalling his bewildered cry of 'Mama!' – a cry from a time when there were no dark-haired girls. He had taken violently against the nurse. Only Anne could manage him, Sally had been informed a dozen times, and fair-haired Anne with her large bones, close-set eyes and beaky nose, was thoroughly Ludbury. 'Of course, it runs in the family,' Aunt Bunny had breathed as she and Sally watched Anne perform a deft manoeuvre to facilitate the patient's comfort. Sally had presumed she meant caring for the sick and was thinking of Great-Aunt Pip. How absurd was this obsession with the family, this suspicion of all who lacked Ludbury markings. It occurred to her that a portion of the odium she had incurred at puberty had been due, not only to an enlarging bosom and a shrinking waist – deplorable though these developments had been – but to their dawning, unconscious realization, that she was becoming not as they were. Apparently, a resemblance to Grandma Ludbury had been insufficiently reassuring. Come to think of it, there had always been a degree of speculation and argument about Grandma – perhaps because of her quiet refusal to be other than herself. I had better go down and confess, she thought, swinging her legs from the window-seat.

'I'm afraid Grandad doesn't recognize mè. He got rather upset,' she told the gathering at the fireside. 'I don't seem to be much use. Can I get the supper? What would people like?'

When everyone had completed their scanty meal – Meg briefly relieving Jim so that he could eat at the table – Sally washed up, then put hot water bottles in the beds.

Jim came down and said he must go. At once Bunny rose, but Anne detained her. 'No, you must go to bed, you're exhausted. The rest of us'll take turns tonight.' But as she spoke, her eyes fell on her sister and she became embarrassed.

'You and I will take turns, Anne,' Meg put in hastily. 'I'll sit up first.'

'Right-oh. Wake me when you've had enough, or if there's any bother. We'll leave the bedroom doors open. But shut yours, Aunt Bunny.'

'You'll wake me if . . .'

'Of course.'

'Come to bed, Aunt,' Sally said gently, taking her arm. And Bunny, who seemed beyond protest, went with her like a fostered lamb.

Sally dreamed she had been banished from Willow Dasset. 'Go, go,' they cried from the yard as she stumbled down the steps. At the bottom she turned and sent them an imploring look. They were implacable – 'Go, go.' She got into her car and turned the key in the ignition. The engine rasped, but failed to turn. She spread her hands helplessly. 'Go, go,' they insisted, pressing down on her. Rah, rah, choked the dead engine, rah, rah . . .

She awoke, but the engine continued its futile rasping. Then she sat up, for it was not rasping, but coughing. A dry cough, Aunt Bunny's cough. 'A nervous cough,' Anne had diagnosed yesterday when Aunt Bunny had suffered a bout of it, for placing a spoon on her tongue and demanding that she say Ah had revealed no inflammation, neither were glands enlarged, nor had her temperature risen. It was a nervous cough brought on by stress and fatigue.

Sally got out of bed and drew back the curtains. A thin light was dawning, and an electric light bulb glowed yellow at a cowshed window. She switched on the bedroom light and looked at her watch. Ten to seven. Not too early to make tea.

Moving from pantry to kitchen to scullery, filling a kettle, setting a tray, peering out across the yard at the cowshed and catching a burst of song, she felt that she had become her grandfather, doing as he had done for so many years. The sounds of tea-making would carry, she knew, to the bedroom above the kitchen. She imagined her eleven-year-old self lying up there in bed, hearing footfalls on the linoleum, on the stairs, and the approaching rattle of china.

Instead of taking the tray to the chest at the head of the landing as her grandfather would have done, she put it on the tallboy near Aunt Bunny's door. Then she crept along the landing to check the situation in the two main bedrooms.

She turned left into her grandfather's room and stood at the edge of the open door. A lamp on the dressing table had been left burning all night. Grandad in the bed, Mother – not Anne, she noted with surprise – swathed in a blanket in the basket chair, were both sound asleep with their mouths open. Her heart seemed to miss a beat as it struck her that each sleeper's attitude exactly mirrored the other's. Their heads were tilted back over pillows, so that their jaws gaped and faint clicking noises erupted in their throats. Their eyelids were thin translucent hoods. The tautness of their sallow skin suggested the straining faces in Brueghel's *Parable of the Blind* – impossible to view these two and not believe they had been created in the same instant by the same hand.

Tea was not yet required.

Across the landing the other room was in darkness. She looked round the open door and after a moment was able to distinguish a mound under the bedclothes. Evidently, Anne still favoured the same sleeping style, hunched under the covers so that it was a wonder she could breathe. No doubt if she were to go and prod her, Anne would fling back the bedcovers, reach for her clothes and launch into a rapid soliloquy.

It would be a shame to wake her.

At the other end of the landing, Bunny got out of bed and switched on the light, thus precipitating a new fit of coughing.

'Get back at once,' Sally said, coming in with a cup of tea. 'Drink this. It might help.'

Obediently, Bunny returned to bed and sat up against pillows pressed to the iron bedstead. 'Thank you . . . it's good,' she spluttered between sips and coughs.

A cardigan had been draped over the back of a chair. Sally took it and wrapped it around her aunt's bony shoulders.

'I'll fetch my cup,' she decided suddenly.

She went back to the landing and poured herself some tea, then took it into the narrow little room and perched on the side of the bed below Bunny's feet.

The coughing subsided. They drank thoughtfully.

It was a little girl in the bed, thought Sally, a frightened little girl in a hairnet, peeping over a cup, trying to be brave. And how brave she would have to be, Sally all at once grasped, for her imminent loss was not only that of parent and home, but of child, the love of her life, her one and only. 'Daddy . . . !' she heard her aunt call again and again in echoes from the years, now reprovingly, now tenderly, now admiringly, always with an undertone of significance. He was her precious one, thought Sally, and her eyes strayed to the chest of drawers in a corner of the room where she had once found gifts from other relatives pushed out of sight, discarded and forgotten in a drawer for fear of distracting the single-minded focus of Aunt Bunny's affection. Did they lie there still? Sally did not doubt it – this year's white nylon petticoat with yester-year's peach silk; this year's good wishes from Sally, Alex and Timmy with an ancient offering from Meg, Henry and the girls. Tokens of affection were required only from the precious one. But the precious one was about to depart. Ahead, for Aunt Bunny, lay the ultimate bereavement.

Sally put her cup and saucer on the floor and reached for Bunny's hand. 'Poor Auntie.'

Tears began to spill over thin cheeks. Sally removed her

aunt's empty cup and took her into her arms. The tears fell faster, a warm velvet flood rushing from the core of Bunny's being. They spread damply over her niece's bosom. 'Oh, oh. Oh, Sally!'

'I know . . . I know . . .' Sally rocked her gently.

At length, Bunny was exhausted and lay back on her pillows. 'What you must think of me!' she gasped shyly.

They smiled ruefully at one another while Sally continued to hold her hand.

'Wouldn't you damn well know it?' muttered Anne, joining her mother at the window in George's room. 'The bloody thing worked as easy as pie – drew off at least a pint.'

They glanced round at the old man in the bed who was sitting up and looking pleased with himself, then turned again to contemplate the garden. 'Well, I shouldn't tell *them*,' Meg warned, thinking of weaker sisters. 'We don't want anymore of that Ooo dear! Should we or shouldn't we?' she said in a put-on, dithery voice. 'Just keep mum and let everything go ahead as arranged.'

Anne nodded.

'I should think you've had about as much as you can stand. Your leave's nearly up, anyway. Talk about a busman's holiday! It's all very well for Bunny to go on about you being the only one who can deal with him, but if this goes on any longer he'll have to put up with a nurse – if they can find one who'll put up with *him*.'

'It was probably a fluke with the catheter, anyway. It worked pretty well yesterday morning, and then look what a day we had of it.'

'Perhaps he's more relaxed first thing.'

'Or not feeling so stroppy. Look at him. Butter wouldn't melt. You can't imagine him fighting like a demon.'

'Can't I, though,' Meg said bitterly, rubbing a deep scabby groove in her arm gouged by horny fingernails.

'You're tired out, too. You should have woken me last night.'

'You were more in need of sleep. Go and get some breakfast. And remember – least said . . .'

As Anne left the room, Meg went towards the bed.

'Barley's coming on,' George remarked pleasantly.

It took her breath away; it was the stuff of a lifetime's intercourse between them – How's the barley, Daddy? Oh, coming along nicely. We'll go and look at it after tea. She sat on the edge of the bed and peered at him. He stared back, apparently in full possession of his faculties.

'The barley, Daddy?'

'Barley?' he repeated, puzzled.

She recoiled in disgust.

'I shall go to market, directly.'

'Will yer now?' she sneered under her breath, and was then seized with remorse. She clasped his hand and shook it. 'Daddy, *Daddy* . . .' She wanted to tell him, to warn him of what lay ahead, that soon an ambulance would come and bear him away from Willow Dasset, that strangers would take charge of him, submit him to a surgeon's knife. She became so anxious for him to escape this fate that she almost sank to her knees and begged him to give in. But then came the mocking memory of how she had applauded his clinging on to life; only this wretched prostate business and the messy cruelty of the catheter had changed her mind. She had always been easily sickened, a deformed calf, a diseased cat, a badly injured dog had all precipitated a cry of 'For God's sake kill it, Daddy.' Put it out of my sight so that I no longer need to think about it, had been the more precise sentiment of her heart. And now,

336

inwardly, she was urging her father: Give in. For God's sake, give in!

There was one thing, though, to be said for her father's predicament: it had certainly taught her a lesson. Catch her hanging on to life at all costs! But at once she was seized by the horrifying knowledge that she could do no other than kick and scream as he did.

My God! Brooding! Getting as bad as Sally! She sprang to her feet and marched to the bedroom across the landing where she ripped the covers from the bed and set about the pillows and mattress.

Sally slipped into the room – they were all at the bedside; Aunt Bunny, Uncle Jim, Mother, Anne – and looked anxiously to see whether her entrance had upset the patient. But Grandad Ludbury looked pink and smug as a newly fed infant.

Outside, the dog began to shout.

'That'll be them.'

'I'll go down,' Jim said.

Sally, with her hands behind her back clutching the windowsill, remained apart from the others.

The ambulance men came upstairs.

There was a hiatus, a moment when nothing happened, might never happen, or perhaps the sky would fall.

Then the men moved on the bed. Sally swung round to face the window.

During the battle that followed, her eyes held to the garden. Plants lay in mouldering mounds on the red-brown earth. Hips, and a few brownish blooms, hung drably from the rose trellis. The trees at the end of the lawn were bare, their leaves raked up and gone. Even the shrubbery had lost its shine. Where are you? she cried silently. Have pity. Come to him. And Grandma Ludbury, who, all the

337

time, had been strolling along the path – only Sally had just this moment caught sight of her – gazed up at the window of the room where she, too, had encountered death. Help him. Teach him. His way is too painful, and utterly, utterly vain.

Gracefully, regretfully, not without sorrow, Grandma Ludbury shrugged.

Of course, she had begged the impossible. It took a lifetime to practise the manner of one's dying. For the second time in her life Sally found herself crying Let me be like you!

The wrenching of the master from Willow Dasset went on – along the landing, down the stairs, into the hall. His leave-taking throbbed with an intention to rend the fabric, but the house could not be moved. When the struggle burst upon the outside world, the dog became frantic, yelped and howled and tried to loose himself from his chain. Upstairs, Sally marked every sound and watched the scene in her mind's eye.

Then all was quiet, heartlessly quiet.

Soon, feet came weightily up the stairs. 'They've all gone,' Jim said. 'Anne drove Meg in the Morris. Bunny went with the Guv'nor in the ambulance. I said I'd be along later, but I don't know . . . It's out of our hands now.'

When Sally failed to turn from the window, he sat down in the basket chair. Watching her still back, it occurred to him that there was no reason not to smoke. 'What yer thinking about?' he asked eventually.

She heard the popping of his lips, and smelt the sweet, soothing aroma of his pipe. 'Thinking of Grandma, actually.'

'What about her?'

'That she got it right and Grandad didn't.'

'Well, now . . .' He considered the matter through a series of puffs. 'Depends . . . what you mean . . . by right. What's right for one . . .'

'I know that, Uncle. I suppose what I'm feeling is that life, as it goes along, ought to reflect progress. We grow up, learn, get better at things, understand more; it's logical to think of it as a progression. To end up a disgusting mass of incoherent rage, roaring and struggling, insensible of everything you ever valued or learned, seems to me to make a mockery of it all. If that's to be the outcome one might as well give up now.'

'I don't know if anyone ever told you, but that wasn't the way your grandmother went.'

'I know.'

'But I've a feeling, Sal, that your idea of life's too high falutin'. We're animals, you know, when you get down to it, and the driving force of every animal is to go on living. That's nature — might as well face it.'

She shuddered and turned. She saw that he was very comfortable in the basket chair, legs thrust out straight, pipe going well; his kindly face was distinctly unperturbed. 'But what it's all about, Uncle, is trying to become satisfactory to oneself. Imagine getting near to achieving that, then tell me how anyone can cling on to life at the expense of losing it? It doesn't make sense. All the same' — she had no desire to ruffle his composure, so she bobbed down and laid her cheek against his — 'I'm with you about our basic animal nature. Personally, I've always felt very much at home with cows.'

'Mmm. How about,' he asked thoughtfully, 'a plate of my special scrambled eggs?'

Heavens, she was starving! 'Yes please!'

'Right-ho. You can make the coffee.'

*

339

'Did anyone think to tell Harry?' Meg asked suddenly, on arriving back at Willow Dasset from the hospital.

There was a short silence.

'I'll go and phone Dora,' said Jim.

In the late afternoon, Harry arrived in a temper. Soon, all four of George's children were shouting. (If Harry had come over more often to do his share . . . How dare they go ahead without consulting him? If Harry only knew what they'd been through . . . He'd a darn good mind to go straight down to that hospital this minute.)

'Uncle,' Anne got in quietly, her hands non-combative in her pockets, her expression helpful, her tone that of one reasonable person addressing another, 'we should have kept you in the picture – no question about that. But I'm sure you can appreciate how it happened. We were dog tired – hardly a minute to go to the lav, never mind use the phone. And take it from me, there was no other course left. We'd come to the end of the road, I'm afraid.'

'Well,' Harry said, opting for magnanimity. 'If you say so, Anne. You're a professional, you know what you're talking about. It was just that Dora got it into her head that you'd all got together behind my back. Mind you, it's her speciality – getting the wrong end of the stick. Hello, there,' he called to Sally, noticing her for the first time. 'Long time, no see! How's tricks?'

'Too old for tricks, Uncle.'

The telephone rang in the hall. When no-one moved, Anne said: 'Shall I?' and went to answer it.

They waited in silence for her return.

'Well, the op was successful, and so far, so good,' she reported. 'They said close relatives can pop in about seven, by which time he should have come round properly.'

At twenty to seven, Harry drove his sisters and brother to the hospital in his white Jaguar car.

Sally and Anne found themselves alone in the dining-room.

Anne went to the sideboard and took a bottle of whisky from the cupboard. 'Pour you one?'

'No thanks. Loathe the stuff. Any brandy?'

Anne found an ancient, almost empty bottle. 'Think it's OK?'

'I'll risk it.' When they were both seated by the fire, she asked: 'Do you remember how we used to play that we were doing proper work on the farm?'

'Yeah. Happy days.'

'Now you're here doing immensely skilled work, really powerful, significant stuff.'

'Well, we grew up, didn't we?'

Sally swirled the brandy in her glass and peered suspiciously at some grainy bits caught on the side. 'Trouble is, I still feel as if I'm playing – not doing real work – just playing – with ideas, mostly.'

'I suppose my line's more practical.'

'You've grown up without hiccups. A nice smooth progression. I bet they didn't warn *you* not to hang around the men.'

'Hang around the men? Is that what happened? I assumed you'd got too good to mess about with the rest of us. A bit snooty, I thought.'

'Covering up. It was a bit self-conscious making. So no-one suggested you should give it up?'

'No fear. Shouldn't have taken any notice if they had.' She yawned, then tossed back the last of the whisky. 'Christ, I'm jiggered. Mind if I go up and have a bath?'

'No, go ahead. I'll read for a bit.'

When Anne had gone, she went into the scullery and poured the brandy down the sink. The window above the sink, backed by inscrutable darkness, had become a mirror. She saw herself dramatically reflected, her hand on a tap, her body resting against white porcelain. Behind her, every feature of the room was vividly exposed. She stood perfectly still. Her image was as permanent and necessary a part of the scene as the electric cooker, the pans on the rack, the door to the dairy, the scrubbed deal table. The idea of a stranger here and herself banished seemed incredible. But it will happen, she thought. Very soon, now, Willow Dasset will slip away from me for ever. As panic rose, she turned away and went in search of her book.

George's children returned white and shaken. Bit by bit, Sally learned their story. Grandad, on discovering that he was not in his bed at Willow Dasset, had become violently agitated. A cot to contain him had been produced, but its high sides had further enraged him. By the time they had taken their leave – the sounds of his furious struggle hardly diminishing during their journey along the corridor – escape had become the sole focus of his unquenchable will.

His children seated themselves at the great mahogany table.

'Supper?' Sally asked.

'Not yet. We could do with a cup of tea, though – eh, Bunny?'

'Oh, yes; cup of tea.'

'Whisky for you, Jim?'

'Thanks, Harry.'

Sally supplied her mother and aunt with tea, then sat on the hearth rug and poked the fire. Behind her, at the table, they began to talk. Sally thought of the times when she had squatted here, at her grandfather's feet; she could identify the exact spot from the pattern in the hand-worked rug. She shifted herself slightly. Here she had sat, and at this point, here, her grandfather's shiny boots had rested, one crossed over the other. How she had relished him, studied every detail, every line.

'You've got to admire him for it,' her mother was saying forthrightly. 'He may be at his last gasp, but he still won't be bossed.'

'And that sister was bossy,' said Bunny. 'I didn't like her a bit.'

'There's no sense in it, though,' Jim said. 'A bit of thought now and then might have done him good. He might have learned something.'

'Some people'd sit on their backsides all day, *thinking*,' Harry commented sarcastically.

'It's not *fair*,' Bunny blurted. 'It's not fair that this should have happened to Daddy. It was terrible leaving him like that. It was *cruel*.'

'They'll give him something, Bun, something to calm him down. It won't seem so bad tomorrow. Drink your tea before it gets cold.'

'I don't see why he should suffer like this. Daddy never hurt a soul. He was the kindest man in the world.'

'I don't know about that,' Jim said. 'He could be hard as nails when it suited him.'

He could be cruel, thought Sally, recalling the time when she had hidden in the corner by the sideboard and watched the men come in, cap in hand, to be given their wages. He had paid them contemptuously, as if chucking meat to worthless curs. Oh yes, he could be cruel.

And so kind, she thought, as other memories came to her – the day she had taken the Fordson Major for an illicit ride . . . Christmas night, pulling crackers . . . And so loving. Oh, such a warm, big man.

The discussion behind her had grown heated. 'Stop it, you two. Look what you're doing to Bunny. Bun, do pull yourself together. What you need is an early night. We all do. Come on, let's agree to disagree. Don't let's fall out.'

Because none of us has the complete answer, Sally thought, getting to her feet. Or rather, we each focus on the bits of him that made the greatest impression, or the bits we choose to remember. He was full of contradictions. So are we all. 'Would you like me to get supper now?'

In the morning, while trying to climb out of his cot, George suffered a heart attack and died.

The following day was sunless and cold. After breakfast, Bunny and Sally put on their coats and went out into the garden.

'I must go soon,' Sally said.

'Oh, must you?'

'Soon,' she repeated, but in a modifying tone to reduce the urgency.

'You'll stay for the funeral?'

'I don't think so. I was here at the end – that seemed the important thing.'

Bunny stopped to pluck a weed from the border. 'The garden will go to pot,' she said, looking at the weed in her hand as if uncertain what to do with it. She laid it carefully on a flat border stone for retrieval later. 'And there'll be a sale. Hordes of people trampling about . . .'

'I'll come again soon.'

Bunny looked up at the house. 'We are all of us going to lose Willow Dasset.'

It was kind of her to allow others to share in her grievous loss, Sally thought. Gently, she took her arm.

Then, she, too, looked up. There was a figure behind the dark glass of an upstairs window. In the dull light, only a white gleam told Sally it was Rebecca. You, she said silently, you will remain in possession.

344

8

Willow Dasset . . . It was ten years since Grandad Ludbury
had died, and not once during her many visits to Uncle Jim
at Horley-in-the-Hedges had she been tempted to drive
past and see whether and how it had changed. All pro-
posals to go there she had resisted, fearing the intrusion
of the present into the past. Horley-in-the-Hedges was an
enjoyable part of the present and belonged as much to
Alex and Timmy as to herself. But Willow Dasset lay deep
in long ago – distant and evocative as a myth or dream.

But now, it occurred to her, she was alone and driving
south within a few miles of the place. She could approach
it in private. No-one would know she had been.

Distant hills drifted, fields by the roadside sped by. Sally
burst into song. Yes, today, for the first time in all these
years, she could take Willow Dasset in her stride, for
during the last few hours she had won a great success;
she had proved herself! To savour and prolong her sense
of triumph, she rehearsed her telephone call, last night,
to Alex.

'Darling, darling . . .'

'Sally! Don't say you got it?'

'Yes.'

'You clever angel! But last night you seemed down –
sure the cocky chap had got it . . .'

'I wasn't the only one. All the candidates I spoke to
had the same impression. He was so pally with a couple
of bigwigs on the panel it seemed a foregone conclusion

– the job was already his. I couldn't believe it when it was me they called back in this afternoon. Oh, Alex, I feel like jumping into the car now and rushing home to you and Timmy . . .'

'Can't you?'

'No. I've promised to stay another night. There's some-one the Dean wants me to meet in the morning. Never mind. First thing tomorrow you can hand in your notice at that dreary school.'

'Perhaps I'd better look at sits vac in County Durham . . .'

'Don't you dare! Just get on and write that masterpiece. I'd better ring off now – a celebratory sherry with the Dean . . .'

'Great stuff, Sally.'

'I should be able to set off mid-morningish tomorrow.'

'Can't wait to see you, darling.'

Powerful, she felt *powerful*, she exulted, dropping into third gear, accelerating smoothly round a bend. It was that old 'I can do it' feeling – the most marvellous feeling in the world. Suddenly, a vision of herself on the Fordson Major – prompted by the remembered words of her grandfather – rose in her mind. 'Never seen anything like it in me life: little girl roarin' round Bailey's Field, pigtails flyin', cheeks like a couple of boiled beetroots.' She had heard him with guilt, for she had undoubtedly sinned, but beneath her shame-faced mask she had been triumphant.

She parked the car on the grass verge and walked back to the gateway. There was no gate, just a cattle grid, but behind the spreading oak – a well-remembered sentinel – a piece of stout fencing led from a scanty hedge to the old gatepost. She stood on a rung of the fence and leaned against the tree.

In the scudding light and shade, old landmarks seemed faded and apologetic amid brash, bright additions. A new Dutch barn dwarfed its old companion, and the dull purple slate of old barn roofs looked tired and worn beside the metallic roofs of new farm buildings. Near at hand, the tied cottage showed signs of intensive occupation – a line hung with washing, a battered car by the gate, toys left out on the path. Old Willow Dasset cowered amid new life.

Only the house at the heart of things appeared free from new embellishment. From her vantage point she could see the window of her grandfather's bedroom overlooking the yard, the window from where he had watched comings and goings, and which he had once pushed open in the small hours to thrust out his gun and take a shot at Benjamin, forgetting in his disturbed-from-sleep state that the shepherd was on night-time lookout for foxes. (That incident, she recalled, had hugely tickled Aunt Bunny who had never tired of recounting it.) She was too far distant to detect the unevenness of ancient window panes, but she could imagine their wavy depths and imagine, too, the window on the other side of the room overlooking the garden. Her eyes dwelt on the high trees, and she wondered if the hallowed ground they shielded remained as her grandmother had ordained – the paths free from weeds, the borders bright with flowers, the trellis smothered in blooms, the staddlestones encrusted with mosses, the shrubs fragrant, the lawn well mown. Was it, she wondered, a fit place, yet, for a haunting? And then she knew the true reason for her return to Willow Dasset: she longed to know whether, now and then, white light might be glimpsed against an upstairs window, or a brief shining against the dark of the shrubbery. Did she walk there still? Did she watch over the garden?

Investigation was impossible, but unnecessary, Sally decided. The blank innocence of the scene was deceiving, for among the trees and cobbles, along deeply rutted tracks, in meadows and paddocks and cool, shadowy, sweet-smelling interiors, she had encountered the inconsistencies that sharpen awareness – and the mystery of a woman's quiet, unshakable self-possession. So much had been absorbed, and with such immediacy and passion, it was unaccountable that she could detect no mark, no sign, to show that these things had been.

She stepped down and walked along the grass verge until she came to the gate that closed Bailey's Field to the road. No-one was about. Swiftly, she climbed the gate and dropped down into the field. Tall hedgerows enclosed it. Here, she could believe that nothing had changed, or that time had flown backwards.

Nothing is lost, she thought, looking about, marking the place where the binder had stood, and where the harvesters had rested over their tea, telling tales, teasing, flirting, laughing. Every detail of what had been was a part of her. She, herself, was the mark, the sign.

But the pure feeling of that time had gone for ever; it could not be relived. Suddenly, the memory of perfect happiness seemed the saddest thing in the world. A sharp ache grew in her, and as she caught her breath, the clouds parted and sunlight set the field ablaze. She put up a hand to shield her eyes. A flash of colour moved beneath the beech in the far corner of the field. A young girl in a red-spotted dress rose from the bank and began to run along the side of the hedgerow, legs pounding, pigtails flying, a ringlet of flowers held high in her raised hand.

The light was too strong. She lowered her head and felt the sun's warmth fade. When she looked again the field was empty; dull and still, it seemed to declare, as it

348

always had been. Not so, she thought, climbing back over the gate, for she could clearly hear the throb of a tractor, the clatter of a binder, feel the hot, flying dust, and smell the ripe grain of perfect summer.

In the car she sat and waited for her trembling to pass. Then she took stock – looked at the map, consulted the clock on the dashboard. It was one o'clock. Eagerly she turned on the car radio. 'The World at One,' announced a familiar voice.

'Yes, yes, come in world, come in!' she cried thankfully, and steadily, with no backward glance, drove away from Willow Dasset.

THE END

A SCATTERING OF DAISIES
THE DAFFODILS OF NEWENT
BLUEBELL WINDOWS
ROSEMARY FOR REMEMBRANCE
by Susan Sallis

Will Rising had dragged himself from humble beginnings to his own small tailoring business in Gloucester — and on the way he'd fallen violently in love with Florence, refined, delicate, and wanting something better for her children.

March was the eldest girl, the least loved, the plain, unattractive one who, as the family grew, became more and more the household drudge. But March, a strange, intelligent, unhappy child, had inherited some of her mother's dreams. March Rising was determined to break out of the round of poverty and hard work, to find wealth, and love, and happiness.

The story of the Rising girls continues in The Daffodils of Newent and Bluebell Windows, finally reaching its conclusion in Rosemary for Remembrance.

THE QUIET WAR OF REBECCA SHELDON
by Kathleen Rowntree

The Ludburys were a clannish and dominating farming family —
Rebecca was the new young bride they didn't like.

Rebecca first met George Ludbury when she was eleven years old. Her mother had died that morning and George was the only one to giver her comfort. She loved him from that moment on.

But George's family were a different matter. The Ludbury's — an affluent Midlands farming family — were snobbish, possessive, malicious, and in the case of Pip, downright mad. The matriarchal Mrs Harold Ludbury was enraged when George — for whom she had planned better things — insisted on marrying Rebecca. From that moment on the family did their best to wreck the marriage, win back George to the family farm, and alienate Rebecca's children from her.

It took thirty years of gentle compliance and evasive pleasantness before Rebecca won her private war and achieved exactly what she wanted.

0 552 13413 9

A SELECTED LIST OF FINE NOVELS
AVAILABLE FROM CORGI BOOKS

THE PRICES SHOWN BELOW WERE CORRECT AT THE TIME OF
GOING TO PRESS. HOWEVER TRANSWORLD PUBLISHERS RE-
SERVE THE RIGHT TO SHOW NEW RETAIL PRICES ON COVERS
WHICH MAY DIFFER FROM THOSE PREVIOUSLY ADVERTISED
IN THE TEXT OR ELSEWHERE.

☐	12387 0	Copper Kingdom	Iris Gower	£3.50
☐	12637 3	Proud Mary	Iris Gower	£3.99
☐	12638 1	Spinners Wharf	Iris Gower	£3.99
☐	13138 5	Morgan's Woman	Iris Gower	£3.99
☐	13315 9	Fiddler's Ferry	Iris Gower	£3.50
☐	13316 7	Black Gold	Iris Gower	£3.99
☐	10249 0	Bride of Tancred	Diane Pearson	£2.99
☐	10375 6	Csardas	Diane Pearson	£4.99
☐	10271 7	The Marigold Field	Diane Pearson	£2.99
☐	09140 5	Sarah Whitman	Diane Pearson	£3.50
☐	12641 1	The Summer of The Barshinskeys	Diane Pearson	£3.99
☐	12607 1	Doctor Rose	Elvi Rhodes	£2.99
☐	13185 7	The Golden Girls	Elvi Rhodes	£3.99
☐	133094	Madeleine	Elvi Rhodes	£3.99
☐	12367 6	Opal	Elvi Rhodes	£2.99
☐	12803 1	Ruth Appleby	Elvi Rhodes	£4.99
☐	13413 9	The Quiet War of Rebecca Sheldon	Kathleen Rowntree	£3.99
☐	12375 7	A Scattering of Daisies	Susan Sallis	£2.99
☐	12579 2	The Daffodils of Newent	Susan Sallis	£2.99
☐	12880 5	Bluebell Windows	Susan Sallis	£3.50
☐	13136 9	Rosemary For Remembrance	Susan Sallis	£3.99
☐	13346 9	Summer Visitors	Susan Sallis	£2.95
☐	13545 3	By Sun and Candlelight	Susan Sallis	£3.99

All Corgi/Bantam Books are available at your bookshop or newsagent, or can be
ordered from the following address:

Corgi/Bantam Books,
Cash Sales Department,
P.O. Box 11, Falmouth, Cornwall TR10 9EN

Please send a cheque or postal order (no currency) and allow 80p for postage
and packing for the first book plus 20p for each additional book ordered up to
a maximum charge of £2.00 in UK.

B.F.P.O. consumers please allow 80p for the first book and 20p for each
additional book.

Overseas customers, including Eire, please allow £1.50 for postage and
packing for the first book, £1.00 for the second book, and 30p for each
subsequent title ordered.

NAME (Block Letters) ....

ADDRESS ....

....